HALE

Yes

JADE DOLLSTON

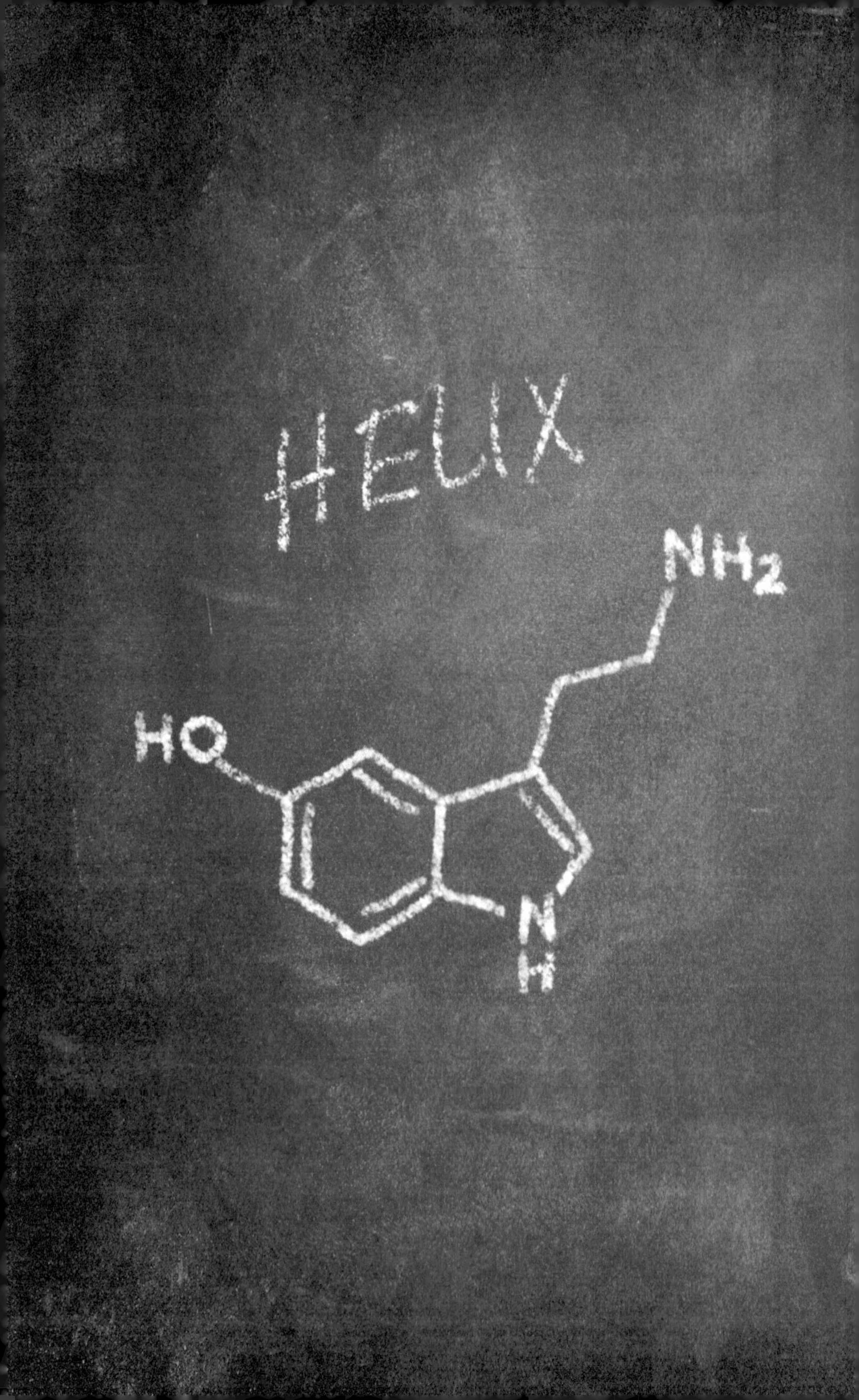

HELIX
NH2
HO
N
H

Prologue

HELIX HALE

FIVE YEARS AGO

I, Helix Hale, have the most ridiculous twin brother in the history of shared uteruses. Or is it uteri? I'm pretty sure either is correct, but I'd have to look it up to be certain.

Anyway, like I was saying, Phoenix's idiocy knows no bounds. The entire week, he's been sporting a different T-shirt in the lead up to his wedding. Last Saturday, for the pre-wedding gala, instead of wearing a button-down shirt beneath his tuxedo jacket like the rest of the normal men, he sported one of those goofy tuxedo tees with *Groom to Be* imprinted on it.

For the record, yes, I do believe a pre-wedding gala is incredibly pretentious. Like the wedding itself isn't going to be gala-esque enough. But that's what Beatrice and her father wanted, and what the Bettencourts want, the Bettencourts get.

But I digress... back to my brother's abysmal wardrobe decisions. Monday at the cocktail party, he sported a red shirt that read *I'm going to marry the shit out of Beatrice.* I thought for sure his bride would tell him to change, but she simply smiled that tolerant, placid smile she always does. The one that's not really a smile but merely a slight lifting of her lips. Like maybe she farted and is trying to look like she didn't.

Then at the wedding golf tournament—*yes, I know*—he showed up in a polo shirt imprinted with a sombrero and *Nacho Average Groom*. And the only reason he wore a polo instead of a T-shirt that day was out of respect for the dress code at the fancy country club.

There were other questionable shirts throughout the week, but I think I've blocked them from my brain. Tonight though? I'm not sure I'll ever be able to scrub this one from my mind.

First of all, it's neon pink. So neon, I think it's bleached all the photoreceptors in my retinas. Even Barbie would see this shade and recoil in horror.

Second, there's a cartoon groom kneeling before his bride. The text beneath reads *Under New Management*. It may be the single most cheesy thing I've ever seen.

But Phoenix is thrilled to be getting married. I don't think he's stopped smiling for almost a year, and if my twin is happy, then I'm happy. For the most part. I'd be positively ecstatic if he were marrying anyone but Beatrice.

Are you catching on that my brother's betrothed isn't my favorite person? How very astute of you. I'm sure Beatrice—*please don't call me Bea*—Bettencourt would be a perfect wife for some bland, rich guy with no personality whatsoever, but for Phoenix? Absolutely not.

Not that my brother's not rich. We all are, but Phoenix is so much more than his wealth. He's got a big personality and an even bigger heart. He's the kind of guy who would take a bullet for you.

Of course, he's probably also the reason you're getting shot at in the first place, but still...

Someone shoves a tequila shot into my hand, and I down it, refusing the lime Phoenix tries to hand me. My eyes connect with Remington's, and though he's not my twin, he's still my brother, and we can communicate without words. His eyes are blaring the same thought running through my head. *Can we leave now?*

I give a subtle shake of my head. *Not yet.* Though I'd love nothing more. This loud, crowded nightclub in the heart of Houston, Texas isn't exactly my scene. I prefer a quiet pub with good beer or a small sports bar with games on the television screens.

Actually, if I'm being honest, I'd rather be in my lab than

anywhere else. I'm a scientist in the research and development division of our family's company, Hale Cosmetics. I'll run the lab one day, but for now I'm an assistant. And that's cool. I'm twenty-seven and completed my doctorate in biochemistry last year. My time will come.

Remington is the oldest of us three brothers, two years older than Phoenix and me. I'm probably most like Remi, quiet and reserved, though I don't have the broodiness my older brother exudes. Phoenix, on the other hand, is always the life of the party, the center of all conversation.

I guess that makes me the uninteresting one, though maybe that's not entirely true. I have a condition called synesthesia. This phenomenon can take a lot of different forms, but the one I have gives me the ability to visualize actual colors around another living being. Kind of like seeing their auras. It doesn't happen with every person I meet, but for those I have a connection with, I can *feel* the colors that define the person.

Yeah, I admit it's a little woo-woo for me. I have a scientific brain that's hard-wired for facts and hypotheses, so this isn't something I've ever shared with another person. Well, except when I was five and asked Phoenix what color he thought I was. He gave me a confused look and told me I was white, though I got more tan in the summer. That's when I realized I was different.

If my twin were a color, he would be a vibrant blue, bright and eye-catching, the kind of blue that holds a person's interest. Remington is deep purple, a little dark but a color that is compelling the more you stare at it.

And me? Fuck if I know. It's not easy to see these things in yourself. There's some quote I heard once about self-reflection being necessary to gain an understanding of life, but I'm not sure about that. I'm a simple creature. My life consists of reading, work, and swimming. What more is there to understand?

If I had to assign myself a color, I guess I'd be gray. A light, plain, uninspiring shade like limestone. Though there are times when my gray turns darker, as if it was pulled from the edge of a shadow. But I don't let that side show. I force myself to be light. I'm Helix Hale, the quiet guy who keeps his head down and focuses on work. That other part of me doesn't exist.

Only... I know better. I'm not stupid enough to believe a person can completely get rid of certain desires. But with enough control, you can lock them in a room and forget about them. The only problem? Sometimes they want to come out. Burst through the tightly locked door and take over.

But no, I can't... Kayla wouldn't...

As if the mere thought of her somehow summoned my girlfriend, my phone buzzes against my hip. I know it's her before I even look because everyone else I'm close to is either in this room or wouldn't disturb me since they know I'm at my brother's bachelor party.

Sighing, I check the sixteenth text I've received from Kayla in the past three hours.

> Kayla: Why are you ignoring my calls?

I tap out a response and nod to the bartender, signaling for another round of shots for our group. I could use some mind numbing right about now.

> Helix: I've talked to you twice already since I've been here, Kayla.

> Kayla: But I've called two more times, and you didn't pick up.

I resist the urge to type in all caps.

> Helix: Because I'm with my brothers.

> Kayla: Are you dancing with anyone?

> Helix: Have you ever seen me dance?

> Kayla: I guess not. Who else is there?

I can literally hear her demanding voice even though we're only texting. Fuck me. I'm not sure how much longer I can do this. Glancing around the group in the VIP section of Titanium, the club we're at, I type back.

> Helix: Few guys from Phoenix's frat. And Dutton.

Our cousin, Dutton Hale, shouldn't fit in at this swanky club with its shiny metallic interior. He's a cowboy, through and through, and he's dressed as such with a pearl-snap shirt, starched Wranglers, and his trademark black cowboy hat. At least he's wearing his nice boots tonight and not his dirty shit-kickers.

But Dutton can fit in anywhere. He's a lot like Phoenix in that regard. With sandy-brown hair and an ever-present smile, he's one of the most likable people I've ever met.

And if you're wondering, in my head my cousin is the color of a golden retriever.

> Kayla: There's no one else in the club?

Jesus fucking Christ. My patience is being tried right now. Gritting my teeth, I reply.

> Helix: There are several hundred people here. Would you like for me to go around and get all their names and assemble a spreadsheet I can send to you?

> Kayla: You don't have to be so mean about it. I was just asking.

Cue the tears. I don't have to see her to know she's crying, so I heave out a sigh and, after downing another shot, excuse myself and work my way toward the hallway that runs in front of the restrooms. It's a little quieter back here.

Trying to find some patience I don't feel in the slightest, I tap my phone to place the call.

"H-hello?" Kayla's voice sounds meek and hesitant.

"What did you need?" I ask sharply, hanging onto the end of a very frayed rope.

"Oh, I... uh..." She fumbles for a reason for the multiple calls, and when she can't come up with anything, she finishes lamely. "When are you coming home?"

"Tomorrow. Tonight I'm staying at the hotel next door with Phoenix." Then I add pointedly, "Like I already told you."

To be completely honest, I'm not a hundred percent sure I'm going to stay at the hotel tonight because all I want to do is go home and crash in my own bed. My mattress is better than anything you can find at even the most luxurious hotel.

"But I'm waiting for you in your bedroom," she purrs, and my decision shifts automatically. I'll suffer through the hotel's sub-par bed rather than going back to my house.

And that's when I know the end has finally come. I'd rather give up my comfort than go home and fuck my own girlfriend. Kayla isn't an overly sexualized woman, but she uses it when it benefits her, and I willingly accept every opportunity. But not tonight.

If I'm being honest, the end should have been six months ago. In fact, I'd been on my way to Kayla's apartment to break up with her back in November, but when I got there, she told me the doc had put her grandmother on hospice care. While I'm not in love with Kayla, I'm not a complete dickhead, so I stayed.

Her grandma died two days later, and I couldn't do the breakup while Kayla was actively grieving. And here we are in May. Six months is an appropriate amount of time to stay in a relationship I'm desperate to get out of, right?

"I told you I wouldn't be home because tonight is about Phoenix."

"But..."

I try to keep the coldness I feel out of my voice and aim for resolute. "Good night, Kayla. I'm turning off my phone, and I'll see you at the wedding tomorrow." Before she can reply, I hang up.

Dick move? I don't really give a fuck right now. All I wanted was one night with my brother, his last night as a single man, and Kayla couldn't even give me that without calling or texting every few minutes. And it was stupid shit too.

Mr. Snuffles has sneezed twice. Do you think I should take him to the cat emergency room?

I'm thinking about wearing the yellow dress to the wedding tomorrow instead of the blue one.

Can you get me a bottle of Hale's new perfume? I want to try it.

I have a mosquito bite on my ankle.

Yeah. Not exactly life-altering conversations that couldn't wait until fucking tomorrow.

Turning off my ringer and pocketing my phone, I return to the bachelor party to find a busty blonde hanging all over Dutton. Her voice is a high-pitched coo.

"Like, a man in a cowboy hat is totally the hottest thing, like, everrrrr. It like, totally makes me hot."

God kill me. Like, totally.

I turn to the bar and order a Suffering Bastard—because why the hell not at this point?—leaving a generous tip when the bartender slides the chilled glass toward me. I take a sip, appreciating the slight bitterness combined with the warm bourbon followed by the spicy kick of ginger beer.

When I join our group, I notice Phoenix's frat boy friends heading down the stairs with a group of women, and I look questioningly at Dutton.

"Strike out with blondie?"

He laughs raucously. "Hell, son. You know better than that. I promised her I'd dance with her as soon as the deejay plays a country song."

Phoenix tips his beer bottle at our cousin. "I swear, dude, you pull more tail than a toddler at a petting zoo."

"You didn't do so bad yourself before you got snagged."

My twin grins like a damn idiot. "I've changed my ways, cuz. I'm about to be a married man." He points at the nonexistent ring on his left hand.

Dutton's eyes flit between me and Remington. "And which of you will be next?"

"Not me," we say in unison, like we're back in grade school and trying to get out of a chore our mom asked one of us to do.

Phoenix bumps me with his shoulder. "What about you and Kayla, brother? You thinking about wedded bliss?"

I shake my head. "No, not even close. I nominate Remi."

Remington lifts his middle finger from his glass of scotch to let me know what he thinks about that idea. "I'm focused on my career. Maybe I'll think about marriage later, but it's too much fun playing the field right now." His forehead scrunches. "They all want to get too serious too quickly, and I'm not ready for that."

Dutton rolls his eyes. "Because you're going out with women who know you're a rich bastard. They all want to be Mrs. Remington Hale."

Phoenix nods appraisingly. "That's true. You pretty much date only within our societal circle, and they all know the kind of money our family has." Then he adds wryly, "You're certainly not getting laid due to your personality."

"Fuck off," our older brother grumbles, proving Phoenix's point. "I can be charming." Remi tends to be on the broody side, and his scowl belies his last statement.

My twin's eyes sparkle, and I can tell he's up to something. That feeling is confirmed when he leans closer with a wicked grin on his face. "Remi, I bet you can't hook up with a regular girl, someone who's completely unaware of your net worth." He leans back with a look of satisfaction on his face, laced with a side of challenge.

Remi, never one to back down from a brotherly bet, lifts his chin. "I most certainly could."

Dutton and I watch the interaction with interest, both of us knowing Phoenix has Remi exactly where he wants him. "Prove it."

Remi swirls his tongue around his inner cheek and glares. "Fine. What did you have in mind?"

Phoenix doesn't crow, but he might as well because his smirk is one of pure satisfaction. "You take a girl from this bar home tonight."

"No problem," Remi returns, looking just as smug as my twin. "Hold my scotch."

Then Phoenix delivers the kill shot. "One of our choosing."

Our brother's dark eyebrows inch together over his brown eyes. "Who gets to pick? I don't mean to sound like an asshole, but I don't trust you, Phe."

"I'll pick," I offer, and Remi's eyes shoot toward me before he nods.

"Okay, I know Helix won't do me dirty. What are the terms?"

Phoenix taps his chin with a well-manicured finger. "Hmmm. If I win, you have to slow dance with me tomorrow night at my wedding reception. Like junior high style with your arms over my shoulders."

Dutton and I crack up because that is classic Phoenix... utterly ridiculous. Remington is not so impressed if the sigh he blows out is any indication.

"Fine, and if I win, you have to play golf with me every Saturday for the next year."

My twin grimaces. We all play golf, but none of us are as fanatical as our older brother. "I'm only asking for one dance, and you want me to give up my Saturdays for fifty-two weeks? Completely unreasonable."

Remi, ever the negotiator, counters with, "Okay, once a month for six months."

"Deal," Phoenix says, shooting his hand out to seal the arrangement. "But if it rains, you forfeit that month, and I don't have to make it up." My brothers shake, and Remington turns his bleak gaze to me, like I'm the grim reaper coming to take him away.

"Who are you choosing, Helix?" His head swivels slowly from side to side, assessing the women in the VIP area.

"Nope, not gonna be someone from up here. I'm picking someone down there," I tell him, striding to the floor-to-ceiling glass separating the exclusive section from the rest of the club. The group follows me, and I cross my arms over my chest as I scan the women down below.

Remington was right to trust me. I'm not going to screw him over, but I am going to make him work for it. That means no wealthy party girls. Skipping the dancing bodies, I let my eyes flit across the seating area on the far side of the room.

Two women are sitting at a high, round table on the edge of the dance floor, a brunette and a redhead. The brunette stands and tugs on the other woman's hand, but red pulls her hand back and shakes her head. *Hmmm. Is she a little shy?*

I watch as her friend joins another group of women on the dance floor and finds her groove to a Gwen Stefani tune. My eyes go back to red, who is still seated. She fidgets with the top of her dress, as if she's uncomfortable with the amount of cleavage she's showing. She appears to want to be anywhere but here.

If I'm reading the scene correctly, brunette dragged red to this club tonight, probably insisting she wear a skimpy dress. Brunette would be the easier target for my brother, but I need to make this a bit more of a challenge for Remi.

After another quick scan of the area, my eyes are drawn back to red. She's beautiful, her hair cut in a cute bob of dark auburn waves. When she attempts to pull the bottom hem of her dress down to cover more of her legs, I smile. *Bingo.*

"Her," I tell my brothers and cousin as I point. "The redhead at the fifth table from the left."

Turning my head, I find Remington with his nose practically pressed to the glass. "Fuck," he breathes, eyes trained on the beauty. "Thanks, Helix. You're the best brother ever."

Phoenix snorts and smacks Remi between the shoulder blades. "She seems like a wallflower. Good luck with that, bro."

"You better get your putter polished, Phe," he warns, backing away from the window and adjusting the collar of his black shirt. "Watch and learn, boys."

Dutton grabs his elbow and stops him before he can head toward the stairs. "You're supposed to look and act like a regular guy, not a dude with money coming out of his ass."

Remi holds his hands out to the side. "What the fuck? I look regular."

We survey him from head to toe, and Phoenix snorts. "Hate to tell ya, Rem. Regular people don't wear thousand dollar shirts, Brioni loafers, and a Patek Philippe watch that costs more than a Toyota."

Our older brother rolls his eyes. "Fine. I'll go down there naked, but then it will be gravy. I look awesome naked."

"Just take off the watch and change your shirt and shoes," Dutton suggests.

Remington pats his pockets sarcastically. "Well, shit, I seem to have left my spare shirt in the car."

"Switch with one of us," Phoenix suggests.

Remington eyes each of us, quickly dismissing our brother's neon pink monstrosity and Dutton's western shirt. His gaze falls on my simple charcoal-gray button-down. It cost me about eighty bucks, so definitely a far cry from Mr. Fancy Pants, but it's better than his other options.

"Helix, switch with me."

We duck into a corner and trade shirts and shoes before he removes his watch and buckles it onto my wrist. His eyes hold a healthy measure of gratitude and a hint of warning. "Thanks for not fucking me over, man. And please don't scuff my shoes."

I can't help but chuckle. "You got it, bro. And I'll bring your clothes back to you tomorrow."

When we return to our group, Phoenix is cackling. "Gotcha all set up at the Hampton Inn, Rem."

Remington sets his hands on his hips, the pink of his cheeks showing his indignation. "You expect me to fly this woman to the Hamptons tonight?"

We all burst out laughing. Well, all of us except my older brother, who has his trademark scowl imprinted on his face. "Bro, the Hampton Inn is right down the street," I explain.

His face is a mask of confusion before it hits him and his nose wrinkles. "Like that hotel chain? Did you at least book me the penthouse?"

Cue more hilarity while Remi glares. He's such a snob. "Yeah, definitely the penthouse," Phoenix wheezes between guffaws.

Our brother looks marginally relieved. He's going to be in for a shock when he gets there because the Hampton has four floors at the most, and I'm relatively sure there are no suites.

"I don't know why you didn't just book me next door at The Guild," he complains.

Dutton shakes his head, mirth dancing in his sky-blue eyes. "Because you're supposed to be acting like a regular guy, and rooms at The Guild start at fifteen hundred per night. The average Joe Blow would not be able to afford that."

"Huh, guess that makes sense." Remi adjusts the cuffs on his sleeves. He's an inch taller than me and Phoenix, but I'm the broadest of our group of brothers. My shirt fits him pretty well, though I had to leave his unbuttoned because it's perfectly tailored to fit his slimmer frame. Luckily, I have on an undershirt beneath so I don't look like a porn star.

"You look good, man," Dutton praises. Remington looks unsure but nods. "And try not to look so uptight. Maybe smile a little."

Remington bares his straight, white teeth in something resembling an angry panther, and we all chuckle.

"Yeah, that oughta do it," Phoenix snarks, mussing Rem's perfect black hair a bit with his fingers. "Oh, and don't tell her your real name."

"What the hell am I supposed to call myself?" he huffs in indignation.

Dutton's lips curl up at the corners. "How about Joe Blow?"

Remi's lips flatten. "Anything else?"

I scratch my chin, feeling the hint of stubble appearing there. "Joe Blow wouldn't have a private driver, so you can't use Antonio. You either need to walk to the hotel or take a rideshare."

"Fine," he sighs, glancing out the window again, his eyes softening just a bit when he catches sight of the redhead. "You guys can get Antonio to take you home."

"We'll see you in about five minutes when you strike out," Phoenix taunts.

"I'll see you *tomorrow*," Remington shoots back. Then he flashes the hint of a real smile and pulls Phoenix into a brotherly hug. "Love you, man. I'll come early to make sure you're dressed appropriately."

Phoenix laughs and returns the embrace. "Thanks, and good luck, Rem."

Our older brother walks backward, shooting finger guns and a playful wink at us. "That's Joe to you."

As Remington trots down the stairs, we congregate at the window. "Uh-oh. Another man is trying to step in," I note, seeing a blond guy standing beside the redhead's table. My eyes track Remi skirting the dance floor wearing my shirt and shoes.

"He's toast," Dutton predicts. "She's totally going to dance with the blond dude."

I tap the divot above my top lip. "I don't think so. Look at her body language. She's leaning away from him."

My cousin cackles with glee. "Awww, shit. Remi is approaching. A thousand bucks says they're going to rumble."

Phoenix and I cut our eyes at one another. This is going to be the easiest fucking bet ever. Remington Hale does not *rumble*.

"You're on," I say before Phoenix does.

Two seconds later, Remi taps the guy on the shoulder, and when he turns around, my brother jerks his head to the side and says something. Even from here, we can see a frown crinkle the blond man's forehead.

Dutton tenses beside me, muttering, "Come on, Rem-bo. Let him have it."

But he doesn't. Instead, he dips his head and kisses the woman full on the mouth.

"Ha! The old *hi honey, I'm back* routine," Phoenix crows. "It's a classic."

"Well, shit," my cousin curses, pulling out his western-style wallet and counting out a stack of hundreds as the interloping blond guy storms away. He hands it over, and I absently stick the bills into the back pocket of my trousers.

"Oooh, she's asking him to sit down," I say, fully invested in this ludicrous scheme now.

"And he's actually smiling," Phoenix says like a proud father.

The music changes from the club mix to a George Strait classic, and Dutton tips his hat at us, grinning in that cheeky way he has. "Gentlemen, I have a lady to hold in my big, strong arms."

And then there were two…

Remi and the redhead left together about thirty minutes ago, and then the rest of the bachelor party said their goodbyes, most of them also leaving with women on their arms. Phoenix and I are in a quiet corner with our drinks and our bond.

"Are you ready for next month?" my brother asks as we sit on gray leather padded seats around a small table.

I nod, feeling slightly guilty about drinking while I'm in training, but it's not something I do often. After this weekend, I'll be back to my regular strict diet and schedule.

"I'm ready."

"How's the back?"

I twist from side to side to demonstrate that all's good. I'd been training for the Olympics for years, and four years ago I pulled a muscle during a minor car accident, forcing me to miss the swimming trials. But it's my time now.

"Never felt better," I tell him honestly. "I think I'll definitely qualify for the breaststroke, and I'm hopeful for the two-hundred-meter freestyle as well."

"I can't wait to watch you win gold," he says proudly before narrowing his eyes at me over the table and changing the subject. "So what's going on with you and Kayla?"

"It's time to end it," I say, taking an easy sip of my drink. The lime tingles against my tongue, and my bones seem to relax one by one. It's been a while since I've been drunk or even tipsy, but I'm well on my way tonight.

"It's been time," my brother replies. "She seems to have gotten clingier."

I shove a hand through my dark-brown hair. "Yeah, I don't do well with that, but I couldn't just leave her right after her grandmother passed."

"You'll find someone," he remarks. "But she's not it. I don't mean to sound like a dick, but Kayla's not smart enough for you. You need someone who can challenge your intellect."

He's right, but I don't really like talking about myself, so I shift the subject. "Are you sure Bea is the right one for you?" Beatrice hates being called Bea, so I do it as often as possible.

Phoenix's eyes widen. "Of course she is. Why would you ask that?"

"She just seems more like Rem's type. Driven and ambitious, where you're more easygoing."

My brother shrugs. "We balance each other."

We're silent for a while, and I finally break it. "You think Rem will ever get with Serena?"

Phoenix makes a gagging sound. "Fuck, I hope not. But it's not for lack of effort on her part. She's been trying to get her claws into him for years."

"You think they've ever hooked up?"

He shakes his head vehemently. "Nope. I asked him once, and he assured me they're only friends."

"Fingers crossed it stays that way." I don't say it aloud, but the thought of having Serena and Beatrice both as sisters-in-law makes me want to drink lighter fluid and then swallow a lit match.

I twist my glass on the table and watch the condensation make wet rings against the smooth surface, only looking up when Phoenix leans forward. "Hey, you know what we should do?"

"I'm afraid to ask," I reply wryly.

"We should do some hoodrat shit tonight. Just you and me, like the old days."

I'm just drunk enough to think that doesn't sound like such a bad idea. "What did you have in mind?"

His blue eyes leave my matching ones and search the metal embossed ceiling. "Uhhhh, let's see. Oh! I've got it." His gaze is pure mischief when it returns to mine. "We could go toilet paper Dad's house."

I laugh and pat my back pocket. "I've got a thousand dollars that would buy a lot of fucking TP. Let's get Antonio to drive us to Walmart. We can buy you a different shirt too since that one glows in the damn dark."

Phoenix grasps my hand and squeezes, our eyes locked. "Thanks, twinny."

It usually annoys me when he calls me that, but tonight? Fuck, it makes me feel a little emotional. My brother is getting married tomorrow.

I tighten my hand around his and pat his bicep. "You got it, Phe. Let me pay the bar bill and we can go do all the hoodrat shit you want."

While I'm paying, I shoot off a text to our father.

Y-Chromosome: Do I even want to know
what's going on?

Helix: The groom wants to do some crazy
shit tonight, so we're about to come TP your
house.

Y-Chromosome: Good lord, LOL. You're not
driving are you?

Helix: No sir, Antonio is driving us.

Y-Chromosome: Where's Remi?

Helix: Occupied.

Y-Chromosome: Ah, I understand. I'll let
security know to look the other way for a few
minutes. And I'll warn Rebecca and Perri too
so they don't get scared if they hear two
idiots outside.

I smile at the mention of our seventeen-year-old sister. Well, technically, she's our half sister, but that's just semantics. Perri has been in our
life since she was four. It's a long story.

Helix: Thanks, Dad. I'll come clean up in the
morning.

Y-Chromosome: Call me if you need bail
money.

Three hours later, Phoenix and I fall onto the beds in one of the suite's
bedrooms, still giggling like little kids.

"I can't believe the security guards didn't even hear us," my brother
says, and I grin at the ceiling.

Is it supposed to be spinning like that? We'd gone through an entire
bottle of Remington's expensive-as-fuck scotch in the back of his fancy

car while Antonio drove us to two different Walmarts to buy all the toilet paper we could find. Dad's yard looked like a winter wonderland by the time we were done.

"We were super stealthy," I lie. We weren't.

"Must have been the ski macks... mackiss... masks," Phoenix slurs drunkenly. "That was a good idea to get them at the Walmark."

His face turns toward me from his bed, and I do the same. Even though I can barely see him in the dark, I feel the bright blue of his spirit.

"Tomorrow everything is going to change," I say quietly.

"But we'll always be twinnies," Phoenix replies, his voice uncharacteristically solemn.

"Yeah, we'll always be twinnies."

When I told him everything was going to change tomorrow, I had no idea how true that statement was. Because Phoenix's life didn't just change.

It imploded.

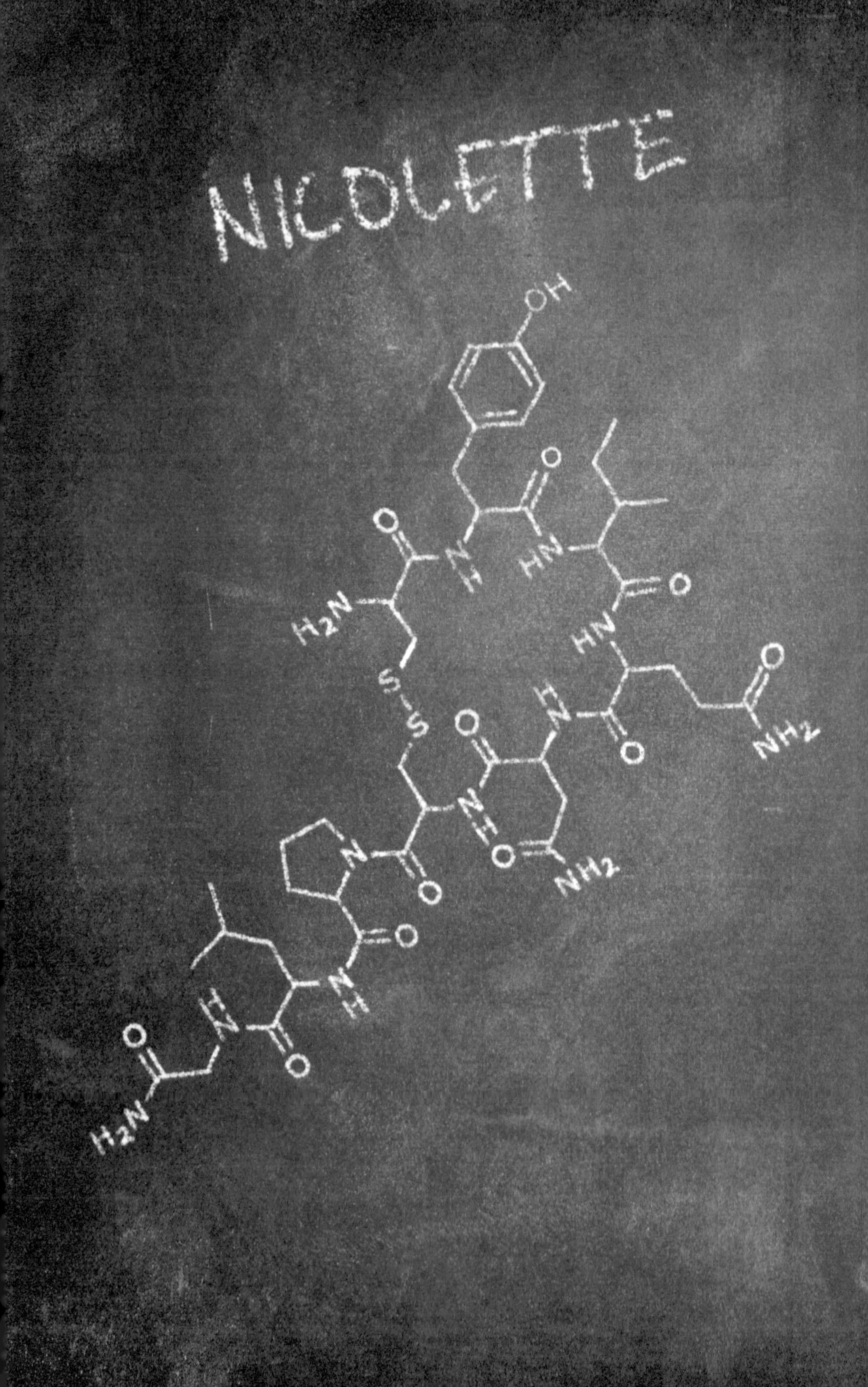

NICOLETTE
OH
H2N
S
S
N
O
NH2
O
NH2
HN
HN
O
O
O
NH2
H2N

Chapter One

IS YOUR MAMA IN THIS HOTEL?

PRESENT DAY

"You're so pretty," the man says as he thrusts inside me. "Your eyes are the color of *Dryophytes cinereus.*"

I lie on my back and try not to wrinkle my nose. Did he just compare my eyes to a goddamn tree frog? What does one even say to that?

My mind is a bit scrambled from the amphibian reference, and I can't seem to remember the guy's name. Carson? Calvin? Hell if I know, so I go with, "Babe. Your huge cock feels so good."

Okay, huge might be an exaggeration, but he's not small either. We'd been flirting from afar all week but finally started talking at the final cocktail party for the American Academy of Clinical Biochemistry conference in Los Angeles. One thing led to another, and now I'm in his hotel room.

"Thank you," the man on top of me says.

Connor grins. He seems to appreciate the dick compliment. Hmm, not Connor, but I'm getting closer. Conrad! Yes, his name is Conrad.

I wrap my ankles around his waist and purr, "Harder, Conrad."

He lifts his head, his brown eyes darting in confusion between my green ones—that apparently remind him of the American tree frog—and I worry I got his name wrong.

"This is as hard as I get," he tells me, flexing his hips, and I groan inwardly.

Outwardly though, I give him my best flirty smile. "I mean *fuck me harder.*"

The corners of his lips tilt upward. He really is quite handsome when he smiles. "Okay, I'll try."

Conrad pulls back and pushes in a little harder. "That's it," I encourage, still wanting more. I grab his ass with both hands and yank him into me with a rough thrust.

The headboard bangs against the wall, and Conrad freezes, jerking his head up and staring like he's never heard that noise before. "That was loud," he whispers.

"It's okay," I soothe because *seriously... move, dude.*

Still staring at the wall, he gnaws his bottom lip. "I'm not used to being loud at home because Mama's room is right next to mine."

Oh, for fuck's sake.

"Is your mama in this hotel?" I ask, tilting my hips to get some friction on my G-spot, though Conrad has completely stopped moving now.

"N-no, but if she found out I was doing this, she'd be mad. What if someone calls hotel security and they call Mama to come get me from jail?"

I search his face. He has a few wrinkles around his eyes, making him look mature, and his name badge told me he's a PhD, but I have to make sure I'm not committing a felony here. Tentatively, I ask, "How old are you, Conrad?"

"Thirty."

Phew! Not a minor, just a mama's boy.

I wrap my hand around the back of his head and pull him down for a long kiss. He seems to relax as I murmur against his lips, "Being at a hotel is the perfect chance for you to get dirty and bang some headboards, don't you think?" At the same time, I clench my pussy around him.

He groans and rests his forehead against mine. "Shit. Yes."

"Then fuck me hard." I'm pretty sure if I ask him for what I really want—like, say, a nice hand necklace?—he'd probably run screaming.

Conrad pushes in hard, banging the headboard against the wall again, and I close my eyes in pleasure. *That's it. Just what I need.* His breathing hitches on his next thrust, and he stills.

With a raspy voice, he cries, "I'm ejaculating my semen."

Fucking hell. My libido takes a nosedive at that very awkward proclamation, and I blow out a frustrated breath while Conrad comes into the condom. Five heaving breaths later, he rolls off me and covers his eyes with his forearm.

"Wow, that was amazing, Nicolette," he pants.

"Yeah," I sigh, pushing to a seated position. "I'm just gonna use your bathroom to clean up."

He uncovers his face and reaches down to remove his condom before holding it out to me. "Toss that while you're in there, okay?"

"Um, yeah, sure," I say, pinching it between my forefinger and thumb while I climb off the bed. Five minutes later, I emerge in my black cocktail dress, hands thoroughly washed.

Conrad sits up with the sheet pooled around his waist and confusion on his face. "Why did you get dressed? I don't care if you sleep naked." He shrugs. "I mean, if we were at my house, you'd have to get dressed and sneak out before six because that's when Mama brings my breakfast. But we're all alone." He says that last part with what I assume he thinks is a sultry invitation.

Instead of being rude, I decide to fib. "Oh, I wish I could, but I have an early flight and still need to pack."

"Can I have your number?" he blurts. "I know you live in New York, and I'll be there next month." His grin is wide and hopeful. "I'm staying at a hotel."

I walk over and kiss his cheek, trying to soften the blow. "I've got a lot going on next month, but I enjoyed getting to know you, Conrad. You're really sweet."

And it's true. Conrad is a sweet and smart man, but I don't want to hook up with him again.

He gives me a boyish smile and blushes. "Okay, you can find me on social media if you change your mind. My last name is James."

I turn to leave, tossing a wink over my shoulder. "Keep banging those headboards, Conrad James." His laughter follows me out the door.

With the straps of my high heels looped over my index finger, I make my way down the carpeted corridor. I'm going to have to scrub the hell out of my feet when I get back to my room, but my arches ache too much to put my shoes back on.

Another woman approaches from the other direction, her stilettos also in her left hand. I recognize her from one of this morning's seminars. We make eye contact, and her lips curve up in a chagrined smile of kinship.

"You doing the post-convention walk of shame too?"

I laugh and nod, stopping when I get even with her. "I guess so." Holding out my right hand, I say, "I'm Nicolette Bell."

The woman's red lipstick is smudged a little when she smirks. "Like I don't recognize you, Dr. Bell. Your lecture on biomolecules in the cosmetics industry was amazing." We shake. "I'm Shay Martin."

"Thank you, and please call me Nicolette." On a whim, I ask, "Hey, would you like to grab a drink down at the bar?"

Her expression brightens. "I'd love that, but do you care if I grab a pair of flats? My feet are killing me."

"God, yes. In fact, I think I'll put on some comfortable clothes too. I'm a few floors up." I don't mention I'm on the top floor. The conference put me up in the presidential suite since I was a featured speaker.

"Meet you at the entrance of the bar in ten," Shay says, walking backward toward her room with a grin on her face.

I'm dressed in black yoga pants, a red tunic top that flutters around my hips, and my black HEYDUDES fitted comfortably on my freshly washed feet. Shay is dressed similarly in black leggings and a green V-neck top that looks amazing with her strawberry blonde hair.

"I was excited to be accepted into the Academy this year," Shay says as the waiter drops off our lemon drop martinis. "I just graduated from pharmacy school two years ago."

"Where did you get your degree?" I ask.

"University of Houston." Her face pinkens a little. "I know it's not like Harvard or Duke, where you went."

Reaching across the table, I pat her hand. "Hey, you got your doctorate, and that's all that matters. I love seeing more and more women in the science fields." I take a sip of my drink and watch as Shay visibly relaxes, her shoulders inching down.

"I was glad to get in at U of H because I grew up in Houston. My mom has diabetes and isn't the best at taking care of herself, so it was nice to be close to her."

I chuckle. "I was the opposite. I was accepted at Columbia and Princeton for undergrad, but those were way too close to my family in Jersey, so I decided on Harvard. And to broaden my horizons a bit, I got completely out of the Northeast for my postgrad degrees. I actually enjoyed Duke. North Carolina is a beautiful state."

Shay's brown eyes are sympathetic. "Don't get along with your parents?"

My nose wrinkles. "My dad tries, but my mom..." I tilt my head back and forth a few times, trying to be diplomatic. "Let's just say she doesn't get me."

Sensing the touchy topic, Shay changes the subject, which I appreciate. "I didn't expect so many people to be hooking up at this conference, but everywhere I looked tonight, couples were leaving together left and right."

I laugh, remembering my first conference years ago. "It's not uncommon once the drinks get flowing. People have been in intense classes for days, so they want to let loose."

Shay giggles. "I get that. I know all the talk about hormones made me feel a little frisky." She tastes her drink and eyes me. "Were you with that tall guy you were talking to at the party?"

I nod, not wanting to talk badly about Conrad. I feel a little protective of the guy. "He was really nice."

My new friend sighs. "My guy too. He had some ink on his arm, so I thought maybe he was a bit of a bad boy, but he was just... nice."

Placing my fingertips on my temples, I close my eyes and hum. "Hmmmm, a tattoo? Let me guess. A model of an atom?" When I open my lids, Shay is gaping at me in shock, and I know I'm right. "Bohr model or Rutherford?"

"Bohr. How did you know that?"

I wave a hand at her. "It's the same tat every biochem guy has. I'm still looking for a guy who has something original or inspiring."

Shay's face turns contemplative, her eyes unfocusing for a second before they widen. "Crap, you're right. I saw at least twenty of them this week."

I twist one of the escaped curls at the nape of my neck. "I've decided to swear off science guys. I've said it before, but I mean it this time."

Shay titters out a laugh. "Same." Her smile softens. "This is nice, having another woman to talk with. Thank you for inviting me."

"Of course. We STEM wenches have to stick together. When I was first starting out, I found it difficult to connect with other people." I shake my head. "Not on a professional level; that came a bit easier for me. But it was hard to find people I wanted to spend time with at the end of the day."

She waves her hand in front of her shoulder. "I volunteer anytime you want to unwind after a conference." Propping her chin in her palm, she says, "If you're ever in Houston, give me a call. I'd love to hang out again."

I think of the email I recently received—the one I haven't been able to stop thinking about—and meeting a new friend from Houston feels like a sign I'm headed in the right direction. "I'll do that," I tell her, adding, "And it might be sooner than you expect."

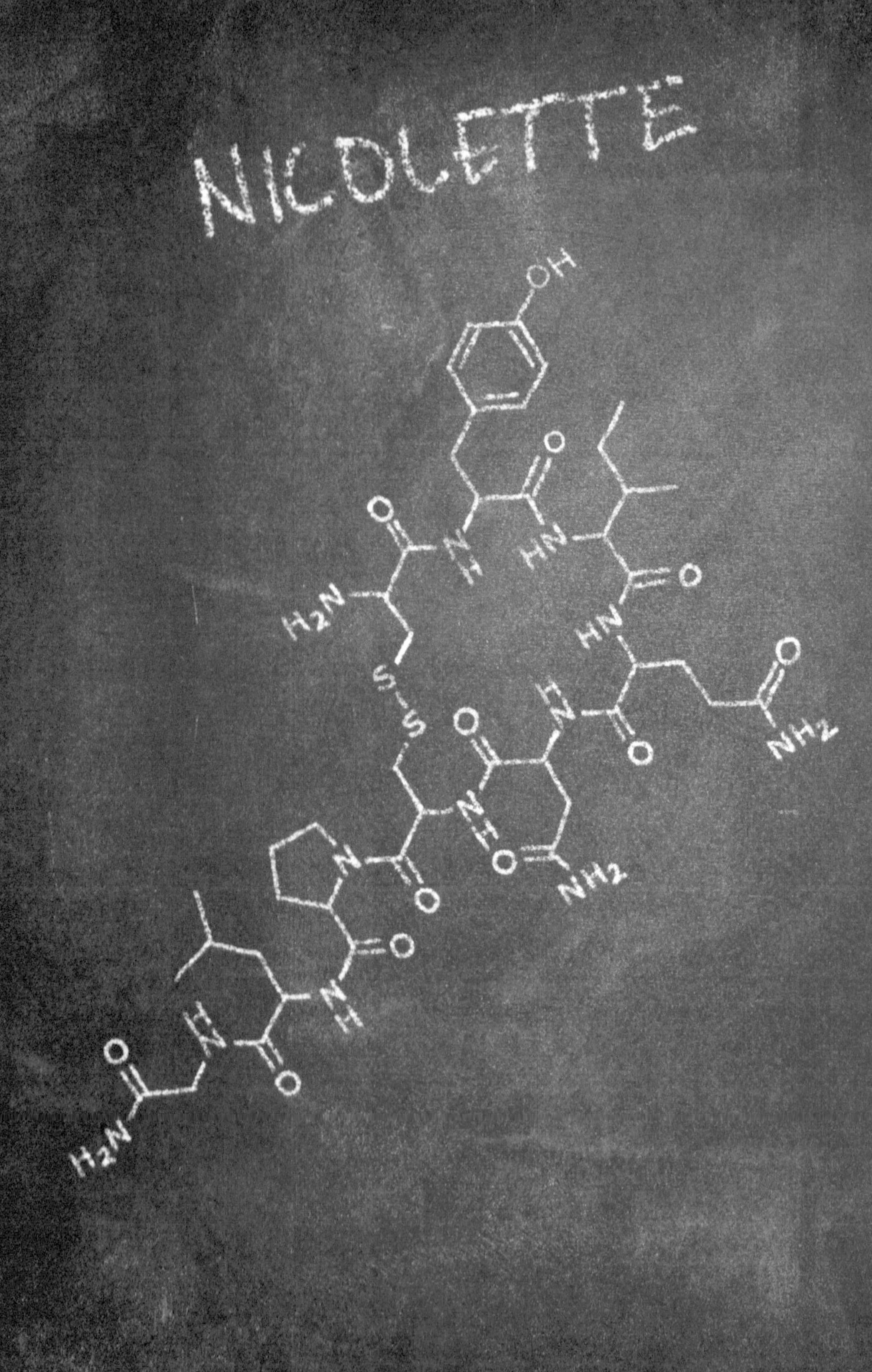
NICOLETTE

Chapter Two

MONDAY CAN GO FUCK ITSELF

I don't like Mondays.

Sure, most people dislike the first day of the week after the weekend, but I *despise* them with every cell in my body. Why, you may ask?

Because this is the designated "family dinner night" at my parents' house. Yay. And I mean that in the most sarcastic way possible.

"The roast is good, Ma," I say, cutting into the tender meat and taking a bite. I'm doing my best to be pleasant in the hopes that if I'm nice to them, they'll be nice to me.

"Thank you, dear. I cooked it in my new Instant Pot." She pats my sister's hand. "Angelica bought it for me."

My eyes flash to my sister, who is smiling sweetly, and I say, "Well, that was nice of her."

"It's more than nice. It wasn't even my birthday or anything." Ma tilts her head and beams at Angelica like she's gazing at the brightest star in an enchanted sky. "She's such a lovely person. So thoughtful."

I don't bother to point out that my lovely, thoughtful sis bought it on my Amazon account. With my debit card.

Beside Angelica, who's sitting across from me, Rory whispers something into her ear, and she giggles. Rory is my sister's boyfriend—who used to be my boyfriend. So yeah. That's fun.

Ma adores him and passes him the tray of meat. "Rory, another slice?"

"Thank you, Mrs. Bell. This is the best roast I've ever had."

She titters and fingers the pearls at her throat. "How is the insurance business, dear? Are you still staying busy?"

Rory drones on for a few minutes, and I attempt to not nod off.

I'm startled back into the conversation when my father asks, "Nicci, how is your work going?"

Dragging a small potato through the brown gravy, I answer. "It's going well. I've proposed a new product line I'm really excited about with—"

"I had two new clients this week, Daddy," Angelica interrupts, and I pop the potato into my mouth so I don't sigh. Maybe if I stick it really far in, I'll choke and then have an excuse to leave.

But Pop smiles indulgently. "That's great, baby. Your beauty shop is really growing, huh?"

Ma looks like she's about to pee herself with excitement, which usually means she's about to jab a thinly veiled insult my way. "Everyone adores our little Angelica," she coos, stroking my sister's long blonde hair. "Such a sweet personality and a smart businesswoman to boot. I certainly wish Nicolette had inherited some of my business sense."

I don't react because it's what she wants.

"Ahh, I think Nicci is doing fine," my father says, turning his questioning green eyes on me. "Aren't you? You don't talk much about your job."

With an indulgent smile, I say, "Everything's fine, Pop. How is the store doing?"

That gets him going until dinner is almost done. He and Ma started Bell Hardware about twenty years ago after Pop got laid off from his carpentry job, and he loves talking about screws, paint, and all manner of household repairs.

When my mother begins to serve the pineapple upside down cake for dessert, Rory pipes up. "Angelica is going to that big hair expo in Trenton in a few weeks. But don't worry about her, Mr. and Mrs. Bell. I'll drive her to make sure she gets there safely."

"Such a darling boy," Ma purrs at him. "Taking care of our baby girl."

I think I should receive an award for not mentioning that thirty-five is hardly a baby.

"Of course," the kiss-ass replies. "Anything I can do for my sweetheart."

"I wish Nicolette could find a nice boy like you."

Again, I restrain myself from pointing out that I did, in fact, have that exact same "nice boy," and then Angelica got jealous and decided she wanted him. Not that I'm sad about it. Sure, I was hurt at first, especially when Ma told me I shouldn't make a fuss about Rory cheating on me with my own sister. Because... *family is family, Nicolette.*

When I look at him now, all I feel is relief. Rory's a brown-nosing douche with a small dick. Also, his last name is Clutterbuck, though in my head I call him Clusterfuck to amuse myself.

Again, Pop attempts to bring me into the conversation. "Nicci, don't you have an, um, expo or something coming up?"

I poke at a syrupy cherry on my plate. "It was last week. The American Academy of Clinical Biochemistry conference."

My dad smiles warmly. "And didn't you tell me you were teaching one of the classes?"

"I was the lecturer for two of the seminars," I reply, forking up a bite of the buttery crust.

"Well, isn't that something," he says proudly. "What were the classes about?"

Since he seems genuinely interested, I tell him, "The first was on the use of biomolecules in the cosmetics industry, and the other focused on the effects of isopropylparaben and isobutylparaben in skin care products."

My glance around the table is met with blank stares, so I explain. "Isopropylparaben and isobutylparaben are examples of what are commonly known as parabens. Chemically speaking, those are esters of parahydroxybenzoic acid and are often used in cosmetics, food, and pharmaceuticals as a preservative due to their antimicrobial benefits. They help to extend the shelf life of products."

"And are these parabens... bad?" Pop asks, and I toggle my head from side to side a couple times.

"Not necessarily. Some foods like barley and blueberries have naturally occurring parabens, but the two I focused on have suspected links to infertility and cancer. They're absorbed through the skin and can integrate themselves into the body's tissues, specifically breast tissue."

"Oh my!" Ma clutches her pearls.

I shift my eyes between her and Angelica. "Make sure to check the labels of your makeup, lotions, and other products. I'll send you a text with the ingredients to look out for." They both nod silently.

Rory shovels in a big bite of cake and talks around it. "Where was your conference, Ni—oof." He's cut off by an elbow in the side from my sister. She doesn't like any attention on anyone but herself, especially from Rory.

I answer anyway. "It was in L.A."

Ma tsks. "Oh, that seems silly to go all the way to California for some meeting. Don't they have something closer to home?"

Don't roll your eyes, Nic. Don't do it.

My eyeballs quiver in their sockets but maintain an even stare. "The Academy holds their conference in a different place each year, Ma. Next year it's in Dallas, and then the next two will be in New York and Miami."

"Well, I think it's ridiculous to spend all that money on flights and hotel and—"

I cut my mother off. "All my expenses were paid by the Academy, and they also pay a generous speaking fee."

Her lips flatten. "Oh. Well." She seems disappointed that I cut off any reason for her to criticize me.

Rory leans forward. "How much do you get paid for something like that?" When I hesitate, he prods, "Five-hundred bucks?"

Angelica flashes her most darling smile, her voice turning syrupy. "Don't embarrass her, honey. It probably wasn't that much, and Nicci just doesn't want to say."

"Twenty-thousand." I blurt out the truth before I can think better of it, and everyone's eyes go wide. Pop's fork clatters to his plate, and Ma makes a little squeaking sound. Angelica looks constipated.

Fuck.

"Dollars?" Rory asks incredulously.

No, pesos, you idiot.

Instead of saying that, I rush to explain. "I was also the keynote speaker for the closing dinner. That's why it was so much."

"Well, that's... that's something else," Pop says.

My eyes flit to my mother. I don't know why I always look to her for approval I never receive, and it annoys the hell out of me that I do.

"I'm sure you did well," she says, and I feel my body relax a little before she adds, "I certainly hope you didn't wear your hair like that if you had to get up in front of people and talk."

I finger the dark curly hair at my shoulder, kicking myself for not putting it in a bun like I usually do. I don't have perfectly straight blonde hair like Ma and Angelica. It's honestly a bit wild unless I use a ton of product in it, which I made a point to do tonight before I came. But it wasn't enough. It's never enough.

Before I show all the emotions that are trying to seep in around my carefully stacked walls, I toss my napkin on the table and stand.

"Thanks for dinner, Ma, but I have a long drive back to the city. Pop, I'll take a look at that computer problem you were having before I go."

And I depart, out of the kitchen and down the wood-paneled hallway to my father's office. An annoying tear attempts to leak out, but I don't allow it. *No fucking tears, Nicolette Bell. You're thirty-three years old, for Marie Curie's sake.*

The chair behind Pop's desk is covered with russet brown leather that's worn in spots from age. I settle into it and boot up his desktop. There's an audible whine from the machine, and I shake my head. He refuses to buy a new one, though this one is well past its prime. I look around for the laptop I bought him but don't see it.

While I'm waiting, my eyes scan over the papers scattered across the aged wooden desk. All of them have some form of *PAST DUE* stamped in red on them. I frown, but before I can investigate further, I hear footsteps, so I face the computer and begin typing.

"Hi, honey." I smell my dad's Old Spice cologne as he sinks into the guest chair, but I don't turn around.

"This shouldn't take me long," I reply as my fingers fly across the keyboard, entering code to help me find the problem.

He's silent for a long while before finally saying, "You know how your mother is, Nicci."

I continue my work, never breaking stride. "I do."

Another few beats of silence. "She's not all bad."

"That's quite an endorsement," I shoot back. "They say Ted Bundy wasn't all bad either. I heard he didn't desecrate the corpses of *all* his victims."

Pop snorts before quickly clearing his throat and attempting to sound stern. "Nicolette, you know Bridget adores you, but she has to make sure Angelica feels important too. Your sister has had such a hard life."

"Yeah, receiving so much affection growing up must have been really hard on her," I scoff, spotting the problem on the screen and initiating a sequence to get rid of the malware. I don't mention that any difficulties in Angelica's life were of her own making.

Pop sounds uncomfortable, and from the corner of my eye, I see him massaging the back of his neck. "Well, I'd like to be affectionate with you too, but I know you don't like being hugged."

I turn my head slowly to face him, my eyes narrow. "What makes you say that?"

He shrugs. "You know, when you were about ten or so, you told your mom you didn't like anyone hugging you. So she let the whole family know."

That's not exactly what I said. I told her I didn't want *her* hugs anymore. Guess she decided I didn't deserve affection from anyone.

I don't like sparring with my father. Though he falls short in so many ways, he's the only one in my family that gives half a damn about me. And half a damn is better than no damns at all.

So I stay silent.

"She suspected you were autistic like in that movie with Dustin Hoffman and Tom Cruise. Uhhh..." Pop snaps his fingers in concentration.

"*Rain Man*," I supply, and he points a finger at me.

"Yeah, that one. Because you were so smart like that guy. She said you must be autistic."

I cross my arms over my chest while the computer works. "Then why didn't Ma ever have me tested instead of diagnosing me from a movie she saw before I was born?"

Pop stares at his shoes. "I don't know. She said we should just be more careful around you. Maybe I should have... I don't know."

It wasn't the first time someone suggested I might be on the spectrum. I'd been called a savant more than once in my educational career, but I don't think I am. Most savants have some sort of neurodevelopmental condition, such as a traumatic brain injury or autism.

My dad's face is flushed bright red, and I take pity on him. "Don't worry about it, Pop. When I got to college, I had myself tested by a neuropsychologist. I'm not autistic; I'm just... gifted and have a high aptitude for the sciences."

The doctor actually told me my IQ score put me in the genius bracket, but I decide not to share that with my father. I've never shared it with anyone because I've been conditioned not to talk too much about myself or my accomplishments. Tonight's dinner is the perfect example of why.

"Oh, well, that's good. You always could take care of yourself, Nicci."

Out of necessity, I don't say aloud.

My eyes flash to the screen, and after a few more keystrokes, Pop's computer is back in working order. I stand.

"Okay, it's all done, but this thing is ten years old. I've installed all the updates it can handle. Why don't you use the laptop I sent you, Pop? It's top of the line and will do everything this old desktop does but better and faster. Plus, it's portable."

He rolls his lips in and doesn't meet my gaze. "I, uh, let Angelica use it. She said she needs it for her business."

Of course.

I try to bite my tongue. I really do, but... "Wasn't the cost of a computer included in her small business loan?" I ask.

A muscle twitches beneath Pop's left eye. "She didn't end up qualifying for the loan, so I, um..."

A heavy breath shoves its way up my throat, ending in a long sigh. "So you're footing the bill for yet another career change. What is this? The sixth one?"

Pop's green eyes, so much like my own, flash with annoyance. "Angelica is trying, and she needed help. I'm her father."

There's so much I want to say, but I'm done with this night. And it never does any good to criticize my sister and her questionable life choices anyway. That only pisses him off. My father's biggest fault is his ability to remain oblivious about the things going on around him. And he insists that everyone else maintain that same level of obliviousness. Don't talk about it, and it didn't happen. Makes for a happy family, right?

I soften my voice and look pointedly at all the overdue invoices on his desk. "You want to talk about this, Pop?"

He follows my gaze and begins gathering the papers into a stack without looking at me. "No, no. It's nothing. Just been a slow month. It happens, you know?"

I watch silently as he finishes, holding the invoices against his chest and faking a smile.

"Do you need me to float you a loan?" I finally ask, and his eyes go round.

"No, of course not, Nicci. I'm fine. Everything's fine."

Nodding, I say, "Okay, Pop. Let me know if you change your mind." I know he won't. He's too proud to accept any help.

As I depart, I'm overcome with the sudden urge to hug my father. But I don't. I haven't had an embrace from anyone in my family in over two decades, and to do so now would just feel... awkward.

The drive back to New York City takes over an hour, and I'm exhausted by the time I trudge into my brownstone in Brooklyn Heights. Because my aptitude for science extends to the computer sciences, I go straight to my laptop and hack into three of the companies I saw listed on some of Pop's hardware invoices. Then I pay the bills in full for him.

Yes, I know I'm enabling him to enable my sister, but goddamn. She's bleeding our parents dry, and I can afford to help. He'll know it was me next time he tries to make a payment and finds out it's already being taken care of. Neither of us will mention it, and we'll carry on like it never happened. That's just how it is in our family.

Then I open my email and find the one from Hale Cosmetics letting me know they'd like me to come for an interview. Clicking on it, I read the words for the hundredth time, and key phrases jump out at me.

...exactly what we're looking for.

...at a time of your choosing.

...look forward to hearing from you.

After staring at it for a good ten minutes, I finally respond that I can come for an interview this Friday. As soon as I hit send, a warmth floods my body like a soothing bath of contentment. Speaking of baths...

Pushing from my chair, I cross the laminate tiled floor and go straight to my bathroom to fill the tub. While I'm waiting, I open the Amazon app on my phone and change my password. Angelica is thirty-five-fucking-years old, and she can open her own account.

She pays for virtually nothing on her own since she moved back home with Ma and Pop last year. And tonight I found out our father apparently paid to refurbish the small house next door to serve as her beauty salon.

As I sink into the warm water a few minutes later, I close my eyes and inhale the scent of lavender. Today is done and dusted, and I couldn't be happier, even though dinner at the Bell household exhausts me.

Yeah, Monday can go fuck itself with a big, smelly, diseased elephant dick.

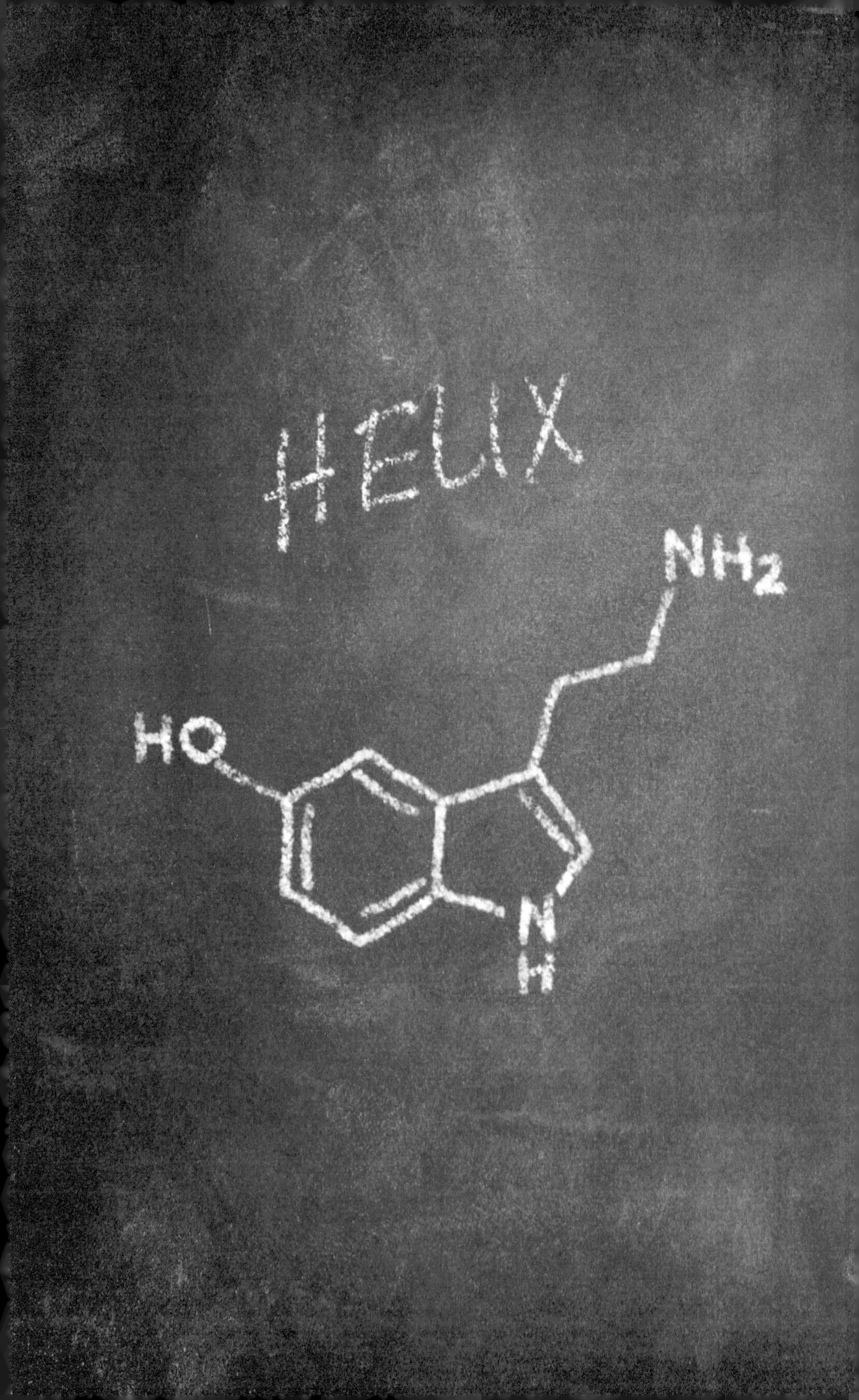

HELIX
NH2
HO
N
H

Chapter Three

IT'S DOUBTFUL SHE HAS A SECRET WILD SIDE

I swing open the door to my house and am struck in the knees by a ball of pure sunshine.

"Uncle Helix!" a sweet little voice squeals against my legs as I fight to maintain my balance.

"How's my doodle bug?" I ask, picking up Reece beneath her arms and lifting her until she's wrapped around my waist. I kiss her downy cheek and inhale the scent of bubble gum. My niece always smells like bubble gum.

She props her thin arms on my shoulders and grins. "I can wipe my own butt now."

I can't help but laugh. "That's good, Reecie. I'm proud of you." Stepping back, I allow Phoenix to stride in and close the door behind him. He sets Reece's pink suitcase in the foyer. "What are your plans tonight?" I ask him, and he winks.

"Oh, you know, the usual."

I'm assuming that means he has a date, or more likely, a hookup, though he never goes into specifics. I don't know why he's so vague about it. No one would judge him for needing a night off from dad duty, and we're all more than happy to help out because Reece is the light of our lives.

Speaking of Reecie, she grabs my face and pulls it around so she has a hundred percent of my attention. "Uncle Helix, what are we doing tonight?"

"Oh, I dunno. I thought we could maybe do some... science stuff?"

She squeals and reaches for Phoenix, and her dad takes her in his arms. Reece pats his face and says gently, as if she might hurt his feelings, "I love you so much, Daddy, but you can go now. I'll be fine doing science stuff with Uncle Helix."

He rubs his nose against hers before peppering her face with kisses. "Love you too, baby girl. Don't blow up the house or anything."

The four-year-old rolls her eyes like a damn teenager. "We won't, silly Daddy." Then she squirms until he sets her down, and she's off like a shot, running toward my kitchen.

"Thanks for keeping her," my twin says. "I'll take her bag up to her room while you go try to save your kitchen."

I lightly slap his arm. "No problem. It's the highlight of my week."

"Sooooo, how is this like science?" Reece asks as she sits atop my gray-and-white marble countertop. She's wearing a little apron that looks like a lab coat. I had it made for her a couple weeks ago, complete with *Dr. Reece* stitched on the chest.

"Because you have to measure every single ingredient perfectly and add them in the proper order," I tell her, handing her the measuring cup. "The recipe calls for one cup of cocoa powder, and if you don't put the exact amount, the brownies will come out gross. Same thing if you forget the eggs or vanilla. Just like if I add the wrong amount of something in my lab, it will mess up the entire project."

I show her how to make sure the top of the cocoa powder is flat and even before letting her dump it into the mixing bowl. We make a terrible mess adding all the ingredients, but it doesn't matter. Reece is having fun.

In my best nasally nerd voice, I say, "And now, you need to turn on the conversion device to transform the compound into a semi-liquid state."

She flicks on the stand mixer and giggles when the ingredients turn into a dark-brown sludge. "It is like science! Can I put them in the oven?"

"I think I'll do that part, since you're not qualified for that procedure yet," I tell her, booping her adorable button nose. "But you can help me scoop batter into the pan and make sure it's smooth."

Once the treats are in the oven, we clean up our mess, and then I sit cross-legged on the floor in front of the oven with Reece on my lap. We watch the brownies rise and firm up as they cook.

"Temperature is important in most chemical reactions. See how they're changing to a solid form with the addition of heat?"

Reece wiggles happily. "Uhh, you mean they're changing to a *yummy* form."

I grin against the top of her dark curls and place a kiss there. I love this kid, and I like teaching her about science in a way that's relevant and easy for her to understand. Science is everywhere, in every aspect of our daily lives, from the technology we use to the hormones that are released when we have certain emotions to the simple act of making brownies.

Reece is brimming with energy, so once the pan is out of the oven, I ask, "You want to take a swim while they're cooling?" She nods vehemently. "Do you need help putting your suit on?"

"Nope, I can do it by myself," she says smartly, tromping up the staircase to the room I have set up for her. I follow her up and go to my room to change. Less than five minutes later, I hear, "Uncle Helix, I need help!"

Smiling, I make my way down the dark-wood hallway to Reece's room, a veritable confection of bubblegum pink. That's the color I sense when I look at my niece. "What's the deal?"

She frowns and holds up the two straps that are supposed to wrap around her neck. "I can't tie them." Her bottom lip trembles, and I kneel down and press a kiss to her forehead.

"That's okay. Girls' bathing suits are complicated." Turning her, I tie the strings into a bow at the nape of her neck.

"Boys sure have it easy," she sighs like she has the weight of the world on her tiny shoulders. "All you have to do is put your shorts on."

I stand and hitch her onto my hip before traipsing down to the ground floor. Before we can head out the back door, I hear a knock at the front of the house. Reece's eyes widen.

"Who do you think it is? An axe murderer?"

I bust out laughing. Where does she come up with this shit?

"We don't get many of those in this neighborhood, doodle bug," I tell her wryly, walking across the parquet flooring to the foyer. I live in River Oaks, one of the most exclusive neighborhoods in Houston. Swinging open my navy-blue paneled front door, I find Perri on the brick doorstep.

"Aunt Perri!" Reece shrieks, practically leaping from my arms to my younger sister's. I stuff my hands into the pockets of my swim trunks and watch the two embrace.

"Hi, sweetie," Perri coos, her eyes closed as she twists side to side in a rocking motion. "I've missed you."

"I missed you too. When did you get home?"

"Last night, and when I heard you were going to be at Uncle Helix's house tonight, I decided to come over." My sister's blue eyes flash to me. "If that's okay."

I grab the back of her blonde head and pull her toward me to kiss her forehead. "Of course it's okay, sis. I'm glad you're home." Perri just graduated from the University of Michigan. We all went to her graduation, but before that, we hadn't seen her since Christmas.

Perri shares a father with me and my brothers, but she has her mother's looks, with pale-blonde hair and eyes that are a couple shades darker than mine and my twin's. Remi inherited our mother's brown eyes, though he also shares our dark hair.

"We're going to swim while the brownies cool," Reece chatters excitedly. "They're *special* brownies."

My sister arches a questioning eyebrow in my direction.

"Not *that* kind of special," I assure her with a chuckle. "Your suit is in the pool house, if you want to swim with us."

"I'll go with you and tie your straps," Reece offers. "Uncle Helix said girls' swimsuits are complicated."

That earns me another eyebrow from Perri, who mumbles under her breath as she passes, "Getting them off or getting them on?"

I shake my head with mirth and start to follow them, but my phone rings from the coffee table. "Perri, I gotta check this call. Keep an eye on her."

"Got her!" she calls back.

Reece is a good swimmer, but I take absolutely no chances with my niece's safety, and she's never allowed in the pool area without an adult.

Swiping my phone to answer, I say, "Hey, Abigail."

She sounds breathless when she replies. "Oh my god. I just got a call from Isla."

I'm the laboratory director now at Hale Cosmetics, and Dr. Abigail Blake is my lab manager. Isla is our administrative assistant.

Instantly on alert, my voice turns sharp. "What's wrong?"

"Not a single thing. Well, aside from Isla being behind on checking emails, but it was a really busy day today. You know that though since you were there. Thank you for lunch, by the way. Everyone really enjoyed the—"

"Abigail," I say sternly to get her back on track.

"Oh, right, right. So anyway, guess who we got an email from today?"

"Mickey Mouse," I say dryly, and there's a long pause before I hear a sharp bark of laughter. Abigail is book smart, but sometimes she doesn't get my sense of humor. Or maybe it was just a lame joke.

"No, Dr. Nicolette Bell," she announces, and I can picture her doing a little flair move with her hand.

Of course I recognize the name immediately. Though I've never met Dr. Bell in person, she's highly regarded in our industry, and I've read several of her articles and papers. In fact, some people call her the queen of modern-day biochemistry.

"Huh. She's with Aquarius Cosmetics now, right?"

"Yes," Abigail gushes. "Her name was on the top of the list from that headhunter we hired last month, so we sent her an inquiry. I never heard back, so I assumed she was happy with where she was, but today we got an email that she's interested in coming for an interview."

The tight tension I've had in my chest since Abigail announced her impending departure from Hale Cosmetics finally eases a bit. "That's really good news. I look forward to speaking with her."

I can practically hear my manager's wince as she hisses out a breath. "Yeah, there's a slight problem with that. She asked to come for an interview on Friday, and you're leaving for London tomorrow."

"Shit," I curse, pinching the bridge of my nose. "I can't put off this trip. I need to finalize everything for the new European skincare launch next month."

As well as being the lab director for the U.S. division, I'm also the head of research and development for all Hale laboratories worldwide. And this trip is extremely time-sensitive.

"I've heard that Dior and Estée Lauder are also looking to hire for their labs this year, so I think we need to strike while the iron is hot. It's not very often that someone like Dr. Bell becomes available."

That's true. What the fuck is Aquarius thinking by not doing everything in their power to hold onto someone with her qualifications?

"That's not helping my stress levels, Abigail," I warn as a headache begins to throb in my temples. "I know you're wanting to retire before your first grandchild is born in a couple months."

"I *am* retiring," she reiterates firmly. "What if I do the initial interview with Dr. Bell on Friday? I mean, it's almost a foregone conclusion that we'll hire her, as long as she's not a total psycho in person. She's by far the most qualified person we could get."

My face scrunches. "I don't know, Abigail. Don't you think it would be insulting if the head of the department isn't even there to meet with her?"

"I've been thinking about that," she replies quickly. "So just hear me out. I could explain about your trip and that you really wanted to be here, and if everything goes well, I could take her to meet your father. Don't you think meeting with the CEO of the entire company would be impressive? You know they usually keep us lab rats locked in our little science cave."

I can't help but chuckle because it's true. Our lab is housed in its own building next door to the corporate offices.

"Okay, I think that might work but let me respond to her email. I think a personal note from me might help to smooth things over."

Sometimes extremely brilliant people can be prickly, and I don't want to blow this chance.

Abigail's voice trembles slightly, probably because she's doing the shoulder shimmy she does when she's excited. "I have a good feeling about her. I think she could be the one, Helix."

Those words hit me in an odd way directly in the center of my chest, and I rub my fingertips across the spot. "I hope so, Abigail."

After hanging up, I go to the back door and peer through the paned glass to check on the girls. They're splashing in the pool, so I stick my head out to tell them I'll be just another minute.

Then I carefully draft an email to Dr. Nicolette Bell.

Dr. Bell,

I'm so pleased to hear that you're interested in joining us at Hale Cosmetics. We strive to be the best in the industry in both quality of products and quality of life for our employees. At our core, we are a family-run business, and we like those who work with us to feel like they are truly a part of the Hale family.

I understand you'd like to come for an interview this Friday. That can definitely be arranged, though I will be out of town for the week. I hate that I can't be there to meet with you personally, but my lab manager, Dr. Abigail Blake, would be more than happy to conduct the interview and show you around. Dr. Blake has been with the company for over a decade, so she can answer any questions you may have.
I apologize deeply that I can't be there in person, but I have time-sensitive business at our London offices. I hope you don't perceive this as a slight to you in any way. If you'd prefer to meet at a different time after I return, I'd be happy to schedule that at your convenience.

Feel free to email me at any time if you have questions or concerns.

I look forward to your reply.

Sincerely,

Helix Hale, PhD, Laboratory Director and Head of Research and Development - Hale Cosmetics, Inc.

I read over it again before hitting send. Then I walk out to the flagstone surrounding my pool and stride to the side, tucking away my professional persona and fully embracing my fun Uncle Helix side.

"Look out, girls," I call, taking two long strides before launching myself into a ball over the water. "Cannonball!"

"I like these pajamas, Reecie," I tell my niece, pulling the satin top over her head.

"I love dragons," she announces like I'm not fully aware of that fact.

"Did you know there's going to be a new football team in town? They'll be called the Houston Dragons."

"No way," she breathes, her blue eyes going round. She looks so much like Phoenix when she does that.

"Yes way," I retort, picking her up and tossing her onto the middle of my bed, where she bounces with a giggle. "And it's a ladies' football team."

Reece scrunches her face and squeals, clasping her tiny hands in front of her chest. "Do you think we can go to a game? Huh? Can we? Please, please, please?"

"I think that could be arranged. Now get under the covers and read your book while I take my shower."

She scoots beneath the dark-blue sheets and flops back onto the silky pink pillow I keep on my bed just for her. I kiss her forehead and go into the en suite.

When I return a few minutes later, Reece is looking at *Azmina the Gold Glitter Dragon*, which is book two in the *Dragon Girls* box set I got her for Christmas last year. Even though she's only four, she's already reading at a first-grade level, thanks to her nanny. Ms. Lorraine is in her sixties, a retired elementary school teacher with empty nest syndrome and a love of reading. Phoenix was lucky to find her.

I'm dressed in black pajama pants when I emerge and climb in beside Reece. Yes, she has her own room at my house, but I'm a sucker for her sweet little face, so I don't even argue with her about it anymore. One day she'll be too old to want to snuggle with her Uncle Helix.

"What's this word?" she asks, and I wedge my arm beneath her head and peer at the book.

"Let's sound it out. What is T-I-N-G?"

"Ting?"

"Yep, and when you add the rest it's…" I watch as her lips move and her brain works through it.

"Tingled!" she exclaims. "Her fingertips tingled."

"That's right, doodle bug. Do you want to read the rest of it out loud to me?"

Seven minutes later, Reece's words are coming slower and farther apart as her eyelids begin to droop. I take the book and place it on the nightstand before my niece rolls toward me and cuddles into my side.

Her shampoo gives off a sweet, fruity scent, and it sparks an idea. Our company makes high-end hair products for adults, but what if we developed a shampoo and conditioner line for kids? Maybe different formulations for straight hair versus curly hair, like Reece has.

I pick up my phone to make a note of it when I notice an email from Nicolette Bell. She replied that she's happy to meet with Abigail on Friday and completely understands about the scheduling conflict. Feeling better, I dig into some research on the biochemist.

Damn, her credentials are impressive. Dual doctorate degrees in biochem and medicine. Did her residency in dermatology. Also has a strong background in microbiology. And she's only thirty-three years old, a year older than me.

I also note with interest that she was the keynote speaker at the recent American Academy of Clinical Biochemistry conference. I'm a member of the Academy as well—it's by invitation only—but I hardly ever go to conferences or meetings, only enough to obtain some continuing education hours. I'm not exactly the social type.

I locate tons of photos of Dr. Bell, all with her hair in a prim bun and with black-rimmed glasses over her green eyes. She's pretty enough, though she appears to be very straitlaced. Not surprising. The woman has more degrees than a thermometer, so it's doubtful she has a secret wild side. Not that I care about that. All I'm concerned with is that she's qualified to do her job.

Removing my own glasses, I set them aside and turn off the lamp, hoping Dr. Nicolette Bell will fit in well with me and the rest of the team.

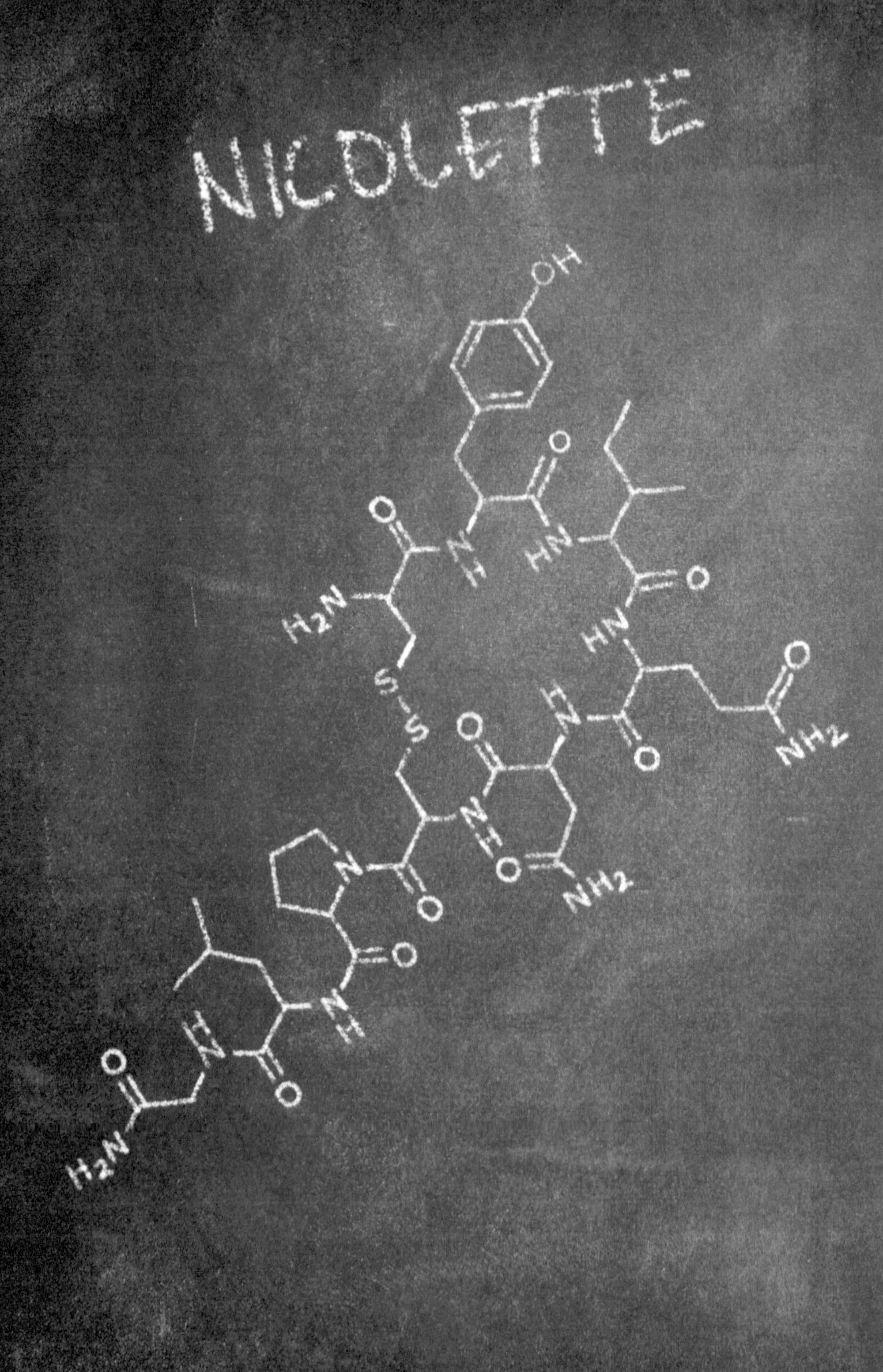

NICOLETTE
OH
H2N
NH2
NH2
H2N

Chapter Four

HE'S PROBABLY A BIT OF A DUD

"Hey, I just landed," I say to my friend Lehra when I step onto the concourse in the Houston airport on Friday at ten in the morning.

"Switch to FaceTime so I can see how gorgeous you look," she says. Changing the call over, I see my adorable friend with her blonde curls and wide smile.

"Here I am in all my professional glory," I say dryly.

"Let me see the fit," she demands. "My husband wants to see too." Lehra and Cruz Estrada recently got married, and she loves to say the H-word every chance she gets.

Cruz's handsome face squeezes in beside hers. He's Cuban, with brown skin and brilliant blue eyes, and he's an absolute dreamboat. After her prior relationship, Lehra deserves a man who treats her like she's everything, and Cruz is most definitely that man.

"Me too! I wanna see," a familiar voice says in the background before our crazy friend Artie seats himself on Cruz's lap with a flourish. Cruz just shakes his head good-naturedly as they all jockey for position. "Okay, show us."

Stepping into an alcove, I pull the phone back and drift it down my body, showing off the new black suit I'd treated myself to for this interview.

"I'm just wearing the tennis shoes until I get in the car," I inform them. "I have my black heels in my bag."

"Oh my god, you look stunning. That lipstick is the perfect shade of red," Lehra says, dabbing at her eyes with her napkin like a mom watching her firstborn head off to kindergarten.

"Agreed," Artie chimes in. "It looks very professional... and not in a sex worker kind of way."

I can't help but laugh. "Well that's good since I was definitely not going for the hooker vibes."

"You're gonna knock 'em dead," Cruz says with a small smile.

"Because she's a fucking queen," Artie adds with a snappy hand gesture.

I swear, these people are good for my soul.

Another voice I recognize hits my ear. "What can I get y'all today?"

"Oh, you're at the Butterfly?" I ask, referring to the Butterfly Martini Bar in Manhattan.

Charmaine, our favorite server, somehow manages to wedge her face in among the others from behind their table. "Hey, girl. You headed to your interview? You look great."

"Thanks, and yes. They're sending a car for me."

"Good. Kick some interview ass." She bops Artie on the head with her butterfly-shaped notepad. "What do you want to drink, you little freak?"

I fight a grin as I await his answer. Artie always gets the same drink, but he... *embellishes* his order each time.

"Give me a dirty martini."

"How dirty?" Charmaine asks, playing along like she always does. Last time we were there, he said he wanted a martini that was *anal sex with a hobo* level of dirty.

Artie's lips curl up at the corners. "I want it to be as dirty as the inner rim of a gas station toilet after chimichanga night."

Charmaine makes a gagging noise before taking the rest of the drink and lunch orders. Once she's departed, Lehra leans her chin on her hand and returns her attention to me.

"Are you nervous?"

I wrinkle my nose. "No, just... anxious, I guess. I've been with

Aquarius Cosmetics since I graduated, so going to a new company will be a whole new world."

What if they don't like me?

"They're going to love you," Artie says as if he can read my mind. "You're the coolest nerdy bitch I know."

That makes me laugh. "Thanks, but I need to go. I still have to find my driver."

Cruz and Artie wish me luck, and Lehra blows me a kiss. "You've got this, babe. I'm so proud of you."

She has no idea how much I needed to hear someone say those words to me.

Calvin, the man driving the town car that was sent to pick me up, is a burly red-haired southern gentleman with a deep, soothing drawl. He's also an excellent tour guide, pointing out landmarks and attractions as he weaves through the Houston traffic and into the downtown area.

"Now down yonder is the medical center," he says, pointing a thick finger toward a busy road.

I chose to sit in the front seat with Calvin rather than in the back, and I duck my head to see numerous hospital signs in the distance.

"Is MD Anderson down there?" I ask.

"It is," he says, casting a glance toward me. "Are you... I mean, do you have... Sorry, I'm prying."

His cheeks go ruddy, and I rush to assure him. "No, I don't have cancer, but a friend of mine from med school did his oncology residency at MD Anderson. I know it's ranked as the top cancer hospital in the country."

Calvin nods in the affirmative. "It is. My mother had stage four breast cancer, and they saved her. She's still kicking along, even at age eighty."

"It's wonderful that you still have your mom."

"I agree. And here is Hale Cosmetics," he informs me as we pull up to the curb. "The tall building has all the corporate offices, but you'll be going into that one there. That's the lab." He points to the three-story structure to the right of the larger one.

Both buildings are made of blue mirrored glass, though the office building is at least ten stories with the Hale Cosmetics logo near the top. "Thanks for the ride, Calvin. And for the excellent conversation."

"Of course. Stay right there, and I'll get your door for ya." The driver is spry for such a big guy, rounding the car quickly to pull open my door. "Good luck to you, Dr. Bell. I hope to see you again soon." He tips an imaginary hat to me and grins widely.

"I hope so too."

"Ah, there's Dr. Blake. Isn't she ugly?" he asks, gesturing toward a woman striding toward us from the laboratory building. When I gasp in surprise at his rude comment, he bursts into loud guffaws. "I'm the only one allowed to say that because she's my sister."

That relaxes me into a laugh, and I recognize the family resemblance as she gets closer. Dr. Abigail Blake has short, flame-red hair interspersed with gray, and her hazel eyes twinkle like her brother's.

"Dr. Bell," she greets, shaking my hand enthusiastically. "So pleased to have you here. I hope Calvin didn't fill your head with any of his bull."

"He told me he has the most brilliant and beautiful sister in the world," I tell her teasingly, and she cuts her eyes suspiciously at a grinning Calvin.

"Hmm, I guess I'll let him live another day then." She rises on tiptoe to kiss him on the cheek. "I'll text you when we're ready to go to lunch."

"I interrogated Dr. Bell like you asked and learned all her secrets," Calvin says in a mock whisper.

"Did you waterboard her?" Abigail whispers back.

"No, but if she didn't fess up, I was going to make her listen to my entire discography of Willie Nelson until she spilled the beans."

His sister shudders, and I laugh at their sibling banter. "That wouldn't have worked on me," I inform them. "I like Willie."

"Ah, a woman of refined taste," Calvin booms. "Hire her immediately."

Abigail shoves his shoulder. "Go on, you big goofus. And thank you for picking up Dr. Bell."

"You're welcome to call me Nicolette," I offer. Yes, I worked hard for my degrees, but I'm not one of those people who insists my colleagues call me doctor every time they address me.

Her already friendly smile warms by about twenty degrees. "Excellent, and you call me Abigail." She gestures with a hand toward the mirrored glass front doors, and we begin walking. "I think you'll fit in just fine here, Nicolette."

I. Love. Hale. Cosmetics.

My interview went well—great, in fact—and we've just completed a tour of all three floors of the laboratory building.

Everything about this place is freaking fantastic, from the high-tech lab facilities to the people. The only drawback is the location. Due to the humidity in Houston, if my hair weren't tamed into its customary bun, I'd be looking like a poodle right now.

But I can overlook the tragedy my tresses will be if I ever wear my hair down because *the lab*! It's seriously one of the best I've ever seen. Judging by Dr. Helix Hale's extremely formal tone in our email exchange, I'm guessing he's a bit of a stick-in-the-mud, but the man does know how to organize and run a laboratory, so I can overlook that. It's totally fine because I'm not looking for a friend, just a colleague that respects me and my work.

"I thought we'd grab a bite of lunch, and then I'll introduce you to our CEO," Abigail says.

My eyebrows shoot upward. She's going to introduce me to Haywood Hale? I'm pretty sure the CEO of my current company, Aquarius Cosmetics, has no clue who I even am. I passed him in the hallway last month, and he called me Nelda.

"That sounds great," I reply.

"Do you have any specific dietary requirements or allergies?" she asks.

"No, I pretty much eat anything."

Abigail leads me out of the building where Calvin is waiting beside the fancy town car. "Great. We'll go to Pappadeaux. It's seafood with a Cajun flair, and their bread is to die for."

The drive to the restaurant doesn't take long, and we arrive at a brick building with a wide patio that's surrounded by a short, black, iron fence. When I suggest Calvin join us for lunch, he declines, citing his seafood allergy.

"We could have eaten somewhere else so your brother could have come," I tell Abigail once we're seated on the patio. It's June, but the fans and the shade keep the Houston heat under control.

"He's fine. He usually has lunch on Fridays with a couple of his old Army buddies at a burger restaurant."

I smile. "He looks like a former military guy."

"He was on the boxing team in the Army before he suffered a retinal tear. The docs repaired it, but they told him he could potentially lose his eyesight if he gets hit in that eye again."

My forehead furrows with a wince. "Ouch. At least he listened to the doctors' advice."

Abigail shakes her head and smirks. "The stubborn fool would have kept right on fighting, but his superiors put a stop to it." She greets our server warmly when she approaches and sets a basket of bread and whipped butter between us. "Thank you, Candice."

We order our food and drinks. I'm tempted to get a mixed drink but decide against it since I'm technically still on an interview, so I get the same thing my lunch partner gets... sweet iced tea. When in Rome and all that.

"Do you like working at Hale?" I ask Abigail, and her smile is nothing short of beaming when she replies.

"I love it. I'd stay here forever, but my daughter is expecting her first baby soon. Childcare costs are insane, so I decided to retire and focus on being the coolest babysitting grandma ever." She leans slightly across the table and lowers her voice. "Do you mind if I ask you a personal question, Nicolette?"

"Not at all." Candice drops off our drinks and I take a sip. It's not bad. A little sweet, but I think I could get used to it. "Ask me anything."

"Why do you want to leave Aquarius?"

Ugh. This is a difficult question. It's bad form to badmouth your employer while on a job interview, but I also want to be honest, so I choose my words carefully.

"I'm looking for a change in leadership."

Her lips twitch at the corners as she reads my meaning without me having to spell it out. "Who is the director of your current lab? I know Dr. Tate retired last year."

And that's when my discontent began. I'd hoped to get Thomas Tate's position when he retired, but I was passed over for the promotion.

"Joyce Davidson," I reply, trying to keep the bitterness from my voice.

"Hmm, I don't think I know Dr. Davidson," Abigail muses, pulling off a chunk of bread and coating it lightly with seasoned butter.

"She's not a PhD," I reply. "She has a bachelor's degree in women's studies."

Abigail's hands stop, and she gapes at me in amazement. "How is she qualified to run a cosmetics lab?"

I barely manage to hold back the "she's not" that's on the tip of my tongue and instead reply with what I hope is a neutral tone. "She's the CEO's niece."

She slumps against the back of her chair and shakes her head. "I think I understand."

I knew she would. Dr. Abigail Blake is a sharp woman. Changing the subject, I ask, "How is it working for Dr. Hale?"

Abigail's face breaks into a smile. "He's utterly brilliant. I'd say he's fairly easy to get along with. Definitely demands the best from anyone who works there, but he's fair."

"Do you feel like he listens to you and is accepting of new ideas?"

Her head tilts to the side in thought. "Helix can be a bit stoic, but he appreciates innovation, no matter if it's his idea or someone else's. He's a man of few words, but I feel like he always listens to me. I like to tease him that his ears work better than his mouth." Abigail eyes me over the rim of her glass as she takes a sip. "Do you feel like you're not being heard in your current job?"

Again, a sticky question with an equally sticky answer. Aquarius hasn't had a single new product line since Joyce took over a year ago. I have ideas, but she poo-poos them as unnecessary because *things are going fine. Why mess with a perfectly good formula? If it ain't broke, don't fix it.*

So I temper my response and answer as diplomatically as I can. "I enjoy new development. I prefer to push through the stagnant old ways and discover fresh, vibrant new products that keep consumers interested."

Abigail nods thoughtfully. "That's Dr. Hale's approach as well, so I think you two will mesh well. I appreciate your honesty." She winks. "And your very diplomatic answer. Helix would appreciate that as well. He values loyalty above all else."

Loyalty. Hence the reason I didn't call Joyce a complete moron and say she's running the development lab at Aquarius into the ground.

As the server sets my plate of Texas redfish with crawfish étouffée in front of me, I tell Abigail, "Dr. Hale sounds wonderful. I look forward to meeting him."

Though in the back of my mind, I'm thinking he's probably a bit of a dud.

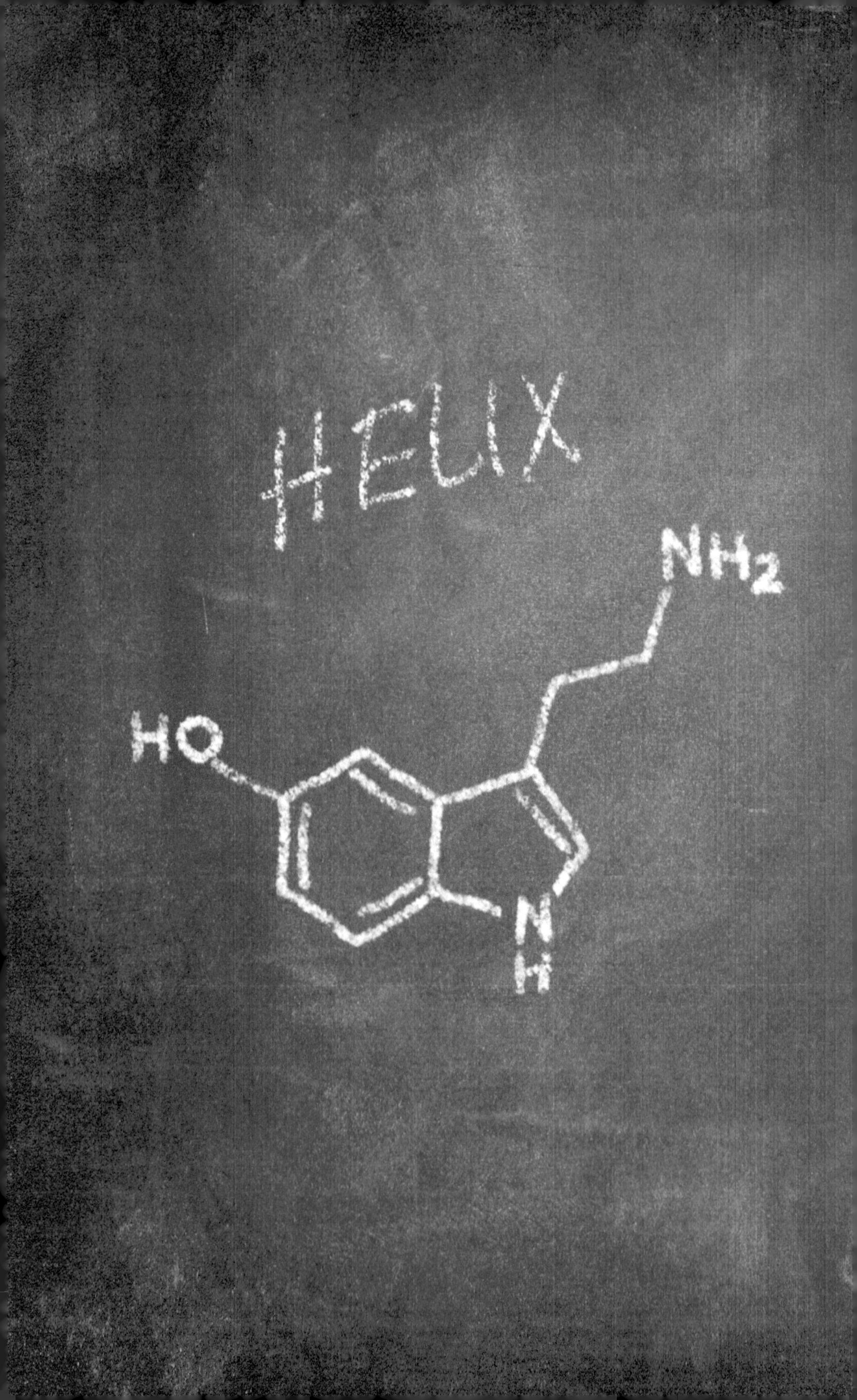

HELIX

NH2

HO

NH

Chapter Five

THE FUCKMEISTER HAS ARISEN

"I think she would fit in really well here, Helix. We both know her qualifications are impeccable, but she seems like a good person too. She was so kind to Calvin, and he definitely approves of her."

I'm at Remi's flat in London, and I relax back onto his black leather couch as I speak with Abigail on the phone. Her report makes me feel better, especially the part about Calvin. I don't stand for anyone being condescending toward him. I actually refused to work with one supplier after their salesman copped an attitude and made a rude comment about our driver.

While Calvin may not have the academic brilliance of his sister, the man is a gem. He's loyal and kind, and I regard him with the utmost respect for his service to our country.

Rubbing the back of my neck, I ask, "And she seemed like she would fit in well with the rest of the team? You know I don't like drama and shit."

Abigail hums thoughtfully. "I don't think you have to worry about that. Nicolette got along with everyone. She even took time to stop and engage with Cody and Marla while they were homogenizing some samples of that new under-eye gel." Cody and Marla are two of our graduate students who are working toward their PhDs.

"Cody didn't say anything stupid did he?" While he's a highly intelligent kid, sometimes he can be a bit awkward.

I can hear Abigail's grin through the phone. "He asked her what her favorite amino acid is."

I shake my head in amusement. It's not the weirdest thing he's ever said. "And what was her answer?"

"Phenylalanine."

"Mental acuity and mood. That's a good one," I muse. "I trust you, Abigail, and if you think Dr. Bell is a good fit, I'll make her an offer."

She sounds pleased. "Good. I was afraid if we didn't find someone to replace me, you might hold me hostage in servitude."

A smile crests my lips. "Distinct possibility, though I would have treated you well and let you out of your cage for bathroom breaks at least twice a day."

"Well, aren't you sweet," she drawls sarcastically. "Though I am a little sad I don't get to work with Dr. Bell. She's brilliant."

"And what am I? Chopped liver?"

"Meh, you're okay," she teases, "but I do think we may have found someone who's actually smarter than you, boss."

"We'll see," I say mildly, though after reading Nicolette Bell's extensive resume, I think Abigail may be correct.

And I'm surprisingly okay with that.

"Everything go okay with the interview?" Remi asks when he wanders back into the living room with two glasses of fine scotch.

"Yep, Abigail likes her. I just emailed Dr. Bell an offer, so we'll see what happens."

My brother hands me a glass and settles into the black recliner adjacent to my seat on the couch. "How's Phoenix doing?"

I think about my twin as I take a sip. The liquor tastes warm and buttery-smooth going down. "Seems like he's doing well. He has one of us keep Reece every Tuesday, but he's kinda tight-lipped about where he goes on those nights."

"Probably getting some pussy," Remington remarks, crossing his legs at the ankles. "God knows he needs it."

"Maybe, but it's weird. You know how he is. He'd tell me if he were hooking up with someone. Phe has never been shy about his body count."

Remi shrugs. "Could be that he's getting serious with someone and wants to see where it goes before telling the family."

"Could be," I admit, "though he swore he'd never get serious about anyone again after Bea."

My brother's nose wrinkles at the mention of Phoenix's former fiancée. "I know what happened was fucked up, but I'm glad we never have to see her again."

"Amen, brother," I say, lifting my glass in a toast.

"I hear we signed one of the players from the women's new football league to do a campaign for us."

I nod. "Yeah, Houston's getting a team, the Dragons, so Phoenix thought it would be good to get one of the players from our home team. Jordie McNamara is her name."

Remington takes a sip of his drink. "I think that's a smart move. Women's sports are on the rise, and it seems like this new league is going to be very popular. And Jordie is fantastic." At my raised eyebrows, he chuckles. "Don't look so surprised. I watch more than the golf channel."

I laugh with him. "There have been women's football leagues for years, but this one has the full backing of the NFL, so I think you're right."

"This is a good opportunity for Hale Cosmetics and for Jordie." Remi pauses and rolls his eyes. "As long as Phoenix doesn't try to fuck her."

My head tilts to the side in thought. "He won't. She's way too young for him." I lift my glass to my lips and drain the contents. "Now what are we eating tonight?"

The vibe of the London steakhouse is almost Gatsby-esque with its boisterous elegance. I cut into my Scottish grass-fed fillet, swirl it through the truffle mustard, and take the first bite.

Remington smiles at my quiet moan. "Good, huh?"

Swallowing, I nod. "Very. It's been a while since I had a steak."

My brother's knife slices through his Japanese Wagyu as smoothly as if the meat was a slab of warm butter. "Did you get the glitch worked out with the samples today?" he asks before placing a small hunk of steak into his mouth.

I take a sip of my delicious red wine. "I should have it sorted by Monday. I'll head up to the lab in the morning."

"I knew you would. So what's going on at home? Anything new?"

"Perri got home this week, and Reecie learned how to wipe her own ass."

Remington covers his mouth with his linen napkin, but it barely muffles the snort. "Sounds like cause for a party."

I pop a potato into my mouth, and my eyes almost roll back into my head at the salty, crispy outside and tender inside. "These fries are amazing."

My brother lifts an eyebrow and corrects me. "They're called chips here. This restaurant fries them in beef drippings. That's why they're so good." His gaze drifts to something over my right shoulder, and his entire demeanor changes. When his brown eyes darken, so does his deep purple aura.

Ah, he's spotted something that interests him. Or someone.

My thought is confirmed a second later when a British female voice says, "Remi! Don't mean to geg in, but I wanted to say hi."

Remington gives a jerk of his chin, and, like she's been summoned, the buxom brunette rounds the table and kisses him full on the mouth. She's wearing a short sparkly black cocktail dress with tiny ruffles at the shoulders.

My brother whispers something into her ear, and she giggles when he palms her ass right in the middle of the restaurant. He looks around her and speaks to me. "Do you mind if I have company later?"

A smirk pulls at my lips. "Not at all. I'm going to bed early tonight."

Six hours later, I regret that permission. The woman is not quiet, and these two have been going at it for the past four hours. Four. Fucking. Hours.

After the noise finally ended and I managed a couple hours' sleep, I'm fully dressed and making a cup of coffee in Remi's kitchen. He strolls in wearing only loose-fitting pajama pants and a road map of scratches all over his torso.

"Well," I say dryly, "the fuckmeister has arisen."

Unaffected by my irritated tone, he steals my coffee, adds some sugar, and takes a long sip before handing it back to me. "Sorry, I forgot how loud Aster can be." His voice is filled with the grit of someone who got zero sleep and gives zero fucks about it.

"Are you on some kind of supplements or something, Rem? Because good god!" Seriously, I like to think I have stamina in the bedroom, but four hours nonstop?

His hair looks like a mother pterodactyl has begun building a nest in it, and he runs a hand through the dark locks, which doesn't help. "No. I sometimes practice tantric sex. It can last a while."

My eyebrows lift. "I've heard of that but haven't looked into it much. Isn't it where you're looking for a deep emotional bond with someone?" Remi shrugs and turns to open the refrigerator. "So this Aster is someone important to you?"

The slam of the refrigerator door startles me, and I cup my coffee mug with both hands to steady it. Remington turns slowly, his eyes diminished to narrow lines that barely show a hint of blue iris.

"No, she's nothing to me but a fuck. And no, I'm not playing her. Aster knows what I'm able to give and what I'm not, and she's good with that." He leans his shoulders back against the fridge and rubs at his chest. "I don't get with her often because I don't want to lead her on. Just every couple of months or so."

I prop my ass against the countertop and take a sip of my coffee, wincing at the too-sweet taste. "Sorry, Rem. I didn't mean to get you all riled up. I just thought the tantric stuff was something you were supposed to do with... a partner. Like a real partner you're trying to connect with."

His gaze falls to the wood floor, and his voice goes quiet, contemplative. "I'm trying to find something I had once. Only once."

After a few beats of silence, I understand. "The girl you were with after Phoenix's bachelor party." It's not a question because it doesn't require an answer. I already know because all I heard for weeks afterward was about his *one perfect night.* Remi nods anyway.

"Yeah, Minnie." He shoves away from the refrigerator, the movement almost violent as he strides to the pantry door and opens it. "I'm looking for another connection like that. I remember thinking that night that being with her was almost tantric."

What he's looking for is dawning in my brain. "So you studied tantra so you could try and find the same thing with someone else?"

"Yes," comes his clipped answer as he moves things around on the top shelf.

"Have you ever thought maybe it was the woman and not some arbitrary experience with a stranger that you can recreate with another person?"

Remington's head drops, and he blows out a sigh. "Of course I have. But I can't have her." He turns, and his face is pinched with... pain? "Why did she leave in the middle of the night, Helix? I thought—no, *I knew* she felt it too. So why?"

For five years, everyone has been focused on how that weekend changed Phoenix's life forever, but it seems Remi was just as affected.

And if I'm being completely honest...

I was too.

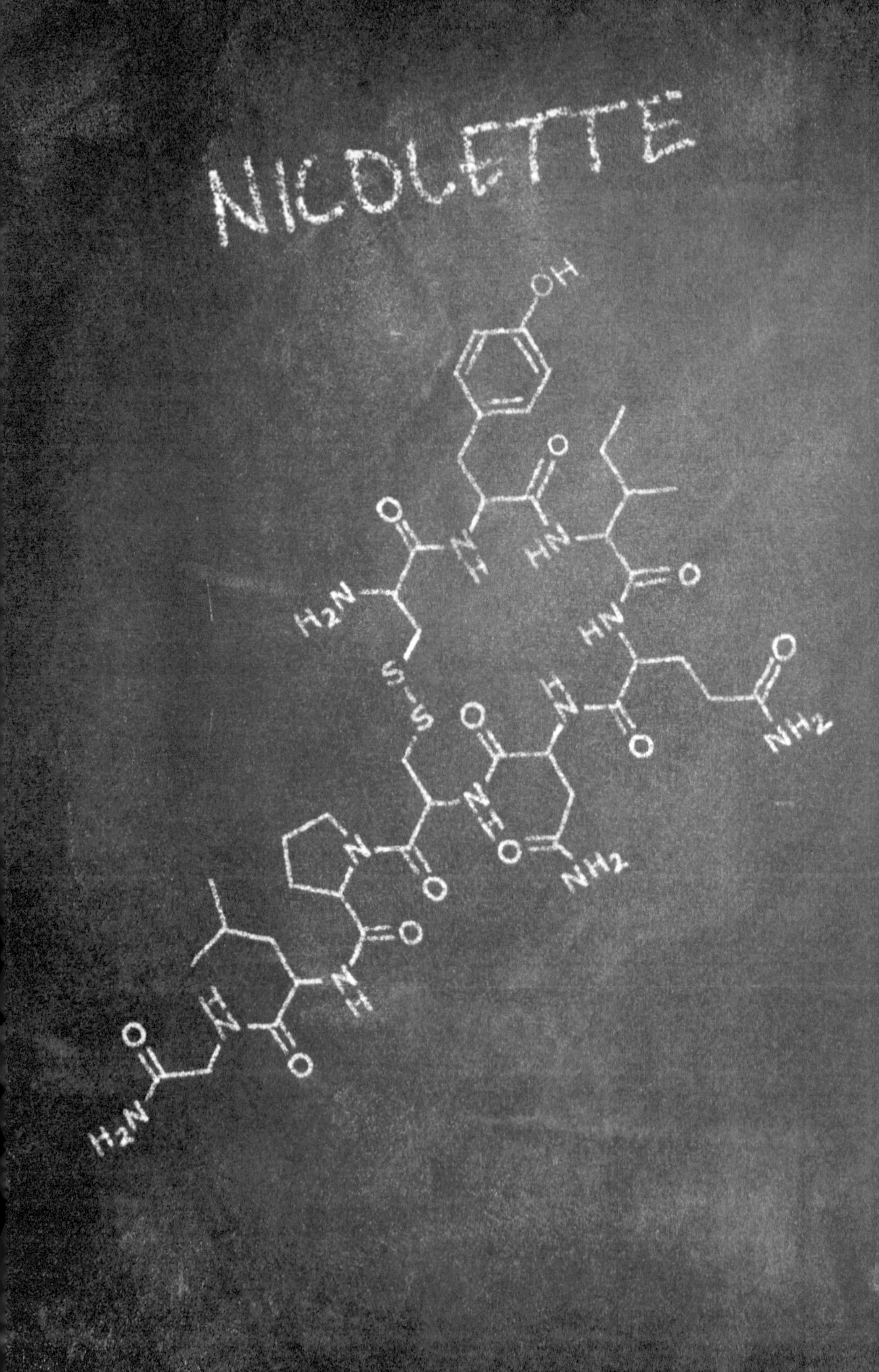
NICOLETTE

Chapter Six

THE BIRTHDAY

"Happy birthday!" Artie yells into my face on the sidewalk outside the Butterfly Martini Bar in Manhattan. Then he grabs me around the waist and squeezes me tightly.

"My turn to hug the birthday girl," Lehra, my other best friend, announces, pulling him away and embracing me herself. My friends are very huggy, and it took me a while to get used to that when I met them a few years ago. For a while, I did this weirdly stiff shoulder pat thing, but they just kept hugging me every time I saw them. And now I relish the affection these two dole out and even return it.

"Thank you both," I laugh as Lehra releases me. "You smell amazing."

She sniffs her own wrist. "I do, don't I? It's one of Hale Cosmetics' fragrances. As soon as you told me you accepted the job offer, I went out and bought a bunch of their products in support." Lehra purses her lips, showing off a pretty peach lip gloss that suits her flawless pale skin. "Got this too."

"Great color on you," I tell her as we enter the bar, which also serves the best comfort food. The dim entryway is almost like a grotto, the darkness offset by neon-colored butterflies hanging from the low ceiling. I love this place.

"Can we be in Charmaine's section?" Artie asks the hostess, and a minute later, we're being seated in a round, purple leather booth.

"My husband texted that he'll be a couple minutes late. He was tied up in a meeting," Lehra tells me once we're settled. There's that H-word again, and I freaking love how excited she is about being married to Cruz.

I met Lehra a few years ago during my dermatology residency at Columbia. My chief resident invited a few of the residents to attend a charity event at our hospital, and Lehra was there with a group from Bouvier, the fashion company where she works. We were seated beside each other at dinner and immediately hit it off. A week later, she introduced me to her friend, Artie, and they became my people.

"Let's see what I want today," I say as I pick up the card with the drink specials.

"You're drinking during lunch on a workday?" Artie questions in surprise because I would normally never do that. Drinking and working in a laboratory don't mix.

My lips roll into a smirk. "This morning I handed in my resignation, and Joyce panicked. Told me she would see about getting me more money and then went all conciliatory." I raise my voice to replicate Joyce's annoying tone. *"Gosh, you should take the rest of the day off since it's your birthday, Dr. Bell. No, really. I insist."*

Artie strokes his ginger beard. "Isn't that the same chick who griped when you were doing mercury testing and wanted to know what the planets had to do with cosmetics?"

I laugh. "Yep, that's her. I honestly felt relieved when I handed her the resignation letter. I think this is the right move for me."

"I agree," Lehra says, but her smile holds a hint of sadness. "It's bittersweet though because we're going to miss you."

"I'll miss you too," I tell her honestly. I didn't have a ton of friends in school because I was so much younger than my classmates. Lehra and Artie taught me how to give and receive unconditional friendship, and that's the greatest gift I've ever been given.

"We'll just hijack the Bouviers' private plane and come visit you," Artie suggests with a flourish of his hand, like that settles it.

"I'm pretty sure that would get Lehra fired from her job," I remark.

Lehra recently took over as the personal assistant for CEO Auburn Bouvier when his previous one retired.

Charmaine approaches and greets us before asking, "What can I getcha?"

"Gimlet and the house salad," I say, smiling up at her.

Lehra tilts her head and hums. "Ummmm, a Moscow mule for me and a sweet tea for my hubby. We'll split a large order of the Irish nachos."

Charmaine turns to a smirking Artie. "And what will your crazy ass have?"

"Loaded fries and..." He pauses dramatically. "A dirty martini."

Our server puffs out a breath and a weary, "How dirty?"

His grin turns wicked. "I want it to be *two syphilitic sheep fucking in an outhouse* dirty."

"Jesus, where do you come up with this shit?" she mutters, though her lips are twitching in amusement as she wends her way through the tables and back to the kitchen.

"I think we're her favorite diners," Artie announces, opening his satchel and pulling out a slightly wrinkled gift bag. "For you, babe. It's from all three of us."

"I'm here," Cruz announces, setting down the box in his hand, squeezing his big body in beside Lehra, and gripping her chin before giving her a soft, lingering kiss on the lips. "Hi, wife."

"Hi, husband," she coos. They stare at each other like the world would end if they looked away.

"Dear god, cut it out! I'm getting the diabetes just from watching you two," Artie whines, and the couple finally breaks eye contact with self-deprecating chuckles.

"Cruz, have you heard from Gianna or Auburn today?" I ask. "She called me yesterday to say she can't make it for lunch because the baby is sick." Gianna is married to Auburn Bouvier, and their daughter, Eliana, is only a few months old.

Cruz's face pulls into a grimace. "Yeah, they ended up taking her to the emergency room last night. She has a stomach bug and the docs were worried about dehydration, so they gave her IV fluids and kept her overnight. Auburn said they got home early this morning, and she's a lot better."

"Aww, poor little thing. Are the twins sick too?" he asks, referring to the Bouviers' eight-year-olds.

"Thank goodness, no," Cruz replies. "They're staying with Gianna's dad and Tora so they don't get exposed to the germs. Auburn hired a service to come deep clean the house while they had Eliana at the hospital."

"In the middle of the night? I've never heard of a service that—" Lehra begins before shaking her head with a smile. "Never mind. I forgot they're freaking billionaires."

Which isn't hard to do, especially where Gianna is concerned. She's a Texas girl who moved to New York and snagged the most eligible bachelor in the city, though she's still one of the most down-to-earth people I know. Of course she always dresses fabulously when they go to an event, but it's not uncommon to see her in an old sweatshirt and holey leggings when she's hanging out around the house. Auburn, on the other hand, always looks the part of a wealthy fashion CEO, and I imagine his underwear probably costs as much as the GDP of a small country.

"Poor Eliana," I say. "And her parents. I wish we could do something for them." Gianna has become a good friend to all of us in the past couple years.

"I'll send them a care package and put all our names on it," Lehra offers. "Some food for Auburn and Gianna and Pedialyte for the baby. Oh, and there's this fantastic baby wash and lotion with lavender that I found at a baby boutique downtown. That might help soothe Eliana."

Cruz is looking at his wife like he'd love to toss her on the table and make their own baby right here in front of everyone, if that subtle lick of his lips is any indication.

Artie leans over the table and inspects something on Cruz's face. "What is that in your beard? It's pink."

Cruz's cheeks go tomato-red, and he scrubs at a spot near his jaw. "Just a temporary... uhhh... shit. I thought I got it all."

Lehra giggles, her face also blushing. Artie's face, on the other hand, is ripe with glee.

"You kinky fuckers were role-playing again, weren't you? Give us all the deets. Who were you? Strawberry Shortcake?"

Artie's eyes twinkle even as Cruz glares at him, but the conversation is stalled when Charmaine returns with our drinks.

I swear Cruz and Lehra have the most fun sex life of anyone I've ever met. They thrive on fulfilling each other's fantasies. She told me once about a "viking warrior" who busted into her house and took her roughly against the wall. Cruz dyed his hair and beard for that one as well.

The big man with pink in his beard effectively changes the subject by handing over the large box he walked in with. "Here you go, Nic. When I talked to Auburn, he asked me to grab this from his office. Happy birthday."

"Thank you," I say, my heart thumping with grateful emotion. Opening the box first, I find a killer black blazer dress and red leather wedge sandals and matching leather earrings from Auburn and Gia. Lehra, Cruz, and Artie got me a gift card for a fancy day spa.

"You guys, this is way too much," I tell them, my eyes bugging out at the dollar amount on the card.

"It's enough for a one hour hot stone massage, a facial of your choice, and a hair treatment in the salon," Lehra explains. "We wanted you to feel relaxed and fabulous for your move."

"That's... so sweet." My voice sounds slightly strangled, and I roll my lips inward and bite down. I truly have the best friends ever.

"Food's here," Artie chirps, nodding toward Charmaine approaching with a tray. She distributes the food, sliding the Irish nachos between Cruz and Lehra.

"Have you decided where you're living?" Cruz asks.

"I haven't had a chance to look yet. You grew up in Galveston, right?"

He nods through a bite of fried potato piled with meat, cheese, and veggies. "Uh-huh. Just south of Houston, so I'm familiar with the city. You want to live in the suburbs or closer to work?"

"Close to work would be good."

"The River Oaks and West University neighborhoods are the nicest, but homes there are in the seven-figure range, and it can be... stuffy."

Chewing thoughtfully, he adds, "Rice Village is great and has more character. I think you'd vibe well there."

"Okay, I'll check it out."

"Lehra and I could fly down with you to look around," he offers, and his wife gazes up at him like he hung the moon.

I smile. "That's really sweet, but I moved away from home for college at sixteen. I'm used to doing things for myself." From the corner of my eye, I see Lehra's lips turn down at the corners, so I rush to put some cheer into my voice. "I wouldn't say no to some restaurant recommendations though."

Cruz gives me a tight smile. "That I can do."

Artie nudges me with a pointy elbow. "What's up with your lunch, Nic? You never get just salad."

I fork up a cluster of greens. "I'm going to dinner at my parents' tonight, and my dad always makes his red beans and rice with andouille sausage for my birthday. Ma makes my favorite strawberry cake. Just wanted to save room."

Lehra is still looking at me with something akin to pity in her eyes. Probably because of the comment I made about being on my own at a young age. Hell, I don't need pity. Things weren't great around my house back then, so I was more than happy to go.

She hugs me again. "I hope you have the best birthday dinner ever."

"I hope so too."

Yeah, that doesn't happen.

Traffic was a bitch today so I'm three minutes late to dinner. I still take a minute to check my bun in the rearview mirror to make sure there are no little stray curls poking out.

As I enter my parents' house through the front door, I call out, and Pop yells that they're in the dining room. Making my way down the short corridor, I search for the scent of the spices my father uses in his red beans and rice recipe, but my nostrils aren't picking it up. His family is originally from south Louisiana, and they moved here when he was little, though his mother taught him all her recipes as he grew up in Jersey.

"Hey!" I greet, earning me a glare from my mother, who's standing beside the table with a large metal pot in her hand.

"You're late," she snaps, and I hide my wince as I sit down across from Angelica and Rory.

"Yeah, sorry. Traffic."

"Well, we almost started without you," she grouches, dipping a large spoon into the pot and pulling out not red beans and rice, but chicken and dumplings. Angelica's favorite. The disappointment hits hard, but maybe Pop had a long day at work today.

I pick at my food as we eat and make small talk throughout dinner, thinking I may have two slices of strawberry cake to make up for not getting the Cajun dish my father usually makes for me. When we're almost done, I decide it's time to tell my family about my new job and my upcoming move to Texas.

"I have an announcement."

Pop smiles at me. "What's going on, Nicci? Something good, I hope."

"I think so. I got—"

"We have an announcement too," Angelica breaks in, elbowing Rory until he stands.

Okaaaay, go ahead then. It's not like I was talking or anything.

My ex then drops to one knee and pulls a ring box from his pocket. Ma squeals. Pop gapes. Angelica gasps like she's surprised, even though this was obviously pre-planned.

Then Rory proposes to my sister with a diamond ring and an excessive amount of flowery language. At one point I believe he said something about her being a perpetual box of treasures that he looks forward to opening for the rest of his life.

I hope to god the treasure box he referred to wasn't her vagina, or I might puke up the few bites of chicken I consumed only minutes ago.

After Angelica inevitably says yes, Ma jumps up and throws her arms around the couple, openly sobbing about her baby and her new son. Not exactly the time to mention my news, so I paste a smile on my face as Pa congratulates the couple. Then I do the whole obligatory *congratulations, I'm so happy for you both* thing as I try to figure out when I should bring up my news.

Ma is still beaming a few minutes later when she says she has a special dessert for us and dashes into the kitchen. My mouth waters in anticipation of the moist strawberry cake with pink frosting that she's about to bring out.

But when she returns, there's no pink cake. It's white, though there are two lit candles on top. My heart sinks to the floor when I notice that the chunky candles aren't a three and a four. No, there's a three and a six.

"I realized earlier that we're going to miss Angelica's thirty-sixth birthday next month when she goes to New York, so I thought we'd celebrate tonight," our mother gushes, and it hits me.

They forgot my birthday. They fucking forgot.

Not that I'm the kind of person who needs a big deal made out of their birthday. I don't want surprise parties and lavish gifts, though actually being remembered by my own family one day a year would be nice.

The cake has sliced bananas all over it, which everyone knows I don't like, but Ma plops a slice in front of me anyway. It's fine. Everything is fine. It's no big deal.

I repeat that to myself until everyone is done with their dessert, and then I carry the dishes to the kitchen while Angelica opens her gifts from Rory and our parents. It would have been nice to know Ma planned this early birthday party for my sister so I could have brought a gift as well. Now I just feel left out. As usual.

After loading the dishwasher, I walk back through to the dining room. "Hey, guys. I'm headed back home."

Pop rises. "I'll walk you out, honey." He follows me out the door to my dark-blue Audi. When we reach the end of the sidewalk, he asks, "Are you okay, Nicci? With Rory and Angelica? I know that has to be hard for you."

I turn to face him in the yellow light from the streetlamp and smile. "I'm perfectly fine, Pop. Totally over all that."

He nods and waves at a neighbor couple walking by on their nightly stroll. "Okay, baby. I just wanted to make sure."

"I'm moving," I blurt out, and my father's head swivels around to face me again, his brow furrowed.

"To a new apartment?"

My lips purse as I blow out a breath. "No, I got a job at Hale Cosmetics, so I'm moving to Houston."

His eyes pop wide. "Texas?"

"That's the one," I say on a chuckle.

The creases in Pop's forehead deepen. "But... that's so far away."

I bite back the retort that that's one of the most attractive aspects of the move. "It's a really good company," I say instead.

"I hate to think of you so far away." His lips tip up on one side in a half-smile. "I know you're an adult, Nicci. And so independent. Hell, you're almost... you're..."

I see it the second the realization dawns on his handsome face, his expression flitting from concentration to horror. "Oh my god, it's... it's your birthday. Today."

"I know, Pop," I tell him quietly.

"But—" The wrinkles above his brows have turned into troubled trenches. "God, Nicci. I'm so sorry. I got distracted with your Ma planning this for Angelica, and—Shit. That's no excuse."

No, it's really not.

"It's all right," I lie. "I had a nice lunch with some friends today, so it's fine."

He shakes his head. "No, it's not." He scrubs his fingers through his thinning hair, making it stick up on top. "I'll make your favorite dinner next week, honey. I'll even do the garlic bread with crawfish on top like you love."

I swallow hard and look down the street, focusing on the circles of light cast by the tall streetlights, my eyes tracing the darkened umbrae surrounding them. "I'm not coming back next week, Pop."

My father is silent for a long moment, and when he speaks, his voice is quiet and not quite steady. "Because we forgot your birthday?"

I want to tell him yes, for forgetting my birthday and for all the other tiny little things that prove I'm a secondhand citizen in my own family. The things that prove I don't matter.

But it's hard to say those truths to my dad. Despite everything, I love him. So I settle on a half-truth. "I'm just going to be busy getting ready for my move."

Pop searches my face, his eyes sliding side to side between mine. The slight tremble of his chin is barely visible in the dimness, and it almost breaks me, so I reach forward and grip his hand. His skin is rough and warm, and I can't remember the last time I even touched his hand.

"I'm sorry, Nicci," he whispers. "For everything. I love you so much."

"Love you too, Pop."

But in the back of my mind, I'm thinking... *But you never loved me enough to do anything about it.*

NICOLETTE

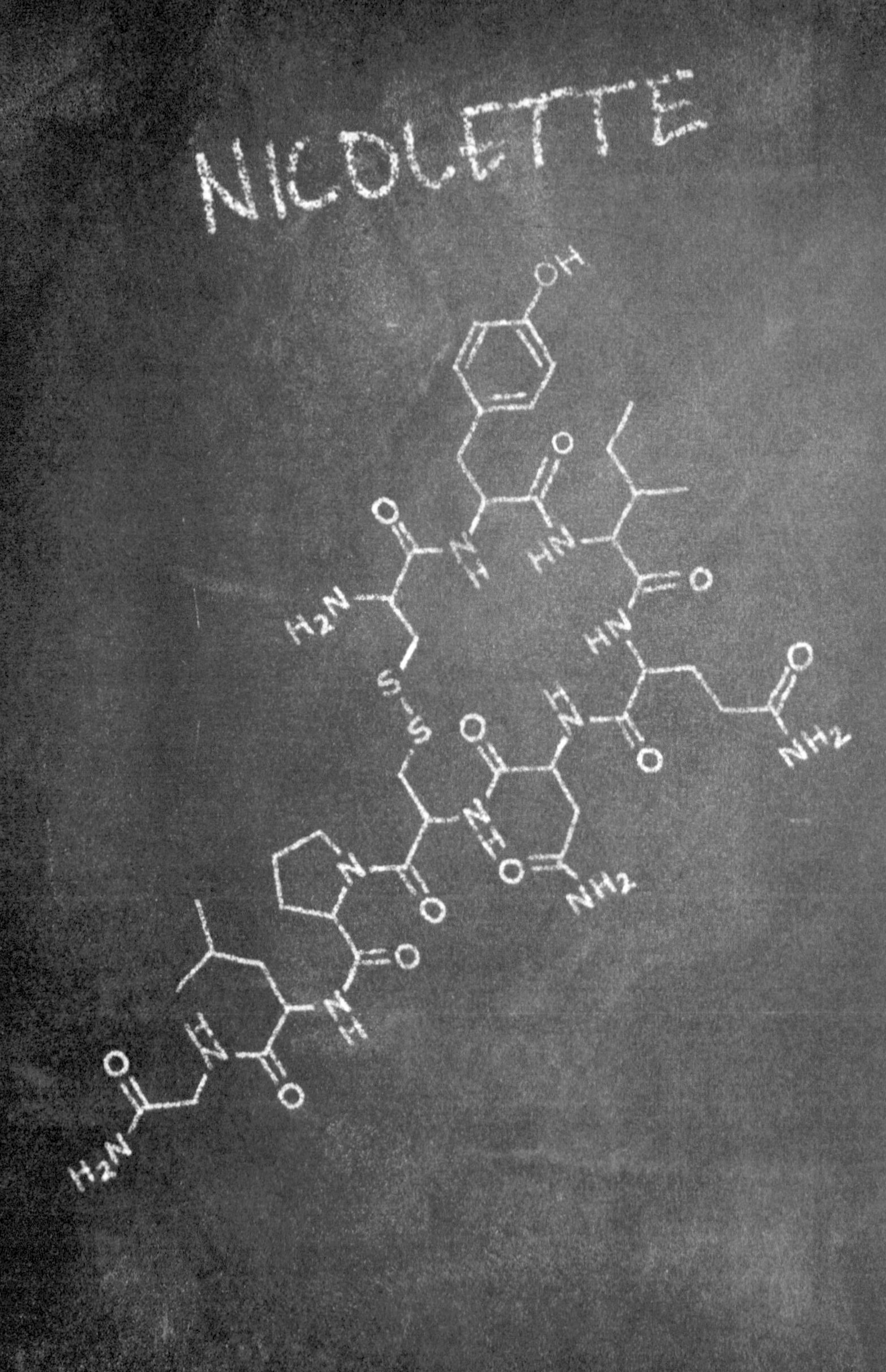

Chapter Seven

HELLO, TEXAS

I'm almost shocked out of my fuzzy bunny slippers—don't judge me, they're comfy—the next Monday when my father shows up at my brownstone in Brooklyn Heights.

"I brought dinner," he says simply, holding up a recyclable grocery bag that smells like Louisiana goodness.

I gape at him for a long moment before finally stepping back. "Come on in. It smells fantastic."

As I'm closing the door, I hear footsteps outside, and for a second, I'm worried he might have brought Ma with him. Until I hear Lehra's voice.

"Hold the door, please!"

I swing it back open to see a pile of boxes moving toward me. Well, it's actually Lehra carrying the boxes, but they're stacked so high I can't see her head.

"You look like a box monster," I laugh, grabbing the top three as they begin to topple.

"Pshhht, more like a superhero. I want a cape with a big double B for Box Bitch."

Her husband, who's right behind her, lets out a soft growl. "Fuck yeah. And one of those skintight outfits to go along with it." She giggles, and I'm pretty sure superhero sex has just been added to their rotating list of role-playing antics.

Cruz is also carrying a huge load of boxes, but he seems to be handling his stack better than his wife. The man is built like a brick shithouse.

"Just set them down over here," I say, leading them to the already packed boxes I've been working on in the living room. "My dad just arrived to surprise me with dinner."

"Oh, gosh. We can leave," Lehra frets, setting down her load and brushing away a damp blonde curl that's stuck to her cheek. "We don't want to intrude."

"Nonsense," my father's voice comes from behind me. "If you like Cajun food, there's plenty for everyone. I'm happy to meet some of Nicci's friends."

Ten minutes later, we're seated around my oak dining table in the breakfast nook. Pop is scooping the beans and andouille sausage on top of beds of white rice in my pretty cobalt-blue bowls.

"You weren't kidding about having plenty," Cruz comments, and Pop adds another scoop to his bowl before handing it over.

"Here ya go, big guy. You look like you can put away some groceries."

"No lie," Lehra comments, shooting a playful look at her husband. "Thank goodness both of us work so we can pay our dang grocery bill."

Pop spoons crawfish in a savory sauce over thick chunks of garlic bread on small plates and passes them out too. "Where do you work now?" he asks my friends.

"We both work in the Bouvier building," Lehra tells him. "I'm Auburn Bouvier's personal assistant, and Cruz is head of security." She smiles proudly at her husband. "He worked personal security and was on the Emergency Service Unit before that."

"Like an EMT or paramedic?" Pop asks.

Cruz swallows the big bite in his mouth before explaining. "It's like the SWAT detail for the city."

He and my father chatter about interesting assignments Cruz has taken part in—the ones he can talk about anyway. I notice he leaves out the story about taking down the Cappitani crime family. I'm one of very few people who are privy to that particular tale that had unimaginable consequences for the Bouvier family.

After dinner, Cruz and Pop carry my already packed boxes out to the moving pod on my tiny front lawn while Lehra and I load my non-essentials into the boxes she and Cruz brought.

"What about the furniture?" Pop asks, wiping a layer of sweat from the side of his neck.

"I'm selling and donating it. The townhome I'm renting in Houston comes furnished, so that's less I need to move."

"Are you staying in a safe area?" my father asks, his eyebrows lowering over his green eyes.

I smile at his concern. "It's in a nice area. The HR department at Hale sent me some listings and set me up with their realtor. Cruz helped me pick out a good neighborhood, and the realtor and property manager gave me a virtual tour."

Pop sighs his relief. "Okay, good." He reaches out a hand to shake Cruz's. "Thank you for helping Nicci."

"No problem," he says, ringing an arm around my neck and rubbing his knuckles across my head. "She's like the little sister I never wanted."

"Stop it, you big ass," I tell him, wrangling my way out of his hold with a laugh.

My dad chuckles. "Is there anything else I can do to help?"

I shake my head. "I think that's about it. Thanks for the dinner and for the use of your muscles, Pop. You didn't have to do all that."

His eyes meet mine, and his smile fades. "Yes, baby, I did."

My stomach clenches with affection and sadness. We gather the food containers and place them back in the bag before walking out to Pop's old truck parked at the curb.

"This was nice. I'm glad you came," I tell him, and he turns to face me, his eyes filling with tears.

"I'm glad I came too. I left you a gift card on top of your purse. A little extra spending money for your trip."

I hate that he did that because I know money's tight for him. At the same time, I'm incredibly touched. To hide the wobble of my lips, I step forward and do something I haven't done in over twenty years.

I wrap my arms around my father's neck.

He hesitates for only a split second before banding his thick arms around my waist. It's tentative at first, as if he's testing me out, but the embrace gradually grows tighter, and I feel his chest hitch against mine.

This should feel bizarre, hugging Pop after so long, but it doesn't. It feels like memories and goodness. Along with a slice of rancor toward my mother for purposely depriving a child—*her own child*—of this comfort.

My dad's wheezing breath is soft against my shoulder, and I feel warm droplets dampen my shirt. "I'm going to miss you, Nicci."

Resting my nose against his neck, I inhale his cologne and the slight tang of sweat, but I don't allow myself to cry.

"I'll miss you too, Pop."

And surprisingly, I mean it.

Two weeks later, at about six in the evening, I pull into the driveway of my new home. The concrete drive is located in the back of the townhouse and leads to a ground-level two-car garage. I'm slightly disturbed to see the garage doors are blocked by a person... until I recognize her from the virtual tour. It's the property manager, Bonnie Clyde.

And yes, her name is actually Bonnie Clyde.

She's blonde, about my age, and dressed in a sunshine-yellow blazer and pencil skirt with a black silky top beneath. Her black heels and huge black hoop earrings lend to her resemblance to a bumblebee. Even the way she flits toward the driver's side of my vehicle is remarkably insect-like.

"Nic-o-lette," she coos as soon as I open the door to my Audi. "So nice to meet you in person." Bonnie grabs my hand and pumps it enthusiastically before I can even push myself to a standing position. "I'm Bonnie."

"Nice to meet you too," I tell her, finally extricating my hand long enough to get out of the car.

"And your accent! Oh my god, it's so cute! I just love you."

I crack up because, to my ears, she's the one with the accent, a distinctive Texas drawl that seems to elongate around each vowel. Then she holds up a set of keys and jingles them at me with a huge smile on her face.

"Oh. Is there a problem with the unit or something?" I ask. "I thought you were leaving the keys in the lockbox." She'd sent me the code to unlock the box near the front door since I told her I would probably be arriving after hours.

"No, hon. Nothing's wrong. I just wanted to drop off a little something to welcome you to the neighborhood." She holds up one finger. "Gimme a sec. Be back in a jiffy."

Then she dashes over to a midnight-blue Mercedes sedan that's idling in one of the parking spaces, her feet tapping a too-quick cadence given the height of her heels. I would have busted my ass if I'd tried to move that quickly in stilettos. She returns a minute later with a hot-pink plate piled with cookies.

"I didn't know if you were allergic to nuts, so I went with chocolate chip. I do make a dang good praline cookie though, if you're okay with pecans." Her bright blue eyes blink inquisitively at me.

"I love pecans," I tell her, taking the plate and keys from her. "Thank you, Bonnie. This is very kind of you, and to be honest, I'm starving, so this is a nice treat."

She swats me on the butt, and I barely manage to restrain a squeak of surprise. "Well then, get your cute little tail inside and enjoy your new home, missy. I live two doors down thataway, so holler if you need me." Bonnie points to the right to indicate the direction of her house. "Old Mrs. Watts lives between us. She's pretty quiet and sticks to herself, but I check on her a couple times a week."

"And on the other side of me?"

"Oh girl, you have a darling couple that lives there, just absolutely *darling*. Their names are Stefan and Lukas. Couple characters, those two." She bobbles her perfect eyebrows and jerks a thumb toward the townhome that's a replica of mine on the left except it's white where mine is blue. "They're out of town right now, but I think they're coming back on Monday. They're super friendly, so they'll probably drop by to say hello."

"Great. I look forward to meeting them." I've been here for less than five minutes, and I already feel the sense of community here.

"I put ya a cute keychain on there to welcome you to Texas, and you have my number if you need anything. Twenty-four-seven," Bonnie tells me as she walks backward toward her vehicle.

Glancing down at the keys, I see a sparkly red-and-blue Texas-shaped keychain with a white star in the center. I laugh at the text: *I wasn't born in Texas, but I got here as soon as I could.* There's also an attached fob that I assume opens the garage doors.

Bonnie departs with a wave, and I drive into the right side of the garage before grabbing my new keys and the cookies. I studied the floor plan before signing the lease, so I know there's a guest bedroom and bath on this level.

Taking the stairs to the second floor, I find the living room, dining room, and kitchen exactly as they looked on my virtual tour. Except now there's furniture. Bonnie had told me they have a warehouse of furniture and sent me color palettes to choose from. I'd selected one with lots of blues and yellows.

The couch is plush, a deep royal-blue—the same as the adjacent armchair—and butter-yellow throw pillows add a splash of brightness. It's homey and inviting, and I like it. The coffee table, two end tables, and six-seat dining set all appear to be made of rustic wood, but they are smooth to the touch. There's a small powder room tucked down a short hallway next to a laundry room.

I place the cookies in the kitchen and scoot up the stairs, where I find the master suite. The microbiologist in me is thrilled to see the queen-sized mattress still has tags on it. The furniture up here is also wooden, a couple shades darker than the honey-hued, wide-plank flooring.

The attached bathroom has a pretty goldenrod and cream pattern with an ivory lavatory and claw-foot tub. The shower is also tiled, and though it's not fancy, it is bigger than the one I had in Brooklyn.

Satisfied that everything is in order, I head back downstairs to retrieve my two suitcases of essentials from the car. I grab a cookie on the way out and groan. They're still slightly warm, and the chocolate melts against my tongue as I haul everything inside, including a small bucket of cleaning supplies.

Bonnie told me the place would be professionally cleaned before my arrival, but I'm going to clean my bathroom and kitchen anyway before using them.

Forty minutes and three cookies later, I'm sinking into the sparkling tub, surrounded by the scent of the lavender and eucalyptus bath salts I remembered to tuck into my suitcase. The movers will be here tomorrow, but for tonight, I'm going to enjoy my bath and my new bed.

I smile and recline as I close my eyes, letting the water and salts soothe my tired body.

"Hello, Texas. I'm here."

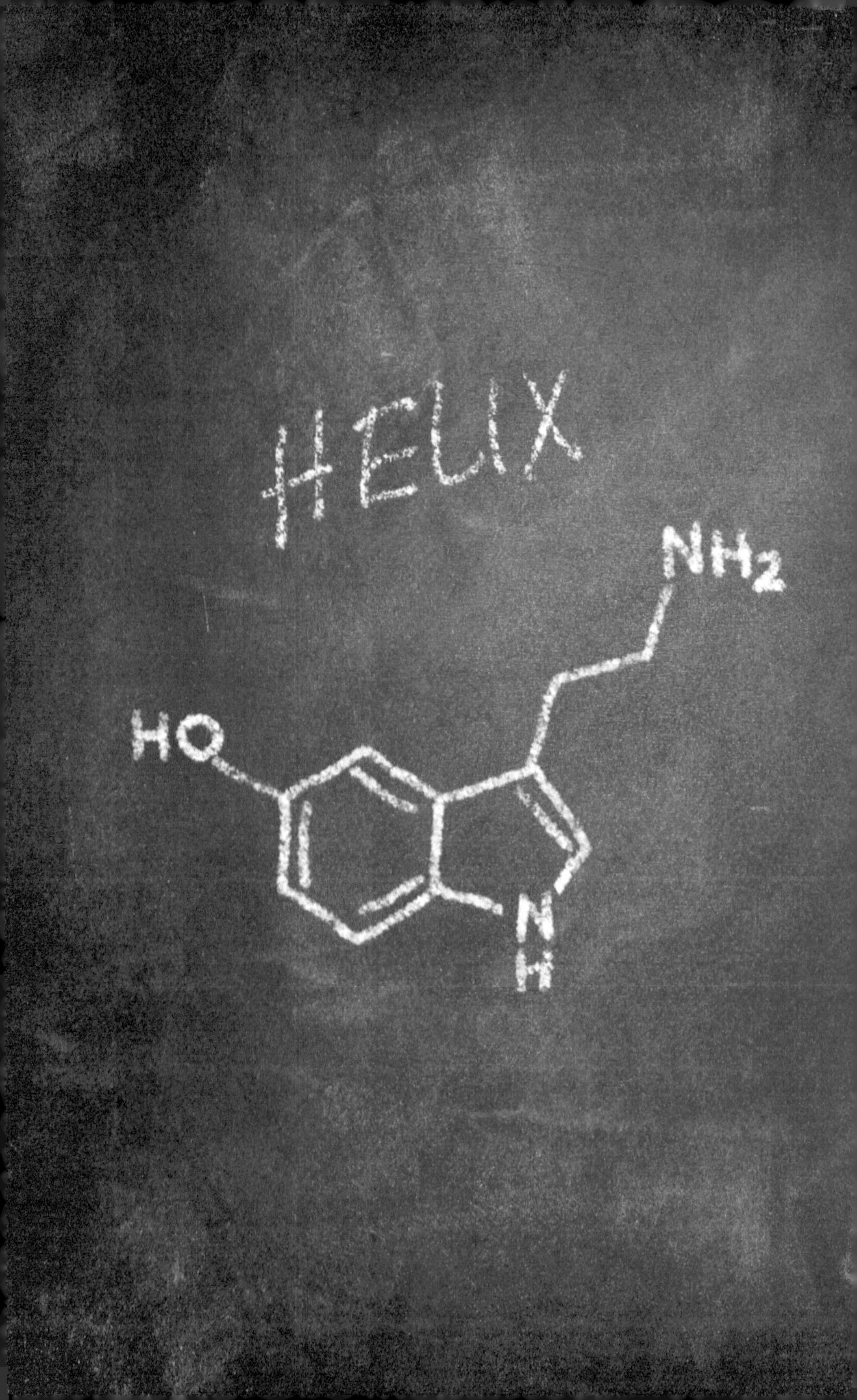

HELIX
HO
NH2
N
H

Chapter Eight

THAT COULD SPELL TROUBLE

It's Wednesday, and Phoenix, Dutton, and I lounge on the pool chairs while we watch Reece and River running through the sprinkler I set up for them. River is Dutton's son, who is only three.

Our cousin has been through some shit in the past five years. He's no longer the fun, light-hearted cowboy he was at Phoenix's bachelor party. Hell, none of us are the same as that night, but Dutton has changed the most. He's dark now, only showing his softer side when he's with his little boy. But I guess that's understandable after what happened to him.

"When does the new lab manager get to town?" my twin asks.

"She arrived in Houston yesterday to get settled," I say, taking a swig of my beer. "She starts work on Monday."

"Hopefully she'll work out. I know it's hard losing Abigail."

"Definitely, but she deserves to retire." Abigail has actually been with the company longer than me but had no interest in becoming the director, so that position went to me when our old director had to retire for health reasons.

"What about you, Dut?" Phoenix turns to our cousin, who's staring at the kids. "Anything new with you?"

"No," he says gruffly. "River, the ranch, that's it." He sits up as his little one runs over.

"Daddy, we want to go shwimming," he announces in his adorable little voice.

"I'll get in," I offer, but Dutton shakes his head.

"I got it." He takes River's tiny hand and pads across the stone to put his arm floaties on him.

"Poor guy," my brother mutters, watching him kneel and gently get his boy ready to swim.

"How's the ad campaign going with the football player?" I ask Phoenix, and he grimaces.

"She's a pain in the ass and so damn hostile toward me."

That surprises me. Everyone likes Phoenix, especially those of the female persuasion. "What's the problem?"

He shrugs. "Hell if I know. I'm charming as fuck, but it doesn't seem to work on her."

I roll my eyes. "You're not hitting on her, are you? She's pretty young."

"Not at all," he says quickly. Maybe a little too quickly. "Jordie just isn't a makeup kind of girl, so I'm trying to make her feel more comfortable."

"So let me get this straight. You offered a huge endorsement deal from our *cosmetics* company to a woman who hates *cosmetics*?"

He sighs. "Yeah, maybe not the best idea. She's completely gorgeous though and will look great in the print ads and videos once we get started filming."

I let an idea ruminate for a moment before speaking again. "Why don't you play up the more natural angle and her all-American looks? You know, instead of trying to make her some glam queen?" Phoenix swivels his head toward me, his eyes searching my face as he nods slowly.

"Yeah," he draws out, "that might work. I want her to be comfortable."

"I'll work on a color palette for her, something softer." I picture Jordie McNamara in my mind. She is a pretty young woman with blonde hair that's always in a ponytail, and I don't think I've ever seen her with makeup on her face. "The Dragons' team color is purple, right?"

"Purple and silver," he affirms.

"We could do lavender for eyeshadow."

Phoenix crosses his legs at the ankles and thinks about it. "That could work. All she cares about is football, so if we correlate the makeup to her team, she might like that." He takes another sip of his beer. "She's very authentic, and I don't want to hide that. It's one of the reasons she's the golden girl of women's football."

"And because she's extremely talented," I point out, and my brother laughs.

"That too." His gaze seems to defocus as he stares at a spot on my tall wooden fence. "Jordie's eyes are the most stunning color of aqua. I've never seen eyes like hers before."

The dreaminess in his voice has my eyebrows making a trek up my forehead. "And you're sure there's nothing going on with you two?"

He snaps his face toward mine, his cheeks a brilliant pink color... and I'm pretty sure it's not from the hot July sun. "Nothing at all." His brow crinkles. "I think I annoy her."

"Understandable. You annoy the shit out of me too."

My brother flips me off before setting his empty bottle in the drink holder and standing. "Come on, asshole. Let's get in the pool."

Pushing out of my chair, I walk behind Phe toward the pool. I'm going to have to keep an eye on him because I think he has a bit of a crush on a certain female football player.

And that could spell trouble.

After my swim on Monday morning, I shower and get dressed in charcoal-gray trousers, a pale-blue button-down, and navy suspenders, the last being a tribute to my Grandpa Hale.

As I drive to work, I get the sense something is on the horizon. Something big, though I can't put my finger on what it could be. The only new thing about today is that Dr. Bell will be starting at Hale

Cosmetics. Maybe it's like a premonition that she will bring something new to the company.

That must be it. Fresh eyes, new perspective, incredibly brilliant mind. Yeah, Dr. Bell will definitely be a difference maker.

For the lab, that is.

I arrive at the building before anyone else, stopping first at our microbiological and chemical analysis area on the second floor to flip on the lights and equipment before taking the elevator up to the third floor. The motion-detection lights come on one by one as I walk down the dove-gray corridor. I do the same for the quality control area and then head for the development lab, where I get everything ready for the day's work.

When I'm done, I unlock the door to my corner office and take a seat behind my sturdy walnut desk. Most of the administrative offices are on the first floor, the exceptions being mine and Abigail's. Or I guess Dr. Bell's now.

I pull up her personnel file on my computer and review it, something I do with each new hire who will be working for me. My eyes scan down the medical section, noting Dr. Bell doesn't have any known allergies or major medical conditions. It may seem invasive to ask those questions, but they are things we need to know for safety reasons. For example, if the employee is diabetic or has epilepsy, we'll know how to handle any emergency situations.

My head lifts and tilts to the side when I hear a noise from the lab manager's office next door. Rising, I put on my white lab coat and exit my office to find Dr. Bell's door standing ajar.

A woman with dark hair pulled into a tight bun stands in front of the desk with her back to me, and I clear my throat to get her attention. She makes a squeaking yelp and spins around, bobbling the pair of glasses in her hand. In two strides, I'm in front of her, catching the frames before they hit the ground. The woman reaches for them at the same time, and her small hand closes around my fist. I cough to cover the sharp intake of breath at the electricity that shoots up my arm. *What the fuck was that?*

Now, a normal person would hand over the glasses and apologize for startling her, but I seem to have lost all my faculties as I stare into the most piercing green eyes I've ever seen. They are sharp and incisive, surrounded by a frame of dark lashes. Her rosy lips are parted, showing off a hint of her pink tongue.

And why the fuck am I looking at my lab manager's tongue? I've never looked at Abigail's tongue. Or any of my employees' for that matter. This is strictly a non-tongue-staring establishment.

My brain does a color assessment of her aura in about two seconds. *Red. She's scarlet red.* Like a red flag, maybe? Or like fire? Probably best not to ruminate on that too much.

"Dr. Hale, I presume? Rescuer of spectacles?"

I can't help but laugh, and she smiles too. She's really pretty when she smiles. "I am. And you're Dr. Bell?"

"That's what it says on my jacket," she says, and my eyes drift down to the name embroidered on her chest. And now I'm looking at her boob. Fuck's sake, at this point, she's going to file an HR complaint before lunch.

However, I still find myself looking at the soft round shape when she asks, "Um, Dr. Hale, can I have my glasses now?"

That's when I realize I'm still clutching her glasses and hand them over with a mumbled, "Yeah, sorry about that."

My eyes sharpen on the parting of her lips when she blows a light mist onto the lenses and then uses the tail of her coat to wipe them clean. I have no idea what's come over me today with all this lip and tongue and boob scrutinizing I'm doing.

"I'm really happy to be here," she tells me, fitting the glasses back onto her face. They don't detract at all from the vibrant color of her eyes. If anything, they make her more attractive. "Your facilities are very impressive."

"We're lucky to have you," I tell her, taking a step back because I'm standing way too close to Nicolette Bell to be work-appropriate.

"Knock, knock," someone says from the doorway, and I recognize the voice immediately as Abigail. I turn and find her smiling with a familiar bakery box in her hand.

"What are you doing here, Abigail? I thought we got rid of you," I tease.

"Well, I just wanted to drop these off for Nicolette's first day." She lifts an eyebrow. "But if you're gonna be an ass, I'll just take these goodies home and eat them all myself."

Nicolette raises her hand. "I'd just like to point out for the record that I'm not being an ass."

We all laugh, and Abigail sets the box down on the desk. "Okay, I'll leave them and let you decide if you want to share any with the boss." She checks her watch. "I need to skedaddle. My daughter has a doctor's appointment, and I'm going with her. Nicolette, I hope you have a great first day."

Once Abigail is gone, Nicolette lifts the lid off the box, and the aroma of fresh blueberry muffins fills the room.

"Wow, these smell amazing. Would you like one, Dr. Hale?"

Damn, I like the way *Dr. Hale* sounds coming from her lips... which I'm definitely not looking at. Nor her pink tongue. It doesn't escape my attention that I didn't notice Abigail's tongue a single time while she was here.

I can feel myself sinking into troubled waters, and I know I need to tread carefully. This woman is an employee of my family's company, and she will be an incredible asset to my laboratory. I can't lose her over something stupid.

So I'll remain completely professional, aloof even, and that starts with *not* having breakfast with her.

"I think I'll just grab one and eat it in my office. I have some things to do before everyone else gets here." I select one and give Dr. Bell a curt nod. "See you in the development lab in fifteen?"

Something trickles down my spine when her smile fades a bit. I don't want to hurt her feelings, so I'm going to have to work hard to walk a tightrope between formal and cold.

Because if I don't, I could see myself toppling off and crashing to the ground.

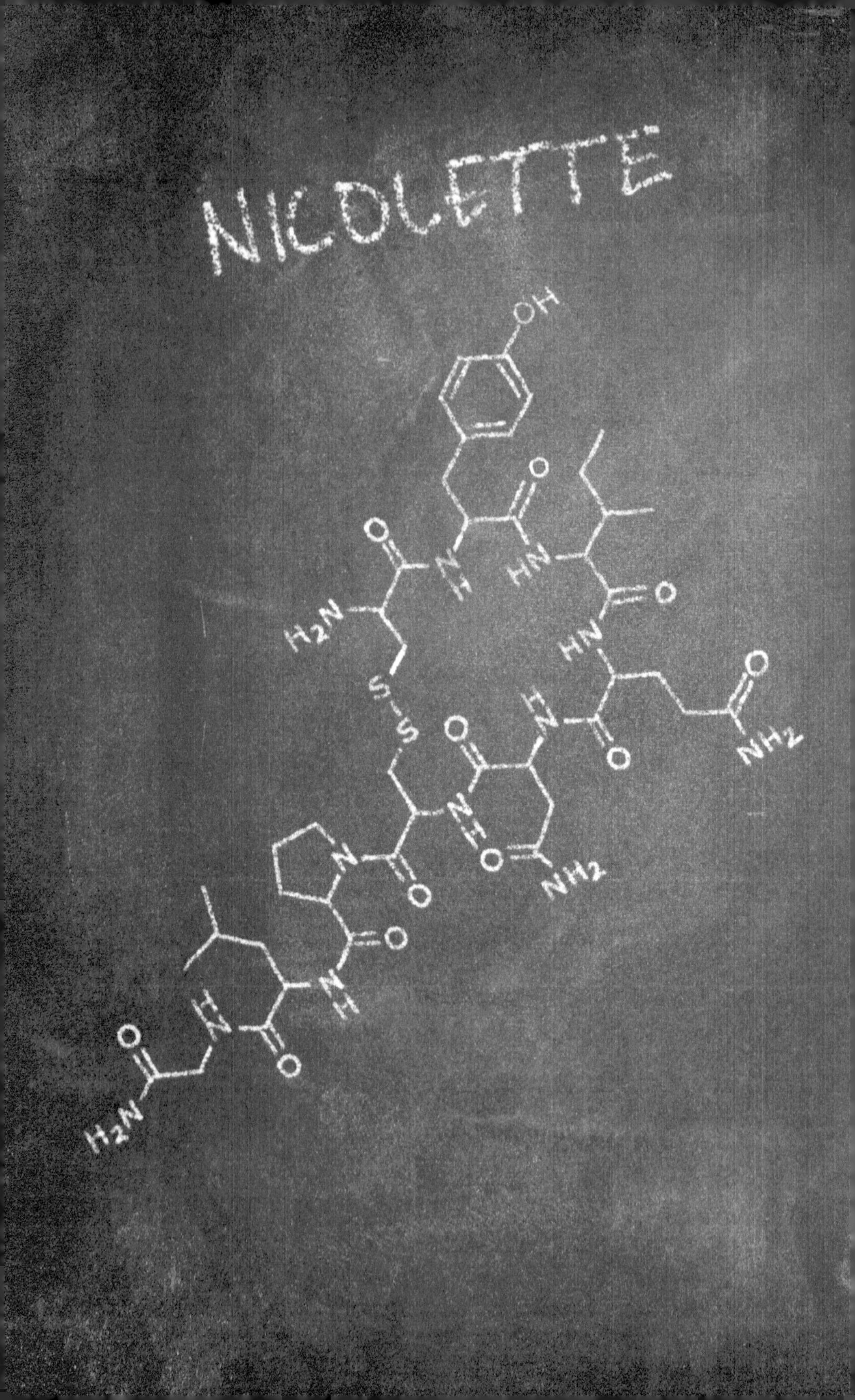

NICOLETTE

<h1 style="text-align:center">Chapter Nine</h1>

IT'S A GOOD THING I'VE SWORN OFF SCIENCE
GUYS

Okay, it's admission time. I'm a sucker for a hot nerdy guy. Give me a man with glasses and a brain, and I'm toast. And my new boss fits neatly into the *hot nerd* category, which leaves me feeling quite toasty.

But it's not just the glasses. The man is tall... like so tall I have to crane my neck to look up at him. He seems broad beneath his lab coat too. And his face? He's so handsome I checked the floor of my office after he left to make sure I hadn't produced a puddle of drool—or other bodily fluids.

If you looked up square jaw in the dictionary, they would most assuredly have a photo of Helix Hale with arrows denoting the rugged lines of his face. And his eyes are so blue, I would think they were contact lenses if he weren't wearing glasses. Though I guess he could be wearing them for cosmetic reasons.

And I'm not even going to discuss his lips.

Okay, okay, since you asked nicely, here goes. They are the softest shade of rose and perfectly plump, though not full-on Kardashian. He has the kind of mouth that would make me wail in despair if he grew a bushy mustache and covered the pronounced cupid's bow with its soft peaks and gentle center dip.

There. I hope you're satisfied because I'm not discussing Dr. Hale's mouth anymore. Speaking of names, he called me *Dr. Bell* all morning. I noticed he called Abigail by her first name, but he's been very formal with me while we moved about the lab, so I reciprocated by calling him by his official title like the other employees do. Everything is just so… polite. Maybe he's simply not comfortable enough with me yet to be on a first-name basis.

Which is fine. I'm here to do a job and not make friendship bracelets with my new boss. It's not like we're TayTay and Travis.

Late in the morning, as I peer into a microscope, I become aware of someone standing beside my stool. Pulling my eyes away from the device, I slip my glasses back onto my face and peer up at the star of my thoughts.

"Sorry, didn't mean to disturb you, Dr. Bell. I just wanted to let you know I'm headed to lunch. I'm sure Abigail showed you when you toured, but there's a cafeteria on the first floor with a nice selection. Everything from comfort food to more healthy options."

"She did," I say, giving him a friendly smile. "I'll grab something in a bit when I'm done with this." I bob my head toward the microscope.

Dr. Hale nods, his eyes dropping to my lips for a second before he jerks his gaze away. "I'll… just be going then. You have my number if you need anything."

He shrugs off his jacket, and holy beakers! He's wearing suspenders. Like the glasses weren't enough. Why does he insist on perpetuating this whole hot nerd scenario with suspenders as well?

I don't miss the way the buttons of his baby-blue shirt strain across the wide expanse of his chest while he removes the jacket, and then he folds it over his forearm and turns to leave. My gaze is drawn to his very tight butt beneath the fine fabric of his gray pants, and *the audacity* of this man to have such a brilliant mind while also being built like an athlete.

It's a good thing I've sworn off science guys.

Twenty minutes later, I make my way through the cafeteria line, choosing meatloaf, steamed broccoli, and a side salad that looks super fresh. Turning toward the seating area, I'm suddenly taken back to my first day of high school as a twelve-year-old in the lunchroom with kids who were able to drive and some who were even old enough to vote. I feel like that girl again... the one with frizzy hair, a flat chest, and no friends. Though I do have boobs now.

"Dr. Bell?"

I twist my head to the side to find a man standing beside me holding a tray. I think I recognize him as an assistant in the microbiology lab, but I don't recall his name.

"Hi," I say.

"I'm Theodore Nguyen," he says. "From the micro lab. Would you like to sit with us?" He tilts his head toward a round table with three other people sitting around it.

"Sure," I say, trying not to let the relief I feel ebb into my words. "Thank you."

Once we're seated, I'm introduced to Grace Arnold, Ned Wright, and Isla Martinez. Grace has a PhD and supervises the microbiology lab, while Isla is Dr. Hale's admin. Ned is a lab assistant and has the curliest blond hair I've ever seen and resembles a tall, skinny baby with his boyish, freckled face.

"How is your first day going?" Grace asks. She's a pretty dark-skinned woman with black wavy hair that hangs down her back in a low ponytail. I love that this company doesn't shy away from putting women in positions of power. It's not always that way in STEM-based organizations.

"Very well. I think I'm going to like it here."

"The perks are amazing," Isla says with a glint in her eye, and she and Grace share a smirk.

"Yeah, the benefits package is impressive, and the work environment seems perfect, busy but not hectic," I reply.

"That's not the package they're referring to." Theodore wings an eyebrow at me and announces wryly, "Every straight female here is in love with Dr. Hale."

"And some of the men," Ned adds, his face turning the color of a McIntosh apple.

Isla rushes to add, "But we're just looking. Dr. Hale is completely professional and would never get involved with anyone who works here. I'm not sure he even dates."

For some reason, that both comforts and disappoints me. Before I can blurt out that odd thought, I shove a bite of meatloaf into my mouth and try not to groan at the savory flavors that burst on my tongue.

"Mmm, this is good. Better than my mother's," I declare.

"All the food is fantastic here," Grace tells me. "They have a couple really good chefs that prepare the menus each day."

By the end of lunch, we're all chatting comfortably, and Grace and I end up in the elevator together. "It's really nice to have you here, Dr. Bell," she tells me, her smile soft and wide.

"It's nice to be here. Everyone has made me feel so welcome. And please call me Nicolette, if that's something you're comfortable with."

"Good, and I'm Grace," she tells me before stepping off the elevator on the second floor. "See you tomorrow."

The afternoon goes much like the morning. Dr. Hale is reserved and cool, though he's not a dick or anything. Most of the workers are in quality control this afternoon, so there are only a few of us in the development lab.

Near the end of the day, I ask, "Are there any particular projects you want my help with?"

My boss rubs at the creases that have formed in his forehead and sighs. "Actually, I'm working on some things for the McNamara ad campaign. Jordie McNamara, the football player," he clarifies. "Phoenix—he's my twin brother and head of the marketing department—wants to play up her more natural looks. I'm struggling with the colors I want to use."

"There are two of you?" I blurt out. I want to kick myself, but at least I didn't voice my next thought: God help the women of Houston.

Dr. Hale cracks a grin, causing a small dimple to appear in one cheek, and that does *not* help my attraction to him one little bit.

"You have no idea how many times we heard that growing up. I was a pretty chill kid when I was by myself, but Phoenix always seemed to drag me into some mischief when we were together."

"Your poor parents," I laugh.

"My mother likes to name her gray hairs after us. The majority of them are named Phoenix."

Ahh, so Dr. Helix Hale does have a sense of humor.

"What would you like me to do on the McNamara campaign?"

He walks around the lab table and slides some color cards, photos, and sample jars across to me. "Maybe give me another set of eyes to help me finalize? It's weird. I'm usually really good with colors," he says, an amused smile turning up the corners of his lips like he just told himself a private joke. *I wonder what that's about.*

"Of course," I say, pulling a picture of Jordie from the stack and studying it. She's a stunning natural beauty, not plain at all, just a really pretty young woman without makeup.

Dr. Hale is silent while I flip through photos of her and read the campaign proposal.

"Okay," I finally breathe. "First of all, Jordie is very popular. I'm not even from Texas, and I know who she is. What if we develop an eyeshadow palette with her name on it? She's young and fresh, and even though she doesn't seem to wear a lot of makeup, I bet she would have fun selecting some colors to go in it. Maybe some lipsticks as well. Your marketing department could even make a logo label with a football shaped like a heart or something."

My boss's blue eyes seem to glitter with excitement. "Yeah, I like that idea. It might make her feel like a part of the whole process instead of just showing up for photo shoots while people primp her."

I examine the sample jars and slide one over to him. "I like the neutral lipstick you picked out, but I'd use this foundation. It's more sheer and will let her freckles show through. Play up her youth and appeal to the younger demographic." Glancing at her picture again, I say, "She doesn't need a lot of coverage because she has the kind of flawless skin women die for."

"You have really pretty skin too," Dr. Hale says a second before his eyes pop into rounded orbs of panic. "I mean, objectively speaking, you have nice skin. As a professional, that's my professional opinion. Professionally."

Despite my attempts to hold it in, a small snort escapes at his rambling. "Don't worry about it, Dr. Professional. I'm not offended."

He huffs a relieved breath. "Okay, I just didn't want you to think I'm... because I'm not... Dammit, why aren't my words working today?"

Running a hand over his handsome face, he shakes his head. "I apologize for cursing in front of you, Dr. Bell."

I wave a dismissive hand. "I grew up in Jersey. You'll have to come at me with something a lot stronger than *dammit* if you want to offend me."

That stupid dimple makes another appearance with his crooked smile. "I'll remember that. Now what else?" He leans forward with his forearms on the lab table, and I catch a whiff of chlorine.

"I like the idea of a soft purple eyeshadow for the photo shoot, but I think this one," I tap the top of one of the tiny jars, "is too bright. Maybe something a little more earthy. I can mix up a couple samples for you to look at, perhaps add a little taupe to tone it down."

His head bobs us and down. "I look forward to seeing what you come up with."

I pull one of the color cards and point to an aquamarine color. "Jordie's eyes are the first things that jump out at me when I look at her photo. A touch of this would make a beautiful complementary color to the purple and really make her pop."

This isn't the most scientific part of working in a cosmetics lab. There's so much testing and regulation that goes into making products that are safe and effective. But it sure is the most fun.

"Anything else?"

"Out of the two blush colors, I like this one." I slide one of the samples toward him. "The other is too pink. This has a more peachy tone if we're going for the girl-next-door look."

"Good, good," he mutters almost to himself as he scratches down notes on a spreadsheet that rests on his clipboard. My heart flutters a little at the fact that he's writing down my ideas. It's been so long since anyone has actually listened to me at work. I've felt almost obsolete for a while, like a well-trained monkey could do my job just as effectively.

"I'll get started on the lavender samples," I say, and Dr. Hale pops his head up from his clipboard before glancing at the digital clock at the end of the room.

"It's almost time to call it quits for the day. Why don't you knock off a little early? You can do the samples tomorrow."

"I don't mind," I argue, but he gives me a scowl that makes my core tingle for reasons I'd rather not think about.

"I insist," he says, his voice dropping about an octave.

I clamp my jaw shut before it can go slack. Damn, there's something about a commanding man. After straightening my area, I say goodbye to Dr. Hale and the other two employees who are at the farthest table working on paperwork.

Since I seem to find myself with some spare time today, I head to the medical center and locate The Woman's Hospital of Texas, something I've been meaning to do since I moved here.

Then I take a deep breath and enter.

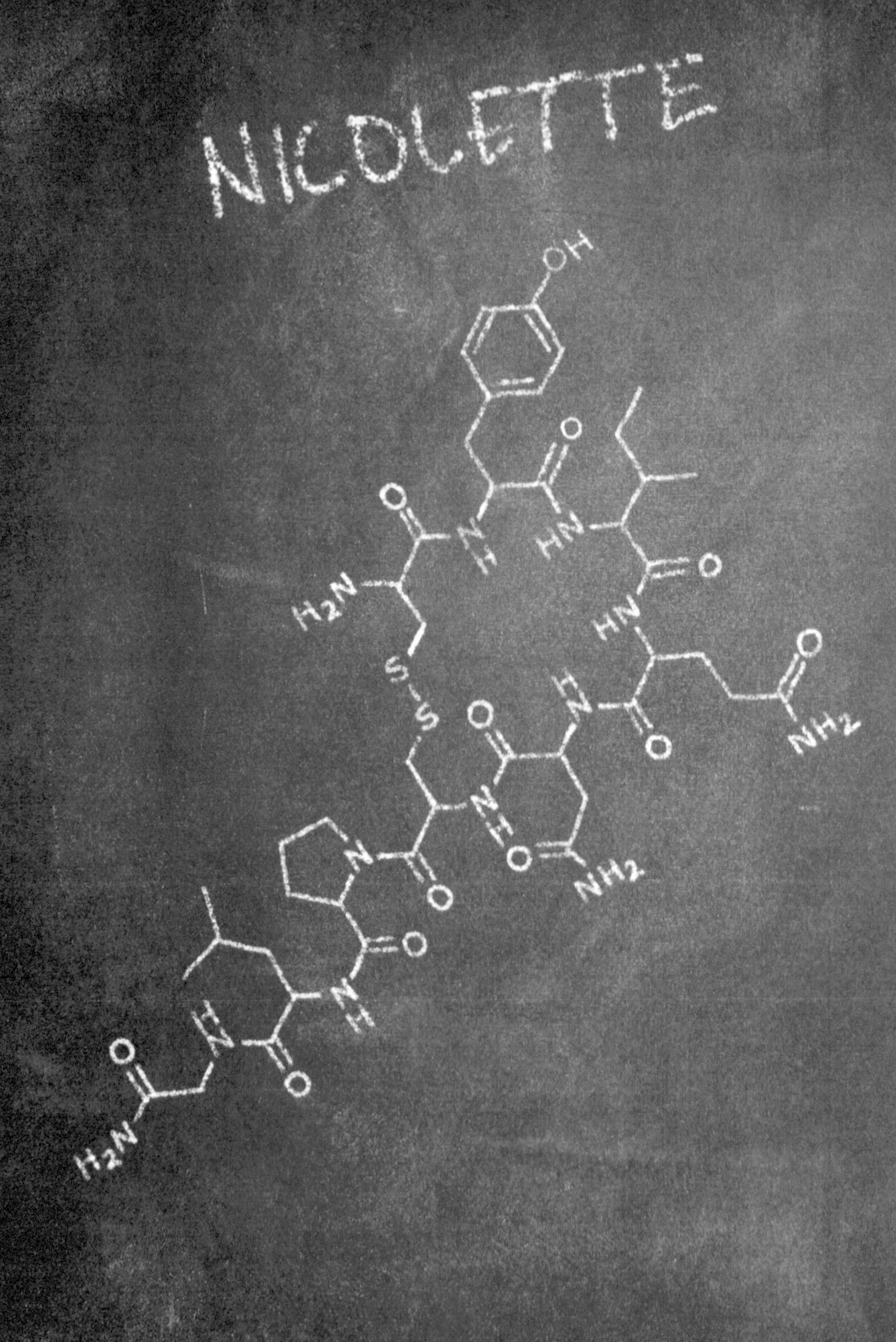

NICOLETTE

Chapter Ten

SIR POOPOO THE TERMINATOR

When I arrive home later that evening, I collect a couple packages that arrived for me today. I'd ordered some sheets and a comforter for the downstairs guest room, so I rip open the boxes and toss the linens into the washer. Lehra and Cruz said they would come for a visit once I got settled, and I want to have a room ready for them.

As I'm about to head upstairs, I hear a knock on my front door and backtrack. Swinging open the door, I find two men and…

"Is that a goose?" I ask, craning my head to inspect what the tall man is holding.

The snowy white bird honks and sways its head from side to side in response. *Guess that answers that question.*

"Yes, this is Pookie," the tall man answers.

"Tell her his real name," the shorter one scolds.

Tall guy rolls his eyes and sighs. "This is Sir PooPoo the Terminator."

I snort, and the bird emits a loud WAHNK in my direction, almost startling me out of my skin.

"Excuse me, Sir PooPoo. I didn't mean to offend," I tell him, feeling a bit silly to be apologizing to a goose, but I'm nothing if not hospitable.

The shorter man tuts. "Don't worry about it. He's quite the drama queen." He holds out a soft, pudgy hand, and I shake it. "I'm Lukas, one of your neighbors."

"And I'm Stefan," the other one says, shifting Sir PooPoo to one arm so he can also shake. He has slightly rougher hands with long, well-manicured fingers. "I'm the sweet one."

"Like hell you are," Lukas argues before focusing on me again. "Don't let him fool you. He gets all precious and up in his feelings sometimes. Then he likes to pretend he has a personality. I assume you're Nicolette?"

"Oh, yes, sorry," I say, feeling equal parts flustered and amused. "I was a little distracted by your feathered friend."

"Understandable," Stefan says, his voice a bit more formal than his friend's. "Not every day two well-dressed men show up on your doorstep with a goose." They are dressed nicely, their trousers and dress shirts of obvious fine quality. Stefan is also sporting a paisley ascot.

"And we brought treats," Lukas adds, handing over a blue polka-dotted box.

"That is so sweet. Thank you," I say, accepting the box and peeking through the top window to see a selection of colorful and intricately decorated cake pops. I'm going to turn into a lardass if all these Texans keep bringing me sweets as welcome gifts. "These are beautiful."

"They're store-bought," Stefan informs me.

Lukas huffs. "You didn't have to tell her that. Maybe our new neighbor thinks I look talented enough to make these masterpieces."

Stefan's tone is dry as the Sahara. "Lukas, you couldn't run an Easy-Bake oven."

These two are freaking hilarious, and I instantly want to know more about them. "Would you like to come in? I'll make some coffee, and we can share the cake pops." I glance at the goose, who seems to be wearing a diaper of some sort. "Pookie is welcome as well."

"We'd love to," Lukas accepts for all three of them, and I guide them into the living room.

A few minutes later, we're all seated around the coffee table enjoying our food and drinks. Lukas pulls out something from his pocket and holds it up to the animal's beak.

"Are you feeding the goose a cake pop?" I ask in shock, though I really shouldn't be surprised at anything these three do.

"No, too much sugar," he answers as Pookie takes surprisingly delicate nibbles. "I wad up a piece of bread and put it on a stick so he feels like he's part of the family."

"And do you mind if I ask how Pookie got such an... original name?"

Both men share a look and a chuckle. The affection between them is obvious, but I'm still not sure if they're partners, just friends, or relatives. The latter seems unlikely because they look vastly different. Stefan is long and lean with blue eyes and blond hair, gray peppering through at the temples. Lukas, on the other hand, is squatty with raven hair and warm chocolate eyes. He appears to be at least a decade younger than Stefan. Then I remember Bonnie referred to them as a couple, so I'm guessing they're partners.

"Lukas told his nephew he could name our adopted pet, and he decided on Sir PooPoo the Terminator."

"He was four at the time," Lukas explains.

"Ah, that makes sense." I bite into a pink and purple cake pop with a white drizzle and moan. "Oh, that's good."

"The Sweet Tooth makes the best desserts," Stefan explains. "It's a few blocks down that way." He points out the window, and I take note of the direction because I'll definitely be finding my way to this bakery in the near future.

"So Bonnie tells us you're working at Hale Cosmetics," Lukas pipes up.

"Yes, I'm a biochemist in the lab there. I'll be doing a little of everything, but I love the research and development side of the business."

Stefan bites into his own treat, this one chocolate with shreds of coconut. "Oooh, I love their products. Any plans for a men's skin care line in the future?"

"I've wanted to do that for a while actually, but today was my first day at the company. I have no idea what plans are in the works, but I hope to suggest it to Dr. Hale at some point."

"That would be fantastic," he comments.

"What do you do for work?" I ask, curious.

"I'm a stay-at-home goose daddy," Lukas announces, stroking Pookie's feathery head. "And Stefan is my sugar daddy."

I laugh and turn my attention to the tall man holding a now-snoozing goose on my couch. "And you? What do you do to support your sugar baby?"

"I'm a musician. Mostly piano, though I'm classically trained in voice as well."

"Stefan can play almost any instrument known to man," Lukas brags, smiling up at his partner with pride shining in his dark eyes. "And he composes music for orchestras and bands. Meanwhile, I take care of everything around the house."

"Except for the yardwork. I do that because Lukas is strictly a house gay."

A laugh snorts from my nose, and I cough. "You two are too much."

Lukas pretends to cast an affronted glare at Stefan. "I helped you carry wood last winter at your mother's house."

Stefan lifts his nose haughtily. "Ah yes. You carried two sticks the size of my pinkie. You're a regular lumberjack, Lukas."

"Hmmph. You know I would have carried more, but I got that darn splinter." Lukas holds up his index finger, and Stefan kisses it.

"Yes, dear. It was a tragedy I'll never be able to unsee." His reply is droll, but it's accompanied by a twinkle in his blue eyes as he takes a sip of his coffee.

Seriously, these two are a riot, and despite their constant back-and-forth, it's obvious they adore each other… and that bickering is their love language.

"I'm so happy you two came over." I reach for another cake pop, this one a glossy caramel color. "How did you two meet? Was it in some kind of goose-tending class?" They both chuckle.

"Nooo," Stefan draws out. "We met at a drag club fifteen years ago. We're both queens." He lifts a perfectly arched eyebrow, as if waiting for judgment, but he's not going to find it here.

I squeal. "Oh, I love drag shows. I used to go with my friend Artie all the time in New York." Resting my elbow on my thigh, I prop my chin in my hand and look at my new neighbors with an assessing gaze. "Who do you two portray?"

"Uh-uh-uh," Stefan says, waggling one long finger at me. "That's top secret information. You'll just have to come to a show and find out for yourself."

I cover my lips with my fingertips. "Seriously? You wouldn't mind? I promise I'm not a rude looky-loo or anything. I just really enjoy all the glam of the shows."

Lukas laughs. "We'd be honored. The club is shut down right now for renovations, but it should be open again in a couple months." They give me the date, and I make a mental note of it.

"We can get you two tickets to the grand reopening so you can bring a date or a friend if you want," Stefan offers.

"I'm new in town, so I don't really—Oh, I'll see if my friend Shay wants to come. I met her at a conference recently, and I've only gotten to see her once since I've been in Houston because she cares for her mother. She could probably use a night on the town."

As we chat for another fifteen minutes, Pookie continues to sleep in Stefan's lap, occasionally emitting small honks on his exhales. The men take turns petting his back.

"We'll let you get back to your evening," Lukas tells me, pushing to his feet and taking the goose so Stefan can stand. "Would you feel comfortable exchanging phone numbers? In case you ever need anything."

"Of course," I reply.

"Just don't call too early unless it's an emergency because Sir PooPoo is not a morning goose," he advises.

We exchange numbers, and Stefan shoots me a sly grin as he hands back my phone. "I probably should have warned you ahead of time, but Lukas likes to send GIFs." He quirks an eyebrow. "Incessantly."

"GIFs are the greatest creation since fried pickles," his partner retorts as I walk them toward the door.

Stefan wasn't joking. By the time I get the dishwasher loaded with our coffee mugs, I have eight GIFs from Lukas's number, the last one being one of a cartoon goose with wide eyes and the word *flabbergoosted* emblazoned across it.

I laugh and reply with a breakdancing goose. Switching to my contacts list, I find Shay Martin's number and give her a call.

"Nicolette, hi!" she answers.

"Hey, how's your mom?" Her mother was hospitalized last week.

"So much better," she gushes. "She was referred to an endocrinologist, and I really like her. She changed up some of Mama's medicines, and her sugar is really coming under control."

"Good, I'm so happy for her. And you."

She lowers her voice. "I was getting concerned that I was going to have to cancel the cruise I'm surprising her with for her birthday, but Dr. Kumar said if Mama keeps progressing like this, it should be safe to go."

"When is your cruise?"

"Mmm, let's see. This is July, so…"

Disappointment courses through me when she lists the same weekend in September I have tickets to Stefan and Lukas's show. "Aw, okay. I just met my neighbors, and they're drag queens. They're getting me two tickets to the grand reopening of their club, but it's the same week you'll be gone."

"Crap, that sounds like a good time. Can we go another time? I know it won't be the grand opening, but I'd still like to go."

"Sure. That sounds good."

"I hate for you to go by yourself. Do you want me to set you up with someone for a date?"

I huff out a laugh. "No, that's okay. I don't mind going solo."

Once we hang up, I fill my floral Stanley cup with iced water and take a long drink, trying to think of someone else who could go with me. Grace from the microbiology lab might want to come.

And if not, I meant what I said to Shay. I don't mind going by myself.

After all, I've been doing things alone most of my life.

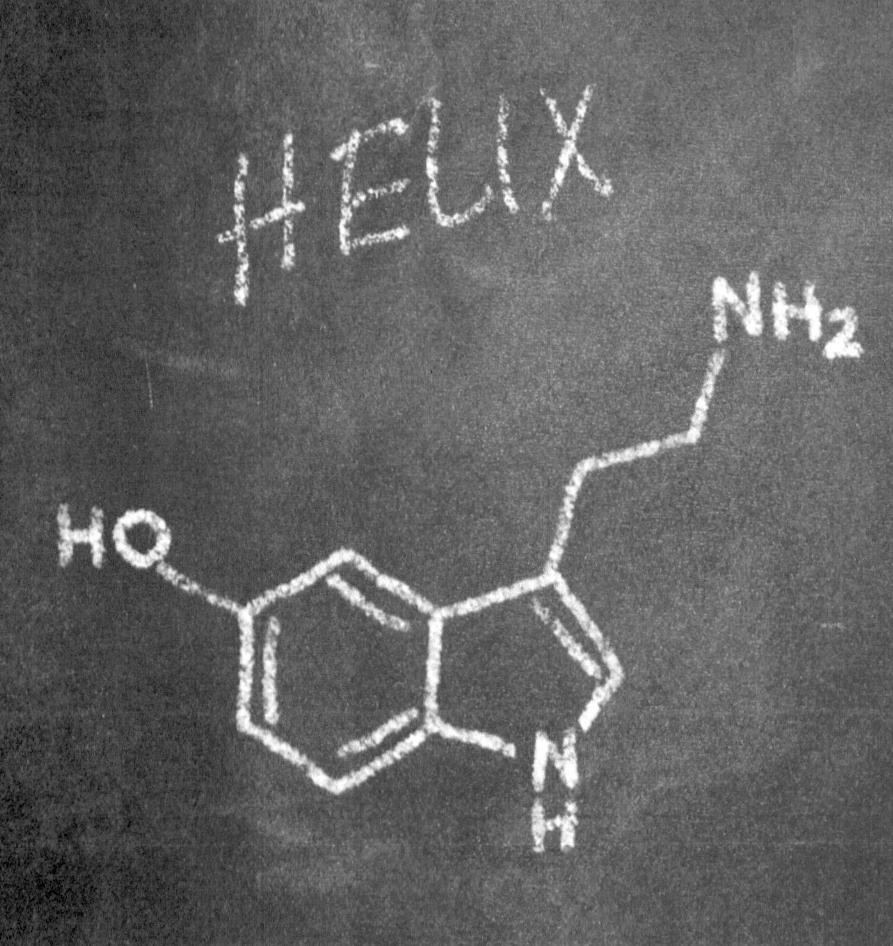
HELIX
NH₂
HO
NH

Chapter Eleven

IT'S JUST DINNER...

Four days later, we're meeting with Jordie McNamara to select the colors for her signature eyeshadow palette. She's fresh-faced and wide-eyed as she looks over all the samples.

"Wow, I can't believe I'm going to have my own eyeshadow line," she breathes, looking up at Nicolette with a worried frown. "But are you sure you want me? I'm not a huge makeup girlie. I mean, I don't mind wearing makeup. I wear it to weddings and stuff, but I don't when I play football because I just sweat it all off."

Nicolette's responding smile is kind. "Of course, Jordie. You're an excellent representative for the Hale brand." She's standing beside the football star's chair and bends to get eye level with her. "I'll tell you a little secret. When I was a teenager, I felt... unseen."

Jordie's lips turn down at the corners. "At school or with your family?"

Nicolette lifts one shoulder and then lets it fall. "Both, really." Phoenix's eyes catch mine in a silent question. *What's that all about?*

I give him a slight shake of my head. *Not sure.*

But my lab manager continues, her focus solely on the young woman in front of her. "I never fit in at home. Then I got bumped up a few years in middle school, so I was a lot younger than my high school classmates. I used makeup to try and make myself stand out, to fit in. I used colors that were way too bold for me, and looking back, I know now I looked pretty ridiculous, but I felt good about myself at the time. You, Jordie, have the self-confidence to choose not to primp yourself to the nines just to go to the grocery store. I love that about you, and it makes you so relatable to young girls who may be struggling with finding who they are... who they want to be. So just have fun with it. Pick some soft colors. Pick some wild colors. Whatever catches your eye, even if you might not wear that color yourself, it's okay. It will appeal to someone out there and maybe give them the confidence they need to be themselves." She shrugs. "Maybe even someone like me whose brain was bigger than her boobs in high school."

Jordie giggles, and Phoenix reaches over to close my lower jaw, which I hadn't realized had dropped open during that little speech. Nicolette Bell had confidence issues? That shocked me to my core. She's fucking brilliant and a very beautiful woman, though I guess being a pre-teen in high school would have been difficult. But what the hell was that about her family? They have got to be utterly proud of her and her accomplishments. I find myself wanting to know more.

After that, Jordie seems to relax and do exactly as Nicolette requested. She has fun choosing colors for the eyeshadows and then the lipstick line, and I can feel my twin's tension ebb away. I know this ad campaign is important to him as the head of marketing, but it seems like he's wholly invested in a more profound way. And I don't miss the way his eyes never leave Jordie after we head over to the studio for the photo shoot. I, on the other hand, keep darting glances at Nicolette, who is standing behind the photographer at Jordie's request. The two seem to have bonded throughout the day, and I'm weirdly jealous of that. And that she asked Jordie and Phoenix to call her Nicolette, but I'm still calling her Dr. Bell... out loud anyway.

As I watch Nicolette joke around to make Jordie more comfortable, I'm becoming more and more intrigued by her. She's smart and personable, and she was one hundred percent on the money with her makeup suggestions. Jordie looks both approachable and fierce in her black-and-purple Dragons uniform.

I have to root my feet to the ground to keep from walking over and pulling all the pins from Nicolette's hair to see what she would look like with it down and wrapped around my fist.

Fuck me. I shift on my feet to accommodate the growing bulge behind the zipper of my black pants. Bending my lab manager over the closest flat surface while I bury my hands in those dark locks is the last thing I should be thinking about.

And yet I know that exact scenario will be playing in my mind later tonight when I'm alone in my bed.

For the next three weeks, I'm a rock of strength and determination at the lab. I work alongside Dr. Nicolette Bell while keeping my demeanor cool and detached.

What I do at night in my bed—and in the shower and once in the living room—is my own damn business.

The woman is a temptation without trying to be. I'm convinced this attraction is completely one-sided because she's nothing if not professional. She's absolutely brilliant, and her brain captivates me as much as her green eyes and those small curls that inevitably escape from her tight buns by the end of each workday. There are always a couple that frame her delicate face and sometimes one that coils against the nape of her neck.

What is happening to me? Why am I focusing on her stray hairs? I know the answer, but I'm doing my best to suppress it.

I stopped by my mom's house after work today, and now I'm driving through Rice Village on my way home. It's Friday, and I'm ready to relax and go for a swim. Until I see a figure that looks both familiar and foreign walking down the sidewalk. Familiar because I've memorized the curve of my lab manager's hips when she walks and foreign because this woman is not wearing a bun. A riot of dark curls cascades down her back, and I can't stop staring as I pass.

A horn honks, and I realize I've veered into the lane beside me. Jerking the wheel of my silver and black sports car, I whip into a parking space and watch her through my rearview mirror as she approaches. Yep, it's definitely Dr. Nicolette Bell.

She stops in her tracks and looks around, her gorgeous curls bouncing around her shoulders as she swivels her head from side to side as if looking for something. Her gaze drops to her phone, and she frowns before searching the storefronts again.

She seems to be lost or something, and the sun will be setting soon. It would be wrong to not try and help. Right? Sighing at my transparent excuse, I exit my car and step up onto the busy sidewalk. The street is lined with shops and restaurants, the plate-glass windows emitting warm yellow lights that bathe passersby in softness.

Nicolette is looking at her phone again, giving me the chance to fully take her in. She's wearing a red one-shoulder top and a black pleated skirt that shows off her pale, creamy thighs. Her black patent leather Mary Janes have chunky heels that give her a couple inches of height, though she's still a good six inches shorter than me.

She looks good... damn good.

Stay professional, Helix. You only stopped to see if she needs help. You're a Good Samaritan. That's it.

Yeah, that's what I tell myself as I approach. "Dr. Bell?"

Her head jerks up and she blinks rapidly like she doesn't recognize me at first. "Oh. Dr. Hale. Hi." The August heat has a few beads of sweat pearling around her hairline, and she swipes them away with one palm.

"I was just passing by and thought I recognized you. Are you lost?"

She makes a huff of frustration and checks her phone again. "I'm looking for a Spanish restaurant called La Mariscada. The address Cruz gave me said it should be right here."

First of all, who the fuck is Cruz? I'm irrationally angry at the thought she may be on a date. A muscle tics in my jaw, but I keep my tone even and conversational.

"Are you meeting someone?"

Nicolette nibbles on the corner of her lips, which are painted a darker shade than she normally wears to work. "No, I'm going to dinner by myself. It was a recommendation from a friend."

That eases my tension slightly. "La Mariscada closed down a couple months ago," I tell her, and she visibly deflates.

"Crap, I was looking forward to some Spanish food."

I throw every bit of good sense I possess to the wind and say, "I know a good Spanish place. I can take you there."

She looks surprised, which makes sense. We've never shared so much as a meal together in the month she's worked at Hale Cosmetics. "Are you sure I'm not messing up your plans?"

"Not at all. I was just going to heat up some leftovers at home." I gesture toward my car, and she takes a tentative step in that direction.

"Uh, Dr. Hale, was your car designed by NASA?" Then her eyes lift to mine, and they look so green and sparkly in the fading light. "Ooh, are we eating on the International Space Station?"

I can't help but laugh, even though I'm still wondering *who the fuck is Cruz?*

"No, the place definitely isn't that far away," I tell her, opening the car door for her. She slides in, and my eyes catch a flash of pale upper thigh as she slides into the sleek customized blue seat.

"Keep it together, Hale," I mutter to myself as I walk around the vehicle, taking a series of deep breaths. "Just dinner. It's just dinner with a colleague."

I lower myself into the driver's seat and put on my seatbelt, waiting for Nicolette to do the same before pulling back out onto the surface street.

Her curious eyes dart around the interior of the car. "This is a Bugatti, right?"

"Yeah, it's a Chiron with an 8.0 L quad-turbocharged W16 engine."

"Sweet. I've never ridden in one before. Thank you for picking me up like a stray puppy."

"I almost didn't recognize you," I admit. "I've never seen you with your hair down."

Nicolette makes a little squeaking noise and touches her hair before rummaging through the small red cross-body bag hanging off one shoulder. "I forgot. I can put it up."

I stop her movement with my hand on her wrist. Her skin is warm and impossibly soft. "Why? I wasn't complaining." For some reason—

most likely a perverted one—I don't want her to tame those wild curls into submission.

"My mother doesn't like when I wear it down."

Making a show of looking around the interior of my car, including the non-existent back seat, I lean closer to her and whisper, "Is your mother in the car with us right now?"

She laughs and shakes her head. "No, I just..."

"Leave it down," I command, and her hands instantly still. The corner of my mouth twitches, and I dirtily wonder what other commands she would follow.

I hear her audible swallow before asking, "Am I dressed okay? I didn't even ask where we're going."

"It's a tapas bar not far from here, and you look great." I gesture to the clothes I changed into before going to my mother's, a pair of pressed khaki shorts and an off-white linen short-sleeved shirt.

Nicolette is quiet for the next few moments as I find the restaurant and park in the small lot. "There's a side entrance we can go in," I tell her, guiding her toward the unmarked gray door on the side of the brick structure. "I come here all the time and know the manager."

"Really?" she asks, seeming surprised and extremely nervous. Hell, I wonder if I freaked her out with my bossy hair comment. Or perhaps she didn't actually want to go to dinner with me but was too polite to say so.

"Listen, I feel like I may have butted in on your evening. If you want to eat by yourself, I can wait in the car for you and then drive you back home."

"No!" she practically yells, clutching onto my forearm with a shockingly strong grip. "I'm not going in there by myself."

I'm so fucking confused by her almost manic behavior, but I just nod and open the door for her. "Okay, sure. Whatever you want." I can't say I mind the way she's holding my arm like she might float away if I don't anchor her to the ground.

The door we enter is adjacent to a long mahogany bar that's shined to within an inch of its life. The bartender, Alonso, immediately lifts a hand in greeting. "Dr. Hale! Give us just a second, and we'll get you a table."

Before Alonso can even summon him, his father, Vicente, walks swiftly from the front of the restaurant, greeting me warmly with a hearty slap on the back. "Dr. Hale, I haven't seen you in so long. I was beginning to get offended."

I chuckle at his mild scolding. "I was just here last week, Vicente."

"Well, that's too damn long." Then he turns to Nicolette, and his accent seems to intensify tenfold as he takes her hand and kisses the back of it. "Ah, bienvenido a The Tapas Table. I am Vicente, the manager. And what may I call you?"

"The Tapas…" Nicolette blinks rapidly about a hundred times, and then her face breaks into a wide grin before she laughs. She seems utterly charmed by the Spaniard.

"Gracias, Vicente," she responds in perfectly accented Spanish. "Soy Nicolette. Su restaurante es hermoso."

The man wiggles his eyebrows at her. "El doctor Hale nunca ha traído a una cita aquí."

I watch with rapt attention as she replies, again in Spanish. "No soy su cita. Somos compañeros de trabajo."

No idea what they just said. I heard my name and picked up a few other words, but my Spanish is rusty. So I ask her as soon as we're seated at a table notched into the arch of a bay window that overlooks the restaurant's courtyard.

"What were you and Vicente saying? Trabajo means work, right?"

Nicolette takes a sip of water and eyes me over the rim. "He said you'd never brought a date here before." She smirks, her tone casual. "And I told him I'm not your date. I'm a prostitute."

Choking on my own spit, I cover my mouth with my napkin. "Wh-what?"

Her laughter is a rich, warm sound that swirls around the table. "Kidding. I told him we're coworkers."

I snag my own water goblet and take a large gulp to clear my throat. "Thank god. I thought for a second there that I'd never be able to show my face in here again."

Nicolette takes in the space, her eyes roaming from floor to ceiling. "Okay confession time." She bends forward and lowers her voice, and I find my own posture arcing to mimic her. "In the car, when you said you were taking me to a tapas bar, I thought you said *topless bar.*"

A burst of hilarity spews from my mouth again. That's why she was acting so nervous.

"You actually thought I'd take you to a topless bar?"

She grins. "I was so confused. I never thought the straitlaced Dr. Helix Hale would go to a strip club."

Straitlaced. If she only knew. "I'm not saying I've never been to one, but I certainly wouldn't take you there."

"I was afraid we'd show up and the sign would read Cooter's or something with the two O's being nipples," she comments. "I was fully prepared to see women dancing in cages, and I'd probably have to suppress the urge to yank open the doors and yell, 'Free the titties!' like a lunatic."

We both crack up until we hear a throat clear beside us. Vicente sets down a carafe of housemade sangria and two wine glasses. "I walk away for two minutes and come back to this discussion," he says, clicking his tongue in mock disappointment.

Nicolette points at me accusingly. "It's Dr. Hale's fault. He's trying to corrupt me."

"Exactly as I suspected." He waggles a stubby finger at me, his voice teasing. "Don't make me have to come back over here. I'll not have you insulting my new favorite guest."

"I thought I was your favorite guest, Vicente," I tell him, feigning insult.

He waves his hand like he's shooing me away as he makes goo goo eyes at Nicolette. "Let me know if you need my assistance, madam. I can get rid of this pest if he's bothering you. Then you can sit at my table, and I'll treat you like a princess for the rest of the evening."

"You don't even have a table," I scoff at his obvious flirting. "I've been coming here for years, and I don't think I've ever seen you sit down."

"Because I've never had the proper motivation." He turns to Nico- lette. "Have you decided what you'd like to eat tonight, Princess Nico- lette?" I roll my eyes.

"I haven't looked at the menu yet," she says. "Do you mind if we take a few minutes?"

"Of course," Vicente purrs, practically bowing his way from the table, but not before tossing me a cheeky wink.

"He's a piece of work," she chuckles, picking up her menu.

"He's something," I mutter, trying to hide the annoyance in my voice. I know Vicente doesn't mean anything by his blatant flirting, but it still crawled under my skin a little bit. Maybe it's because he's on a first-name basis with Nicolette while she and I are still using formal titles. And yes, I'm aware that's my own damn fault.

"Hmm, might have to try the paella," she muses, her green eyes cast down toward the list of small plates.

"You can call me Helix," I blurt out, and her gaze snaps up to mine. "If you want."

"Okay, Helix," she replies, and I like the way my name sounds from her pretty lips. "And you may call me Princess Nicolette."

I snort in amusement. I can't remember the last time I've laughed this much, though it was probably with Phoenix. He's a lot calmer now that he's a dad, but he's still the funniest person I know.

"I refuse to call you princess," I declare, earning me a quirked eyebrow from my date, er, dinner companion. "You're too good for that. I rather think of you in the queen category."

Nicolette sets down her menu and gives me a sarcastic slow clap. "Well done, Helix." But I don't miss her blush at the compliment.

Fuck, I like her. Not just her looks, though her wild hair combined with that one-shoulder shirt is sexy as hell and not tempered in the least by the black glasses perched on her tiny nose. No, I also like her bite and her wit.

Picking up the wine carafe, I ask, "You like sangria?" She hesitates but then nods. "Don't feel like you have to, Nicolette. I can get Vicente to bring you something else."

"No, it's fine. I actually love sangria, but wine makes me sleepy. I can drink vodka, whiskey, rum, and even tequila, but give me more than one glass of wine, and I'm off to snoozetown as soon as I get halfway relaxed."

"Okay, one glass it is," I agree, pouring some of the stout red wine into her glass.

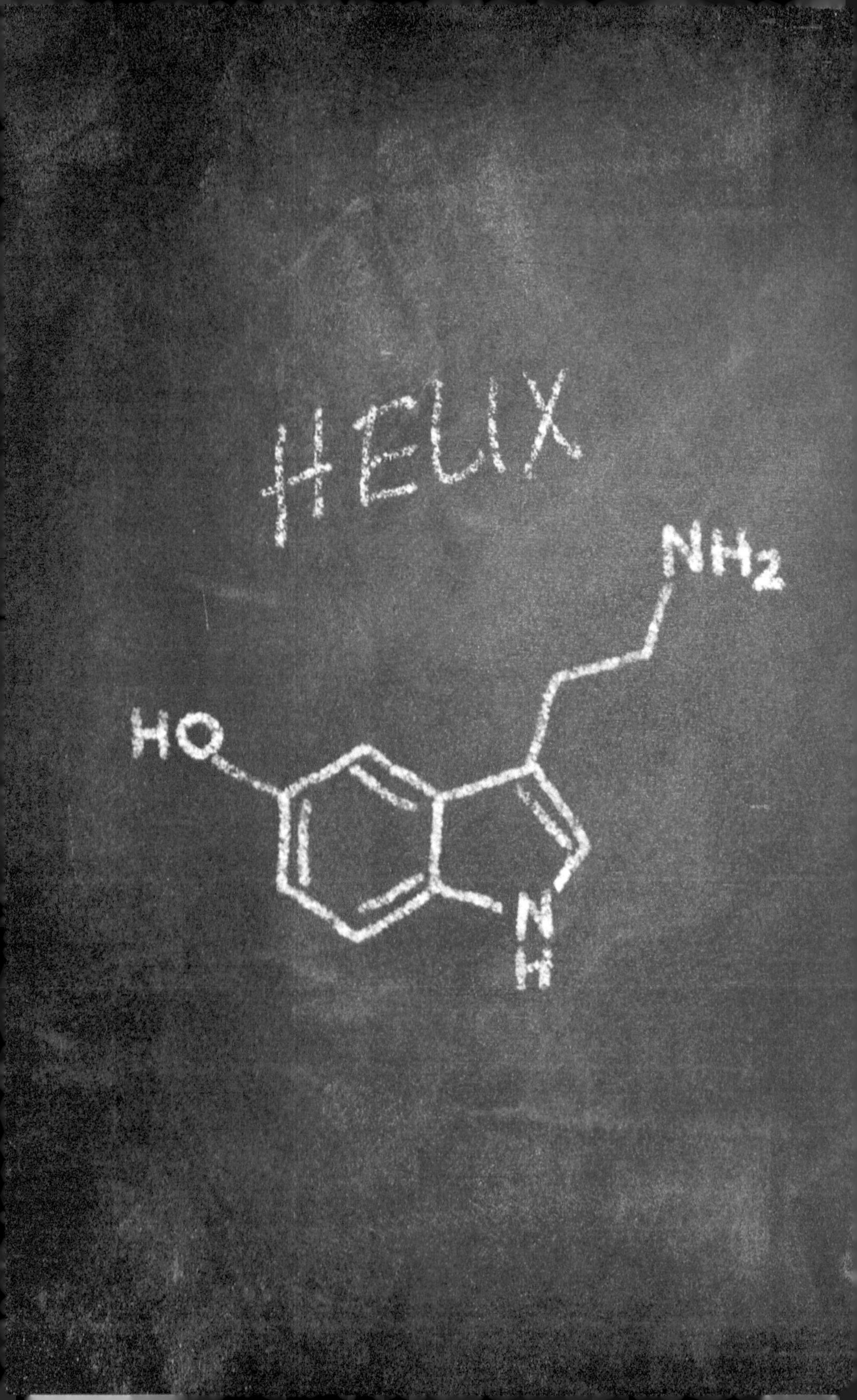

HELIX
NH2
HO
NH

Chapter Twelve

THE GOOSE AND THE GUN

Three carafes of sangria later, Nicolette and I are laughing our asses off. I'd started off sitting across the table from her but moved to the chair beside her about two liters ago as the buzz in the busy restaurant became louder.

"Oh my god! You did not steal an old lady's fake pig from her front yard when you were a teenager," she whisper-yells.

"Yes, we did," I affirm with a grin. "Fucking thing was a lot heavier than it looked. It was made of some kind of stone."

"Let me guess, from what you've told me, this was either Dutton or Phoenix's idea." We'd talked enough about my family tonight that she was able to make that assumption correctly. However, every time I've tried to ask about her family, she's deftly turned the conversation to another topic.

Pressing my hand into my chest, I used my best wounded voice. "You think I couldn't come up with such a stellar idea? I'm hurt, quee-nie." And yeah, that nickname happened about one liter ago.

With a mock solemn face, she replies, "Oh, pardon the hell out of me. I'm sure you were perfectly capable of instigating such mischief. Where was this anyway?" She takes a sip of her wine, her eyes ripe with interest.

"It was in the small town near where Dutton's ranch is located north of Houston." I dumbly point upward like that actually denotes north.

"So what happened next?"

I groan and swipe a hand down my face. "Turns out the old woman the pig belonged to was a widow. She put a personal letter in the local paper begging whoever stole Precious the Pig to bring her back." Wincing, I finish with, "Because it was the last gift her husband gave to her before he died."

Nicolette covers her eyes with her hand. "Oh my freaking hell. Please tell me you took it back."

"We did," I assure her. "Along with a note thanking her for letting us take Precious on a most excellent adventure, signed anonymously, of course. Then we detailed said adventures."

Her brows pinch together. "Like what?"

"We just made up a bunch of stuff that sounded adventurous. Climbing Mt. Everest, whitewater rafting down the Colorado River, eating croissants at a little café in Paris."

Nicolette's face softens. "That was actually really sweet. Probably made her feel better about missing her prized possession while she was abducted."

"It did. The ranch manager from Dutton's farm overheard the widow talking about it in the General Store. She was laughing about it."

"Did anyone suspect you guys?"

"The ranch manager did. He's the one who showed Dutton the newspaper and told him if the pig wasn't replaced by the next day, he was going to find out who stole Precious and shoot them." I can't help the grimace that crosses my face as I stroke my chin. "I think he was only half kidding."

"Yikes!" Her eyes follow the movement of my arm when I lower it to the table. "I've been trying to look at your tattoo all night. May I?"

"Of course." I turn my arm over to expose the inside of my forearm.

She mouths the words she sees there, and my skin tingles when she drags her soft fingertips over the ink. "Pursuit of..." I see it the second she recognizes the molecule of serotonin, and her eyes meet mine with a big smile on her face. "Pursuit of happiness. I love that."

"Do you have any ink?" I ask. *Perhaps a tat on your inner thigh you'd like to show me?* Thankfully, I don't voice that thought aloud.

Nicolette swivels in her chair and pulls her hair to one side, revealing the outline of an oxytocin molecule on the back of her left shoulder. There's a pink rose with the curvy stem entwined around the lines of the molecule. It's the perfect mix of smart and feminine.

I feel a certain pull toward this woman because of our congruous tattoos. Oxytocin and serotonin are two of what are known as the "happiness hormones," the others being dopamine and endorphins.

But oxy, specifically, is considered a love hormone, present during birth and bonding moments. "So you're looking for love?" I ask, and her nose wrinkles when she turns around and releases her hair.

"No, not necessarily. I got this as soon as I turned eighteen. I was in college and feeling... down, I guess." Nicolette picks a slice of wine-soaked orange from her glass and nibbles on it. "You know that high you get when oxytocin is released into your system while someone is hugging you?"

I nod. "Yes, some people refer to it as the hugging hormone because of that."

"Right. I was craving that, so I got the tat to remind me that one day I'd find that feeling again."

"That makes sense. You lived away from your family. I hope you got lots of hugs when you went home for the holidays."

Her lips tighten into a humorless smile. "They're not really the hugging type." She mumbles the next two words, and I know they're not meant for my ears, but I hear them anyway. "With me."

Before I can ask what that means, Vicente appears beside the table. "More food or sangria?" On top of the three carafes of wine, Nicolette and I shared six small tapas.

"None for me," Nicolette answers immediately.

Her eyes turn questioningly toward me, and I shake my head. "I'm good."

When Vicente hands over the check, she attempts to reach for it, but I playfully smack her hand. "Don't even think about it."

"I can pay for my own food and drinks," she argues, but I ignore her protests, handing over my card. After the manager departs to run my card, she glares at me. "Are you always this bossy?"

I meet her gaze. "Yes."

She snorts at my blunt and concise answer. "I'm going to run to the restroom. I'm not even sure how long it will take me to walk home."

Walk home? "You've lost your mind if you think I'm letting you walk home, Dr. Bell," I tell her, reverting to her official name for stern emphasis. We have a staredown for a long moment before she sighs and rolls her eyes.

"Fine," she snaps before standing and stomping to the back of the restaurant.

I watch her go as that little skirt swishes with each step, only pulling my eyes away when Vicente brings my debit card back. "She's fantastic."

"I know that," I say shortly.

"Bring her back. I want her to try our bacon-wrapped figs next time."

My eyes narrow at him. "She doesn't like figs." Okay, I have no idea if that's true or not, but he's getting on my nerves.

"She'll like my figs," he replies with annoying confidence.

"You keep your figs away from Nicolette," I growl, but he just laughs good-naturedly.

"Bring your lovely mother in next time as well."

"Why? So you can flirt with her too?" I've suspected for a while that Vicente has a crush on my mother, despite being ten years younger than her.

"So I can share my figs with two beautiful women," he replies, bobbing his eyebrows before turning to walk away.

"I'm not leaving you a tip, smartass," I call to his back, and I can hear his deep laughter until he reaches the front of the restaurant. I sigh and leave Vicente a very generous tip.

My phone vibrates in my pocket, and since Nicolette is still in the restroom, I check it to find a message from my mother.

> X-Chromosome: I want to meet your new girlfriend.

I stare at my phone like it's an alien.

Helix: What girlfriend?

X-Chromosome: The one you're having
dinner with at The Tapas Table.

Glancing toward the front of the restaurant, I see Vicente grinning at me. The fucker.

Helix: She's not my girlfriend. She's the new
lab manager.

X-Chromosome: Great! I want to meet your
new "lab manager." Bring her to lunch
one day.

Helix: We don't eat lunch together. This was
a one-time thing, so don't start, Mom.

X-Chromosome: You really shouldn't make
your "lab manager" eat alone.

Helix: Stop with the quotation marks. I've
gotta go. Love you.

X-Chromosome: Love you too, sweetheart. I
look forward to meeting your "lab manager."

For fuck's sake. Houston is one of the largest cities in the nation, but sometimes it feels like a tiny little town with the way gossip spreads. I shake my head and put my phone away.

Thank you for dinner. This place was amazing," Nicolette tells me as I guide her out the side door to the parking lot. She stifles a yawn as I open the car door for her. "I'll have to tell Cruz that other restaurant he recommended is closed, but I bet he'll love The Tapas Table."

My curiosity heats the back of my neck as I walk around and slide into the driver's side. "Who is Cruz?" I ask, but there's no answer.

Because Nicolette Bell is fast asleep in the soft leather seat of my Bugatti.

I pull into the driveway behind Nicolette's townhome. We discussed this at dinner, and she told me which street she lived on and that hers was the blue one. Just to be certain, I hop out and peer through the window on the garage door to find her Audi safely tucked inside.

Going back to my car, I pull open her door and squat down. "Nicolette, you're home." She doesn't respond, so I shake her gently. "Nicolette, can you wake up for me?"

Absolutely no response... unless you count the loud snore she emits. Hells bells, she wasn't kidding about wine knocking her out. I try three more times to awaken her before finally deciding, fuck it, I'll just carry her inside.

Tentatively, I pick up the small bag in her lap and unsnap it. This makes me extremely uncomfortable. My mother taught me to never go through a woman's purse after she caught Phoenix and I stuffing her tampons into our Nerf guns and shooting each other when we were seven. But I really don't have much choice. She's not waking up, and I can't exactly leave her in the driveway.

Luck is on my side when I see her keys directly on top. Pulling them out, I search them in the glow of the car's overhead light, finally finding one labeled BD. I can only assume that means back door. I jog over, and sure enough, the key unlocks the door on the side of the garage.

Once I have Nicolette unbuckled and in my arms, I bump the car door closed with my hip. Then I almost scream when I turn around and find...

"Is that a goose?"

"No," an unamused voice says, "it's a Rottweiler."

He steps fully into the light, and I see a blond man wearing a baby-pink bathrobe with boa feathers around the neck. He is indeed holding a goose in one arm with a .44 Magnum in the other hand. And the handgun is pointed directly at me.

Well this isn't ideal.

"Look buddy," I say in my calmest voice. "I don't want any trouble. Just back away, okay?"

He doesn't budge. "If you don't want any trouble, why do you have an unconscious Nicolette in a dark alley?"

"You know her?" I'm not sure, but I think this is good news. At least he's not some stranger roaming the streets with a goose and a gun, though that wouldn't even be the weirdest thing you'd see if we were in the Sunnyside neighborhood.

The man scoffs. "Of course I know her. She's my neighbor and my friend. And who are you?"

"I'm Helix Hale, her boss. We had dinner and drinks, and she fell asleep as soon as we got into the car."

His head tilts in what feels like an accusation, but his gun hand never wavers. "Did you feed her wine? She gets terribly sleepy after drinking wine."

"I'm aware," I say dryly, hefting her body up to readjust her in my arms. She's not big, but I am holding a whole-ass person right now. Something niggles my brain, and I ask, "Are you Cruz?"

The man semi-recoils. "No, Cruz lives in New York. He's Nicolette's best friend's husband."

His last three words relax my spine a bit, like I've been shot with a tranquilizer dart. Though I'm not sure relaxation is exactly what I should be going for right now *because there's still a goddamn gun pointed at me.*

"Can you tell me your name then?" I ask.

"You can call me Dirty Harry," he delivers without a smile, though he narrows his eyes in an uncanny representation of Clint Eastwood.

"Okay, Harry. Can you put the gun down and let me get Nicolette safely inside?"

"How do I know you're not some crazy person who drugged her and wants to do her harm?" he asks, tilting his head the other way.

"With all due respect, I'm not the one outside in a pink bathrobe with a goose and a gun," I very reasonably point out. Or so I think.

The man's eyes narrow to the point that I don't know how he can see. "Are you judging me for wearing pink? Because light-pink is in my color wheel." The goose honks so loudly in concurrence, I almost drop the woman in my arms.

I rush to assure him. "No, not at all. It actually looks great with your complexion." This has got to be one of the strangest conversations I've ever had.

Dirty Harry nods as if that was the correct answer. "Thank you. Though I do concede the rest of it may appear a little bizarre."

Understatement of the century, buddy.

"Stefan, what's going on?" a voice says a split second before another man toddles quickly from the shadows of the home next door. He's dressed exactly as Harry—or Stefan, I guess—except his robe is purple and he's wearing what appears to be a mud mask on his face. "Oh my gawd! Is that Nicolette?"

"Yes, Lukas. This gentleman claims to be Helix Hale, her boss. He said they had dinner and wine together."

"Oh, you should never give Nicolette wine," Lukas tells me, shaking his head from side to side. "It makes her extremely sleepy."

"I'm aware," I grit out, hitching her sagging body up again. How the hell is she sleeping through all this commotion? "May I please take her inside now?"

"Give us a minute," Stefan says. "I'm going to have the LBI look into your story."

Sweat seeps from my back and neck, making my shirt stick to me. "What is the LBI?"

"The Lukas Bureau of Investigation," he informs me imperiously. "It's like the FBI but much more efficient."

Lukas, who's obviously the head of the LBI, taps on his phone before holding it up for his partner to look. "I Googled Helix Hale. He appears to be telling the truth about that." The shorter, dark-haired man looks at me. "Where did you have dinner?"

"The Tapas Table," I say wearily.

Lukas holds up a finger to quiet me as he brings his phone to his ear and turns his back, strolling a few feet away. Two extremely long minutes later, he's back.

"Vicente confirms Dr. Helix Hale was there tonight with one Dr. Nicolette Bell. They had three carafes of sangria, the gambas al ajillo, calamares fritos, paella, crab empanadas, the fried eggplant, and lamb meatballs. He also vouches for Dr. Hale's character."

"They didn't have the bacon-wrapped figs?" Stefan queries, eyeballing me like I committed a major crime.

"His shipment was late," I say, my voice tight.

Lukas nods. "That's exactly what Vicente told me. He said they should have fresh figs by next week."

"We should make a reservation. I do love his figs."

"Already done," Lukas replies, looking smug. "Next Saturday at eight."

"Look," I groan, "I'm glad Nicolette has this very insane neighborhood watch thing going on, and I appreciate you caring about her safety, but can we please get this show on the road now that the LBI has cleared me of any wrongdoing?"

"Of course," Stefan says, finally lowering the .44, his tone shifting to that of a perfect gentleman rather than a psycho vigilante. "Thank you for respecting the process, Dr. Hale."

The goose honks his approval.

"We're just going to take Sir PooPoo for a walk so he can... well... poo poo," Lukas tells me. I'm assuming Sir PooPoo is the goose. At least I hope so.

"But we'll be keeping an eye on this house, and if you're in there for more than five minutes, we're coming in," Stefan warns, his eyes going all slitty again. He drops the gun into the pocket of his thin robe, making it sag on one side.

I can't wait to tell Phoenix about this whole scene. He'll probably be jealous he wasn't here to witness it.

Once inside, I shift Nicolette to carry her over my shoulder since the staircases are narrow. She doesn't rouse in the slightest. One of my arms wraps around her thighs while my other searches for an appropriate place to rest. I press my palm against her lower back to steady her, though my mind goes to a darker place. If she were awake and willing, that hand would be directly on the supple ass that's pressed against the side of my head.

Stop it, Hale. She is fucking unconscious.

After trekking up the stairs, I locate her bedroom on the top floor and cross the room in the darkness to flick on the bedside lamp. I smile at her bedding. The duvet is a soft tangerine color in contrast to the crisp white of her sheets and pillowcases. The bed is unmade, and I straighten the covers before laying her down and placing her purse on the nightstand.

Miraculously, she's still fast asleep. She must have wine-induced narcolepsy. I'm not sure that's actually a thing, but it should be. Sitting on the edge of the bed, I pull her feet into my lap and unbuckle her shoes before pulling them off. The Nobel committee really should award me some kind of commendation for not letting my eyes linger on the smooth thighs that are exposed in this position.

I roll her onto her side and look at her for a long moment, my eyes falling on the oxytocin tattoo. Then I lean over and do what I've wanted to do since she shared her reasons for getting it.

I hug her.

It's chaste and not sexual at all, and I'm rewarded with a small sigh from her. When I release her and stand, I notice a contented smile on her sleeping face.

And that makes me smile too as I flip off the lamp and leave her room.

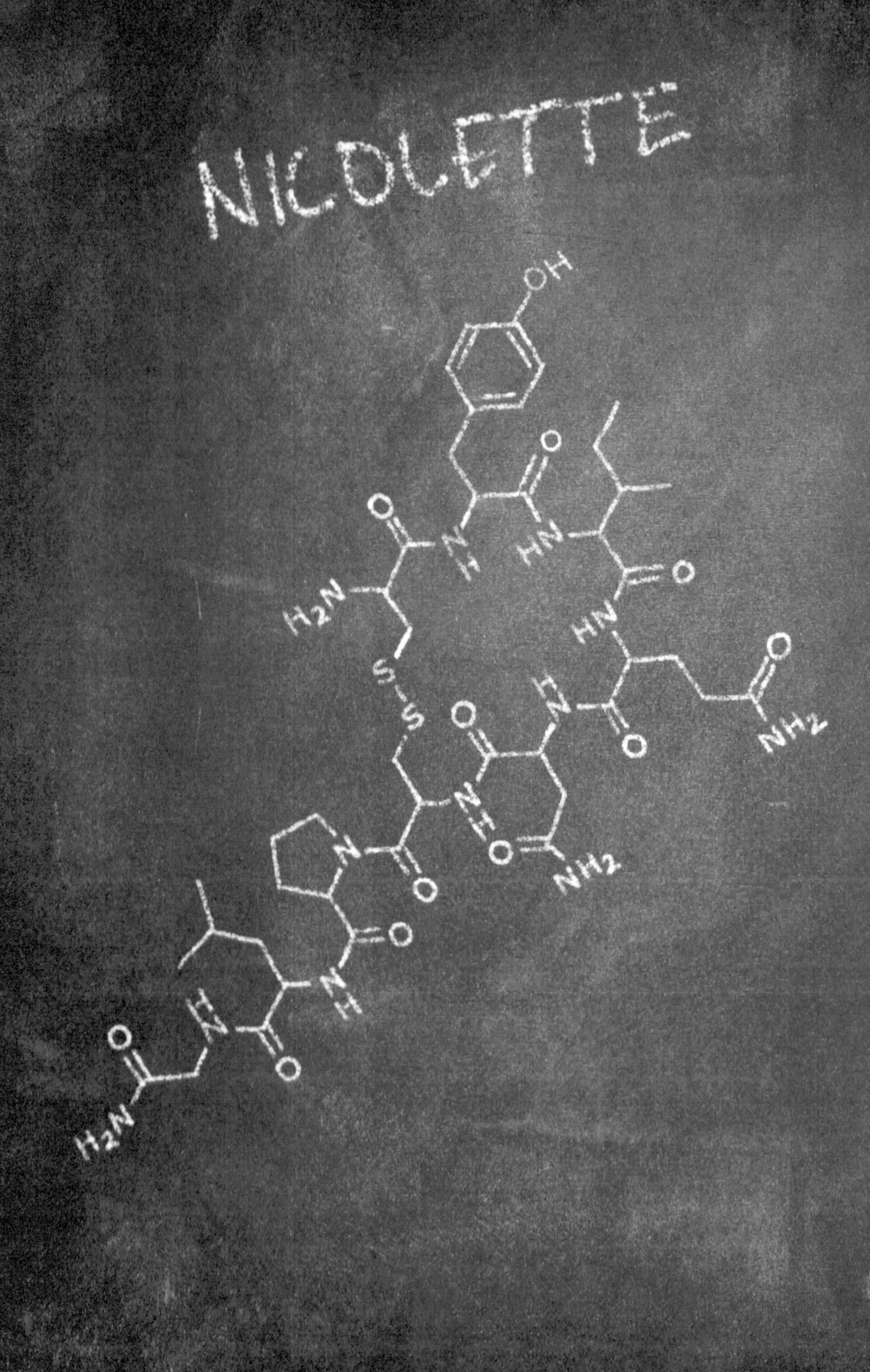

NICOLETTE

Chapter Thirteen

YOGA FARTS

I awaken slowly on Saturday morning and nestle my face against my pillow, noticing my red purse on the nightstand. It's not my usual purse, but I'd taken it last night because it matched my cute shirt perfectly.

Memories of the evening begin to filter in… looking for the restaurant… Helix offering to take me to a "topless bar." I laugh out loud at that. Luckily he found it hilarious as well. He's surprisingly funny, nothing like the stoic man I've come to know in the lab these past few weeks. It was honestly the best time I've had with a man in a very long time, if ever.

And then I remember the wine.

"Shit," I mutter. We drank a lot of sangria last night. I know better, but it was so delicious, and the vibe of the restaurant and Helix's company compelled me to have *just one more tiny glass.*

I sit up in the bed and smooth my curls back. I feel a little fuzzy-brained but otherwise fine. Wine never gives me a hangover. In fact, I usually feel great the morning after drinking wine, but maybe that's because I sleep like a corpse. With a downward glance, I assess my appearance. I'm still in my clothes from last night, but my shoes are gone. Peering over the side of the bed, I see them lined up with sharp precision beside my nightstand.

Who put them there? And how did I get home and then up here to my room?

There's only one reasonable answer, and it makes me cringe. Helix Hale... my freaking boss.

Dammit. I need to message him to apologize. Hopefully he won't think I'm completely unprofessional for falling asleep in his car like a freaking wino. And I'm pretty sure I didn't even make my bed yesterday.

Reaching for my purse, I find that my phone is dead, so I plug it in before climbing out of bed and heading down to the second level to make some coffee. When I get back upstairs with a cup of java in my hand, I see that I have a message from Helix.

> Dr. Hale: How are you feeling today?

> Nicolette: I'm fine. I need to apologize for my behavior last night.

I'm surprised when a message pops back immediately.

> Dr. Hale: Why would you need to apologize?

> Nicolette: I thought that would be obvious. I swear I'm not some wino who randomly passes out in her boss's car. I'm really sorry, Dr. Hale.

> Dr. Hale: I thought I told you to call me Helix.

Even through black-and-white words on a screen, the bossiness comes through as effectively as if he were saying the words to my face. *Or growling them in my ear while he grips my throat and...*

Whoaaa, Nelly. Where did that come from?

Shaking my head as if to ward off the evil, invading thoughts, I quickly change his name in my phone and reply again.

> Nicolette: Okay, I'm really sorry, Helix.

> Helix: No need to apologize. You told me wine makes you sleepy, so it wasn't your fault.

> Nicolette: Thank you for being so understanding.

> Helix: Of course. Though being held at gunpoint was a first for me.

My eyes almost bug out of my head. What the actual fuck?

> Nicolette: I held you at gunpoint?!?!

> Helix: No, silly. You were unconscious. Stefan did.

> Nicolette: My neighbor?!?!

> Helix: Yes, the one with the poo poo goose.

The snort that comes out of my nose chokes me, and I pound my chest as I cough through it. I'm not sure if it was a laugh or a sound of pure shock. Probably a little of both.

I decide this is a conversation where I need to hear his voice to determine whether he's going to fire me, so I call his number.

As soon as he answers, I shriek, "Stefan literally held you at gunpoint?"

"Nicolette." Helix's voice is a balm, deep and soothing. "He thought I was a crazy kidnapper or something. He was protecting you."

"With a firearm pointed at you?" I demand.

"He told me his name was Dirty Harry."

A giggle bubbles out of me before I can stop it. "That sounds like Stefan."

"Look, it all turned out okay. He was trying to protect his friend, and I can appreciate that. He had no clue who I was, so they ran this really weird background check on me and deemed me suitable to get you safely inside your house."

I scrub at my forehead with my fingertips, a headache forming there for reasons unrelated to the wine. "That's a lot to unpack. A background check?"

"Apparently, Lukas runs the LBI. You'll be happy to know I was quickly cleared of any misdeeds, and they stayed outside until I left."

"The... LBI?"

"Lukas Bureau of Investigation. It seems like a stellar organization."

I can't help but laugh at his wry delivery. "You're taking this awfully well."

"I feel partly responsible because of the whole wine thing. We'll have to avoid that next time we eat together. Do you go into a coma with any other adult beverages?"

"No, just wine. And I don't lose my memory or anything. I simply get sleepy," I assure him, my brain stuck on two other words he mentioned. "Did you say next time?"

"Of course. You mentioned at dinner you have a list of places to try in Houston. I can go with you." There's a pause. "Unless you'd rather go by yourself."

I pull the phone away from my ear and stare at it for a second before replacing it. "After last night, you still want to go somewhere with me?"

There's a long pause, and his voice sounds mildly defensive. "You didn't enjoy yourself?"

"No. I mean, yes, I enjoyed myself." God, why am I all flustered? "I had a very good time with you, Dr., uh, Helix."

"Good. Next Friday okay with you?"

"That's... fine."

"Cool. Where are we going next?"

I search my brain to remember. "It's a barbecue restaurant. My friend said it's the best one in Houston."

"Carver's?" Helix asks.

"That's the one," I confirm.

"Great. What time do you want me to pick you up?"

I shake my head, still confused by this entire turn of events. Apparently, I now have my very own foodie tour guide. "Seven?"

"I'll be there." Amusement tinges his voice when he adds, "And don't worry. Carver's doesn't even have wine on the menu."

Smartass.

"I've never seen anyone so excited about a yoga class," I say to Shay Martin, the pharmacist friend I met at the Academy meeting in L.A. earlier this year.

We push through the glass doors to a swanky looking gym, and Shay checks in and adds me as a guest. "Because I guarantee this will be the best class you've ever been to," she replies.

"No lies detected," the pretty lady behind the desk adds with a glint in her eyes. "You got here just in time, Shay. You got the final two spots."

My eyes flit around the room, taking in the high-end machines as we walk through to the back, where Shay opens the door onto a beautiful garden. A group of mostly women—though there are a few men scattered in—gathers excitedly on a large covered wooden patio.

A few people wave at Shay as we find a spot to one side of a circular, raised wooden stage that's in the center of the patio. The aromas of flowers and foliage mix with the palpable scent of eager anticipation swirling in the air. As I people-watch everyone hurriedly finding their spots, I notice all eyes are gazing in one direction, a spot to my right.

"Oooh, here come the yogis," Shay hisses.

A collective sigh goes up around the space, and when I shift my eyes to the right, I see why.

Oh. My god.

Two men make their way through the adoring crowd and climb onto the stage. They're both barefoot, wearing cowboy hats and Wrangler jeans that fit so tightly a person could easily determine if a coin in their pocket is heads or tails. Or if they're circumcised. Both are, for the record.

The blond one is slightly taller and shirtless, and the brunette makes a show of unsnapping his western shirt. I'm pretty sure not a single eye in the place blinks while he shrugs it off, showing off a similar Adonis-like physique as his co-yogi.

"Holy shit," I breathe, and Shay giggles beside me.

"The world could be on fire, and I wouldn't miss this class," she whispers back.

Without taking my eyes from them as they prepare, I ask quietly, "Are these guys qualified yogis?"

"Do you care?" my friend shoots back, and I stifle a laugh.

"Good point."

The blond, who introduces himself as Atlas, leads us through some meditation and breathing exercises while the dark-haired guy, Duke, walks around the space and blesses everyone with his broody presence. One woman, a petite blonde with a sleek ponytail, looks completely naked in her flesh-colored Lululemon sports bra and matching shorts. She makes a lot of mistakes each time Duke passes her, most likely on purpose, because he bends to correct her.

Then they begin the practice, both men on the stage guiding everyone through the poses. Several women groan when the guys do the bridge pose, lying on their backs and lifting and lowering their hips from the ground. To be honest, I may have been one of the groaners.

Plank pose seems to be another crowd favorite because it shows off the thick bulges of the cowboys' forearms. When Atlas and Duke show everyone the low lunge, I gape in amazement. *How the hell are they doing that in those tight jeans?*

From the corner of my mouth, I mumble, "I really need to know what kind of denim they're wearing. Because that's some tenacious fabric. They should use that to build the space shuttle."

I hear Shay snort. "I think we're all hoping one day they'll split their britches."

I double over in laughter, earning me a glare from Duke, which only makes it funnier. Shay gets tickled as well and covers her face with her hands, completely abandoning her pose. I'm too busy grinning at her to notice Atlas approaching until he's directly in front of us.

His voice is low and rumbly as he rests his hands on his narrow hips. "Ladies, is everything okay over here?"

We both do our best to control our features. I feel like I'm in elementary school getting scolded by the principal for talking in the lunch line.

"Yes, we're—"

"Nicolette passed gas, and it made me laugh," Shay interrupts, pointing a finger at me. "Sorry for the disturbance, Atlas."

I'm. Going. To. Kill. Her.

"I—I didn't," I begin, shaking my head rapidly, but Atlas pats my sweaty shoulder with his meaty hand.

"It's okay. Yoga farts happen to everyone sometimes with all the bending and stretching during asanas." A smile crooks his lips. "Even beautiful women."

Then he tips his cowboy hat and swaggers off, giving Shay and I a view of his tight backside.

My eyes shoot to Shay's guilty face. "You're dead to me," I grouse, and she rolls her lips between her teeth.

"Sorry, I panicked. I didn't want to get kicked out of this class. It's the closest thing I get to any action."

I flash her a smile, half forgiving and half wicked. "Next time, let me handle it. I'll tell him you shit your pants."

She snickers and returns her attention to the cowboys on the stage, who are now moving into downward dog. We both do the same. I focus on straightening my back and imagining there's an invisible string pulling my butt to the ceiling. The stretch feels amazing.

And that's when it happens. I fart for real. It's loud in the peaceful garden, and I squinch my eyes shut, pretending it didn't happen.

"Dammit, you jinxed me," I hiss at my friend, whose face is the color of a tomato with her restrained laughter.

I can never show my face at Cowboy Yoga again.

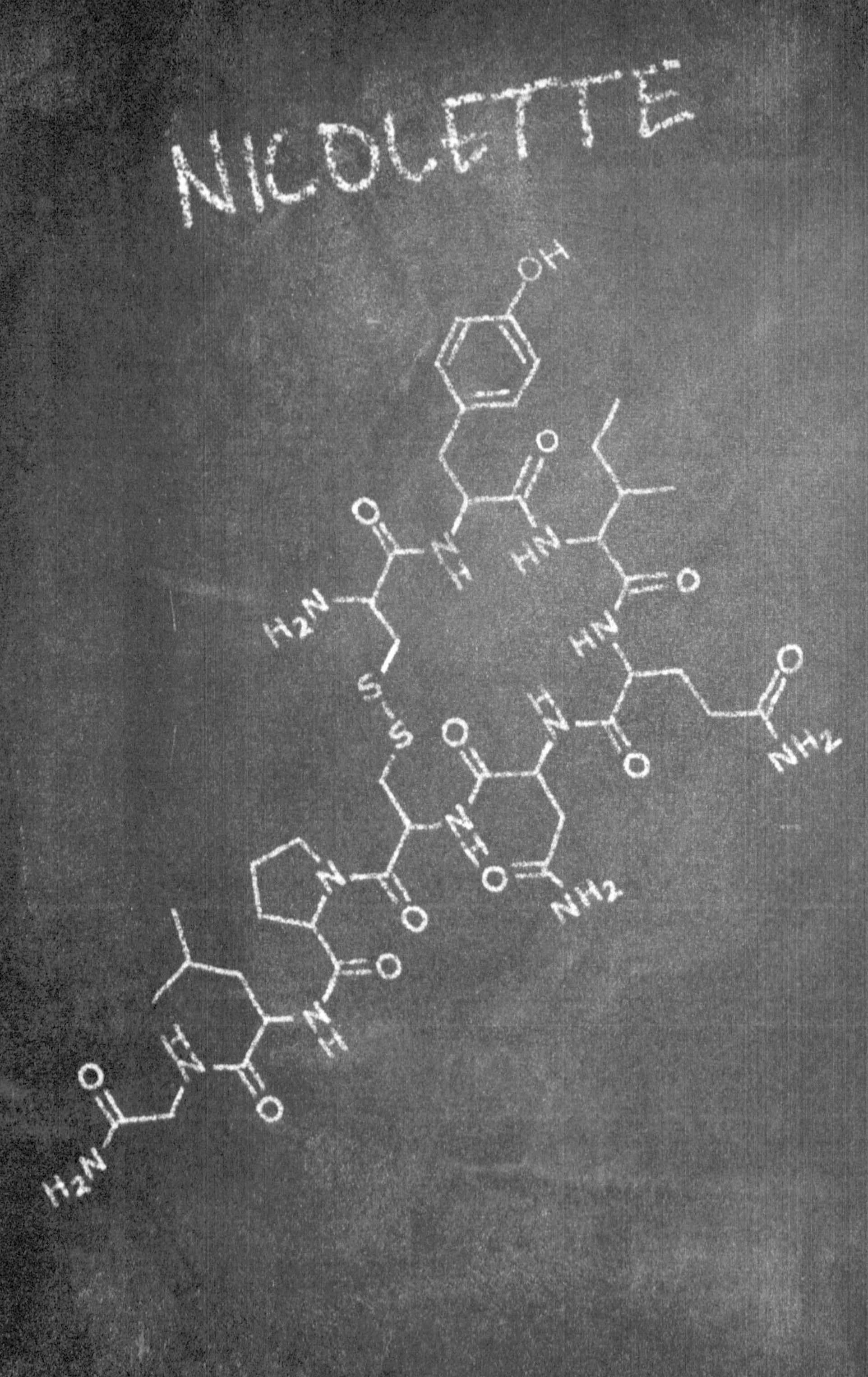

NICOLETTE

Chapter Fourteen

FOREPLAY... TEXAS STYLE

That Friday Helix picks me up in his spaceship car and drives me across Houston to Carver's Family BBQ restaurant. It's rustic, with wood beams crisscrossing overhead and simple light fixtures hanging down from the ceiling.

I let Helix order, and he got us two Coors Lights and a two-person sampler platter. Though platter might be too generous a word.

"Here ya go, sweeties," a woman named Opal says, plopping down a sheet of butcher paper laden with all kinds of smoked meats and sides. Then she stretches out two more lengths of butcher paper, cuts them with a pocketknife, and slaps them down in front of Helix and me. Apparently, these are our plates.

Glancing around the restaurant, I look for a side table with forks and spoons. "Where do we get silverware?"

Opal laughs like that's the funniest thing she's ever heard. "Guessing this is your first time at Carver's, honey."

"She grew up in New Jersey," Helix explains with a playful glint in his crystal eyes.

Opal winks and produces two giant serrated knives from her apron and places one in front of each of us before sauntering away, tossing, "Have fun, Jersey," over her shoulder.

"No forks allowed," Helix explains. "That's why they don't serve potato salad or beans or anything else requiring a fork."

"So we just..."

"Get down and dirty and eat with our hands. It's part of the charm," Helix replies with a grin.

"Excellent," I say, wiggling my fingers in preparation for the feast as I survey the selection. Though I feel a little twinge in the pit of my core at the *down and dirty* line.

There are ribs, sliced pork loin, jalapeño-cheese sausage, and sliced brisket, as well as a large block of cheddar cheese, a full onion with the ends cut off, and a bowl of pickle chips. "What are those?" I ask, pointing at two piles of sides.

"Fried okra and Carver's potatoes."

"Hmmm." I take a little of each meat, one potato, and a small pile of okra. "I've never had fried okra, only boiled or sautéed with tomatoes." I inspect the piece in my hand. It appears to be coated with corn meal.

"It's good like this, and the potatoes are excellent. They toss the slices in butter and seasoning and then roast them."

Popping the okra into my mouth, I feel my eyes widen. It's crispy, salty, and utterly delicious. Then I pick up a potato slice and bite into it, assaulting my taste buds with the flavor of butter and garlic.

"Okay, I'm a fan," I say, eating the rest of the potato. "And I haven't even tried the meat yet." Following Helix's lead, I grab a few dill pickle chips—with my fingers—before using my big knife to cut off a slice of onion and a hunk of cheese.

And then we chow down. Every single thing is fan-freaking-tastic, and there are only scraps left by the time we're done. I drag my last piece of brisket through the barbecue sauce I squirted on my butcher paper and stuff it into my mouth.

My fingers are coated with sauce and seasoning, and I waggle them at Helix. "Are we allowed to use napkins?"

"Sure, but there's a better way to clean up." With a wicked grin, he proceeds to suck each of his fingers into his mouth. That really shouldn't be so damn hot, but there's something incredibly erotic about his thick fingers sliding between those perfect lips as his tongue swirls up every last bit.

I follow suit, savoring the flavorful remnants, and don't miss the way his eyes also track my movements. Jesus, this is like foreplay... Texas style. Picking up my beer, I drain it in an attempt to cool my libido.

"What'd ya think, Jersey?" Opal asks, sliding up to our table and tossing some Wet-Naps onto the surface. She's gotta be in her seventies, but she moves with the spryness of someone half her age.

"Excellent," I tell her, opening one of the packs and cleaning my hands with the damp, lemon-scented napkin. "Best barbecue I've ever had."

She beams at me, her dark-skinned face as sunshiny as the yellow of her Carver's Family BBQ T-shirt. "My niece is the pitmaster here. Took over the business after her daddy had a stroke."

"Really?" I ask, feeling a little guilty that the idea of a female pitmaster would come as a surprise to me.

"Yeppers. You'll probably get to meet her in a minute. She usually makes the rounds about this time." Her eyes shift to the left and brighten with pride. "Ah, there she is. Shonda, honey, come meet Jersey."

A pretty woman with skin a few shades lighter than her aunt's walks over, her tall frame towering over Opal's. Her dark hair is pulled back into a low ponytail, and small lines around her eyes and mouth tell me she probably smiles a lot.

"I'm guessing you're Jersey," Shonda says, greeting me with a firm handshake. "Shonda Carver-King."

"Nicolette Bell," I respond.

"Nah, you're Jersey from now on. My aunt gives everyone a nickname."

My eyes shoot to Helix. "What's yours?"

He winces and rubs the back of his neck while Opal cackles and answers for him. "This here is Rib Bone."

An indelicate snort rips from my nose. "Rib Bone? Sounds like there's a story behind that."

Helix rolls his eyes, but Opal looks positively gleeful. "First of all, Carver's has been open for fifty-two years, and I've been here since day one, so I've been around a minute or two. This fella used to come in with his family when he was a boy." She smacks Helix on the shoulder.

"The kid could polish the meat off a bone like nobody's business, so I started calling him Rib Bone."

"I feel like I got off lucky with Jersey," I share. "Now I'm curious. Does Phoenix have a nickname too?"

Opal nods, her face creased into a grin. "Sure does. Booger." I laugh and wiggle my fingers at her to let her know I need this story. She willingly complies. "That boy was a mess. One time he announced to the whole restaurant that he had a giant booger in his nose. Turns out, he'd just stuck a piece of fried okra up in there."

My words come out in gasps between my laughter. "That's hilarious."

Helix chuckles and shakes his head at the memory. "Dad tried to get it out, but we ended up in the emergency room that night."

"Never a dull moment when the Hales came to eat," Shonda says with a grin. "Do y'all want some dessert? We have banana pudding."

At my skeptical eyebrow, Opal adds, "We do allow spoons for the pudding."

Her niece nudges her. "Except Rib Bone doesn't need a spoon. Remember when his brother dared him to eat the entire bowl with just his mouth?"

Opal bursts into laughter. "Yeah, that was a couple years ago." She gives Helix a pointed look. "That was an impressive display, young man. I'd still like to know where you acquired that kind of skill."

His face reddens, and he clears his throat, obviously wanting a change of subject. "Oh, I forgot, I brought something for you two." He turns to me. "Will you be okay if I grab something from the car?"

I wave him off. "Of course." For the next couple minutes I listen to Shonda and Opal's stories of life in a family restaurant before my boss returns with two small swag bags. But my mind keeps going back to the fact that Helix Hale can eat a bowl of pudding with no utensils. Christ, what else can he do with his tongue?

"These are samples of our new lipsticks for women of color," he tells the women, handing each of them a turquoise bag with the Hale Cosmetics logo on them. "Let me know what you think."

"Ooh, you got new bags. Fancy!" Opal exclaims, and Helix smiles at me.

"Jersey designed them. We just got them in yesterday."

"Oh, you work together?" Shonda asks curiously, her amber eyes darting between us.

"Yes, Nicolette is a biochemist in the lab now. So you should probably call her Dr. Jersey."

"If you call me Dr. Jersey, you have to call Helix Dr. Rib Bone," I tease. "In fact, I think you should put that on your resume."

Shonda eyes us again, her lips tipping up at the corners. "You two are too cute together."

For some reason, I blush at that. I really need to get my shit together and stop having flirty thoughts about this man. But it's hard because he's pretty much perfect in every way except one.

He's my boss.

We decide we need some exercise after our big dinner, so we take a walk in a pretty park that's close to the restaurant. It's late August and the sun is just making its descent toward the horizon.

"This was a good idea," I say. "I think my ass may turn into a brisket after all I ate."

"You have nothing to worry about," Helix remarks, his eyes dropping down my body for the briefest of seconds before jerking away. We stroll beside a large pond and pause to watch a mother duck gliding across the water in a serpentine pattern with three ducklings right behind her.

"Thank you for coming with me tonight. I usually don't mind eating alone, but you made it a lot more fun."

His little half-smile is so damn cute with that stupid dimple. "It was my pleasure. Hale Cosmetics is lucky to have you, and I want to make sure you're happy here in Houston."

Disappointment trickles down the back of my neck at that statement. "So you just offered to go out to eat with me because you want me to keep working at the lab?"

"What? No. I mean, I do want you to stay here, but I've enjoyed the past two Friday nights with you. As a person, not just an employee."

That makes me feel marginally better. "I do like it here." I slap at a mosquito attempting to dine on my forearm. "Except for these damn mosquitoes."

Helix's laugh is deep and rumbly. "They're so aggressive, though I've heard they're even bigger in Alaska."

I pretend to make a slash in the air with an imaginary pencil. "And crossing a trip to Seward's Folly off my to-do list." Chewing on the corner of my lip, I say, "I am happy to be working at Hale. I feel like you listen to me."

His brow wrinkles. "Why wouldn't I? You're very incisive, Nicolette. That idea you brought to me last week about the men's skin care line was genius." He shakes his head. "I don't know why I've never thought of that before. We're completely missing the opportunity to market to half the population."

A sense of elation fills my chest at his praise. "Thank you. I've been thinking about it for a long time, but Aquarius wasn't receptive to the idea at all."

Helix makes a scoffing sound. "Their loss. Like you pointed out, men's skin is different from women's, so a dedicated line for guys is definitely a niche we can fill." He shrugs. "Guys need clean faces and moisturized skin too. I actually use our women's line, but I make myself a batch in the lab without the added girly scents."

"I've been focused more on actual skin care, but adding some masculine scents would be a great idea."

He smiles at me, and Jesus, he's absurdly attractive.

"We brainstorm well together. Do you have any ideas for our new fragrances for next year?" When I hesitate, his smile falters, and his blue eyes bore into mine with hypnotic force. "What's that look?"

"I do have an idea, but it's... different."

He never breaks eye contact. "Different is good."

Bolstered, I ask, "What if we added something that evokes pleasant feelings?"

"You mean like pheromones?"

I wave my hand at him. "No, those have been done to death, and that's more to attract another person. I was thinking more like an additive that gives the actual wearer a sense of contentment. Makes them happy to be in their own skin, not just because they smell good but because they *feel* good."

Helix's eyes defocus for a second while he contemplates what I've said. "Like that calm, content feeling you get from an oxytocin release?"

"Exactly!" I tell him, smacking his bicep, which is much firmer than I would have expected. The good doctor apparently doesn't skip out on arm day at the gym.

His head bobs up and down a few times, and I can practically hear his brain whirring. "I like that. But oxy is difficult to administer in its organic form. It has to be spritzed directly up the nose, and even then, only a small amount will cross the blood-brain barrier. Not enough to actually make much difference. There was a study I read about somewhere... maybe from Ireland?"

"Scotland," I correct. "And you're right. It would have to be something absorbed directly into the skin, something that would work through the bloodstream instead of needing to reach the cerebrospinal fluid, which is where you usually find neurotransmitters."

His excitement leaves with the slight droop of his shoulders. "So it's impossible."

I tilt my head to the side. "Not necessarily. I've been working on synthesizing something that resembles oxytocin but is effective in the bloodstream."

Helix's eyes widen in amazement as he guides me to a forest-green bench, and we sit on the slatted surface. "You're shitting me."

With a giggle, I assure him, "I'm not. It actually works pretty well. On me anyway. I haven't tried it on any test subjects, but I can show you the formula and the mechanism if you're interested."

His smile is everything. "You'd share it with me? Like we could actually use it for our new fragrance line?"

"Of course. Why would I develop something I didn't want to go to market?" I nibble the corner of my lip. "There's one small problem. It works well on its own, but it doesn't smell very good. When I try to add scents to it, it loses its effectiveness."

He leans against the back of the bench and stares out at the pond.

"Huh. I'd have to see the formula, but maybe if we put our two brains together, we could come up with a solution." His face jerks to mine. "That is, if you want my help. I didn't mean to assume."

"I'd love to collaborate our minds," I tell him, leaving out my innermost thought—I wouldn't mind collaborating some other body parts as well.

Good lord, I need help.

Slapping his thighs, Helix grins. "Great. This calls for a celebration. Have we walked enough to deserve dessert since we turned down the banana pudding?"

I quirk one eyebrow. "What did you have in mind?"

He glances behind us. "There're a couple food trucks back there. I know the gelato place is really good."

Though the sun is dipping and not full force, it's still August in Texas, and a cool treat would hit the spot. "That actually sounds great."

He pulls up the gelato truck's website on his phone, and we peruse the flavors.

"The pina colada one sounds good to me," I decide.

Pushing to his feet, he says, "You relax, and I'll go get it."

When he's gone, I slump down on the bench and cross my legs at the ankles. A breeze drifts through the oak trees, and I close my eyes, allowing it to cool my warm skin.

Just when I get completely relaxed, my phone rings with a FaceTime notification... from my mother. I jerk upright. What if something happened to Pop?

"Ma?" I answer swiftly, waiting to see her face appear. When it does, I'm surprised to see Angelica sitting beside her. They're both smiling, but that doesn't put me at ease. "What's wrong?"

"Why would anything be wrong?" she purrs, causing the hairs on the back of my neck to rise. "Can't a mother just call her daughter?"

Seeing as how I moved to Houston over a month ago and she hasn't called me a single time, I'm inclined to say no. But I don't say that out loud.

"Sure. I was just worried. Is Pop okay?"

Ma tilts her head and smiles. "Of course he is. We just wanted to call and invite you to a party."

"My and Rory's engagement party," Angelica adds.

"Oh. How... nice," I reply, confused at this invitation.

"I told your father you probably wouldn't be able to come, but he said we should still call to invite you," Ma replies, her lips tight, and suddenly, I get it. They don't really want me there, but Pop insisted I be invited.

Something stubborn rises up in me, and I add a mental spit-shine to my spine. "I'd love to come. When is it?"

It's almost imperceptible, but I see the disapproval in their eyes, and now I'm even more determined to go. Don't ask me why. Maybe it's my way of saying *fuck you* to the both of them. They're being forced to invite me, and I'm damn well going to accept.

"Welllll," Angelica draws out with mock-sweetness, "I'd love to see you, but the party is couples only. Would you be able to find a date by next weekend?"

"N-next weekend?" I stammer. Shit.

"It's fine if you can't come," Ma pitches in quickly, pretending to be disappointed, though I can see the glee shimmering in her eyes. "I'm sure you're busy with your work stuff and haven't had time to make friends."

Angelica snickers. "Or a boyfriend. Can you even imagine Nicolette with a boyfriend, Ma?" They both laugh like we're in the middle of an Eddie Murphy standup routine.

My shiny spine dulls in a split second, and I can feel my confidence retreating into itself until it disappears with a pop.

"We'd love to come," a deep voice says from behind me, and my eyes widen. I recognize that voice. It's my boss.

He leans down over my shoulder and works his face into the frame of the camera with mine, grinning with a winning white smile. "Hi, I'm Helix, Nicolette's boyfriend. Is the party on Friday or Saturday?"

Every single one of my mom and sister's flabbers have been gasted, if their gaping mouths are any indication.

Then Helix hands me a small cup and kisses my cheek. "Here's your gelato, honey."

Boyfriend? Honey?

What the actual fuck is going on here?

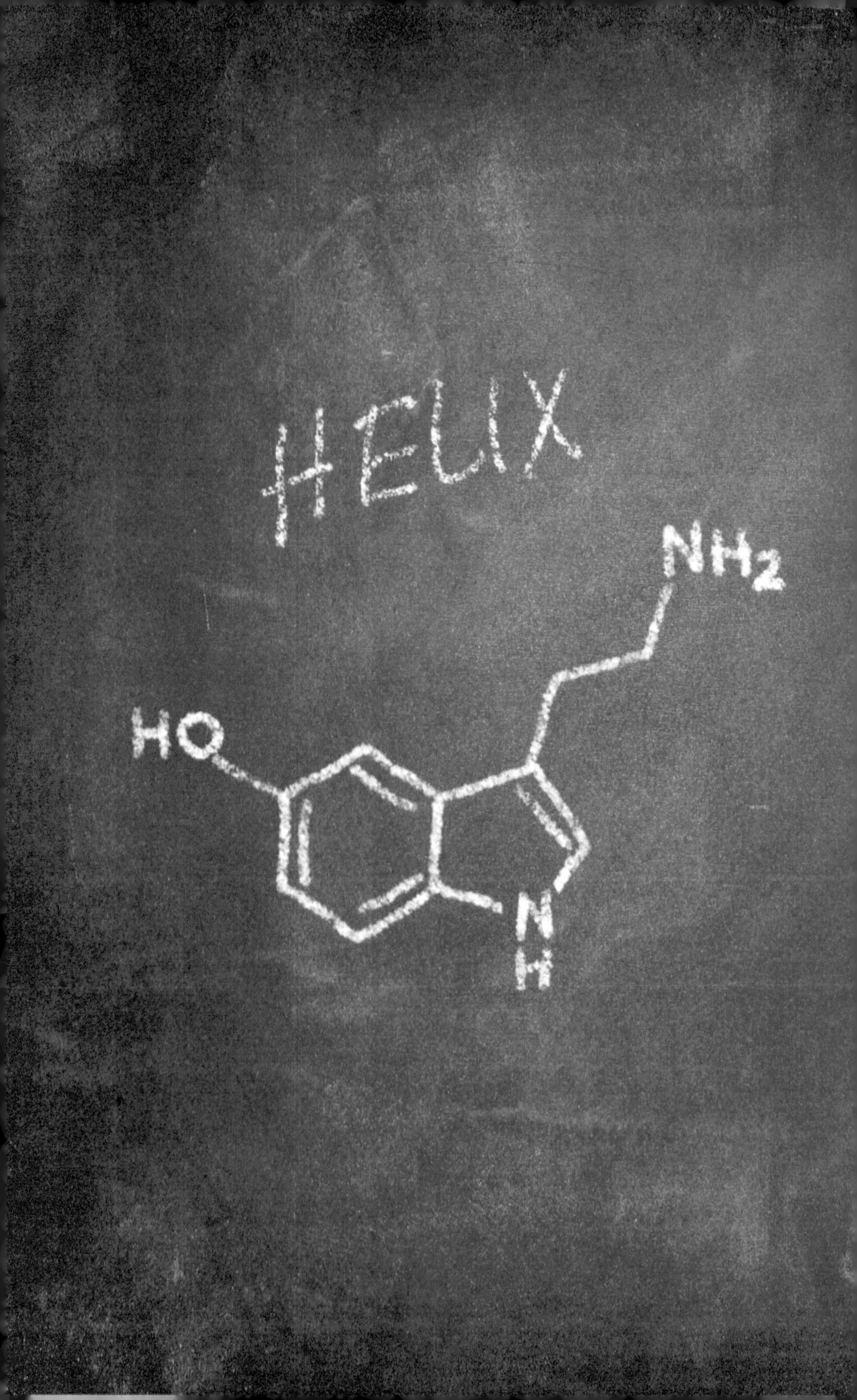

HELIX
NH2
HO
N
H

Chapter Fifteen

THE BABY ELEPHANT STORY

Yeah, I just did that.

Was it a rash and stupid thing to do? Most likely. Am I sorry? Not one tiny fucking bit.

I walked up just about the time those women, who I assumed were Nicolette's sister and mother, extended that insincere invitation. I was about to retreat to give her privacy when the mother got that pissy look on her face and commented that the father insisted. Like they wouldn't have invited a member of their immediate family otherwise.

After that? I eavesdropped without an ounce of shame. Even though I couldn't see her face, I could tell from Nicolette's body language that she was shrinking into herself in the face of their verbal jabs.

And that was absolutely unacceptable. So I did the only thing I could do and inserted myself into the situation as Nicolette's "boyfriend."

And here we are.

I rest my chin on her shoulder as the two women on the screen flounder for at least twenty seconds before the mother finally answers, "The, um, party is on Saturday evening."

The sister is scowling like someone pissed on her favorite blanket.

"But you really don't have to come. It's a long way, and I know this isn't much notice."

That makes me wonder how long they've been planning this shindig and if they purposely waited until the last minute to invite Nicolette.

"No problem," I answer with the fakest smile I can muster. "That's what planes are for, and we wouldn't miss it for the world. You're Nicolette's *family*, after all." Emphasis on *family* for their benefit.

"Okay, well..." the mother says, seeming to be searching for what to say next. She's not so fucking strong when the person she's bullying has backup. "I guess that's that. We'll see you both next weekend."

"Just send Nicolette whatever we need to know. Time, location, dress code. I look forward to meeting you all," I say, and their faces disappear a second later without another word. Coming around the bench, I sit beside Nicolette. "Well, they seemed nice."

She ignores my sarcasm, her wide-eyed face turning slowly toward me. "What the hell was that, Helix?"

One of my eyebrows arcs up. "That was your family acting like jerks, so I stepped in with a solution."

"But..." Nicolette shakes her head in apparent confusion. "It's not your job to deal with my family issues."

"I made it my job," I tell her calmly, spooning a bite of mango gelato into my mouth.

She stares at me like I've lost my ever-loving mind. "What's going to happen when I show up by myself next weekend and have to tell them you were just joking around? I'm going to look stupid."

"You're not going to look stupid because I'm actually going to go with you." I point at her bulging eyes with my spoon. "Stop doing that with your eyes. You're freaking me out."

"I'm freaking *you* out?" Nicolette questions. Then she closes her lids and dips her head, voice barely audible. "I don't understand why in the world you would want to pretend to be my boyfriend, Helix."

I hate seeing the pain on her face, and her vulnerability drives a stake straight through my chest. Placing my spoon inside my cup and setting it on the bench beside me, I gently lift her chin with my fingers until she's looking at me. I have the strangest urge to lay my lips against hers and breathe in her pain, take it all away. But that would be weird, right?

Yeah, definitely.

Instead, I go with the truth. "Nicolette, your family was bullying you. I don't put up with that shit. What kind of man would I be if I didn't stand up for someone..." I pause before I say my true thought—*someone I care about*—and finish with, "Someone who's my friend?"

She opens her mouth and then closes it almost all the way, blowing out a stream of air. "I don't know."

"I wouldn't be able to respect myself if I didn't step in. If you truly don't want me to go, I won't, but I promise you, I don't mind."

Nicolette runs her bottom lip through her teeth. "I don't know what I want."

I release her chin and nod at her cup. "Eat your gelato and tell me why your mother and sister talk to you like that."

When she doesn't move, I nudge her hand until she takes a small bite. Then I pick up my own cup, cross an ankle over my knee, and gaze out at the pond, sensing she needs the mental space to open up to me. From my peripheral vision, I see her do the same.

After a minute of silence, she finally speaks. "My family prefers my sister. It's kind of a golden child type situation."

I'm shocked to my shoes. "With all your brains and accomplishments, *your sister* is the golden child of your family? Good god, what the fuck has she done? Found a cure for cancer? Brokered a peace deal in the Middle East?"

Nicolette lets out a bitter laugh. "Angelica is on her sixth career change right now, still lives with our parents, and has a substance abuse problem."

I'm genuinely confused, my mind spinning to try and process why. "Do you think it's because she's... troubled or whatever? So they think she needs more attention?"

"No, I learned she was the favorite when I was five and she was seven. Long before any drug problems."

My heart physically hurts, but I can't stop myself from asking, "What happened when you were five?"

She releases a sad laugh. "Christmas happened. All I asked for was a Barbie Dreamhouse. I'd seen it on TV and wanted one so bad. Angelica said it was stupid and asked for a bike and a bunch of craft stuff. She was into bracelet making." Nicolette takes another bite, her eyes going hazy with the memory as she swallows. "So Christmas morning, there were several presents beneath the tree, but I instantly spotted a big, wrapped gift. I was so excited."

"You thought it was the Barbie house?"

Her shoulders lift and fall in a shrug. "It was the Dreamhouse, but the tag had Angelica's name on it."

"But she didn't even want it," I very helpfully point out.

"She did once she realized she got something I wanted. Played with it all the time after that and wouldn't let me touch it." Nicolette's voice should sound bitter, but it simply sounds defeated, as if this kind of thing was commonplace in her life. "My dad seemed surprised when Angelica opened it on Christmas morning, and then he and Ma went into the kitchen for a while. I could hear them arguing, but I couldn't make out what they were saying."

I lean into her, nudging her softly with my upper arm. "I'm sorry, Nicolette. That wasn't fair and must have been really hard for a little kid to deal with."

She nods. "Now that I'm older, I think I know what happened. I think my dad bought me the Dreamhouse, and my mother put Angelica's name on it instead of mine."

"On purpose?" I'm just in shock over this. How could anyone knowingly hurt a child like that? If they couldn't afford the gift their kid wanted, I could understand that. But this story? It's all kinds of fucked up.

"Yes, definitely on purpose. It's like Ma was jealous of me or something. My dad always tried to give me attention because Ma didn't, but it only made her mad." I want to ask why but she answers before I can say it out loud. "Angelica was a planned pregnancy, and I was the surprise baby she didn't actually want."

My anger is at a fever pitch, and I want to fucking destroy that bitch of a mother. No, she doesn't even deserve the title of mother. That bitch of a bitch.

"She said that to you?" I barely recognize the seething tone of my own voice. I haven't been this pissed since... well, it was five years ago. The whole thing with Phoenix.

Nicolette's lips roll in and out between her teeth a few times. "I overheard Ma talking to her friend about it one day. This was after that Christmas with the Barbie house. A few months maybe? Hell, I don't know. I was a kid and not great with time, but that seems about right."

"And your father?"

"Pop loves me," she says simply, spooning another bite of pina colada gelato into her mouth. "I remember he tried to get me extra gifts and stuff for my birthday when he could afford it, but Ma would always make sure Angelica had twice as much."

"For *your* birthday?" I snap.

Nicolette looks at me like I'm the one talking nonsense. "Yeah, Angelica would pitch a fit if she saw me getting anything, so Ma distracted her with her own gifts." Her nose wrinkles. "It's always been like that, so I'm used to it now."

For her to be utterly resigned to being treated like that, I know there's so much more to the story, but I've heard enough to know she needs someone at her back next weekend. And that someone is going to be me.

"Nicolette, have you ever heard the baby elephant story?"

Her mouth twitches. "Are you about to call me an elephant? Because I'm not sure that's what I need to hear right now."

Laughing, I take her empty cup and stack it with mine on the ground beside us. "Just hear me out. You might find it insightful."

She swivels to face me, and I like that. I angle toward her as well as I begin to speak.

"When a baby elephant is kept in captivity, they tie it to a tree with a strong rope."

Nicolette's lips quirk. "My mother was bad, but she never tied me to a tree or locked me in a cupboard under the stairs."

I give her a soft smile. "This story is more metaphorical, not literal." When she nods, I continue. "Since it's in an elephant's nature to roam, the baby pulls and tugs and tries to break the rope or pull the tree down, but he's just not that strong yet. After months and months of trying, he eventually gives up."

With her green eyes glistening, she shakes her head. "That's so sad."

"It is. And the elephant remembers that struggle as a baby, even when he's all grown up. So if he's tied to a flimsy tree with a thin rope, he won't even try to break free. Though he now weighs several tons and is strong enough to easily break the rope or pull the tree out by the roots, he won't do it. Because he's been programmed to expect that he can't."

Her green eyes dart between mine, and I realize our fingers are intertwined. I'm not sure if I made that move or if she did, but I'm sure as hell not letting go now.

"So what are you saying?"

I squeeze her hand. "I'm saying, knock over the goddamn tree, queenie."

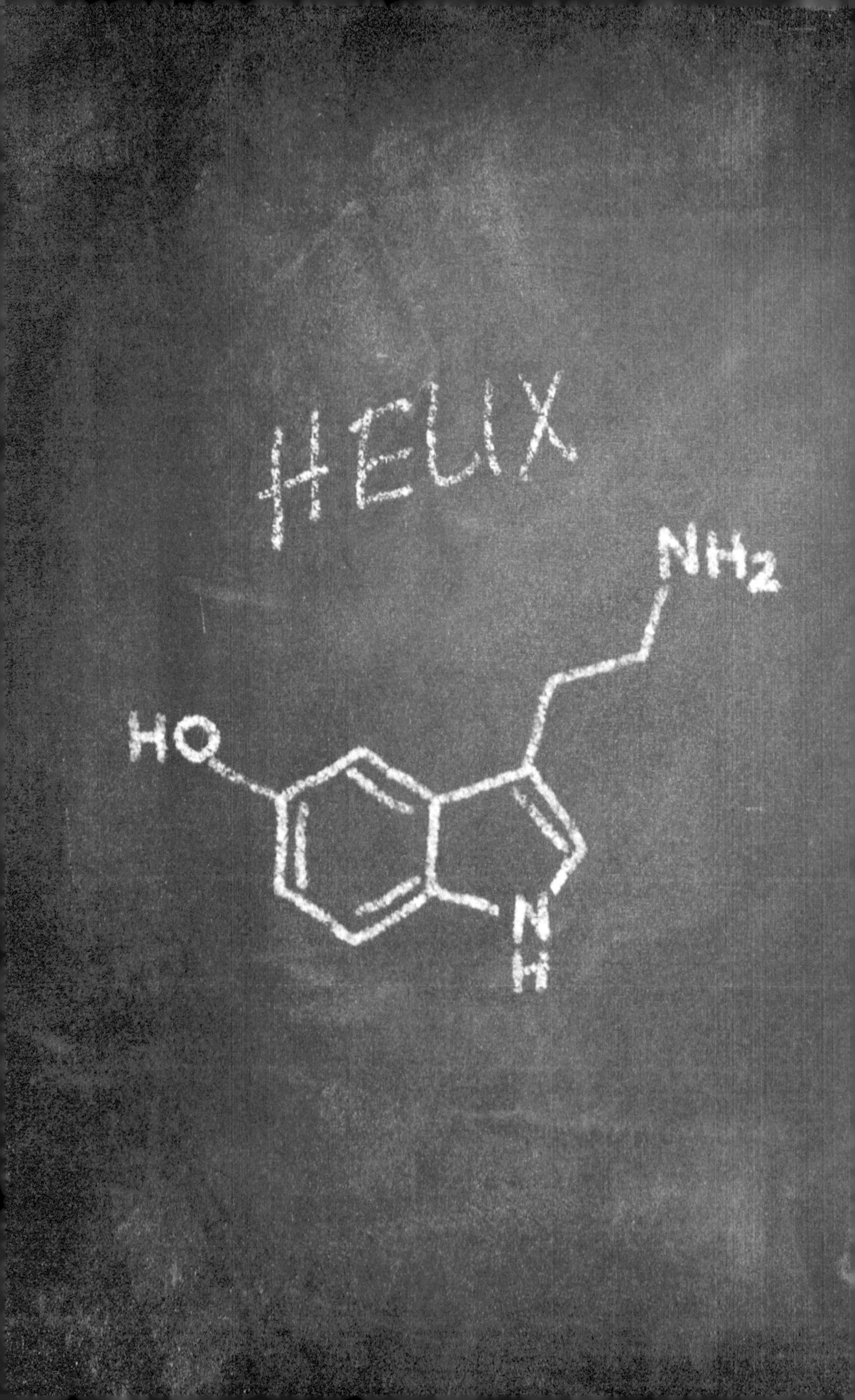

HELIX
NH₂
HO
N
H

Chapter Sixteen

DEAR GOD, AM I BLUSHING?

Nicolette's father called while we were on the way home from the park last Friday night. I only heard one side of the conversation, but her entire demeanor was different while talking to this particular member of her family. She was relaxed and smiling, the way one should be when talking to someone they love—and who loves them.

Her pop was apparently excited about her upcoming visit and wanted us to come the day before the engagement party. After she got off the phone with him, she tentatively brought it up, and I told her it was no problem.

So we left work early this Friday afternoon and headed to the airport. Nicolette has been hounding me all week about getting my information so she could book our flights, but I assured her I had it handled. Then she kept asking how much the tickets cost so she could reimburse me... until we arrived at the private hangar for the Hale family. It houses both our private plane and the company one. Today we're taking the family jet, a Dassault Falcon 8X.

We're seated near the front of the plane in two reclining, cream-colored chairs that sit side by side. "I can't believe how quiet it is," Nicolette says, staring out the window at the clouds below us.

"Advanced soundproofing," I explain. "It's one of the quietest cabins available."

Her eyes shift toward mine. "I can't believe you got your family's plane to fly us to New Jersey. I was planning to buy both our tickets."

"I'm aware," I say wryly. "You've only mentioned it four hundred times."

"Oh shut it," she retorts, smacking my arm. We're both still in our work clothes, and she brushes at her loose-fitting black pants. "I was planning to change at the airport, but would it be okay if I change before we get there?"

"Of course." Then I ask, "Why don't you just change for dinner at your parents' house?"

Her eyes round as if I've said the most ridiculous thing ever. "I can't show up wrinkled. My mother would comment."

Yeah, fuck her mother. What kind of bullshit is this where a kid can't show up at her parents' house in less than pristine condition? Hell, my family's net worth is in the eleven digit range, and I could show up at either of my parents' houses looking like a hobo, and no one would say a thing. It's not like tonight is some formal event. We're just having dinner at their home.

"I showed you the sleeping quarters earlier. You can change back there," I tell her, angling my thumb toward the rear of the plane. When she rises, I stop her with a hand on her arm. "Nicolette, wear your hair down tonight."

It's a demand as much as a request, and she inhales deeply and stares into my eyes for a long moment before nodding. Nicolette mentioned her mother not liking her hair down during our first not-date, so I'm basically daring the woman to say something in front of me. I'll shut her ass down real quick.

As soon as she's gone, my phone rings, and I see it's Phoenix Face-Timing me. "Hey," I say when I answer.

"How's my favorite twin?" he asks with a grin.

"All good. How about you?"

"If I was any better, vitamins would be taking me."

I laugh. "What's up?"

"I was calling to see if you wanted to go to the first Dragons game with me. Dad got us a suite."

"Yeah, that sounds good. I'm excited to watch them play, especially now that I've met Jordie. Is Reecie excited?"

"Thrilled. I got her the cutest little jersey, and she's been wearing it around the house." His eyes narrow and search the screen. "Are you on the Falcon?"

Shit.

"Yeah, just a weekend trip," I answer vaguely.

"Cool. Business or pleasure?"

What I wouldn't do for some pleasure with the woman who's probably half-naked at the back of this plane right now. But I don't say that.

"It's... pleasure, I guess. Like I said, it's just for a couple days."

"Where you headed?"

"Uh, New Jersey."

"What's in..." He stops, his eyes turning shrewd. "Ohhhh, New Jersey, as in where Dr. Bell is from?" The teasing, musical tone of his voice annoys me.

"It's not like that," I huff. "I'm helping her out with a toxic family situation."

"Helping how?"

I sigh and drag my hand down my face. It's always been difficult for me to lie to my brother, so I reply with a mumbled, "I'm pretending to be her boyfriend for the weekend. Like I said, it's just to help her out."

I stare into the very smirky face that's a replica of mine, except Phoenix perpetually rocks a bit of scruff where I'm usually clean-shaven. With a spark in his blue eyes, he looks like a kid on Christmas morning receiving this little tidbit of information.

"I bet you're going to help her out. I saw how you looked at her that day of the photo shoot."

Should have known I couldn't get anything past my twin. Lowering my voice, I say, "She's attractive, okay? That doesn't mean anything is going to happen. I actually have some self-control and don't find it necessary to stick my dick in every good-looking woman I come across."

"You came across her already? Damn, dude." As I mentally kick myself for walking right into that one, Phoenix leans forward and whispers, "Like on her ass or her tits? Ooh, or did you forget a condom and have to pull out and jizz on her stomach?"

"I never forget a condom," I snap. "I don't trust anyone enough for that shit, and I'm not getting trapped in a relationship because of a baby."

His smile dims a little. "Not every pregnancy ends with a relationship, Helix."

I feel a bit like an ass and soften my tone. "I know, brother. If I ended up with a kid like Reece, I'd count myself as the luckiest bastard in the world. You know I think she's amazing. If I could have kids without a woman in the picture, my house would be full of them. I just..." My lips press together so hard they ache.

"I understand. After what happened, you have every right to be skittish. Speaking of that, have you heard anything recently?"

I subconsciously rub the scar on my shoulder and mutter, "No, nothing."

He's quiet for a moment, and I know he's worrying about me, though he's fully aware I don't like talking about what happened to me five years ago. Luckily, he shifts away from that topic.

"You know if you want kids, you can adopt or get a surrogate, right?"

Allowing a grin to crack my face, I ask, "Can I adopt Reece?"

My twin smears a hand down his face. "Don't ask me that right now. I'm so exhausted, I might be tempted. We had dinner with Dad and Rebecca last night, and their housekeeper slipped Reece some candy. She was completely wired until almost midnight."

That's when I notice the dark circles beneath his eyes. "I'll come pick her up when I get home Sunday. She can stay the night with me."

"You don't have to do that, bro. You'll already have her on Tuesday."

"So I get double the time with my best girl this week. What's the problem?"

"I'll be out of town for two nights in a couple weeks. I hate leaving her that much."

"Phoenix," I say patiently, "we're twins, so I feel like Reece is partly mine anyway. I know you feel guilty, but you know she doesn't mind staying with me."

My brother chuckles. "I think she likes you better than me sometimes."

"She loves you more than anything, bro. You've been her sole caretaker since she was born."

His lips press together into a line, as if he's disappointed in himself. "With a lot of help from my family."

"Because we want to, not out of obligation but out of love."

He smiles, and the corners of his lips turn up. "Thanks, Helix. I'll let you know about Sunday."

We chat for another minute, and as I'm hanging up, Nicolette returns to the cabin. She looks stunning in slim black pants and a spring-green top that makes her eyes pop. Her sandals are black and have a small green flower on the toe. Dainty earrings and a simple gold chain are her only jewelry.

And she wore her hair down.

Nicolette is seated across from me, and I watch as she tugs at her shirt, checks her makeup in her phone camera, and then fools with her hair. "Why are you fidgeting so much?" I ask.

Her hands drop to her lap and twist into a nervous knot. "My family is just a lot."

I pop one eyebrow up. "I've told you stories about my family."

She finally laughs, and I absorb the sound, loving the way it feels in my chest. "Your family is a lot in a funny way. Mine is..." Her eyes turn to look out of the panoramic window. "The man my sister is marrying used to be my boyfriend."

Something coils in my stomach. Jealousy maybe? "And you still have feelings for him?"

Her horrified gaze jerks to mine. "God no. Not at all. It's just that my mom took their side when Rory cheated on me with Angelica." I'm in shock, but she continues in a ramble. "Not to mention, my mother looks for any reason to criticize me, from my hair to my clothes, and that makes me a nervous wreck to be around her. I do my best to fade into the background because that makes family dinners easier, but then my dad tries to bring me into the conversation. And that only pisses off my sister because she likes being the center of attention."

Nicolette shoves a hard breath from her lungs and stares at me with a grimace on her face. "Like I said, they're a lot, and I'm... embarrassed that you'll be there to see it."

Sadness wars with anger in my chest, and I take a moment to think about what to say to all that.

"Do you like wearing your hair down, Nicolette?"

She seems startled by the question, and her gaze wanders the cabin for a second as she thinks about it. When they come back to mine, the green irises are resolute. "I do. I like my curls, but—"

I cut her off with a raised palm. "No buts. It's your hair, and if you like it down, fucking wear it down." Leaning forward, I lock our gazes together. "I need you to promise me something."

She scrapes her teeth over her bottom lip. "What?"

"Tonight I want you to be the big, beautiful, strong elephant that you are."

Nicolette bursts into laughter. "I never thought being called an elephant would be the sweetest compliment I've ever heard." I wait for her promise, and she finally relents, crossing her fingers and tapping her chest. "I do solemnly swear I will be the elephant."

My grin is so wide it makes my cheeks hurt. "Good. Not that you need it, but I'll be there for backup. I'll give you a signal if I think you need a reminder to embrace your inner pachyderm."

Her head tilts in apprehension. "What kind of signal? You're not going to trumpet like an elephant are you?"

I think about it for a second. "What if I tap my nose?"

"Hmmm, that's a lot more subtle, but I guess it will work." She fusses with her hair again before stopping herself. "Can you distract me? Tell me something about yourself I don't already know."

The words leave my mouth before I can lasso them into submission. "I have synesthesia."

Nicolette's eyes pop into wide spheres, almost bulging from her head, and I rub my fingers over my lips as if I can erase what I just said.

"The phenomenon where you have sensory crossover? What kind do you have? Ooh, do you perceive shapes when you smell certain things? Or see colors when you're listening to music?"

My disquiet over blurting out my secret slowly recedes. She seems fascinated and not... disturbed by my bizarre condition.

"Mine is face-color synesthesia."

Nicolette's mouth drops open. "That is amazing, Helix. So you see colors when you look at someone's face? Is it constant?"

The rigidity of my spine slowly unwinds, and I relax into my seat. "I don't see it with everyone, and it's not distracting or anything. It doesn't completely cover their face, but it's more of a sensitivity to their... God, I hate saying this because it sounds weird, but... their auras."

Her head shakes almost manically from side to side. "No, Helix, please don't say it's weird. It's not common, but it is a documented phenomenon. I heard Beyoncé and Pharrell Williams are sound-to-color synesthetes. And Marilyn Monroe apparently had taste-to-color synesthesia."

I nod. "I've heard Beyoncé has chromesthesia, but I didn't know about the others. I'll have to read up on that."

"You should. I proofread a thesis for a guy I went to grad school with. He was getting his PhD in neuroscience, and he did it on synesthesia. It was intriguing stuff. He believes it develops in childhood when kids are being exposed to abstract concepts." She nudges me with the toe of her shoe. "What age did you first notice it?"

Surprisingly, I'm starting to feel perfectly comfortable talking to Nicolette about this. "The earliest memory I have of it is when I was about five. I told my mom she looked orange like sunshine and Phoenix looked blue like the sky. She didn't seem to think anything of it and just hugged me. Told me that was sweet."

Nicolette leans forward, her elbows resting on her thighs. "Does your twin have it too?"

"Not that I know of. I tried to bring it up to him when we were little, but he didn't seem to know what I was talking about." My shoulders lift in a self-conscious shrug. "I've never told anyone else."

Her smile is positively glowing. "Really? Thank you so much for trusting me with it, Helix. That means a lot to me."

Dear god, am I blushing?

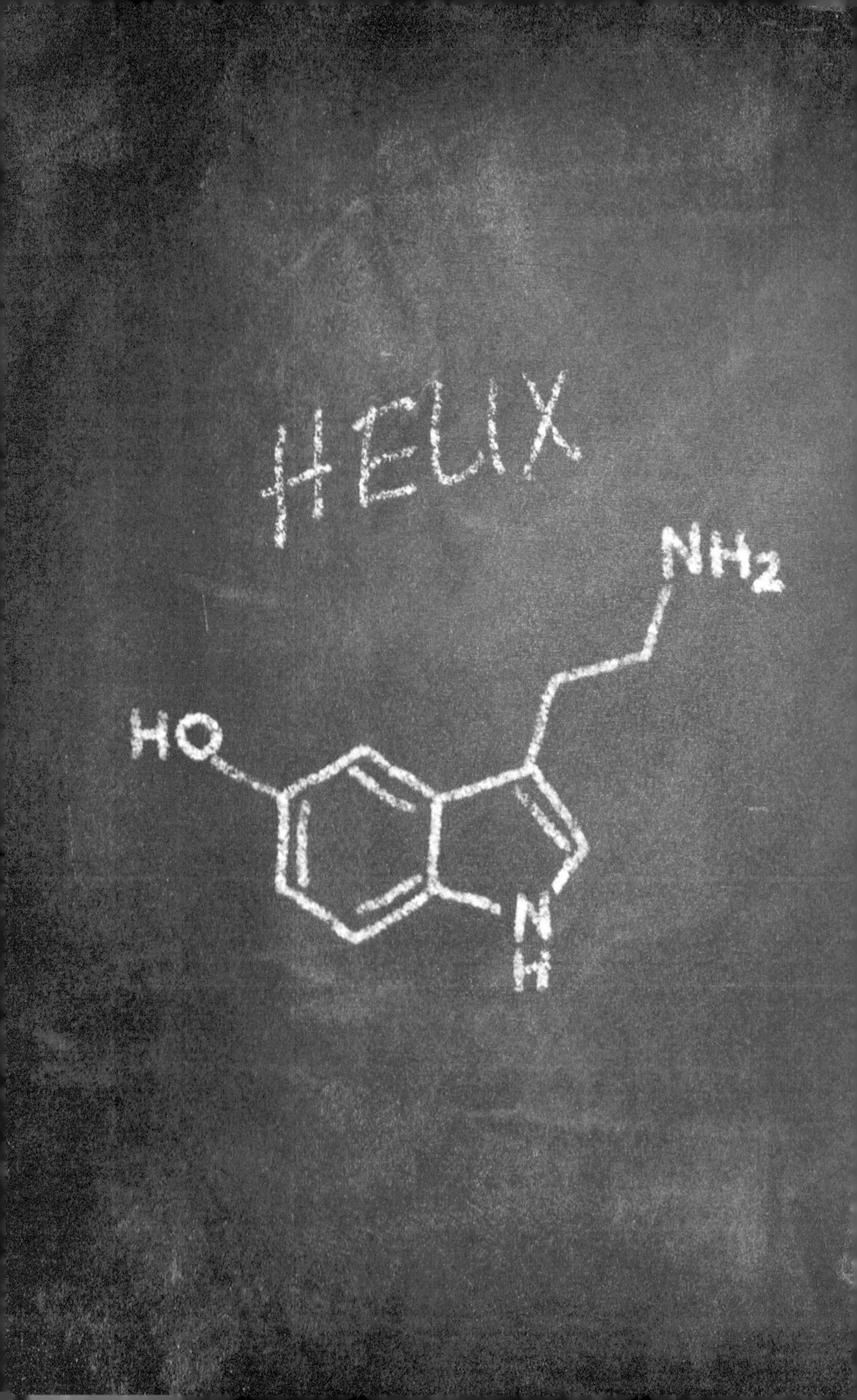

HELIX
NH₂
HO
NH

Chapter Seventeen

THE DICK-CON ONE SITUATION

I don't like these people.

The dad? Well, I'm reserving judgment on Albert Bell for now, but the rest of them can go to hell. At least the father came out and greeted us when we drove up. He seemed genuinely thrilled to see his daughter again, though the tentative hug shared with Nicolette was awkward at best.

The others? They barely acknowledged us when we walked in, other than the sister eyeing me up and down. I also changed clothes on the plane, donning navy pants, a pale-blue button-down shirt, and brown Brioni loafers. Yeah, Remington got me hooked on them when we switched shoes all those years ago at Phoenix's bachelor party, and now I wear them almost exclusively.

I'm using all my good manners at the dinner table though, just like my mother did her best to teach us boys when we were little.

"The meatballs are delicious, Mrs. Bell," I say politely.

"Thank you, Felix."

"His name is Helix, Ma," Nicolette corrects. "With an H."

Bridget glares at her daughter. "I see you forgot to fix your hair today."

I want to come across this table, but I need to let Nicolette find her own elephant, so I nudge her with my knee. When her attention turns to me, I subtly tap my nose, earning me a smile before she turns back to her mother.

"I didn't forget, Ma. I like my hair down," she says calmly, her chin lifting the slightest bit in defiance.

I want to fist pump, but instead, I drift my fingers through the curls and give her a little backup. "I do as well. It's one of my favorite things about Nicolette." Her hair is silky beneath my fingers, and I have to force myself to pull my hand away before I do some inappropriate shit in front of her entire family.

The so-called mother pinches her lips together but shuts the hell up while Mr. Bell clears his throat and gives me what seems to be a grateful smile. "Helix, we're so glad you could make it. Was your flight okay?"

"Very smooth," I reply, taking a sip of my water.

"What kind of aircraft were you on?"

"It was a Dassault Falcon 8X."

The man's green eyes widen. "You took a private jet?"

"Yes, sir. It's my family's craft."

I wonder if I said something wrong because everyone stares at me like I just grew a horn from my forehead. Rory, the cheating prick-wagon, chokes on a meatball, and Angelica scowls at her sister like she did something wrong by having a boyfriend with a private plane.

"Pop is obsessed with planes," Nicolette explains. "You've just made his night."

Her dad nods in affirmation. "I wanted to be an Air Force pilot, but I had a heart valve problem that disqualified me. I enjoy going to air shows every chance I get though."

We talk for a few minutes about the Falcon, Mr. Bell asking about every single spec he can think of before he turns to Nicolette. "Honey, how is your new job going?"

"Really good, Pop. All the people who work there are—"

"Nicci, did you see the new earrings Rory bought me?" Angelica breaks in, pulling her stick-straight blonde hair behind one ear to show off tiny diamond studs.

"Those are nice," Nicolette mumbles, and I can hear the sigh she suppresses at the interruption.

After that, Angelica cuts off her sister three more times when their dad asks Nicolette a direct question, and it's starting to piss me the fuck off. I notice she doesn't do that to anyone else at the table. Only Nicolette. When dinner is almost done, Mr. Bell tries again.

"Nicci, tell me about your new townhome."

She opens her mouth to speak, but this time, I'm the one who stops her with a hand on her arm. "Hold on, sweetheart. You know your sister is going to interrupt you like she has four times already, so let's let her get it out of her system." I don't miss Nicolette's small snort, which she turns into a cough as I direct my most saccharine smile across the table. "Angelica, go ahead and say whatever it is you feel compelled to say so that Nicolette might actually get to finish a sentence some time tonight."

I'm afraid I may have given the woman an aneurysm because her mouth gapes open before she begins stuttering out nonsense syllables. Finally, she grudgingly says, "Go ahead, Nicolette."

My fake girlfriend finds my knee beneath the table and gives me a gentle squeeze as she has an uninterrupted conversation with her father about her new digs.

Rory keeps his gaze fixed on his plate while Angelica blushes furiously beside him. Mrs. Bell's face is so sour, she looks like someone force-fed her a live squid.

But Nicolette seems happy to be talking to her dad, and that's all that matters.

After dinner, Mr. Bell says, "Nicci, I put yours and Helix's suitcases in the blue room upstairs."

I freeze. Well, hell. Somehow with everything I've had going on this week, I seem to have overlooked one tiny detail...

The sleeping arrangements.

Nicolette shoots panicked eyes in my direction, and I try to portray a look of calm, but I'm not. *What the fuck was I thinking?* Of course they'd think we would share a room. You know, since we're *dating* and all. Then her brow furrows, and she turns back to her father. "Not in my room?"

Angelica speaks up, her face once again smug for the first time since I put her in her place at dinner. "I needed extra space for some of my stuff, so I moved it all into your old room."

"Oh. Okay." Nicolette sounds a little freaked out, and to be honest, I am too. But I take her hand and give her what I hope is a reassuring smile instead of an expression of *holy shit, I'm going to be sharing a bedroom with a woman I'm wildly attracted to and yet can't touch because she's my employee.*

"It's fine, babe," I say for everyone else's benefit as we head upstairs.

"I'm sorry, I'm sorry, I'm sorry," she repeats in a whispered hiss the entire time we're walking up the steps and turning down a hallway to the left.

"It's fine," I repeat. "I can take the floor."

Nicolette pops her eyebrows at me as soon as she swings open a door and waits for my response.

"Oh." That's all I've got because this is the tiniest room I've ever seen. I'm not even sure if it could be considered a room. More like a glorified closet. The walls are painted a soft blue, and the bed covers have a blue-and-black diamond pattern that makes my eyes cross.

I stare at the bed that I'll apparently be sharing with Nicolette because there is no floor space to speak of. The bed is pushed up against the left wall, and there's less than a foot of room on the right side because a black lacquered dresser takes up most of that wall. Our suitcases wait at the foot, and the fit is so tight, we have to squeeze around them just to enter.

Nicolette deflates before my eyes. "I'm so sorry about this, Helix. I didn't even think..."

My cock hardens simply from standing beside a bed with this gorgeous woman, which doesn't bode well for me, but I tighten my fingers around hers in reassurance.

"We'll make it work. There's plenty of room." My tone is falsely cheerful, but I smile through it.

She casts me a dubious look because there is definitely *not* plenty of room on the bed... the *double* bed.

Christ on a go-kart.

"You're right. We're both adults," she tells me, making me harder as I think about some very adult things. "Why don't you get ready for bed first? The bathroom is across the hall."

I scoot around her, and the space is so limited, my erection brushes against her round ass. My sharp intake of breath is echoed by Nicolette's. Pretending like my cock didn't just have the pleasure of meeting those soft globes, I quickly grab a few things from my suitcase and hold them in front of my crotch to hide the evidence of what she already felt.

"I'm just gonna..." Jerking my head toward the hallway, I exit like the hounds of hell are on my heels.

Fifteen minutes and one cold shower later, I re-enter the prison cell, er, bedroom, with a settled cock to find Nicolette attempting to gnaw a hole in her bottom lip.

"All yours," I announce. I'm dressed in soft black shorts and a plain white T-shirt, and once she's gone, I contemplate what to do. I normally sleep in my underwear unless Reece is staying over. Then I wear my pants or shorts, sans shirt. I sweat like a motherfucker if I try to sleep with a shirt on, no matter how low I set the air conditioner.

Finally deciding that sweating through the mattress would be more embarrassing than sleeping shirtless, I pull it off over my head and fold it neatly on the dresser. If Nicolette seems uncomfortable with my lack of sleeping attire, I'll put it back on and try my best to deal with it.

I sit on the edge of the bed and scroll through my phone until Nicolette returns, her hair in a messy topknot, her face scrubbed clean, and...

She's trying to kill me. Literally. The woman wants to send me into cardiac arrest. Without my permission, my eyes plunge down her body and to her sleepwear, which consists of a red satin tank top with skinny crisscross straps and lace around the bust. The hemline of the matching shorts slants upward on the sides, revealing a whole lotta damn leg.

The Sahara Desert has apparently relocated to my mouth. Or maybe my salivary glands have malfunctioned because my dry tongue is stuck to the roof of my mouth.

"Hey, sorry. This is all I brought. I didn't know..." She looks uncomfortable, shifting from one bare foot to the other.

I manage to produce enough spit to get my tongue to work, though my voice is croaky. "It's nice. Totally fine." Not sure how many times I've said the word *fine* in the past hour, but I've definitely gone over my limit at this point.

Her chin dips shyly. "Pretty lingerie is my guilty pleasure."

"Mine too," I say before I can stop myself. When her head snaps up, I quickly add with a chuckle, "Not to wear but to... admire."

Our eyes lock and then Nicolette's drag down my body, hanging on the scar on my shoulder for a second. Her brow wrinkles, but she doesn't comment because her appreciative gaze continues its downward trek. It's almost palpable against my bare skin. Without makeup, the pink flush coloring her cheeks is easy to discern. Due to the confined space, I can smell her body wash, something fresh and light. But something else joins the scent. Is that feminine arousal?

Apparently having an excellent sense of smell, my cock makes a resurgent effort in my pants, and I *really* need her eyes to not land that far down. So I say her name.

"Nicolette?"

She almost looks surprised at her brazenness as her gaze returns to my face. Her voice is a sweet rasp, laden with what sounds like desire. "Yes?"

I clear my throat and my dirty mind. "I can wear a shirt if that makes you more comfortable. I just tend to run hot when I'm sleeping."

"So hot," she breathes, her eyes making another dip to my bare torso. Then she catches herself and hastily replies, "No, you're fine. I mean, it's fine."

Guess I'm not the only one overusing that word tonight, I think with an internal chuckle. "Which side do you sleep on?"

"Um, it doesn't matter to me."

Scooting over toward the wall, I slide beneath the covers, effectively hiding my hardening cock. Nicolette's bare lips perk up on one side. "Aren't you forgetting something?"

A good night fuck, perhaps?

I studiously avoid looking at that creamy expanse of thigh when she props one knee on the mattress and leans forward to... remove my glasses. I'm not sure if I'm relieved or disappointed because, for a second, I thought she was going to kiss me.

Relieved. I'm definitely relieved because I know with one brush of her lips against mine, I'd have her beneath me in less than five seconds. And that would be a bad idea.

Or a fucking awesome one, my dick protests.

"How blind are you without your glasses?" she asks as she sets my frames on a small shelf mounted above the iron headboard.

"You're a little blurry, but I can still recognize you from this distance."

She places her own glasses beside mine, and I get a weird—but not unpleasant—feeling in the pit of my stomach seeing them side by side like that.

"I'm about the same," she informs me, turning to switch off the light. The room is draped in darkness, but I feel the dip of the bed when she crawls in beside me.

Rolling onto my side to face the wall, I attempt to make myself as small as possible, which is no easy feat, given my size. I can't see Nicolette, but from the sound of it, she's lying on her back.

"Good night," I say.

"Good night," she replies. "And thank you for coming with me. I feel bad about the awkward sleeping arrangements."

"Not the worst sleeping arrangement ever. I shared a bed with Phoenix until we outgrew it, and you smell a lot better than him." That earns me a giggle, and I ask, "Can I ask you a question?"

"Sure."

"If your sister needed extra space, why didn't she put her stuff in this room?"

There's a long pause. "Because it wasn't mine."

Rage rears its ugly head again, and I mutter, "I don't like her very much."

I hear Nicolette's humored sigh. "I don't either." After a moment she asks, "Can I ask *you* a question?"

"Shoot."

"Do you... I mean, with your synesthesia, can you see... my aura?"

I roll onto my back, and turn my head toward her, even though there's no light seeping through the single high window in the room. "I can."

"What color am I? Or is that too weird to ask."

Unable to control my laugh, I ask, "I tell you I can see people's auras, and you ask if *your* question is weird?" I feel her smile, even in the darkness. "You're scarlet red, queenie."

"Hmmm." After that little hum, she's quiet for a moment. "And what does red mean? I'm assuming you've looked this stuff up."

"I have. It's not an exact kind of thing and can vary from one synesthete to another, but in general, red means vitality and energy." After a few seconds, I add on, "And passion."

"Ooh, I like that one." She shifts a little, and her arm brushes mine, but neither of us pulls away.

When I hear her breathing even out, I turn back onto my side to face the wall and drift off into my own dreamland.

Nicolette is holding my penis.

I repeat: Nicolette. Is. Holding. My. Penis.

She seems to be asleep and completely unaware that she has her hand on my cock, but my awareness is at the highest level. Thankfully she's gripping me over my pants, so there's at least a bit of fabric between us.

A ray of sunlight peeks through the dark curtains, casting a yellow sliver of light against the wall in front of me. My internal clock tells me it's probably six or seven in the morning. Nicolette will be waking up soon too, and I know this predicament will embarrass her. So I gently wrap my fingers around her wrist and attempt to extricate myself.

That only makes her grip me tighter, and I suppress a groan. This has officially progressed to a DICK-CON one situation.

I almost startle when a soft voice mumbles, "One corn dog, please."

Did she... just...

Her hand strokes up and down my length as she continues to mutter. "I love corn dogs."

Yes, yes she did.

"Is this a foot long, sir?"

Not quite, baby, but you're not far off the mark.

I realize that instead of stopping her, I'm now guiding her hand as she slowly jacks me off, my hips arching forward for more.

Dear god, what the hell is wrong with me?

Inching my other hand down, I manage to pry her fingers from my shaft without waking her, though she emits a huffy protest and rolls over onto her other side. A hefty sigh of relief pushes from my lips, and I perform a quite impressive sort of gymnastic move, launching myself over Nicolette and onto the narrow space between the bed and the dresser.

Grabbing my shirt, I slip it over my head and tug the hem down, doing my best to cover the very obvious tent in my pants. Looks like it's time for another cold shower.

And then I might take Nicolette out for some corn dogs.

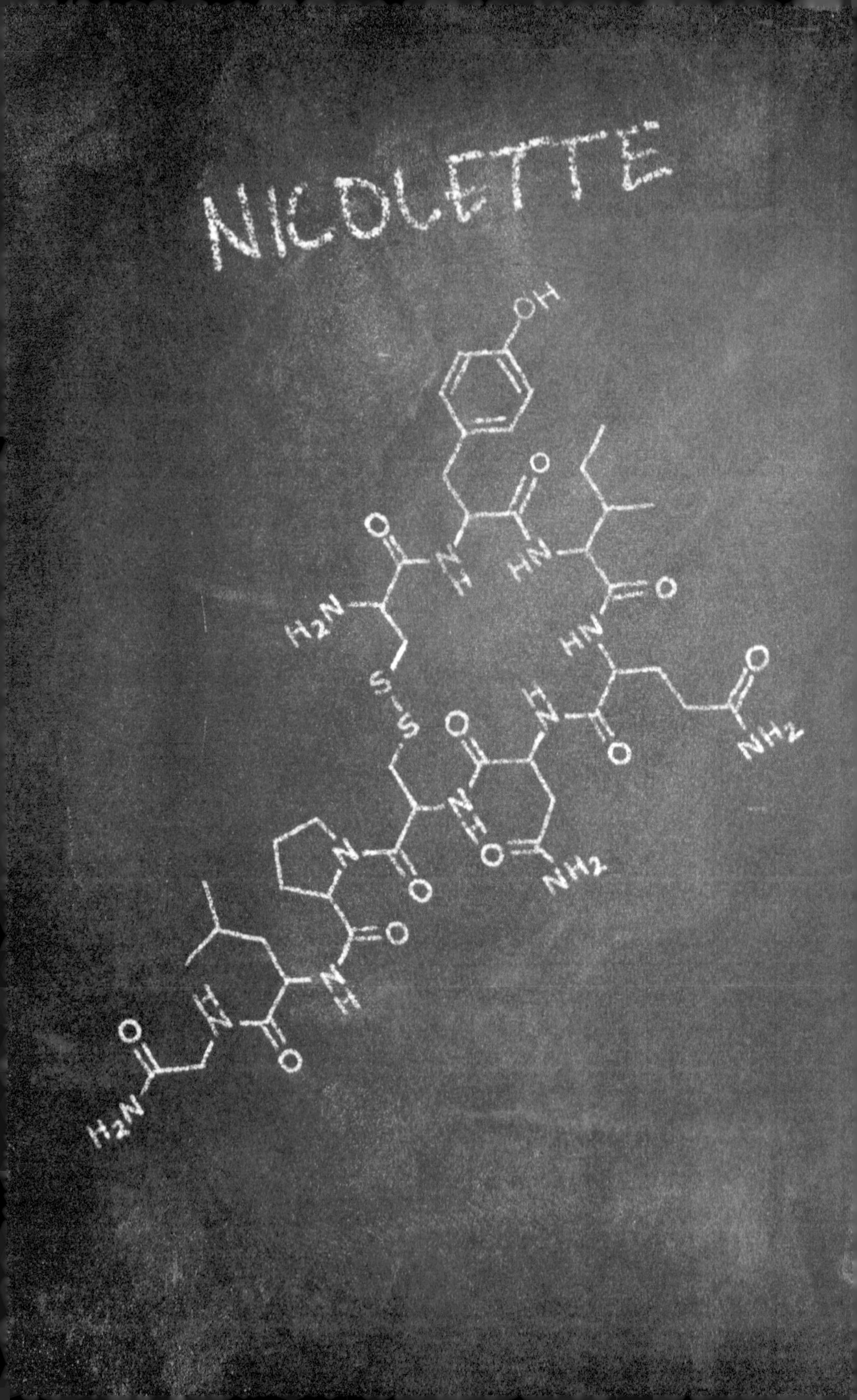

NICOLETTE

Chapter Eighteen

KINKY RECOGNIZES KINKY

For some reason, I woke up this morning craving corn dogs. It was the weirdest thing because it's not something I eat all the time. In fact, I haven't had one since the state fair last fall.

Brushing that aside, I get dressed and go downstairs, finding Helix and my dad cooking breakfast. "Hey, guys," I say, and they both turn to greet me.

"Morning, babe," Helix says, and I get a fluttering low in my belly at the endearment. So I stand on tiptoe and kiss his cheek. I didn't plan to; it just felt like the natural thing to do. He doesn't seem to mind, and dips one eyelid in a wink. Cue more flutters, though these are a bit farther south.

"What are you two up to today?" Pop asks, beating the eggs in a cobalt-blue glass bowl.

Helix flips a piece of bacon in the pan. There's something so hot about a domesticated man. "I thought maybe you'd like to go to the airport and see the Falcon this morning."

Pop's hand pauses and his entire face brightens like Helix just announced we were taking an impromptu trip to the moon where we'd be invited to an all-you-can-eat jambalaya buffet. "Are you for real?"

My boyfriend—*fake* boyfriend—laughs. "Totally for real."

I jump in to help with breakfast, putting biscuits on a pan when Rory enters through the kitchen door. "Morning, everyone."

We all greet him, and then Pop is back to talking excitedly about the morning's plans. "Helix is taking me to see his plane, Rory."

"For real? Can I come?"

Helix's eyes flash to me, and I shrug that I don't really care. "Sure," he replies. "We can all go."

Ma and Angelica come downstairs just as we're putting the food on the dining room table. We discuss tonight's party while we eat, and my sister is in her element, the center of attention, just how she likes it.

Rory rests an arm on the back of Angelica's chair. "Babe, Helix is taking us to the airport to check out his plane. We all get to go. Won't that be cool?"

Her head whips to the side like something out of a horror movie, her eyes burning like lasers. "*We* won't be going anywhere. Have you forgotten our engagement party is tonight?"

He chuckles and darts his gaze nervously around the table before coming back to his fiancée's. "Baaaabe, that's, like, eleven hours away. And you said you got that event planner lady so you wouldn't have to do anything today and could just relax."

An event planner? Who the hell paid for that?

Not my circus, not my monkeys, I try to remind myself on repeat.

After Angelica forbids Rory from going with us and Ma declines, Pop, Helix, and I head to the airport.

My dad is in hog heaven. He's toured the entire plane and even got to sit in the cockpit. Now he's up on one of those moving ladder things with one of the mechanics inspecting the engine.

"You've made his day. Heck, probably his entire year," I tell Helix as we watch Pop check his phone, frown, and tap out a message before sticking his head back near the engine.

"I hope it was okay that I offered. He seemed genuinely interested, but I didn't want to come across as... you know..." He shrugs, and his lips twist to the side.

I grip his bicep, and *holy beakers! This man is firm.* "Not at all. I appreciate you indulging him."

Helix loops an arm around my shoulders, playing the part of the doting boyfriend. Only... the feel of his warm body next to mine makes me wish this wasn't fake.

"I wanted to run this by you before I mentioned it to your dad, but I asked Eliora how long it would take to get a flight plan approved. I thought maybe Mr. Bell would like to go for a quick ride."

Eliora Dubois is the pilot that flew us here. She's a lovely woman in her forties with dark-brown eyes and a no-nonsense raven bob that hits about chin length.

My eyes almost pop out of my head. "He would freaking love that! What did she say?"

"She said for a short trip, the FAA would probably approve it within the hour since it's not too busy here today."

It's impossible to describe how excited I am for my dad, and my affection for Helix Hale grows by leaps and bounds. The cost to just fire up this plane is probably more than Pop makes in a month.

"I think it's been years since he's been on an airplane," I say, "and as far as I know, he's never been on a private jet."

Helix's grin is as big as my own. "Let's talk to him and see what he thinks." He seems genuinely happy, as if doing this for a man he met yesterday brings him actual joy.

I look up at Pop to find him scowling at his phone again as he types. "Pop, can you come down here for a second?" I call, and a few seconds later, he's back on the ground. I nudge Helix since this is his plane and his idea.

When he presents the offer, my father's neck cranes in astonishment. "Are you fucking serious?"

Helix laughs. "Yes sir, Mr. Bell. Can I assume you're interested?"

"Well, hell yes, I am. And call me Albert."

"Okay, Albert. I'll give the pilot a call."

When Pop's phone rings, he checks it and then rolls his eyes as he holds up a finger. "Let me just grab this. It's Bridget."

He walks off and places the phone against his ear. We can't hear my mother's side of the conversation, but we get the gist of it from what Pop is saying.

"I thought we paid the venue extra since they have an in-house florist... Then why do you want me to come back? I don't know anything about flowers... Seriously, Bridget? You need me to come and help you decide where to put the centerpieces? Put them in the damn center of the tables... What? I don't even know what an aesthetic is. Sounds like some kind of anti-inflammatory pill."

I'm getting a bad feeling about this, and when my eyes meet Helix's, I can tell he's getting the same vibe.

Pop throws his hands in the air, and his voice lowers, though it's still audible due to the echoing acoustics in the hangar.

"You made me take out a loan for this party, Bridget, because Angelica just had to have her party at Bridgewater Hall and insisted on this particular party planner... I realize that, but what did I pay the planner six thousand dollars for if you want me to come all the way back and make flower decisions?... Yeah, well maybe someone should pay *me* six thousand dollars since I'm doing her job... And not to mention the costs of renting the venue and catering and every other little thing... Fine, I'll come back, but we're not eating anything but beans and toast for the next twenty years because we're not going to have money for groceries."

He slams a thick finger against the phone screen, and I watch as his back rises and falls with his heaving breaths. When he finally turns around, I quickly pretend like Helix and I are deep in conversation about work.

"I'm not sure I like that name for the new mascara."

My boss catches on immediately and asks, "No? What do you suggest we call it?"

"How about—Oh, hey, Pop," I say, acting as though I just saw him walk up and hadn't been eavesdropping on that whole conversation.

He looks miserable, his voice dreary. "I have to go back. I thought everything was planned to a T, but your mother and Angelica need me. I'm sorry, guys."

Helix's lips droop at the corners. "It's no problem. We'll head back now, and I promise, we'll get you a ride on the Falcon soon."

Pop stares longingly at the sleek silver plane and sighs. "Yeah, I guess." Then he returns his gaze to us. "And it's silly for all of us to go back. I'll just catch a rideshare, and you two go get lunch and have some fun."

I make a fast decision. "Pop, why don't I go help Ma and Angelica so you can go up in the plane? I don't mind, since I've already gotten to ride on it." Okay, that's a bit of a fib because the last place I want to be is with my mother and sister. But Pop deserves a little fun. He works hard with very little thanks.

He shakes his head. "She specifically said me. It will be okay. Why don't you call your New York friends and see if they want to meet up? I'm sure they'd like to meet your new beau."

I argue with him, but he's not having it. My chest almost cracks in two when he glances sadly back at the plane once more before heading out to meet his Uber. I'm fucking fuming.

"Are you okay?" Helix asks, placing his hand softly against the back of my neck. I like the touch way too much.

"Not really. There's no way she needs his help with flower arrangements. Building a shelf? Yes. Working on the plumbing? Also yes. But centerpieces?" I stomp my foot in anger. "She was just pissy because he was having fun with me."

Helix's hand squeezes. "Does she enjoy making other people miserable?" He winces. "Sorry, I know that's your mother."

That makes me smile a little. "No offense taken. Ma likes being in control, and she knows Pop won't refuse if she says it's something *Angelica* needs."

He scoffs. "*Needs*. Yeah, right. Your Pop needs to learn to say no."

My lips twitch. "Maybe he should find his own inner elephant."

Two hours later, we're eating burgers at a diner halfway between New York City and my parents' house in Jersey. Artie, Lehra, and Cruz were all excited to meet up when I called them, and Helix insisted he was fine with going. After all, what else were we going to do with the rest of our day?

Lehra dabs at the tears running down her cheeks with a paper napkin. "No he did not threaten you while wearing a bathrobe and holding a goose," she wheezes through her laughter.

Helix smiles indulgently. "He did indeed."

"Never know what will happen in Houston," Cruz cracks.

"Cruz is from Galveston," I remind Helix. "He's the one who gave me all the restaurant recommendations."

Cruz shakes his head. "I can't believe La Mariscada is closed. My mom used to take me there for my birthdays when I was a teenager."

"When you and Lehra come to visit, we'll take you to The Tapas Table," Helix tells him. "They have a lot of the same dishes." I don't miss the *we* in that offer.

Leaning across the table, I lower my voice. "When Helix took me there, he said we were going to a tapas bar, and I thought he said *topless* bar. I was completely freaked out until I figured it out."

The table erupts in laughter again. We're having so much fun, and Helix fits right in with my friends. He and Cruz begin talking about football while Lehra and Artie ask about everything going on in my life. God, I've missed them.

"Sounds like you have great neighbors," Artie comments after a few minutes. "I mean besides Stefan almost committing assault with a deadly weapon against your boyfriend."

"Shhh," I shush him, waving my hand and glancing at Helix, who is still engrossed in a conversation with Cruz about the best running backs in the league. "I told you, it's only fake."

Artie, the master of dubious looks, lifts a perfectly waxed eyebrow. "Whatever you say, baby doll." Luckily he lets it go and changes the subject. "So you said Stefan and Lukas are drag queens?"

"Yes, and they gave me two tickets to the grand reopening of the club where they work. I wish you were available in two weeks so you could fly to Texas and go with me."

He mock pouts. "I'm going to be in Seattle that weekend or I totally would. Plus, I really wanted to check out that Cowboy Yoga class you were talking about."

I swirl one of my french fries in ketchup. "It's fine. I'll just go by myself."

Helix, who's sitting to my right, turns his head with a scrunched brow. "Where are you going by yourself?"

"Stefan and Lukas's drag club. It's in a couple weeks."

He purses his lips. "Hmm, I'll go with you, if you want."

I gape at him with the fry halfway to my lips. "You don't have to do that, Helix."

With a nonchalant shrug, he replies, "I don't mind. I like drag shows."

"You've been to a show?" Artie asks him, skepticism edging his tone.

"Yeah, when I was a freshman at MIT, my roommate had just come out. He enjoyed going to the shows, so I would go with him." His lips bump up at one corner, forming his cute, dimpled half-smile. "Mark was still a little skittish and wasn't ready for anyone to approach him yet, so I was there as kind of a buffer. But I had fun."

Popping the crispy potato into my mouth, I chew and think. It couldn't hurt anything, right? "Okay, if you're sure you don't mind."

"Not a bit, queenie. After all, what are fake boyfriends for?" He winks, and I'm pretty sure he heard what we were talking about earlier. *Great.*

"Oh. My. God," Lehra says dramatically the second we're in the restroom. "Helix is so hot. Tell me what's going on with you two."

"Nothing, I promise," I say, holding up one hand like I'm taking the witness stand in a trial.

She huffs her displeasure. "You should date him for real."

"He's my boss," I remind her, going into one of the stalls.

As soon as I pull my shorts down and sit, I hear my friend in the one beside me. "That only makes it hotter," she sings. "He's so perfect for you. Smart and sweet. I mean, really, Nic. He volunteered to go home with you and pretend to be your boyfriend when your sister was acting like a bitch."

"He was just being a good friend."

"And," she goes on, ignoring my argument, "he's taking you to dinner every Friday night. Not to mention that bit about him going with his friend to a drag club in college. That's a really good man. He's not some intolerant boob who thinks going to that type of show would lessen his manhood."

"Great. Now I'm thinking about his manhood," I say dryly, and Lehra snorts out a stream of giggles.

"He definitely has a crush on you, and I think you might just be crushing on him as well."

I let that statement hang in the air, grateful to have the excuse to flush so I don't have to answer right away. While I'm washing my hands, my friend exits her stall and meets my eye in the mirror while she takes the sink beside me. She's not going to let me get away with not responding.

"Okay, fine. He's attractive." When she tilts her head, I admit, "*Very* attractive, okay? But I've sworn off dating other scientists. You know this."

She rolls her pretty blue eyes. "I think he could be different though. I bet he could light your Bunsen burner right quick."

"Oh my god, you're so ridiculous," I scoff, though I can't say I haven't thought about Helix's big hands all over my body, setting my skin on fire with every touch. "He's just a really nice guy."

"Mmmm, I bet he's got a hidden dirty side though."

I cut a side-eye at her. "What makes you think that?"

Lehra dries her hands and then taps her temple. "Kinky recognizes kinky, and I think Helix Hale is a freak."

Super. That's just the image I need in my head when I have to share a bed with this man for another night.

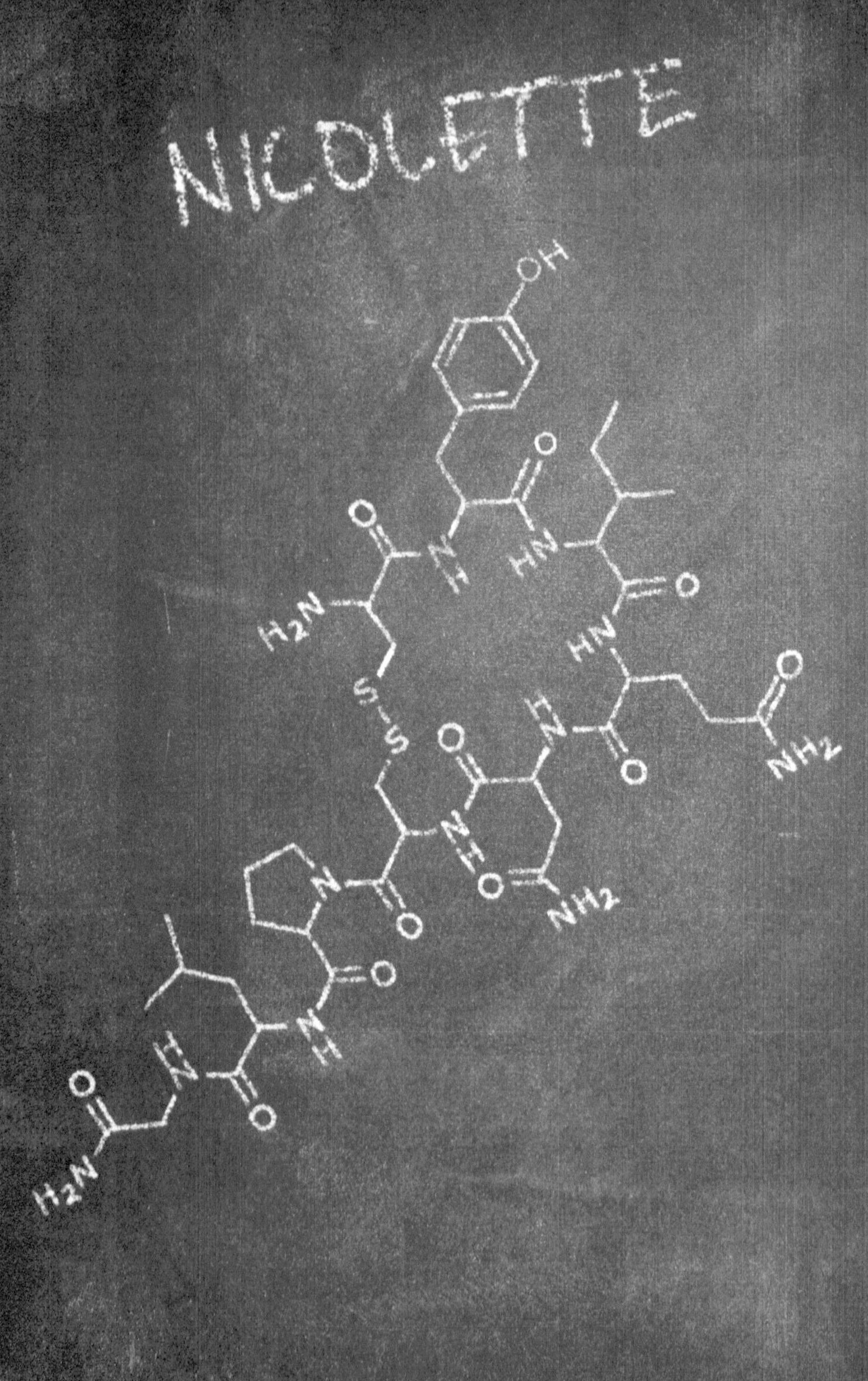

Chapter Nineteen

RAH-RAH, MOTHERFUCKER

I slide a coat of gloss over my ruby lips and pop them, checking my reflection in the mirror. All my makeup is from Hale Cosmetics, of course, and I look pretty fantastic, if I do say so myself. I pulled my hair up on one side with a small clip, and my curls look especially bouncy tonight.

Running my hands down the classic black Bouvier cocktail dress, I swivel to look at the back. It plunges daringly low, and a white satin bow rests just above my butt. I pull my black-and-white Bouvier heels from my suitcase and slip them on, giving me another four inches of height.

Helix got ready in our shared room and then headed downstairs while I was in the shower to give me some privacy. Holding onto the railing so I don't bust my ass, I head down to the first floor.

"Okay, I'm ready," I say, and Helix looks up from his position on the couch where he'd been scrolling through his phone. His eyes widen, and I can't say I dislike the appreciation in his hot gaze.

"Whoa, damn," he says, rising to his feet. "Nicolette, you look amazing."

My eyes roam down his big body encased in solid black, from his pants to his jacket to the pressed shirt underneath. The only diversion from all the black is a pair of glasses I've never seen him wear before, these with tortoiseshell frames. It's a smart look. And extremely sexy.

"You too. I like those glasses."

His focus drags up my body like the touch of a feather before he focuses on my face. "Where are yours?"

"I have contact lenses I wear sometimes," I explain, gesturing toward my spectacle-less face.

His bright blue eyes darken as he stares at me, and I wonder if Lehra was correct. Does Helix have a crush on me? Then he holds out his arm and smiles.

"Ready to go, girlfriend?"

I loop my hand in his elbow. The expensive fabric is like butter against my skin. "I'm ready, boyfriend."

That really shouldn't feel so good to say.

"Well, this place is swanky," Helix says as we walk around the large open space.

"Very," I say, my voice tight. Bridgewater Hall is part of the uber-exclusive Bridgewater Country Club.

"Are your parents members here?"

"No, they'd never be able to afford the membership fees here," I tell him, worry creasing my forehead. "Pop said he had to take out a loan for this party. Can you even imagine what the wedding will be like?"

"I'm sorry. It sounds like your father is in a hard spot with..." He waves his hand around. "All this."

I blow out a frustrated gust of air as Helix guides me to the open bar. "If I ever get married, I'm paying for it all myself so I don't put my family in debt."

"Yeah, it's ridiculous. Phoenix's wedding was insane, but then again, so was his fiancée."

We place our order, a whiskey and Coke for Helix and an appletini for me. "Phoenix is married?" I query. "I knew he had a daughter because you've mentioned her a couple times, but I was under the impression he was single."

"Oh, he definitely is." He takes a sip of his drink. "The wedding was called off at the last minute, but the week before was filled with events every day and night. It was way over the top. They even had a pre-wedding gala."

My face pinches into a grimace. "That sounds miserable."

Helix laughs. "It was. Were you one of those little girls who dreamed of her wedding day?"

A smile teases my lips. "I was. I always wanted a big wedding with a fancy dress where I was the most important person for just one day."

The gap between his dark eyebrows narrows. "You deserve to be the most important person to someone, Nicolette. And not just for a day."

I squirm a little under his intense gaze. So I put on my best smile and shift the conversation, looking around the high-ceilinged hall.

"I came to a quinceañera here once for my friend Muriel. Of course, I was only thirteen at the time since I went to high school early."

"Was that weird? Being so young in high school, I mean."

I take a sip of my drink, the flavors bursting on my tongue with a mixture of tanginess and sweetness. "It was at first, but then a group of older girls took me under their wing. Muriel was one of them." I laugh. "I met her when she needed a tutor for advanced placement chemistry. After that, she and her friends invited me to sit with them at lunch every day. I couldn't hang out with them on the weekends because of my age, but Pop did agree to let me come to her quinceañera."

"Do you still talk to her?"

"Just on social media. She lives in France now with her husband."

"I'm glad you had someone," Helix says. "High school is hard enough without being the odd man out."

Lowering my voice, I lean forward, catching a whiff of his cologne, something with dark notes. Maybe bergamot? It's extremely appealing.

"It helped that none of those girls liked my sister. When they learned she was... you know, like she is to me, they decided I was their new buddy."

He chuckles. "I could totally see Angelica being a mean girl in school."

Speaking of the mean girl, she approaches in a pearl-white dress and matching heels. She's followed by Annette, one of the bitchy girls my sister has known since high school. Angelica roves an assessing gaze up and down my body, the fakest smile ever on her lips.

"You know it's against wedding etiquette to wear white, right? Only the bride is supposed to wear white," she says through clenched teeth.

I feel Helix's hand on my exposed back, and the warmth and strength seem to seep through my skin and into my bones.

"Um, yes, I'm aware," I say. "Have you suddenly gone color blind, Angelica? My dress is black. And as far as I know, this isn't your wedding."

Her nose pops up in the air in that superior expression she's perfected so well. "The bow on the back is white, and you have white on your shoes. I don't like it. You're committing a fashion faux pas at *my* engagement party."

Annette doesn't say anything, but her wildly darting gaze tells me maybe she thinks my sister is overreacting.

"Would you like for me to rip the bow off and hide it somewhere?" I take a slow drink of my martini and smile sweetly. "Because I have some ideas of where I can stick it."

Angelica's blue eyes widen in shock. I haven't talked back to her in years because I was always reprimanded or grounded by our mother when I did. But now I'm a grown-ass woman.

No, screw that. I'm a fucking *elephant*.

Angelica's lips tighten, and I can practically hear her teeth grinding. "Fine, I'll allow it for now but just remember who's the bride here and who's not."

And with a sniff, she stomps off, her friend in tow.

Helix's grin is the picture of gleeful pride. "Well done, Dr. Bell." Then he taps the tip of my nose. "You're the fiercest elephant I've ever seen."

Holy shit! Swoon city, anyone?

We mingle with the crowd, and I introduce Helix to some of my extended family, mostly aunts, uncles, and cousins I haven't seen in years. The food is served by roaming waiters in matching suits and is obviously expensive. I worry how much debt this party is putting my father into and what my bridezilla sister will demand for her wedding.

Again, I remind myself that it's not my problem. Pop has to learn to put his foot down and say the word *no* to Angelica and Ma. I glance over at him. He's handsome in his gray suit, but the man looks tired and browbeaten.

Clarity hits me that that's probably how I used to look when I was around my family. I know I kick ass at my job. It's where I'm the strongest. I can run a lab, supervise employees, and develop new products like a boss bitch. My weak spot has always been with my family. Ma had all the authority over me, and through the years, I've let myself be pushed down and down until I was trained to be nothing more than an insignificant place at the table.

But no more. I feel so much freer now, and I realize all it took was some separation. And a man who told me I was strong and encouraged me to stand up for myself.

Helix.

Damn, I really like him.

He's chatting with one of my male cousins, and I nudge his arm and tilt my head to indicate that I'm going to the restroom.

"I'll walk with you," he says immediately before turning to shake my cousin's hand. "Austin, it was good to meet you, man."

"Same," Austin replies before smiling at me. "Nicolette, nice to see you again. Helix was just telling me how lucky he feels to have you at Hale."

I've always liked Austin. He's a year younger than me, but we played together at family get-togethers when we were young.

"Oh, I think he's a bit biased," I say modestly. "If you ever come to Houston, make sure to give me a call."

"Sure will," he replies with a nod.

Helix's hand lands on my back, and the gesture seems so natural, like that spot was made for him to touch.

I've got to stop thinking shit like that. He's my boss. My hot-as-hell boss, but whatever.

We walk together down a corridor and then turn right down another short hallway to the restrooms. "I'll wait right here for you," Helix says, leaning back against the wall across from the ladies' room with his hands in his pockets.

Going inside, I do my business and then wash my hands before exiting. As soon as I do, Helix holds his index finger to his lips and jerks his head to the left. Pausing, I hear my sister and Annette. It sounds like they're standing right around the corner.

"Can you even believe she wore that dress with white on it?"

Annette sounds unsure. She's always been one of Angelica's minions, but her voice is tentative. "I really don't think it's considered rude to wear something with just a tiny bit of white on it. The dress your mother is wearing tonight has a white collar."

My sister snorts a derisive sound. "Well that doesn't bother me. Just when *my sister* does it. I know she still wants Rory back."

I make a gagging motion at Helix, and he covers his mouth with his hand to hold in a laugh.

"I don't know," Annette says warily. "Her new boyfriend is really handsome, and I looked him up. He's, like, a billionaire or something."

Angelica sounds pissed, and I can picture her squinting blue eyes. "Whose side are you on, Annette?"

"Yours of course," she answers with placating swiftness. "I was just saying, Helix Hale is a catch. And sooooo hot."

Licking my finger, I press it to his chest and make an almost silent sizzling sound. Both our shoulders shake as we try to keep our amusement quiet.

All my hilarity fades at Angelica's next words. "He's probably not even her real boyfriend. I mean, what would he even see in her?"

Shit.

Helix frowns and shakes his head at me as we hear Annette again. "I don't know. I think Nicolette is gorgeous. That dress looks amaz—" She cuts herself off, and I can only imagine the glare my sister is giving her. "I mean, she looks like crap. Totally horrible. You're probably right. I'm sure they're just faking it for the party."

My sister's voice comes through loud and clear. "I know I'm right. Now come with me to the bathroom. I need to pee."

Panic rises in my chest because *holy hell, they're headed this way*, but Helix bends his head and whispers, "Trust me?"

"Yes," I reply without thinking, and the next thing I know, I'm being spun until my back is pressed firmly against the wall. When Helix steps into me, I'm sandwiched between plaster behind me and a large, hard body in front of me.

Then he takes my mouth with his. It's not the usual tentative brush of lips between a couple having their first kiss. No, this is brimming with the confidence of a man who knows how to fucking kiss a woman.

I'm floundering, unable to figure out what to do with my hands, when I hear two sets of footsteps. As if someone told them to do it, my arms slide up and around Helix's neck, my fingers weaving into the softness of his thick, dark-brown hair. He makes a small noise of approval a second before twin gasps sound off from beside us.

And then all outside noise fades away when Helix's tongue breaches the barrier of my lips. Not that it was a very effective barrier in the first place because I parted them without much urging. We're in our very own steamy bubble of need and longing, unaware of the rest of the world.

Helix tastes like sugar and warm whiskey, and I feel a sense of euphoria as our tongues slide and twirl together. I know logically it's simply the effects of various hormones that are released when two people kiss. Serotonin, oxytocin, and dopamine, to name a few. But this is more than simple biochemistry. This is electricity, a carnal hunger for more, more, more.

Our tongues battle, but his is a four-star general, commanding mine to follow his slow but demanding rhythm. Meanwhile, one of his arms belts my waist, holding me to him while the other...

Dear god. His other hand is firmly kneading my ass.

I repeat... His. Hand. Is. On. My. Ass.

A whimper escapes me when he slides it down to the back of my knee because *seriously dude, what are you doing? Grab my butt again.* But that whimper quickly morphs into a moan when he yanks my thigh up around his hip.

And there it is. His penis. Directly between my legs. Either this man is smuggling a lead pipe in his trousers or he is very well-endowed. *For the love of all that's good and holy, please let it be the latter.* I discover it is indeed his very hard cock when I rock my hips in a searching circle.

He growls into my mouth. Literally growls. I've read about this before in romance books, but I've never understood it, and I've certainly never experienced it before. I thought it was one of those things romance authors must have had a meeting about and voted on. Things that only happen in their steamy books and never in real life. You know, like growling, multiple orgasms, and women who fall asleep after sex without peeing and yet never get a UTI.

But when Helix Hale growls at me like a wild animal toying with his prey, I become a fan of the human growl. A huge, pom-pom-toting, foam-finger-wearing fan. Rah-rah, motherfucker.

Helix dips his knees and gives me a forceful upward grind against my clit, and my body lights up like fireworks in the darkest of skies. *He's going to make me come like this. Fully clothed against a wall.*

But then he ends the kiss with one more slow swirl of his tongue and a soft suck against my lips. When I open my eyes, my vision is hazy, and I think maybe the kiss was so hot it dissolved my contact lenses. Then I realize it's merely the haze of pure, unadulterated lust... as well as Helix's foggy glasses.

He removes them and sticks them inside the pocket of his jacket, his gaze never leaving mine. I think he's just as affected as I am, his pupils dilated so widely I can barely see the blue of his irises. When he licks his lips like he has to have just one more tiny taste of me, he might as well have reached down and pinched my clit.

Helix speaks first in a voice filled with grit. "Well, I guess we made our point."

"We made a point all right," I reply.

Speaking of points, I wish he'd *point* that deliciously hard penis back to my vagina. Fortunately, I refrain from expressing that audibly.

He finally pulls his gaze away and glances to his right. "They're gone."

"Who?" I ask before mentally slapping myself. "Oh yeah. Whats-her-name and... the other one." My brain is so addled, I can't seem to remember the names of the people who witnessed that epic mouth-fucking.

Helix's lopsided smile is awfully smirky, but I don't mind. He deserves to be smug after that. The man has a sensuous, talented mouth that's worthy of a large trophy. Maybe one with a big tongue on top and a placard that reads *World's Sexiest Kisser*.

He seems to realize he's still holding my leg around his waist, and he slowly lowers it before smoothing down my dress. "Thank goodness for stretchy fabric." His thumb brushes across my lips. "And Hale Cosmetics smudge-proof lipstick."

My fingers flutter around my mouth. "It still looks good?"

"Mmm, very good." Did his voice just go an octave deeper? "Though your lips are pretty swollen." He seems to be proud of that accomplishment because his gorgeous lips twitch.

"Yours are too," I retort, which only makes him smile bigger.

"I don't mind if everyone sees what we've been up to." He glances down between us where there's a very erect piece of evidence that's tenting the front of his pants. "Though I probably need to get this under control before we go back out there. Don't want to be indecent."

I can't stop my giggle. "Bridezilla would be offended because I doubt she's ever seen one that impressive."

Helix looks like a proud dad. "You think it's impressive, queenie?"

Shoving at his chest, I roll my eyes. "Good grief! Men! Go to the bathroom and..." What was I going to say there? Jack off? "Go splash some cold water on your face and think about baseball or something," I finish.

He backs away and winks. "Might take a while. Like a full inning of baseball thoughts. I'm pretty worked up right now."

When he enters the men's room, I sag against the wall, letting all the air spill from my lungs. My boss just kissed the fire out of me. I know he was just "proving a point" and it will never happen again.

But did I want it to?

Hale yes, I did.

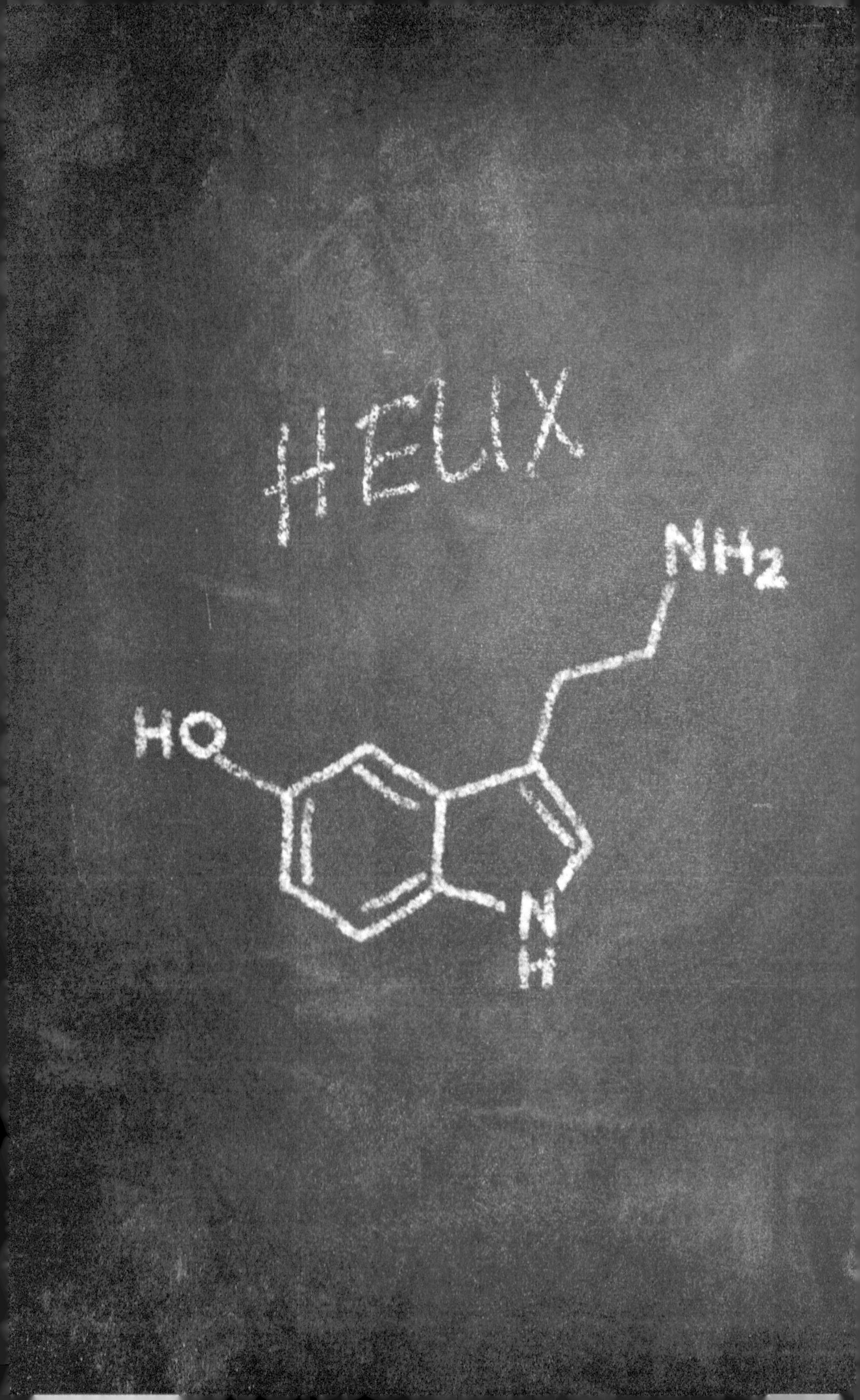

HELIX
NH2
HO
N
H

Chapter Twenty

SOMETIMES THE MOST IMPORTANT THINGS ARE THE HARDEST

I leave work on Wednesday and make a couple stops to pick up the orders I placed earlier. Then I head to The Woman's Hospital of Texas in the sprawling medical center.

As soon as I enter the lobby, I see my sister waiting for me and give her a hug before we take the elevator upstairs. Abigail answers my soft knock on the door with a huge grin on her face.

"Congratulations, you old grandma," I tease, and she squeals, hugging Perri and me with enthusiasm.

"He is so perfect! Just beautiful, with the chubbiest cheeks ever." Then she recounts her new grandson's stats as she leads us into the room where we wash our hands at the sink. She already sent me all the information last night after the delivery, but Perri and I listen patiently anyway.

Striding to the new mother, who's sitting up in the bed, I give her a quick hug and hand over my gifts. "Congratulations, Christi."

"Aww, thank you Helix," she says, smelling the blue-tipped roses before doing the same with the bag of food. "Oh my goodness! Did you bring me Chipotle?"

I chuckle. "Sure did. With extra guacamole like your mother said you liked."

Her face looks tired but in a lovely way, like a brand new mother with a healthy baby. "Thank god. The food here is pretty good, but I feel like I need to eat eight times a day. Breastfeeding ain't no joke."

Perri hugs Christi and sets her gift bags on the small table beside the bed before pointing at each one. "This one is from me, this is from Remington, and the purple bag is from Phoenix and Reece. Reece said to make sure you know she helped pick out the gift."

Christi beams. "She is such a cutie pie. I hope my Noah grows up to be as sweet as her."

I personally don't think anyone could ever be as sweet as my niece. She's an absolute angel; but perhaps I'm a bit biased.

"Dad said he stopped by already, and Phoenix told me to apologize that he's not here in person," Perri continues. "He doesn't think it's a good idea for people with small children to visit new moms and babies. You know, because of the germs from preschool and all that."

The new mommy laughs and pulls a bowl of food from the Chipotle bag. "I totally understand. Thank him for his thoughtfulness. I'm already convinced Noah is going to end up with every disease known to man."

Abigail sits beside her daughter's bed and pats her leg. "When one of the nurses came to get the baby earlier, Christi asked her if she had washed her hands. Thankfully, the nurse took it in stride."

"Okay, maybe that was a little crazy," Christi says around a mouthful of black beans, rice, and grilled chicken—with extra guac. "But as soon as he was born, it was like I was a new person whose only job is to keep my baby safe."

That hits me in the chest because I felt the same way when Reecie was born. I was the first person who got to hold her after Phoenix, and it felt like my heart immediately belonged to her. I assume it's because she's the daughter of my twin, so we're extra bonded or something, but I would do anything for that kid.

We keep our visit short because we know Christi must be tired as hell after delivering a nine-pound baby last night. My motto for visiting new moms is give them food and gifts and get the hell out. They need rest more than idle chit-chat.

Abigail walks us down to the nursery, and we watch through the window as Christi's husband holds up the scrunched-up infant so we can see him through the glass. Perri and I gush appropriately.

Then he begins to wail... the baby, not the husband. "Welp, looks like it's feeding time," Abigail says as Charles brings the baby to his shoulder and says something to the nurse. "I'm going to go to Charles and Christi's house to grab them a few things while she fattens up our boy."

"I could have brought anything they needed," I told her.

She shakes her head and chuckles. "In their excitement to pack every single thing Christi and the baby may need for a six-month stay, they forgot to pack any shirts for Charles." Abigail twiddles a finger through the glass. "That's why he's wearing hospital scrubs today. Luckily, they did remember underwear because as much as I love my son-in-law, I draw the line at touching his unmentionables."

We laugh and embrace once more before Abigail scoots down the wide corridor with an extra pep in her step. She's truly thrilled to be a grandmother, and I'm happy for her.

"I'm gonna head out," Perri says, popping a thumb over her shoulder. "My friend Marie is waiting for me in the car. We're going out for pizza."

I kiss the top of my sister's head. "Okay, shorty. Have fun and call me if y'all decide to have beer with your pizza. I'll come pick you both up."

She throws her arms around my waist. "Thanks bro, but we'll be fine. Only sweet tea tonight."

When she's gone, I wander down to the Neonatal Intensive Care Unit and stare inside, remembering when Reece was here. She was a few weeks early and only had to stay one night in the NICU as a precaution, but the fear was so real.

A woman approaches one of the nurses and hands her a tiny infant. They're both gowned up with protective gear, including masks, but I recognize that dark bun.

Nicolette? What the hell is she doing here? I momentarily panic, worried she might be thinking about changing jobs and going into medicine full time. Is she interested in acute care pediatrics? That wasn't even what her residency was in.

Fuck, I don't want her to leave. That thought is a lightning bolt of fear in my chest. I haven't been able to stop thinking about that kiss last Saturday night. After leaving the party and going back to her parents' home, we got ready for bed and climbed in again.

Luckily, I didn't wake up with her corn-dogging my dick again. Or maybe unluckily, depending on how you look at it.

Since then, everything has been normal, at least on the outside. On the inside, I want more. More of her whimpers, more of that hot little pussy against my cock, more kisses.

I'm not normally big into kissing. I don't mind it during foreplay, simply because I know women like it, but during sex? It's a no for me to that kind of intimacy. That's why I prefer fucking from behind, besides the obviously beautiful visual of seeing a woman's ass as she bends and submits to me.

So why did this morning's little fantasy session in my shower include looking into Nicolette's green eyes while I push into her? Why did I imagine dipping my tongue into that sweet mouth of hers and taking my fill as I fuck her until all I taste are her moans?

I have no idea. What I do know is I came harder than I ever have before. The orgasm doubled me over and almost took me to my knees.

Speaking of being on my knees, I wonder what her pussy would taste like?

I'm roused from that dirty thought before my cock can get too invested in the idea when the woman in question exits the NICU, all her protective gear now gone. She's a few feet away, and her head pops up when she senses me, her face paling in the bright overhead light.

"He-Helix. What are you doing here?"

"I came to see Abigail's new grandson," I reply. Her head swivels back to the NICU, and I quickly add, "He's fine. He's in the regular nursery, but I decided to walk down here for a minute."

"Oh. Okay." Her answers are short, and no color returns to her ivory cheeks. "Guess I'll be going now." She takes a step and angles her body to walk around me.

"Nicolette," I say more sternly than I mean to, and her feet stall. "Are you okay?"

She'd been trying to squeeze between me and the wall, so our bodies are close. Not touching, but close enough that I can smell the sweetness of her shampoo. *Is that jasmine?*

I press the subject because I can't imagine what she's doing here. "Is there anything you want to talk about?"

Her eyes dart everywhere before finally landing on mine with resignation. "Would you like to get a cup of coffee?"

We settle into a quiet corner of a coffee shop near the hospital. The patrons are a mishmash of exhausted medical personnel and people who are most likely family members of patients with their glazed eyes and weary spines.

Nicolette, on the other hand, is full of restless energy, her fingers fidgeting and one knee bouncing. Once the server drops off our drinks, Nicolette takes a long sip of her iced coffee. I don't speak. I don't push. I let her take the lead because she obviously has something of importance to say.

Finally, she stills and clasps her hands together on the table. "I volunteer in a baby cuddling program."

That was the last thing I expected to hear. I have no clue what this program is, despite the obviousness of the name. "A... baby cuddling program?"

She nods. "I'm sure you know how crucial human contact is for newborns. Swaddling, snuggling, and hearing a person's voice aids in their development and emotional wellbeing."

"I agree," I say. "And you volunteer to do this?"

Her green eyes brighten behind her glasses lenses. "I do. I know it's to help the babies, but I think the cuddlers get just as much from it."

In other words, it gives Nicolette something she needs. Instead of diving into that shark tank of possibilities, I ask, "And where are their families?"

"A lot of them have to go back to work after a couple months to keep their health insurance. They want to be there every single minute for their little ones, but the cost of having an infant in the NICU is crazy money that most people don't have. They come in after work, but that leaves a gap in the other hours of the day. The nurses do their best, but they have so much on their plates already."

Taking a sip of my black coffee from a daffodil-yellow mug, I give her a small smile. "I think that's a wonderful thing to do, Nicolette."

Her lips thin over her teeth. "And then there are those cases where the mother isn't able to hold the baby."

From her tightened up demeanor, I gather we're getting into personal territory. "Because the mother is ill or incapacitated?"

"Yes, there's that. Or they're on drugs and aren't allowed," she adds, gripping her glass with so much force I can see the pallor of her knuckles.

Knowing we're getting to the root of the issue, I pick around the edges of it. "When did you start doing this baby cuddling program?"

She tilts her head and looks at me, though her eyes are unfocused, like my image is not the one being projected from her retina to her brain. "I was in college."

I stay silent and let the story unfold at her pace. "I noticed when I came home for Christmas my freshman year that Angelica had lost a lot of weight. I was concerned and asked her about it, but she told me it was none of my damn business." Her smile holds no humor. "You've met her, so no big surprise, right?"

"Not at all," I reply softly.

"Angelica was in her senior year of high school. I'm two years younger, but I had leap-frogged her because I graduated early." Nicolette looks down into the pale-brown of her coffee and gives it a stir with the fat straw. "When I came home for the summer, she looked even worse than she had at Christmas. She's always been thin and willowy, that type of body men love, but she was beyond that. She was a stick."

I disagreed about the body type statement, but this wasn't the time to correct her, so I buttoned my lip and let her talk.

"She had started hanging out with our cousin, Zoey, who was one of those out-of-control teens. Her parents had pretty much given up on even trying to discipline her by the time she was thirteen."

"Did you say anything to your parents?" I ask.

Nicolette's teeth indent her lower lip, and I can see the pain flicker in the green of her eyes. "I did. I sat them down one night and told them I thought Angelica and Zoey were doing drugs. It wasn't just the weight loss," she rushes to say. "Zoey had these sores all over her face, and Angelica had developed a kind of facial tic." She twitches her left eye a few times to demonstrate before she continues.

"Ma, of course, was completely offended that I would dare to insinuate something like that about her precious baby girl. Pop..." She sighs and stares into her drink again. "Pop has always been kind of like an ostrich. If he keeps his head buried in the sand, nothing bad can happen. If he doesn't want it to be true, then it must be a lie."

"He didn't believe you either." My words are a statement rather than a question because I can see it in the dip of her head and the slump of her shoulders.

"It was the only time my father has ever yelled at me." Her voice is so low, I can barely hear it. When she lifts her eyes to mine, I see the fierceness I normally only see when she's working on a difficult problem in the lab. "I knew what was happening, but no one would listen to me. We got into a big fight, and I left early to go back to school."

"Where did you stay?" I ask.

"I'd made friends with the resident adviser in my dorm. I had tutored her in biology, so she let me sleep on her futon until I was able to move back into my room. It was only about a month until the fall semester started."

"Did your parents contact you?"

Nicolette shrugs and takes a long sip of her drink. "Pop did the next day. He apologized for yelling but told me I couldn't just go around saying things like that."

"Jesus, it's not like you posted it on Facebook for the whole world to see. You just had a private conversation with your parents about your concerns for two family members."

She blows out a sigh. "Exactly. Anyway, I told him not to worry. I'd never bring it up again."

"Not your circus, not your monkeys," I say, and Nicolette laughs. I love seeing her laugh.

"I say that in my head all the time." Hooking her straw through the hole in a piece of ice, she lifts it to her mouth and slips it inside before crunching it. "My mother's always been like she is, but that whole blow up changed how I thought about my father. I was still hurt months later, so I chose to go home with a friend for Christmas break my sophomore year and didn't even go back to Jersey. Same with Spring Break."

"Did you ever go back?"

She shakes her head. "I thought I was going to have to for the next summer, but I was offered a paid internship at Aquarius. There was a host family that I stayed with in New York."

I'm truly amazed by her. She was still a teenager then and yet more independent than most thirty-year-olds I know. "So how does that relate to the baby cuddling program?"

"Ah," she tells me with a lift of one brow. "I almost forgot what we were talking about."

"Because you're so much older than me," I tease. "They say memory is the first thing to go."

Nicolette holds up her index finger and pretends to glare at me. "One year, whippersnapper. I'm one year older than you."

A chuckle rumbles my chest. "Okay, fine." Then I mutter so she can hear, "Some people get so testy in their old age."

She gasps and playfully kicks my shin beneath the table. "I'm going to need to speak with your mother, Dr. Hale, because I know she raised you better than to make fun of a lady's age."

I think of that text from my mother asking to meet my "new girlfriend" and laugh again. "You two would probably get along really well." My coffee is cooling, so I drain the rest of it and set down the yellow mug. "Go ahead and finish your story. I'm sorry I interrupted with my abhorrent rudeness."

With a sniff, she says, "Thank you for acknowledging your mistake." She stirs her straw around the almost empty glass.

"Do you want another coffee? Something to eat?"

Nicolette's mouth twists in thought. "It might be a little late for more coffee. Just water will be fine." Her hand goes to her stomach, as if she's testing to see if she's hungry. "And maybe something light to eat?"

"They have a huge club sandwich here. We could split it."

When she nods, I flag down a server and place our order. She returns shortly with our waters, and Nicolette takes a long drink.

"Okay, the baby thing," she says, setting her glass down before inhaling and exhaling slowly. "So I told you I was in New York for the summer."

"I remember."

"Well, I heard through the grapevine that Zoey was pregnant. I'd unfollowed her on all social media accounts because she was always posting wild pics of her and Angelica. It made me sick to see them like that." Her voice turns soft with thoughtfulness. "Zoey was a year older than me, so between me and my sister. She was always nice to me growing up, and it was hard seeing her throw her life away."

Nicolette nibbles on her bottom lip and runs an absent finger up and down the sweat forming on the side of her water glass. "Anyway, that summer I got a call from Pop that Zoey went into early labor, and the baby wasn't doing well."

I'm starting to see where this is headed, and my guts clench.

"They moved the baby to a hospital in New York. Since I lived there, I went to check on things, expecting to see Zoey."

"She wasn't there?" I ask.

Anger takes shape on Nicolette's pretty face, narrowing her eyes and hollowing her cheeks. "No, the baby was born addicted to meth, so they took him away from Zoey. My aunt was there though, wailing that she had no idea how this happened."

I roll my eyes. "Of course she didn't. She'd only been enabling her daughter for years."

The server drops off our sandwich, which she'd separated onto two crystal yellow plates. Nicolette's eyes widen at the thick triangles. "Wow, that is big."

"That's what she said," I blurt out before I can stop myself, and my dinner companion snickers while I whack my forehead with my palm. "Sorry, I've been around Phoenix for too long."

"It's okay." She smiles before taking a healthy bite, and I do the same. "Anyway, my aunt seemed more worried about Zoey than the baby, so she left to go back to New Jersey."

"The baby was a boy?"

She nods. "Noah. I explained the situation to the nurses, and since no one knew who the father was and the baby was kind of an orphan at that point, she let me come up there after work and hold him. She got me signed up with the cuddling program to make me all official and cover her ass."

We're both silent, me in my thoughts and Nicolette in her memories.

"Noah was small, about four pounds. The low birth weight only compounded all the other health problems that come with a baby addicted to drugs." She shakes her head and asks, "Have you ever been around a baby with neonatal abstinence syndrome?"

I shake my head and answer with a soft no.

Her face pinches into a grimace. "It's not pretty. The tremors, the irritability, the trouble feeding. It pisses me off and makes me sad at the same time."

"Same," I grunt, though I mostly feel rage. "Those babies shouldn't have to suffer because of their mother's decisions. And it is a decision. I know drug abuse is a disease, but at any point, she could have sought help. Did she even try?"

"She didn't," Nicolette answers. "She and Angelica kept partying like it was 1999 throughout her pregnancy."

"Fucking ridiculous," I mutter, the anger heating my face on behalf of a baby I'd never met.

"Noah was a fighter though. He held on for two weeks, and then..." She sucks in a breath, and I reach over the table to clench my fingers around Nicolette's. She raises her chin a notch and says, "He had a seizure. They tried, but there was nothing they could do."

"I am so sorry, Nicolette. You sound like you'd grown close to Noah."

Tears rim her lower eyelids but she doesn't allow them to fall. "I held him every evening for those two weeks. Through the unstoppable crying and the shakes, I held him. I thought he was getting better because he and I found a bit of a rhythm. He started falling asleep when I cuddled him instead of crying constantly."

I can't think of a damn thing to say, so I simply squeeze her hand again.

Nicolette's nostrils flare. "Zoey made quite the spectacle of herself at the funeral, wailing and falling out on the floor. She was obviously high again, and it disgusted me. Noah's death was a hundred percent her fault."

"Did that provide a wakeup call for your parents?"

Her short laugh was sardonic. "You would think so, right? But no. I had made a pact with myself not to speak to them about Angelica's drug issues, but I did eavesdrop at the wake. My mother was going on and on about how she was glad Angelica wasn't into that kind of stuff."

I want to slam my hand on the table and yell in frustration, but I keep my voice low. "Fucking clueless."

"Completely. What did give them a wakeup call was when Zoey overdosed a couple months later. Angelica was with her and panicked, calling our dad instead of emergency services. He got there and saw all the drugs and paraphernalia. And the dead body of his niece. That's what really kicked him in the pants."

"It's not like he didn't already know," I say. "He's not a stupid man; he was just in denial, and it's sad that it took two deaths for him to come to his senses."

"He called and apologized for not believing me. Told me they were putting Angelica into a drug rehab facility immediately. I told him good luck."

I'm completely blown away by this woman. In my mind, she acted like a bit of a doormat when it came to her family. Not that I was judging. Family dynamics are complicated, and no one has the right to cast judgment on what a person does to maintain their peace. After all, she was under her mother's thumb for the first sixteen years of her life, and she didn't have much choice.

But Nicolette graduated from high school early, turned seventeen shortly after, and then left the state by herself to go to college. At seventeen fucking years old. Then she rocked her way through undergrad in only three years with perfect grades—at Harvard, no less—and then got accepted into an exclusive program where she worked on her medical degree and PhD concurrently. Completed that in an astonishing six years and was accepted into a competitive dermatology residency.

Yes, I've studied her résumé at length. Shut up. It was for work.

I'm realizing Dr. Nicolette Bell is anything but a doormat. I know now that she used apathy toward her family as a coping mechanism because she had been programmed to believe she was an afterthought. Despite the first half of her life, she rose and grew into the strongest woman I've ever known.

And I think I have a bit of a crush on her.

Not just her body but also her mind and her heart. She was still a teenager when she went to a hospital to hold a screaming premature infant every night because he didn't have anyone else.

There are depths and layers to Nicolette that I never could have imagined, and I blurt, "I'm so proud of you."

Confusion marks her forehead with two lines above her glasses. "Um, okay. Thank you. What did I do?"

I'm not sure what to say, so I go with, "For sharing your story with me. I know that was difficult." Then I release her hand because these sandwiches require both. "Eat your dinner."

"Yes, boss," she replies with a smartass salute.

"So I'm guessing the rehab was successful for Angelica? She looked healthy when I met her."

Nicolette wavers her head from side to side. "Yes and no. She was good for a while. Went to dental hygiene school and got a job. Then a year later, she got fired for stealing a tank of nitrous oxide from the dentist's office. Of course, I learned all this from another cousin. Austin... you met him."

"Yeah, he was a nice guy." I inhale the rest of my sandwich. "Your parents didn't talk about it with you?"

She takes a bite and chews before saying, "Nope. Never brought it up. They sent her off to rehab again. I would talk to Pop about once a week, and he acted like nothing was going on. He's the ostrich in this story, remember?"

"He was probably still embarrassed his teenager saw very clearly what was happening all those years ago, while he was a grown man who ignored the problem and got mad at you for trying to help."

"I think so too." Nicolette's lips twitch. "You should think about a career in psychiatry. You're pretty insightful."

I pretend to shudder. "Talking to actual people all day, every day? No thanks. I prefer my lab work."

She regards me with a scrutinizing gaze that makes my shirt feel too tight. "Not a fan of people?"

"Meh. I prefer to keep my circle small."

"And am I in your circle?"

Her cheeks pinken the prettiest shade of rose, and I'm pretty sure she didn't mean to ask that.

"You are most definitely in my circle, queenie." *And lately, you've been directly in the center of it,* though I don't divulge that part to her.

We share a smile, and then Nicolette reverts to the previous subject. "As far as I know, Angelica hasn't used since that stint, though she does have her other issues."

"Like what?"

Nicolette's tone is weary as she rolls her eyes to the ceiling. "Oh, where do I start? She moved back home with my parents so she could save money. She can't hold down a job for any amount of time because she keeps changing careers." A giggle escapes her, and she leans forward. I find myself doing the same. "At one point she decided she wanted to be a restaurant manager. Now, mind you, she has absolutely no experience in the hospitality industry, so they told her she had to start out as a server."

I shake my head and chuckle, imagining Angelica Bell serving food. "Bet that went over like a pole-vaulting walrus."

"Yep, she didn't last two weeks. Let's see... she applied to be a secretary at a Baptist Church but didn't make it past the interview because she said shit in front of the pastor. Then there was the photography phase. Pop even paid for her to take classes. She started booking outdoor sessions to get started until she had the money to open her own studio."

I'm becoming amused by her Angelica career saga. "How did that one end?"

Her grin is just this side of smirky. "Out of the ten sessions she booked, she only showed up for five because it was too hot or she was tired. Then there was the one with the newborn. Angelica canceled in the middle because the baby was misbehaving."

I'd just taken a drink of water and had to jerk my napkin to my mouth to keep from spewing it all over Nicolette. "The baby was misbehaving?" I ask incredulously.

"She was only a month old and started crying. Angelica said she couldn't work like that and flounced out, like she was a world-famous artist or something. Of course she was raked over the coals in the reviews on her website, so she quit."

I drag my hand down my face. "How are you two even related?"

Nicolette's lips flatten. "Trust me, I ask myself that all the time."

"You really didn't have to walk me all the way to my car. Yours is on the first level."

I huff out a scoffing sound. "If you think I'm going to let you walk through a dark parking garage by yourself, you don't know me very well."

We stop beside her car, and Nicolette looks up at me. "Thanks for listening to me. Sorry it wasn't a very pretty story."

"Not everything is going to be all sunshine and roses. Thank you for sharing with me."

I don't usually feel awkward with her, but tonight I do. It's not because of anything she told me at the coffee shop; it's because I'm dying to kiss her again. So I shove my hands into my pockets to keep from reaching for her.

"Are we still having dinner on Friday night or are you sick of me by now?"

My shoulders relax at her teasing. "You think I'd miss out on the great restaurant quest across Houston? The Cattle Company Steakhouse, right?"

"If that's cool with you."

"I've never eaten there, so I look forward to it."

"Guess I'll see you at work tomorrow," she says, lifting her chin to look into my eyes.

"Yeah. Tomorrow."

Nicolette turns and presses her thumb against the button on her car handle to unlock it, and I suddenly don't want to let her go. So I say, "Nicolette?"

She swivels back to me. "Yes?"

"How often do you do the baby cuddling thing?"

"Usually once a week on Wednesdays, though they'll occasionally call me in if another volunteer can't show up." She looks down at her shoes for a second. "I know Noah is gone, but there are so many other babies out there in need. That's why I still do it."

Her heart overwhelms me.

"Would it be okay if I went with you?" I ask. "I'd like to volunteer too."

Nicolette's lips turn up into a smile of pure sunshine. "I would love that." Then her smile fades. "Just warning you though, sometimes they scream the entire time. It's not an easy thing to do."

I pull my lip through my bottom teeth. "Sometimes the most important things are the hardest."

She surprises me when she steps forward and binds her arms around my waist. I return the embrace and rest my cheek against the top of her head. When the side of her face presses to my chest, I wonder if she can hear the acceleration of my heart.

She's wearing the flat loafers she always wears to work, so she has to look up at me when she finally raises her head. "Thank you, Helix. I needed that."

As I stand with my hands in my pockets and watch her drive away, I quietly say, "So did I."

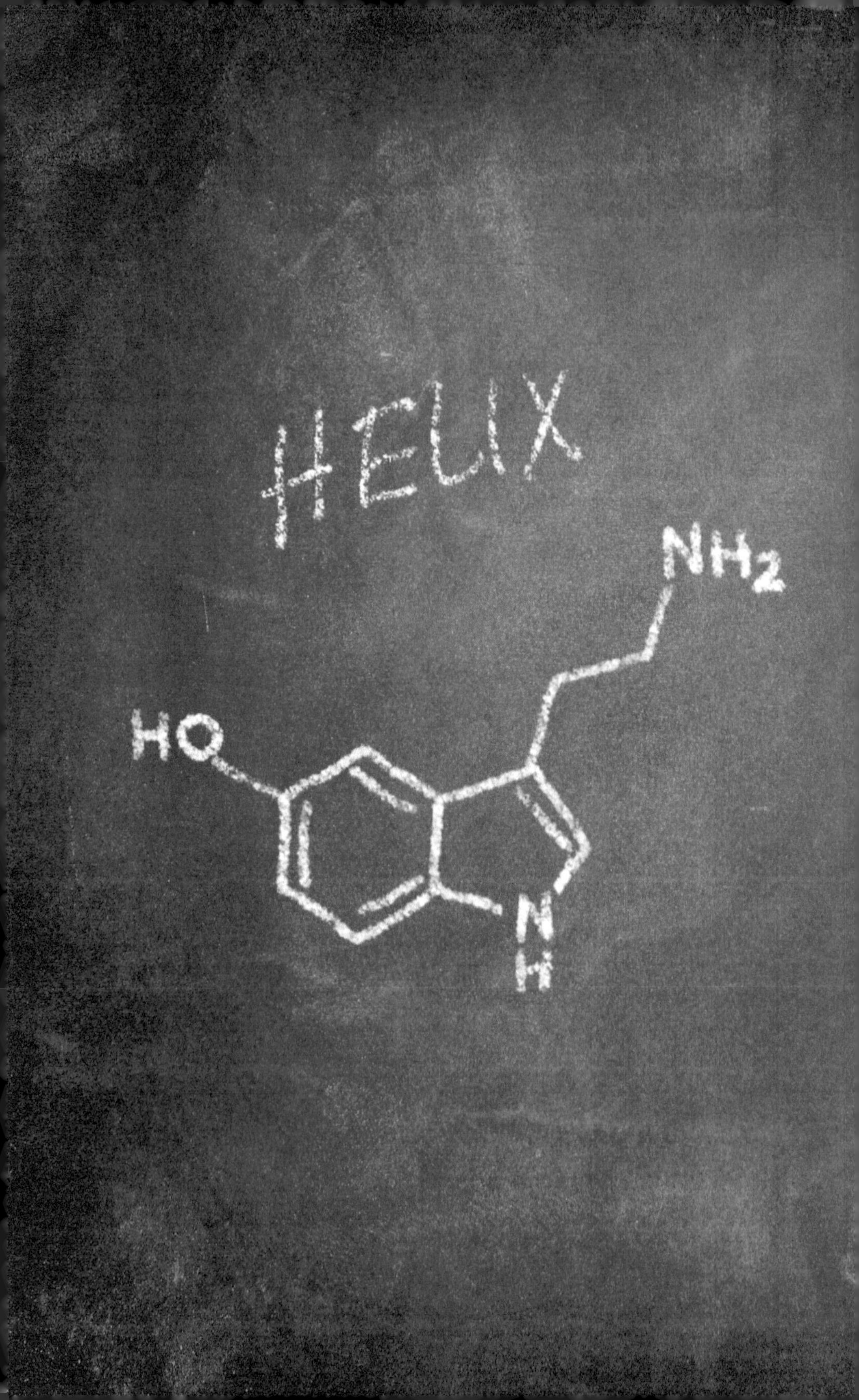

HELIX
NH₂
HO
N
H

Chapter Twenty-One

LATE NIGHTS

"It's so quiet after everyone leaves," Nicolette muses six days after our discussion at the coffee shop. She's across the lab table from me, holding a sample jar to her nose and inhaling. "This one is better."

"I like when the lab is quiet," I say, taking the jar and giving it a sniff. "Yep, definitely less pungent than the last one. We're on the right track."

After finishing Jordie McNamara's campaign, which has been received quite well by the public, our team has been working on the men's skin care line and have started on hair products for kids. That puts Nicolette and me staying late at the lab to develop her formulation for the fragrance enhancement. We decided to keep the idea for it between the two of us until we have it nailed down.

There are no windows in the lab for security reasons. It's not unheard of for other companies to spy and steal ideas, so the security at Hale Cosmetics is top-notch, especially in the laboratory building. Despite the lack of a view to the outside world, I can feel the darkness settling outside.

"It's getting late," I note, and Nicolette lifts her head, seeming surprised when she looks at the clock and sees it's after nine.

"Time flies when you're analyzing formulas," she quips, and I laugh. Biochemistry jokes are the best.

Her eyes look especially green today, and I round the table to get a closer look. "What eyeshadow are you wearing?"

Her hand flutters near her temple. "Oh, it's from Jordie's palette."

"May I?" I ask, lifting my hands to the sides of her glasses. When she nods, I remove them and set them aside before peering at her, seeing the expertly blended browns and greens. "So this is Gridiron Green and Pretty Pigskin?"

"Yes," she replies, and I think her voice is slightly more breathless than it was a minute ago.

Taking her jaw gently in my hand, I tilt her face to the side. I'm doing my best to focus only on the makeup, but I can't help but notice the soft gusts of her breaths on my hand. The filthiest part of my mind works its way to the forefront and wonders what her breath would feel like on my cock after she took me into her mouth. Warm air against wet, thick flesh. *Fuck.*

The cock in question begins to take notice of Nicolette's proximity, and I feel the tip begin to slide against the inside of my boxer briefs as it grows.

I have absolutely no excuse for what happens next. My dick and my hand seem to be in cahoots because my fingers slide down a few inches until my hand is wrapped around Nicolette's throat.

Her rapid inhale is followed by the slow exhale of a sultry moan, and it unravels any rational thought in my head. With a slight shift of my hand, I angle her face to mine and search her eyes. But this time, I'm not looking at eyeshadow. I'm looking for the consent I so desperately need.

My fingers and thumb tighten the slightest amount on the sides of her beautiful, slender neck. Her skin is warm and pliable, and I can feel the quickening beat of her pulse as clearly as if I were holding her bare carotid artery in my hand. She's excited.

"Is this what you like, Nicolette?" My voice has reached a timbre I haven't heard from myself in quite a while, deep and commanding.

Her reply is instantaneous and clear. "Yes, that's what I like."

"Are you sure?"

The corners of her lips journey upward into a bit of a smirk. "Everyone knows women like jewelry, and hand necklace is my favorite."

Mother of god, she is fucking perfect.

I yank her forward by the neck, our lips crashing together like the strongest of magnets, the laws of physics and lust combining to make them unable to stay apart. The kiss is not tender, and it's not hesitant. There's no seeking entrance into her mouth with a soft stroke of my tongue against her closed lips.

No. I take. I devour. I claim.

When my tongue pushes into her mouth, Nicolette responds by wrapping her tongue around mine and driving her fingers into my hair. I wonder if she somehow knows how much I love that... the pulling and tugging on my hair.

Releasing her neck, I drag my hands down her body and grip her waist, hauling her hard against me so she can see what she does to me. She groans and flexes her hips forward in a needy plea. I plan to satiate every single need she has.

My lips finally release hers, and I trail kisses across her cheek and to her ear. "This is what you want?"

Nicolette sighs when I punctuate my question with a hard suck of her earlobe. "If by *this*, you mean fucking me on this lab table, then yes, Helix, I do want *this*."

Hale. Yes.

But I need her to understand the way I am, so I lift my head and meet her gaze. "We work together, and I don't want there to be any misunderstandings or hard feelings between us. This can only happen once, okay? I can't give any more than that."

She doesn't appear to be offended by my conditions. In fact, she grins wickedly. "I understand. You have an extended rebound time and can only get it up once a day."

Damn, I adore her bite.

With a chuckle, I slide my hands around to cup her bottom, something I've been thinking about doing since I felt it in that hallway when we kissed. Nicolette has a fantastic ass.

"You know that's not what I meant, smartass. I'm younger than you, remember?" I point out, earning me a narrowing of her eyes. "So my rebound time is excellent. I just—"

"I know what you meant, and I'm good with that," she interrupts. "I'm not looking for anything, especially something that could get messy with my boss."

Dammit. I forgot for a second that I'm her boss. There's no way I want to stop this, but I also don't want an HR disaster on my hands. Yes, I'm part owner of Hale Cosmetics, but I'd never do anything to hurt my family's company, no matter how great the temptation.

So I grit my teeth and say, "I should probably check on the company policy regarding things of a sexual nature between coworkers."

Again, Nicolette smiles. "Have you forgotten I was hired recently? I read the entire employee handbook cover to cover, so I know what it says." She taps the side of her head, which houses that brilliant brain of hers. "There's nothing forbidding any kind of relationship between employees at our level. If I were an assistant, yes, that would be a problem, but I'm in a managerial position."

"Thank fuck," I say, my mouth back on hers while I'm still uttering the last syllable.

We shrug out of our lab coats and drop them wherever-the-fuck. With our mouths still fused, I go to work on the buttons of her shirt with one hand while cupping her pussy with the other. The heat is evident even through her pants, and it makes my dick throb.

Nicolette, on the other hand, is not quite so dexterous. After a couple fumbling attempts to get my shirt off, she curses and rips the damn thing open, sending buttons pinging to the floor.

It's undoubtedly the hottest thing I've ever seen. She's as anxious for this as I am, and there's nothing that turns on a man more than a woman who is feral for him.

We pull our mouths apart long enough for me to pull my suspenders down and for us to remove our shirts, and I stare down at her blood-red bra trimmed in lace. "This is sexy as fuck," I tell her, dragging a single finger along the scalloped edges that barely cover her breasts. "Did you wear it for me?"

Her mouth quirks. "No, I wore it for myself. It's the one thing I splurge on because—"

"Pretty lingerie is your guilty pleasure," I finish, echoing what she told me in our shared room at her parents' house.

She nods, seeming surprised that I remembered. I flick the clasp open and slip her bra straps down her arms before tossing the garment onto the floor. Her body is fantastic. Her breasts are full and pink tipped, and her waist tapers in before flaring again at the hips.

I haul her against me, loving the feel of bare skin to glorious bare skin. Her tits are soft against my chest, other than the firm peaks of her nipples. I enjoy the contact for a while until I have to touch her cunt. It's not a want; it's an undeniable *need*.

After undoing her pants, I slide my hand inside and groan. I feel lace against the back of my hand, and my fingertips brush against silky skin and a tiny stripe of hair. I think it's called a landing strip, which makes sense because it's directing me exactly where I want to be like an aircraft controller waving a 747 toward its destination. Not that I need guidance. I know my way around a woman's body.

Kissing my way down her chest, I look up at her and circle her nipple with the point of my tongue. Wetness meets my fingers as I continue to tease those pert tips, one after the other while my other hand pets her pussy with soothing strokes. I don't touch her clit yet. I'm enjoying the tease too much.

My voice comes out as a soft warning. "I like being in control, Nicolette."

Closing her eyes, she whimpers, "Yes."

"Do what I tell you, and I'll reward you. Now keep your eyes on me."

Her lids snap open, and I graze my middle finger over her clit. Her hips jerk, and the nipple I'm currently occupied with hardens against my tongue.

"Yes, Helix. More of that. Please. I'll do anything you tell me to do."

"Hmmm, you're a goddamn good fucking girl if I've ever seen one," I purr, allowing another featherlight brush against that sensitive bud in her panties.

She nods, and her eyes go half-mast, though she keeps them on me like I directed. Her hips squirm and attempt to get more friction against her pussy, but I don't allow it. Not yet.

"I need you, Helix. Just tell me what to do."

Taking one nipple into my mouth, I give her a single, hard suck before releasing her with a pop. "I want to hear you beg."

"Please," she whispers, jutting her hips forward. "Please make me come. I promise I'll be so wet for you."

Taunting her, I ask, "And what would you like me to do with your wet cunt after I've made you come?"

Her breaths are rapid pants that make her chest heave back and forth directly in my line of sight. It's a beautiful sight.

"I want you to fuck it. Hard. However you want." She blinks with faux innocence and adds, "Please, Dr. Hale."

God. Damn.

I haven't come in my pants since I was thirteen and MaryJo Dubanowski showed me her tits behind the gym, but hearing those words from Nicolette's kiss-puffed lips takes me right to the edge of embarrassing myself.

Finally giving in to her pleas, I rub a firm circle around her clit, and she emits the most delicious sound of pleasure. Wanting to hear more of that, I take one nipple into my mouth and apply enough suction to make my cheeks hollow. Nicolette's knees wobble, and she grips the edge of the lab table with one hand and uses the other on the back of my head to hold me to her breast. Not that she needs to because I have no desire to be anywhere else.

"Yes, yes, that feels so good, Dr. Hale."

Fuck, why do I like when she calls me that?

I slide my long middle finger into her entrance, and a rumble starts in my chest when I feel how snug she is. I'm going to have to work her over a bit before I can even get a second finger in, much less my cock.

Nicolette grinds downward, and I hold the heel of my hand against her center while gliding my finger in and out of her. It takes a few minutes to get a second digit inside, and I'm itching to feel that silky warmth around my dick.

Watching for her reaction, I switch to the other breast and bite down lightly. My fingers are met with a gush of wetness, and I groan around her. *Hmmm, she likes a little teeth with her suction.*

Pumping my fingers in and out, I move my thumb to her clit and take another nibble of her rock-hard nipple before soothing the bite with the flat of my tongue. That's when I feel the tremors begin in her hot cunt.

Before she can find her orgasm, I slide my fingers from her body and release her breast. She's incensed, huffing out an exasperated breath.

"Why did you stop? I was so close," she complains.

I don't answer right away. Instead, I hold her gaze as I lick my fingers, slowly, one by one. Her green eyes flare with desire, and my cock surges forward at the salty taste of her. Then I step forward and curl my hand around her throat again.

"You will come when and where I tell you to come. And right now, I want you to come all over my face. I need that greedy little clit to quiver against my tongue as I lick you to paradise. Do you understand?"

"Yes," she breathes, and I'm hooked on the sound of her sweet surrender.

I make quick work of her pants, socks, and shoes before I take in the sight of her in the red thong that perfectly matches the bra she was wearing.

"I can appreciate how lovely these are," I tell her, dragging two fingers between her legs and making her gasp, "but they're not even worthy to grace your perfect body." A few seconds later, the panties join the bra where they belong. On the floor.

Nicolette crosses her arms over her chest, and I meet her green gaze, slowly shaking my head, consternation heavy in my eyes.

"You don't hide from me," I instruct, taking her hands and tugging them down and to her sides. "You are perfect." My head tilts thoughtfully to the side as I rake my eyes up and down her body. "Well, except for one small thing."

She swallows audibly. "Wh-what?"

Stepping closer, I herd her with my big body until her ass is against the lab table, and then I trail my fingers up her neck and to the top of her head. With my torso pressed against hers, I begin to remove the bobby pins holding her hair in its customary bun. One by one, I make a stack as her locks begin to unwind.

"Jesus, how many fucking pins do you use?" I grumble after about the fiftieth one.

A soft giggle escapes her lips. "I have a lot of hair."

"Hmph, no shit."

While I'm disassembling her hairdo, she takes the time to run her hands all over my torso, and I revel in the fact that she feels comfortable enough with me to touch me at will. Then her fingers pause to trace the scar on my left shoulder, and I tense, but she moves on without questioning me, thank god.

When her hair is in a high ponytail, I inspect the black band securing it. Deciding against trying to slide it down and over the mass of curls, I loop my index fingers into it and pull until it breaks.

Burying my fingers in the thick, loopy locks, I pull her forward and kiss her, massaging her scalp until I feel waves of softness cover the backs of my hands.

"That's more like it," I say against her lips. "Your hair is sexy as fuck."

Nicolette's tongue delves boldly into my mouth, and her arms wrap around my thick torso, binding our bodies together. She tastes like the sweet tea we had earlier when I ordered dinner delivery, like sugar and a hint of mint. Finally, I pull back and lower my hands to her waist. With an easy lift, I boost her bare ass onto the lab table, making her yelp.

Then I slide two fingers inside her pussy and attack her neck, my mouth exploring until I find a spot that makes her clench around me. And I suck on it.

"Helix!" she gasps. "Don't leave a mark I can't cover up. I don't want Dr. Hale to see it at work tomorrow. He's really bossy."

I chuckle against her skin. "That's what concealer is for, baby. If you need recommendations for a good one, I know a guy..."

Her laugh is music to my ears, and I lean back to find her mouth stretched with amusement. She's so pretty when she laughs. After one last hard press of my lips against hers, I place my hand in the center of her chest and give her a push. "Put your feet on the table and lean back on your elbows so you can watch me eat your pussy."

She does as instructed, and I lower to my knees, spreading her thighs wider for my inspection. I'm now eye level with her pussy, which is pink and glistening with arousal, like a siren's call for my mouth. I kiss my way up her right thigh, my mouth taking little detours to explore new places to nip and lick. When I reach the apex, I hold myself back from diving into where I really want to be—because, god, she smells good— and kiss down her left thigh, building the anticipation for both of us.

"Please, Dr. Hale," she whimpers, and my cock swells in my pants.

The sound of her. The sight of her. The smell of her. It's like my synesthesia has shifted into another form, and all my senses seem to be crisscrossed. I can practically taste her even though my mouth is inches from her heaven. Glancing up at her face, I see her red aura, burning more brightly scarlet than I've ever seen.

So I take the leap, my groan mixing with her quiet noise of pleasure in the air between us as my tongue licks a long line from her hole, over her clit, and up the landing strip. The dark hair is well-trimmed and feels slightly rough against my tongue, in direct contrast to the surrounding bare flesh that's as smooth as satin.

I do it again. And again. She tastes better than any five-star meal I've ever had, her flavors popping on my taste buds like they were made to my exact specifications.

Reaching down, I free my painfully erect dick and give it two tight strokes to appease his need. Then I focus all my attention on Nicolette, burying my face in her heat and nuzzling my mouth in all her perfection.

I lift my gaze to make sure she's watching. She is, her mouth gaping and her eyes heavy-lidded. When I wrap my lips around her swollen clit, she lets out the most seductive moan, urging me to suck harder.

Alternating between lips and tongue, I have her on the edge in less than sixty seconds. "I'm going to come for you," she rasps, and I give her a scrape of teeth before sucking so hard on that little nub, it will probably be bruised tomorrow.

"Good fucking girl," I tell her, my words muffled by her sweet cunt when I taste her orgasm. She grabs my hair with one hand and bucks her hips, grinding herself against my mouth as she loses her damn mind.

"Oh god. Yes, so good, so good," she chants, and I release her clit and hold out my tongue for her to use. When her hips slow, Nicolette collapses back onto the table, spent, as I dot soft kisses over her pussy.

My dick is staging an all-out protest rally between my legs, and I give him a mollifying stroke until I can get inside this sensual woman.

Standing, I place my hands on either side of her body and lean over her. Her grin is one of pure satisfaction, and it makes me smile. Then she bites down on her lower lip as she pushes to a sitting position and scrapes her gaze down my body. Her eyes widen when she gets to my exposed cock.

"Okay, I don't know where you think you're going to put that thing," she remarks, and I can't help but laugh.

"Turn over, and I'll show you." I stroke my hands up her still-quivering thighs as she reaches for me, her fingers encasing my shaft. "Fuck, Nicolette," I growl when she strokes me from root to tip.

My teeth grind together while she eases her hand up and down with aching slowness, her grip perfect. Her palm slides across my tip, gathering the wetness coating my crown, and I press my palms onto the countertop so hard, I'm afraid I may crack it.

"Do you want me to suck you?" Nicolette asks, her quietly delivered question going straight to my balls.

"More than anything, but not tonight, okay? I'm too close, and as soon as you get those pretty pink lips around me, I'll explode."

Not tonight? Why the hell did I say that? This is a one-time thing, remember?

"Will you fuck me with your suspenders on?" When my eyebrows shoot up in amusement, she blushes and explains, "They're hot."

Looping them back onto my shoulders, I lean down and kiss her lips. "Anything else I can do for you, madam?"

Her fingers tighten around me. "I guess you'll do."

With a playful snarl, I grab her by the waist and pull her to her feet before turning her body to face the table. I quickly grab my wallet from my back pocket and locate a condom.

"Bend over and let me see that ass," I grunt as I tear open the package and sheath myself. She does, looking like a wet dream, bent over and presenting her round bottom to me. My hands are drawn to those pale globes, and I separate her to give me a view of the pussy I devoured a few minutes ago. It's swollen and flushed dark pink, and I can't wait to sink into her.

Taking a step closer, I drag the head of my erection through her wet slit a few times, coating myself with her arousal, and we both moan.

"I'd like to amend my previous statement," I say, and Nicolette looks over her shoulder at me. "I don't always like it quiet in the lab. Sometimes I like it loud. Very loud."

With one hard thrust, I'm halfway inside, and she gives me exactly what I need to hear. My name shooting from her lips in a resounding cry.

"Helix!"

"Fuck," I spit out. "You're so goddamn tight, baby." Her pussy ripples around me, the inner walls like warm velvet surrounding my dick.

An overwhelming need to take her all the way overwhelms my body, but I rein it in, rolling my hips to stretch her out. I don't want to push her past her limits. Not this time anyway.

Dammit to hell. There I go again, acting like this isn't just a one-time fuck.

Nicolette's fingers curl against the resin top of the lab table, and I work her slowly until I see them relax. Licking my fingertips, I slide my hand beneath her and use two fingers to massage her clit. That does the trick. She opens up for me like a blossoming rose, and I sink deeper. Then I draw back and enter her again, looking down to see I'm almost all the way in this time.

"That's it, baby," I coo, rubbing her ass cheek with my free hand. "You're taking me so well."

"More. I want more," she pants, her cheek pressed against the black surface, mouth agape.

Holding her ass with both hands, I pull back to the tip and then give her what she asked for, slamming the front of my hips against her ass. Nicolette's scream echoes around the laboratory, and I could come from that sound alone.

She pushes back against me, and I grip her tighter, holding her in place as I begin fucking her with a fast, steady rhythm. The sounds of our flesh slapping together meld with our groans of pleasure, and I feel my balls tighten against my groin.

I can't even describe how good she feels around me. I always enjoy sex, sometimes more than others, but this? It's pure euphoria.

One of my hands snakes up Nicolette's spine and tangles in the hair at the back of her head. Holding her down, I use my entire body to fuck her with one powerful thrust after another. This is what I love, what I crave. The complete control over a woman's body.

Though my own control seems to be slipping, like a wild animal has taken over my body, intent only on one thing. I look down where I'm entering her, and the sight is mind-blowing. Her pussy is stretched to its limit around my thick intrusion.

"You have the hottest cunt I've ever felt, baby," I growl, my fist tightening in her hair. "You're taking every bit of my cock up this tight little hole."

Her inner walls flutter around me, and I know she's close. Hell, I've been right there since the second I got inside her.

"You feel so good," she says on a moan. "So damn big."

The sight of my fingers digging into the flesh of her ass pushes me closer, and I need her to fucking come. Now.

Sensing what she needs, I release her hair and slide my hand around to the front to cup her neck. When I feel her vocal cords hum against my palm, I pulse out little squeezes around her neck to the same rhythm as my relentless fucking. She seems to like it, shoving back against me and panting out little "oh" sounds.

The effort of holding back my impending orgasm has taken over my entire body. My hair prickles and my toes curl inside my Brionis. I barely recognize my own voice.

"Nicolette, I need to feel you coming. I'm not going to stop until you're milking my cock with your pleasure."

"Fuck," she curses, and I feel it then. Nicolette is so tight around me, I can barely move.

Bending forward, I cover her back and pin her to the table, rutting like a beast.

"You're fucking beautiful, baby. Let me hear you come," I say against her ear.

A second later, my name is all I hear. Nicolette is loud, my name ripping from her throat over and over. The cleaning crew doesn't come in until midnight, so we should be safe from getting caught.

My own roar follows as my release shoots from me, surrounded by her warmth. And all I can think is...

Once is *not* going to be enough.

Picking up my shirt and two loose buttons from the floor, I lift my eyebrows sternly at Nicolette. She giggles.

"Sorry, I got impatient."

I walk toward her as she buttons her own blouse and use my destroyed shirt around her back to pull her toward me. Her hands immediately stop their task and rest on my bare chest.

"Don't apologize. It was hot to see you lose control like that."

"But how are you going to get out of the building now?"

My lips steal a quick kiss from her. "Don't worry. I always keep a spare shirt in my office." Then I think of something. "Shit, there are cameras in the hallway."

"I can go get it for you," she replies, and I snicker, dragging my fingers through the mess of her hair.

"You don't look any less fucked than I do, queenie. But at least you're dressed."

Nicolette's lips twist to the side, and she hums thoughtfully. "I can turn the cameras off for a few minutes. I'll grab your shirt from your office, and then I can go to the bathroom and fix my hair."

I shake my head. "No, the cameras are only accessible from the security office in the other building."

She pinches my cheek. "Oh, ye of little faith." Then she pulls from my arms and strides to her laptop on the long desk along one wall. I follow behind her, curious.

"What are you doing?"

Her fingers fly across the keyboard so quickly I can't even tell what she's typing. "Putting the camera feeds on a loop for a few minutes." She stalls and looks up at me with wide eyes. "As long as I have your permission to do it."

I'm not sure what to say here. We're not doing anything wrong, simply saving ourselves from a potentially embarrassing situation. So I reply, "Fine. You have my permission."

"Okey dokey," she says airily, going back to work.

I shake my head even though she's not looking at me. "But there's no way you're going to be able to get access to the cameras. We have the highest level of sec—" I cut myself off when a view loads of the main corridor on this floor. "What the hell? How did you—"

Nicolette shrugs, looking sheepishly up at me. "I'm really good with computers."

My eyes dart between her and the screen, and I wonder if I look as astonished as I feel. "How do you know it's on a loop and not live?"

She stands and walks toward the door. "Just watch the screen." Then she exits into the hallway. There's no sign of her on any of the cameras. She fucking did it.

A minute later, she returns with a crisp pale-blue shirt on a hanger. The one I had on earlier was white, but I don't think anyone will notice. If so, I'll just tell them I spilled something and had to change.

"I have to say, I'm impressed with your hacking abilities," I say, amusement ringing in my tone.

"Hacking is such an ugly word. I prefer *unsanctioned access*. And I swear I don't break into the Pentagon's system or anything," she assures me as she scoops bobby pins into her palm. "Plus, the laptop is hooked to the Hale server, so it's a bit easier to do from the inside."

I hold up one hand. "Wait, you can break into the Pentagon's computers?"

Her cute nose wrinkles. "Of course not. It would take me days to get through all those layers."

"So theoretically, you could."

"Anything is possible when you put *theoretically* in front of it," she shoots back. "I would never do that though. And I wouldn't have messed with the cameras here if you hadn't said it was okay." Her gaze meets mine, and her green irises darken with worry.

"I know you wouldn't," I assure her, sliding my arms into my fresh shirt.

"The way this system is set up, the raw footage is still there if someone digs deep enough, but I figure no one has any reason to go digging." Her teeth chafe against her bottom lip. "And if they do, I guess they'll suspect what we did."

Twenty minutes later, we're in the parking garage, both of us fully dressed and Nicolette's hair in a haphazard bun. I like her looking a little messy. Her assigned spot is directly beside mine, and we pause near the back of her vehicle.

"I'll see you tomorrow. Thanks for, um, staying late to... work with me," she says, a slight rosy tint blooming on her cheeks.

I stuff my hands into my pockets to keep from touching her, from pulling her against me and kissing her until she's breathless.

"My pleasure," I return, unable to hide the smirk on my lips.

A minute later, I shake my head as I climb into my SUV. I can't believe Nicolette was able to get into our system so easily. Maybe I should tell security there's a weakness?

Then again, I doubt anyone else would be able to tap in like that. Not many people have the mind of a genius. If it were anyone else, I'd be worried, but not with her.

Nicolette Bell doesn't have a nefarious bone in her body.

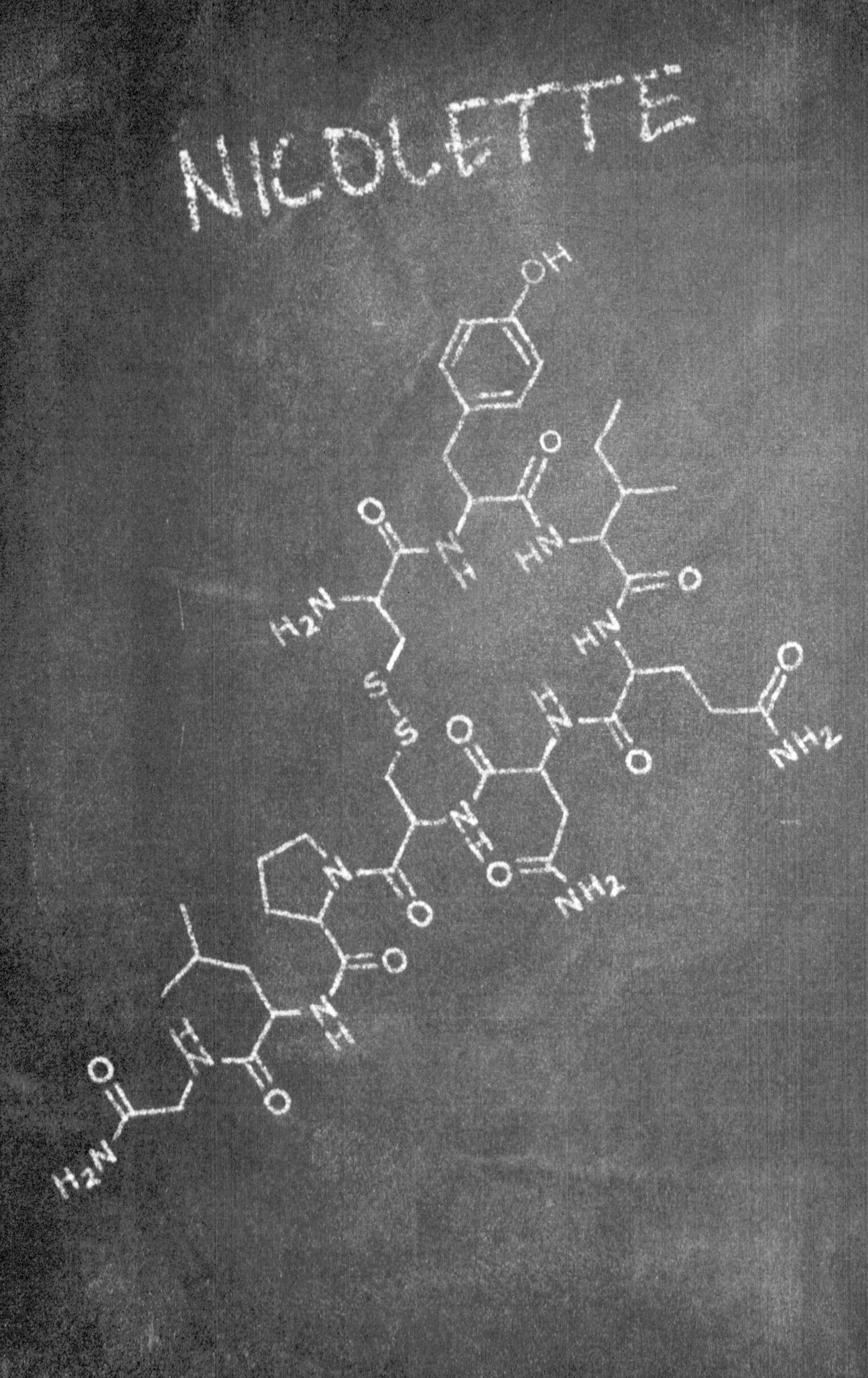

NICOLETTE

Chapter Twenty-Two

FOOTBALL AND FAMILY

One thing I've learned about Texas, they have their own way of doing things. And that's never truer than when looking at the seasons.

It's September, and folks are starting to put out pumpkins, colored leaves, and all matter of "fall" related decor, but here's the thing. There is no fall here. It's a myth. The temperature is hovering at a sweltering ninety-seven damn degrees, but Texans act like it's a cool, breezy autumn afternoon with pretty leaves floating down around them.

Heck, I saw a girl wearing a knitted scarf with her tank top and shorts last week and what I can only assume was a pumpkin-spice latte in her hand. I've been informed by several reputable sources—a.k.a. Stefan, Lukas, and Shay—that my new state will have a couple hard freezes sometime between December and February, and this is what they refer to as "winter."

Another thing about Texas? They love their football. I don't dislike the sport. I watched Giants' games with my dad sometimes when I was a kid, but I can't say I'm a huge fan.

Nevertheless, I'm at the new Houston Dragons stadium on a Saturday because Helix invited me a couple weeks ago. That was way before our little lab rendezvous on Thursday.

Yeah. That. Also known as the best damn sexual encounter of my life.

I was concerned about going to work yesterday. In fact, I almost called in sick to avoid the awkwardness, but I thought that would be too obvious. All in all, we acted pretty normal on the day after, other than a couple shared glances that lasted a beat too long.

Thanks to Helix's massive dick, I still felt some soreness between my legs, which I did my best to conceal. But we worked in the microbiology lab yesterday, and their stools aren't as well padded, so I tended to shift in my seat a lot. I'm pretty sure Helix noticed because I caught him smiling as he looked through a microscope. The smug, sexy man.

After showing my identification at the stadium, I ride with a guard in an elevator that opens on the top floor, where the suites are located.

"This one right here, ma'am," he says, gesturing to a silver door near the center with a dragon logo on the outside.

I tug the hem of my jersey down and stare at the door. Crap, I'm not sure if I should knock or what. The decision is made for me a moment later when the door swings open, revealing a smiling Helix.

"Hey, Nicolette. They messaged that you were on your way up," he says quietly, his gaze eating me up as he takes in my outfit. "I like the boots."

"Oh, um, thanks. Stefan and Lukas helped me pick out everything last night." I wave my hand toward my fitted Dragons jersey, fringed denim shorts that show off my legs without being obscenely short, and black cowboy boots.

His smile fades a little, and he leans in slightly, enveloping me in his delicious scent. "I'm really sorry I couldn't go to dinner with you last night. My brother's home from London."

"I know. It was totally fine." I pat his arm in what should be a completely platonic gesture, but it makes the back of my neck hot when I have a flashback of his thick arms and strong hands holding me to the table while he...

"What are you thinking about, queenie?" he rumbles, snapping me out of my daydream to find him fighting a knowing smile that tells me he knows damn well what I'm thinking about.

"Just wondering if you're going to make me stand out here all day," I say, keeping my voice light.

With a laugh he steps back and lets me in. I have to consciously keep my mouth from gaping open like an uncultured boob when I take in the space. It's phenomenal.

A full kitchen sits to the right as I walk in and it's tiled in the Dragons' team colors of black, silver, and purple. The countertops are lined with an array of food, buffet-style, and even the cabinet handles are shaped like dragons.

Beyond that is the lounge with a textured black concrete floor and several plush rugs beneath purple couches and chairs. Low brushed silver tables provide a place for the occupants to set their drinks, and one curved wall is covered with television screens showing various games from across the nation.

"This is amazing," I gush.

"I agree," Helix says. "I'm glad the new league went all in and did things right. There's more seating down there."

He points to a set of stairs that leads down to a lower level with rows of luxurious reclining chairs. An enormous wall of windows provides an excellent view of the field that's visible from both the lounge and the lower seating area.

"Nicolette!" I turn at the sound of a voice to find Phoenix striding toward us. Good grief! It's a tad disconcerting to see two of the best-looking men on the planet in the same space.

"Hey, Phoenix," I reply, accepting his quick hug. "Thanks for having me."

"Of course. You're part of our family now." He steps back and looks me over. "Look at you being all Texan with your cowboy boots. I like it."

I laugh and lower my voice to a conspiratorial whisper. "I wasn't sure what to wear, so my neighbors went shopping with me. They assured me this was standard attire for Texas football."

"It's perfect, and to be honest, I'm a little jealous of those denim shorts."

Helix casts a flat stare at his twin. "Really, Phe? You're going to talk about jorts again?"

"Hell yes, I am. Why do people look down on men wearing them?" His replica lifts his chin defiantly. "I think we should normalize jorts for men."

Helix shakes his head at this pronouncement, but his lips tug up at the corners. "Thank god we're not in the fashion industry, bro. You would single-handedly bring down the entire family business with your choices."

"Seriously though, I don't understand why women can wear denim shorts and men can't. It's borderline discriminatory."

I can't help but laugh at this nut. "You should really be some kind of ambassador for human rights, Phoenix."

He looks pleased, but Helix groans. "Fuck's sake, don't encourage him."

"What are we talking about?"

I glance up at the new voice, and *good lord have mercy.* There's another Hale brother. While the twins have dark-brown hair and blue eyes, this one—Remington, I presume—sports jet-black locks and brown eyes that are just this side of broody.

"Phoenix is complaining about the inequality surrounding the wearing of jorts," Helix informs him.

"Again?" the newcomer sighs before turning his attention to me, a flash of interest adding flecks of gold to his dark eyes. "And who might you be?"

Helix's displeasure is evident in his cool voice. "She might be off-limits. This is Dr. Nicolette Bell, the lab manager for Hale Cosmetics."

You didn't think I was very off-limits two nights ago when you had me bent over a lab table, I want to tease, but I keep that to myself and hold out a hand to Remington.

"Please, call me Nicolette."

He takes my hand and pumps it twice. "I'm Remington Hale, but you can call me Remi."

"Or asshole," Helix mutters.

"She wouldn't be the first one," Remi jokes. "Nicolette, it's a pleasure to meet you and to have you at our company. I've heard only good things about you."

"Thank you. I appreciate that."

The oldest brother gives me a once-over with his brown eyes, so quick I almost miss it. "Can I get you something to drink? Beer? Cocktail? Wine?"

"No wine," Helix and I say in unison before we crack up. He loops an arm around my shoulders and explains, "Nicolette tends to fall asleep after more than one glass of vino."

The other two brothers regard his apparent familiarity, and they share a look that conveys a thousand words. *Shit, they know.* Helix seems to notice as well and separates himself by a step, letting his arm fall to his side.

The three of them are striking together. Dressed in Dragons' gear and shorts—not jorts—they're all big men, though Remi is about an inch taller than his brothers, while Helix is a bit broader through the shoulders and chest than the other two. I'd venture to guess he has the dirtiest mouth as well.

You have the hottest cunt I've ever felt, baby.

The memory of Helix's words from two nights ago hits me directly in the vag, and I shift from one foot to the other.

"Do you need me to show you where the restroom is?" he asks, obviously noting my discomfort, and I take the opportunity for a little space.

"Yes, the restroom. Definitely."

I need that greedy little clit to quiver against my tongue as I lick you to paradise.

Crap, I need to banish Helix's filthy words from my mind and stop this train of thought before it leaves the station. We agreed it would only be one night. One *very hot* night that would forever be etched into my brain, but still.

I enter the lavish restroom and take a calming breath before doing my business and washing my hands. I thought finally having Helix would sate my needs, but it only seems to have cultivated them. Exponentially.

"All good?" he asks when I emerge, and I nod. "Let's get a drink."

There's a small bar in the kitchen with an actual bartender on duty, and he greets us with a friendly smile. "What can I get you folks?"

"I'll have a bloody mary. Spicy," I request.

Helix nods. "I'll have the same."

A couple minutes later we both have our drinks in tall purple-tinted glasses with seasoned salt around the rim. "What are these?" I ask, inspecting two long green things poking up out of my glass.

"Pickled green beans," he replies. "They're really good."

"Hmmm." I slide one out, intrigued, and suck the juice off before it can drip on my shirt. When I notice the flare of Helix's nostrils as his eyes drop to my mouth, I shamelessly give the bean another very slow suck before biting off the tip.

The flavor is crisp, tangy, and a little bit spicy, but I barely have time to notice before a deep voice—that voice he used Thursday while giving me orders that had nothing to do with work—says, "Careful, queenie."

You will come when and where I tell you to come.

He's like my own personal soundtrack that someone put on repeat and then left the room with the remote. I haven't been able to stop thinking about his filthy words.

I swear, Helix Hale's dirty talk could serve as a creative writing course for spicy romance authors. And I'm sure he has enough material to last for two entire semesters.

"Or what?" I taunt, and his expression hardens. God, I love when he lets this side of him show.

"Or you might just find yourself in trouble, Dr. Bell."

"Well, that sounds..." I pause, giving him my very best flirty eyes. "Horrible."

I can feel his chuckle in my chest as he licks some salt from the rim of his glass and takes a sip. There's no doubt that tongue will have a starring role in my fantasies tonight.

"Are you trying to make me hard?" he asks so quietly only the two of us can hear.

"Is it working?"

The hint of a smile teases at his lips, and he lifts a single dark eyebrow, as if he's daring me to find out. *Mission accepted, sir.*

My eyes journey down his body, over the abs I didn't miss the few times I've seen him shirtless, and directly to his crotch. Helix moves one hand down and lifts his purple-and-black jersey a bit, just for a split second, but it's long enough for me to see the bulge growing in his black shorts.

"Helix, hello, darling."

His sexy demeanor vanishes immediately, and he rolls his eyes in annoyance. "And it's gone," he mutters.

I take a drink to keep from laughing. Were we seriously just discussing his boner in a crowded room full of his family?

Helix turns and plasters on something that I assume is supposed to be a smile as he greets the newcomer. "Hello, Serena. I didn't realize you'd be coming today."

"Remington invited me," the woman gushes. She's beautiful with dark-blue eyes and raven hair cut into a stylish, stick-straight bob that halts abruptly at her chin. And she's wearing a suit. No fucking lie. A royal-blue fitted skirt and jacket with an ivory silk shell beneath. To a football game.

"Interesting choice of attire," Helix remarks, obviously noting the same thing as me.

"Oh, thank you," she purrs, drawing out the last word in the most annoying way ever. "I got it last week in London when I went to visit Remington."

Helix downs the rest of his bloody mary like he needs the liquid strength. I deduce that he does not care for this Serena person. I'm astute like that. Is she an ex of his? That would explain Helix's hostility. Serena seems to talk about Remi a lot, so maybe she's *his* girlfriend.

"I didn't realize you made the trip across the pond."

The woman simpers and tilts her head, allowing her hair to brush one shoulder. "He asked me to. You know how Remington is about me." Her eyes dart around the suite. "Where is my best friend anyway?"

Ah, the best friend, though she's giving me the vibe she'd like to be more.

Helix gestures down the stairs. "He's watching the pre-game warm-ups down there." Serena's head whips around like a lion hearing the rustle of a rabbit in the bushes.

"Fabulous. I'll just go say hello," she says in a posh accent that sounds forced as she twiddles her fingers at him. "Ta ta!"

"Be careful going down the stairs, Serena. Wouldn't want you to fall in those heels," Helix warns to her back, though by his tone, I get the feeling he wouldn't mind all that much if she busted her ass.

"She seems nice," I quip when she's gone, and Helix's face relaxes as he turns back to me.

"She's just as nice as your sister." He places a hand on the small of my back and guides me toward the bar again. "Sorry if I was rude for not introducing y'all, but I wanted to get rid of her as soon as possible. Christ, I need another fucking drink."

"Who is she?" I ask, moving my booted feet quickly to keep up with his long strides.

"That," he tells me, "is Serena Greenfield. She's been friends with Remi since practically birth. Our families used to be close."

"Is she running for office or something?" I ask, earning me a quizzical look, so I clarify. "Because of the way she was dressed."

Helix snickers. "She always dresses like that. Her father was a financial adviser, so she likes to dress like she's one too, even though she's never held down a job before."

"Her father *was* a financial adviser?" I repeat. "Did he die?"

After ordering us both another drink, Helix leans one arm on the leather bar top and speaks in a hushed tone. "Mr. Greenfield went to prison for embezzlement a while back. Their family lost almost everything." He pushes a frustrated breath from his nose. "Though you'd never know it from the way Serena dresses and acts. I guarantee Remi paid for her to go to England last week."

"Are they..."

Helix shakes his head hard, making a sliver of his hair fall across his forehead. I resist the urge to swipe it back in place.

"Hell no. At least I don't think so, though it's not for lack of trying on her part."

Our conversation is interrupted when a small blur of purple and dark curls bursts into the kitchen. "Uncle Helix!"

His face looks like someone just handed him a billion dollars when he turns around and scoops up the blur beneath her arms. Propping her on his hip, he grins as the two rub noses.

"How's my doodle bug?"

Nose rubs? Doodle bug?

Gahh, talk about cuteness overload. My ovaries give him a raucous standing ovulation.

"I'm good. I got dragon wings," the little girl announces, wiggling her body so the sheer purple wings flap. "Pawpaw and Mimi got them for me."

Another voice, this one older, says, "Gotta make sure my granddaughter is properly outfitted." I turn to see Haywood Hale, the CEO of Hale Cosmetics himself, approaching. "Since she's my only grandchild." His tone is pointed, and his blue eyes twinkle at his son, as if telling him to get on the damn ball and produce some more little Hales for him to spoil.

A voluptuous blonde follows Haywood. I assume she's his wife since I saw a large family portrait in the CEO's office with this woman sitting beside him.

"Don't start with me, old man," Helix warns though his words hold no bite. "Have you met Dr. Nicolette Bell?"

The older man turns to me with a genuine smile and a warm handshake. "I have. On the day she interviewed. I like to think I sealed the deal in getting her to come to our company," he teases. "How are you, Nicolette?"

"Very well. Thank you, Haywood." It seems weird to call the patriarch of one of the richest families in the country by his first name, but he insisted the first and only time we met. "And you're correct. You were definitely the clincher for my decision."

"I knew it," he crows before guiding the woman into our little circle. "Nicolette, I'd like to introduce you to my wife, Rebecca."

Mrs. Hale has blonde hair and big blue eyes and looks at least a decade younger than her husband. She extends her hand and speaks with a lilting southern drawl. "It's a pleasure to meet you."

"You as well," I reply politely before pivoting back toward Helix and dropping my voice to a fake whisper and shooting a glance at the child in his arms. "And who's the dragon? Should I be afraid?"

The little girl thinks this is the funniest thing she's ever heard, and her peals of laughter are contagious, spreading to the entire group.

"You don't have to be afraid of me, silly. I'm a nice dragon."

"Phew!" I say dramatically, wiping non-existent sweat from my forehead.

"Tell her your name," Helix prompts his niece.

"I'm Azmina," she says proudly, and her uncle flashes her a look that says to cut it out. "Okay, fine. I'm Reece." The little one sounds completely exasperated from having to reveal her real name. She is freaking adorable and has her dad's dimples.

"I'm Nicolette. It's so nice to meet you," I say, shaking her pudgy little hand. "So you like *Dragon Girls*?"

Her eyes form impossibly wide circles of childlike astonishment. "Yes, you've read those books?"

"Back in New York, I kept my neighbor's daughter, Marley, a couple times when she got called in to work. She was a big fan."

Reece reaches for me, and I take her without pause. "We like the same books, and we have the same hair, so we're twins," she announces, holding a piece of her curly hair up to mine to compare. "Just like my daddy and Uncle Helix."

I laugh. "Okay, twin. Are you excited about the football game today?"

She nods enthusiastically. "Yep. I got to go to the Dragons' first game too, and they won, and there were sliders on the buffet. Those are like baby hamburgers. They're really good." She turns to Haywood, who seems as amused by her rambling as I am. "Pawpaw, are there sliders again?"

Her grandfather laughs. "I told the chef to make sure of it."

"Oh, goody." Her eyes shift to the bar where the bartender just placed our drinks. "What are those?"

"Um, that's a bloody mary," I answer.

Her eyelids pop wide again. "Oooh, is there real blood in them? Can I have one?"

We all chuckle, and Helix answers. "No, they're made with tomato juice, doodle bug, and you don't like tomato juice, remember? You tried it at my house one time."

"Oh. Yeah. I'm thirsty though."

Helix leans to the bartender and says something I can't hear because Reece is discussing dragons again. A minute later, the man hands Helix an orange juice with what looks like purple sugar around the rim and two cherries floating on top.

"Your cocktail, madam," Helix says with a formal accent to his niece.

"Thank you, sir," she says, matching his fancy tone while frowning into the glass. "Why doesn't mine have green beans in it?"

I fight a smile and answer. "Because you have a sweet drink so yours has yummy cherries instead."

Her lips twist wistfully and she sighs. "Okay." She perks up a second later when the bartender hands her a plastic cup with three long beans in it and winks.

"There ya go, Reece. You can eat those after you're done with your juice."

But the kid has different ideas. She plucks the pickled beans from the cup and plops them into her orange juice. I grimace and glance at Helix, who has rolled his lips between his teeth to keep from laughing.

She clinks her drink with mine. "Now we're twinsies again, Nicolette."

"For sure," I tell her.

"Come on, sweetheart," Haywood urges. "Let's go get some sliders to go with your, uh, creation."

I set her down, and she waves before heading off with her grandparents, leaving Helix and me alone.

"I have to say, that's the grossest mocktail I've ever seen," he mumbles, still watching his niece.

"Not gonna argue with you. Reece is darling though."

He gives me that lopsided grin that hits me straight in the nipples. "You have to say that since you're her twinsie now."

Taking a sip of the spicy drink, I return his smile. "You seem really good with her. Do you want kids of your own?"

Helix's shoulders bunch and his jaw tightens. "I do but..." Pursing his lips, he blows out a stream of air that seems to make his body relax. "It's complicated. How about you? You want munchkins?"

I nod. "I do. I'd love to have a kid or two."

"You'd be a good mom," he says quietly, locking me in his mesmerizing blue gaze.

"I hope so. I worry that because of my childhood, I won't. I mean, what if I'm a shitty person who's incapable of—"

"You're not a shitty person, Nicolette," Helix interrupts harshly before softening his tone and brushing a stray curl from my cheek. I lean slightly into his touch as his voice goes raspy. "You're one of the best people I know."

The tender moment is interrupted by the PA system announcing the Dragons are about to take the field, so we retreat to the lounge and take our seats on a purple leather couch.

During the game, Helix introduced me to the only Hale sister, Perri, who sat in the lounge with us. She was the spitting image of her mother, Rebecca, with doe-like blue eyes and soft blonde hair. She was also a very energetic chatterbox, but I liked her.

"That was such a good game," she gushes as time ticks down on the clock. "And I loved watching those female athletes shine. I wish I was athletic."

The Dragons won a hard-fought victory, topping Orlando by a touchdown. The game had been fast and exciting and held my attention the entire time... when I wasn't stealing looks at Helix from the corner of my eye.

"Agreed," I say, clasping my hands over my head to stretch out my back after hours of sitting. My jersey rides up, and I don't miss Helix's gaze on the exposed strip of my stomach.

Unfortunately, Perri doesn't miss it either. The smile on her pretty lips is loaded with mischief as she looks between the two of us. "Helix, I'm going to ride home with Mom and Dad. Why don't you make sure Nicolette gets to her car safely?"

I lower my arms and wave a dismissive hand. "No, I'll be fine."

Helix's brow furrows. "Perri's right. I'm walking you to your car."

So, I guess Mr. Bossy Pants has decided that's final, I think wryly.

People start to file up the stairs of the suite, and Reece appears, dragging Phoenix by the hand and toward the door. "Hurry up, Daddy. Jordie said I can go on the field, and I want her to see my dragon wings."

He rolls his eyes good-naturedly and waves goodbye as he lets his little one lead the way. Perri hugs us both and then bounces up and down on her toes before tossing her brother a very obvious wink.

Helix leans toward his sister and lets out a yap that sounds like the bark of a small dog, and she huffs, flipping him the bird before flouncing away.

"What the hell was that noise?" I ask with a laugh, and he grins widely, showing off that cute dimple.

"When Perri was little, I told her she was part chihuahua. You know, because she's so high-strung? Then when she was eleven, I had her convinced I'd run a test on her and it concluded she had canine DNA in her chromosomes."

"Stop it! No you didn't," I snicker, smacking him on the shoulder.

"Sure did. I even made up a fake lab report proving it."

He guides me toward the exit, and we make our way down to the VIP floor of the parking garage. Helix gave me a parking pass earlier this week to get into this section.

"Thanks for inviting me," I say when we reach my car. "The game was fun, and the food and drinks were fantastic."

"And the company?" he asks.

I wobble my hand from side to side. "Meh. Not bad."

He tries to fight it, but his smile seeps through. "That's not what you said on Thu—" Cutting himself off, Helix closes his eyes and shakes his head, unease taking some of the light from his eyes when he reopens them. "Sorry about that. And up in the suite before the game. For the flirting, I mean."

"Nothing wrong with some harmless flirting," I reply, keeping my tone light. "If I didn't like it, I would've told you." In fact, I rather enjoyed it.

His nod is sage, though he still appears a little unsure. "I'm glad you came. My family liked you."

"I liked them too. Your dad and mom are nice." I wince when I realize my faux pas. "Sorry, I meant your stepmom. Does your mother get along with them?"

Helix snorts. "Not at all. There's some bad blood there since the divorce." He glances around to make sure no one is listening. People are filing by, but no one is paying us any mind. "Perri was born before my parents were divorced," he says in a low voice.

"Oh. Wow. Okay, I never realized that." Haywood Hale seemed like such a nice man, and I didn't have him pegged as a cheater.

"It's not something anyone talks about. I think there were a couple articles questioning the timing a long time ago, but they've been pretty much buried. Most likely the company's damage control team." His nose wrinkles. "Of course, none of us condone cheating, but it's been over two decades since all that happened. There's nothing that can be done about it now, so we all pretty much just roll with it since Perri is our sister."

"I can understand that."

"It's kind of strange, but my mom and Perri actually get along really well. Mom was always kind to Perri because she was a little kid and none of this was her fault."

A smile curves my lips. I've never met Helix's mother, but I think I already like her. "Are we still on for Friday night at the drag club?"

Helix pulls his bottom lip into his mouth and licks it. He seems uncomfortable. "I've been wanting to talk to you about that. Do you think it's a good idea for us to, you know, hang out after..." He makes a couple vague loops with his right hand.

"After making circles in the air with our hand?" I ask, feigning innocence at his question.

His resulting laugh warms my insides. "No, I meant after Thursday."

"Thursday... Thursday..." I tap my chin, pretending to think about it. "Hmmm, that was chicken spaghetti day in the cafeteria right?"

He drops a glare on me that makes my panties feel suddenly damp. "Nicolette." My name growled from between his clenched teeth doesn't help matters in my lower region one tiny bit.

"Ohhh, are you talking about..." I lean forward until our faces are inches apart. "The S-E-X?"

"You know damn well that's what I'm talking about. Do you really think it's a good idea for us to be together after work given that two days ago, I devoured your pussy, bent you over, and then fucked you until your cunt was raw?"

Well, when he puts it like that...

I shift my feet so I can cross my right leg in front of the left, attempting to apply a little friction to my now-throbbing clit. The needy bitch.

"Given that all that took place in the lab, I'd be more worried about us being alone together there. But if you'd prefer not to see me outside of work, I understand." Surprisingly, my voice sounds cooler than I feel.

Helix seems to deflate, and his shoulders droop. "That's not actually what I'd prefer at all." One of his hands lifts and then falls, as if he'd been about to touch me but thought better of it. "I like spending time with you, Nicolette."

"I like spending time with you as well, but if it makes you uncomfortable, we can just see each other at work." I didn't expect the wave of disappointment that washes over me when I say those words. I'd developed a bit of a dependency on seeing Helix every Friday night, eating meals with him, laughing.

"I love working with you, but I like non-work Nicolette just as much. You're easy."

I tilt my head and arch my eyebrows. "Wow, you get railed by your boss *one time*, and all of a sudden, you're labeled as easy."

Laughter barks from him, and he lightly pushes my shoulder. "Stop. You know that's not what I mean." His smile turns boyish and almost shy. "I feel like I can be myself around you."

A tingle of emotion forms at the back of my throat, and I swallow it down. "I feel the same. Would it be better if we took separate cars when we go out? Like today?" He'd had family stuff to do before the game, so I told him I would drive myself.

He crosses his arms over his chest, and frown lines appear on his forehead. "No."

No? That's it? Just no?

My lips twitch. "Are you pouting, Dr. Hale?"

"I don't pout," he says, still obviously pouting. With a roll of his eyes, he uncrosses his arms. "Okay, maybe a little, but there's no need taking two cars when we're going to the same place. As responsible members of the scientific community, we have to think about the environment and conserving resources."

"This is true," I add, trying not to laugh at his apparent attempts to justify us riding together.

"I can still pick you up, and then simply drop you off at your town-house at the end of the night. That way we still get to enjoy each other's company without any of the, uh..."

"Any of this?" I suggest, crudely poking the finger of my right hand in and out of the circle of my left fist.

He snorts out another laugh and shakes his head. "Definitely no more of that." His voice goes deeper, and... *is he standing a few inches closer to me?* "Not that I didn't enjoy it very much, Nicolette."

"I did too," I whisper, feeling the sexual tension like a rubber band between us, stretching to its limits until it either breaks or snaps us back together.

I watch as Helix's Adam's apple bobs up and down a few times, and then he steps back, leaving me with prickles of sweat on my neck that have nothing to do with the humidity.

"Okay, I'll pick you up at seven Friday night. Do you still want pizza since we'll be all dressed up? Or I could make a reservation somewhere nicer."

"Pizza sounds good. I like getting a little fancy and then going to regular places. Makes people wonder what you're up to."

He chuckles. "Daddio's Pizzeria it is."

I reach for my door handle, but Helix's hand is already there, and I repress a shiver at the feel of his warm skin, remembering the expert way he touched me a couple nights ago. He swings it open, and I toss my small bag on the passenger's seat before turning to him.

"One more request."

He nods. "Okay, what is it?"

With a boldness that comes from god-only-knows-where, I stroke a finger from his shoulder down to his firm abdomen.

"Wear your suspenders Friday night... Dr. Hale."

I don't miss his low groan, and when I climb into my car and back out, I'm pretty sure I see him adjust his groin as he watches me.

We may not have sex again, but flirting with Helix is something I don't think I can stop. It's too much damn fun.

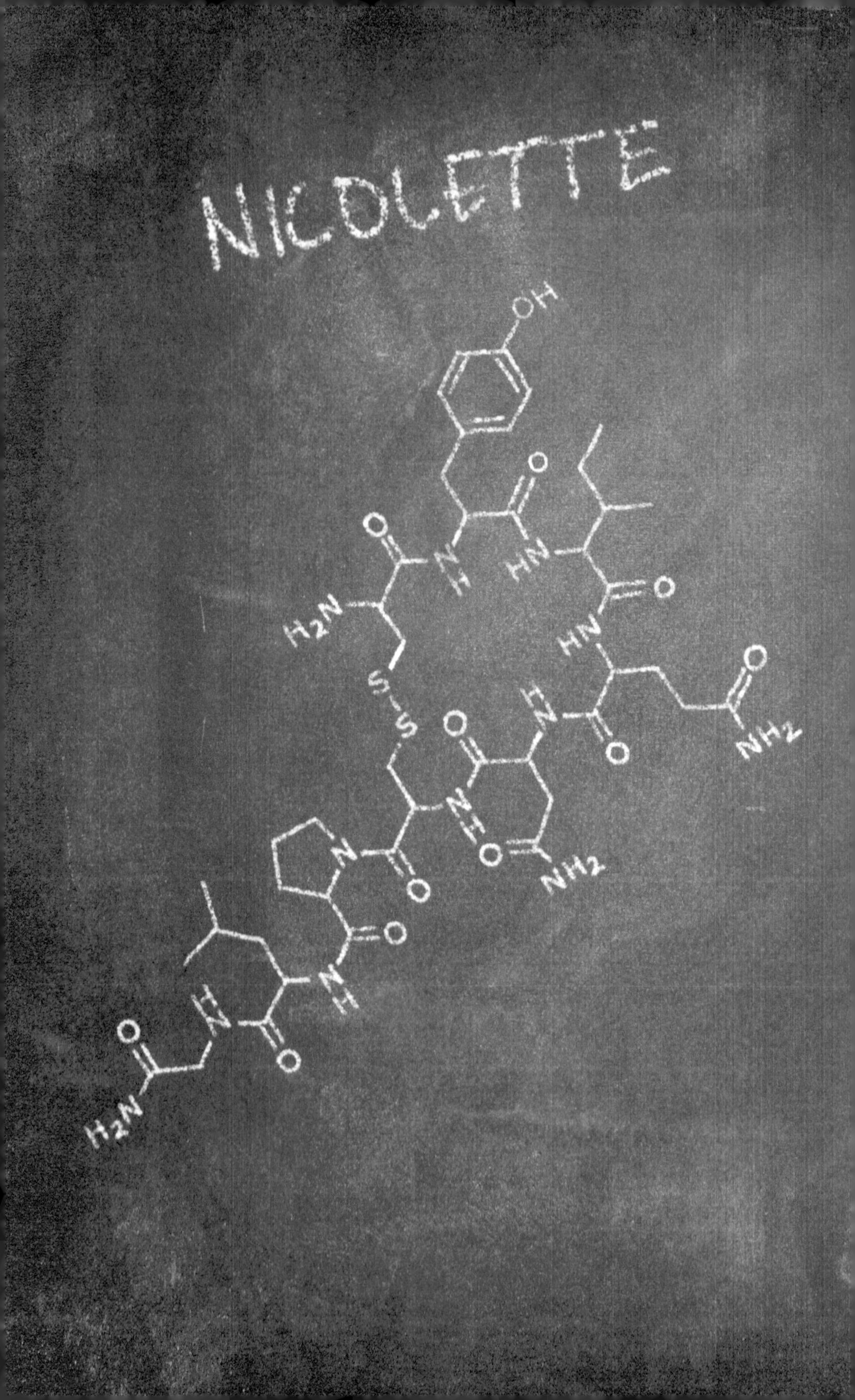

NICOLETTE
OH
H2N
S
S
O
O
N
H
HN
HN
N
H
N
O
NH2
NH2
O
NH2
H2N
NH
N
H
O
O
O
O
O

Chapter Twenty-Three
PURPLE SUSPENDERS AND FISHNET HOSE

On Friday night, I look over my menu at Helix. "I just realized you're not wearing your glasses."

"You're not the only one that has contact lenses," he remarks, not looking up from his perusal of the pizza selection on the page.

It gives me time to look him over. He did indeed wear suspenders tonight, these a vibrant purple color, and I wonder how many sets he has. His shirt is white and must be custom tailored because it fits his form perfectly, showing off that broad chest and shoulders. Black trousers and loafers complete the look.

I, on the other hand, chose the black blazer dress that Gianna and Auburn gave me for my birthday, along with black fishnet hose. My waist was cinched with a wide black belt, and the red leather heels with matching earrings completed the outfit. Like Helix, I also went with contacts tonight.

"What are you getting?"

He flashes his blue eyes up at me for a second. "Not sure. So many good choices."

Daddio's Pizzeria is like taking a step back in time, the decor reminiscent of a 1950s diner, complete with red vinyl booths and a black-

and-white checkerboard floor. But the menu is modern and fun with chef-inspired toppings.

"I'm trying to decide between the Italian Orchard and the Atlas."

He reads the descriptions aloud. "Hmm, prosciutto and thin sliced apple or chicken, gorgonzola, and fresh basil. Both sound good." He lowers his menu. "What if we get one of each and share?"

"Sounds like a plan."

After the waitress in an old-fashioned diner uniform takes our order and departs, Helix leans his forearms on the formica tabletop. "What's the worst thing you could put on a pizza?"

I purse my lips and think about it before answering with, "Uranium."

That cracks him up. "Good lord, woman, I never know what the hell you're going to say."

Patting my hair, I sigh dramatically. "It's part of my enviable charm."

Both pizzas turn out to be delicious. The Atlas has a slightly sweet glaze that I love drizzled on top, but I think the apples paired with salty prosciutto takes the top prize for me.

The conversation flows easily. We flirt a little but keep it relatively harmless, and I can feel something changing inside me with every minute I spend with Helix.

As much as I try to tell myself it's only physical attraction, I'm afraid I might be falling for him.

"Holy crap, this is gorgeous," I say, my eyes darting around the space. It's a refurbished old theater that's breathtakingly opulent.

The theater chairs have been removed and replaced with tables arranged on four descending levels. Helix and I are led to the lower level where our table is situated front and center, directly in front of the stage. Background music fills the air with an upbeat tune.

"Looks like we got the best seats in the house," Helix remarks as we sit on magenta padded chairs behind an hourglass-shaped illuminated table. All the tables are lit from the inside, the frosted plastic muting the rainbow of colors scattered throughout the seating area. Ours is a pretty blue color that reflects Helix's eyes.

I buff my nails on my shoulder. "I don't like to brag, but I know people."

"I'll remember that if I ever need a favor."

My very naughty mind thinks I'd like to do him a favor or three. I avert my eyes before he can read the desire there and gasp when I catch sight of the ceiling. Helix automatically wraps a protective arm around my shoulders and braces a palm on the table like he's about to jump up and kick someone's ass.

"What's wrong?" he barks.

I giggle and pat his thigh. Beakers on a hot plate, that's one firm quadricep. "Nothing's wrong. Just noticed the ceiling."

He visibly relaxes but doesn't remove his arm. I'm not complaining. His eyes go to the ceiling. "Dang, that looks like something Michelangelo would have painted. And the chandeliers are like something out of *The Phantom of the Opera*."

The lighting here is amazing. There are three enormous fixtures with lights that mimic actual long taper candles, complete with intermittent flickering, as well as subtle recessed lights around the perimeter. I'm assuming the latter is a more recent addition, probably the result of the renovation efforts.

After the server brings our drinks, a Slutty Shirley Temple for each of us, Helix picks up the folded card on the table and reads it before summarizing.

"It looks like the Sky Theater opened in 1890, and when the original owner died in 1911, it was purchased by a church to house their large congregation. They had it for about ten years, and after that, there were rumors that it was a speakeasy during prohibition."

I glance around the room, imagining women in flapper dresses and cloche hats dancing with men in dapper suits and fedoras. "I can totally see that." A wide grin pushes my cheeks upward. "Why do I love the thought of a secret speakeasy where a church used to be? There's something so deliciously sneaky about that."

"Because you're a troublemaker, queenie."

"Not denying it," I say smartly. "I totally would have been a boot-legger in the twenties."

"I could see that." Helix glances back down at the card. "The Sky Theater fell into disrepair due to lack of funds and was abandoned. Then a former actor purchased it in the sixties and sank six million of his own money into it to bring it back to life. When he died, he left it to his partner who turned it into a drag club and renamed it The Rainbow Sky Theater. It underwent additional renovations this year, including a restoration of the fresco on the ceiling, which was done by the great-great-great grandson of the original artist."

"Oh, I love that. Brought it back full-circle."

As we chat, the perimeter lighting slowly dims, and we turn our attention back to the stage. Helix bends to whisper in my ear, and the feel of his breath against my neck, makes me shiver involuntarily,

"Who are Lukas and Stefan in this show?"

I turn slightly so he can hear me, and his nose brushes my cheek. I feel air sliding over my flesh as he sucks in a deep inhale.

"They wouldn't tell me. They said I had to come to find out."

His question is partly answered when one of the queens emerges from stage left. She's got huge jet-black hair and is dressed in a full-body, shiny leather jumpsuit that resembles a Catwoman outfit.

It takes me a second, but I recognize the face behind all the makeup and lashes. "Oh my god, Helix, that's Lukas."

He rears his head back, his eyes popping open wide. "Wow, okay, you're right." Tilting his head to the side, he remarks, "He—or wait, is it she?"

"Lukas usually uses he, but I believe the custom is that when they're in drag, they embody that character, so you use the pronoun of their character. Unless the performer has a different preference."

"Gotcha. Okay then, she looks very... svelte."

I can't help my snicker. Lukas is a doll but a little on the pudgy side, but not in this getup. "I wonder what kind of Spanx she's wearing."

The crowd is cheering, but only Helix's voice stands out in my ear. "Did you say you want to be spanked, Nicolette?"

Oh Jesus, Mary, and Joseph.

I pinch the inside of his thigh and hiss, "Stop it, you reprobate.

Spanx is a brand of undergarments made to smooth out problem spots on a person's body." I glance back up at Lukas, who's strutting slowly toward the microphone at center stage, much to the delight of the crowd. Lukas is an outstanding strutter in five-inch patent leather heels.

"That didn't answer my question," Helix says. I turn to face him, and the heat in his gaze could set this entire building ablaze. "Do you want to be spanked?"

"Yes." It's merely a whisper but he must have read my lips because he smirks and nods.

"Noted."

Then he turns his attention back to the stage where Cat Lukas has finally reached the center. I shakily exhale a breath and watch as my friend cracks a whip until the crowd quiets.

"Greetings, fair patrons of Rainbow Sky. I'm your mistress of ceremonies, Madame Simone." We all cheer, and she preens at the attention. Her eyes meet mine for a brief second, and she winks. "I'm so happy to see all my precious kittens here tonight."

After an introductory speech thanking everyone for attending and acknowledging the benefactors who made the transformation of the theater possible, the show begins. We watch act after act, most of them musical, but there was one Joan Rivers standup routine that was so funny it had us almost peeing our pants. She even picked on Helix a bit for his suspenders, but he just grinned and took her barbs like a champ, blowing her a sarcastic kiss.

The choreography is fabulous, the staging is glamorous, and we even get to see a drag king in the form of Elvis Presley. I know the end is drawing near, and I lean closer to Helix. His arm has stayed around me the entire show, his thumb rubbing against the oxytocin tattoo on my shoulder. In turn, I left my hand on his leg when I wasn't clapping.

"Have you seen Stefan?" I whisper. I'd searched the faces of the main acts and the backup dancers, but I hadn't found my other neighbor yet.

"No, maybe he wasn't feeling well." He glances at the Madonna performer on stage, bouncing around with her cone-shaped boobs. "Or he could have had a wardrobe malfunction or something. I'm sure all this takes a lot of... adhesive."

I sit back and relax as Madonna wraps up her act and shakes her cones at the audience on the way offstage. Then Madame Simone is back on the microphone.

"We're so glad you joined us for the grand reopening tonight. And now I'd like to introduce you to our final act." The atmosphere in the place is already electric, but it seems like it amplifies tenfold with the loud cheering and clapping that ensues. Simone cracks her whip. "Settle down, kittens. I know you're excited, and since you've been such good little kitties tonight, I won't make you wait a second longer."

She pauses dramatically for at least ten seconds, knowing she has the crowd in the palm of her hand. Finally, in a cooing voice, Simone announces, "The Rainbow Sky Theater is ecstatic to introduce the always fabulous... Dolly Parton."

Dolly strides onto the stage in a hot-pink rhinestone pantsuit with an acoustic Martin guitar on a strap around her neck. It takes me a second because I'm dazzled by all the bling, but when I realize that's Stefan up there, I let out a squeak of surprise.

Helix stiffens beside me, and I know he's come to the same realization. We both cheer loudly right along with the rest of the audience.

"Hey, y'all!" Dolly says, and my jaw almost hits the table. Stefan has nailed the country singer's voice and demeanor to perfection. "I'm so happy to be with you tonight."

"I love you, Dolly!" someone yells from the back, and laughter floats up from around the room.

She points and says, "I love you too, honey, but did I say you could remove your ball gag?"

The place erupts, and she grins before breaking into a fantastic rendition of "Jolene," strumming her guitar with precision, despite her long pink nails. There are no backup dancers or fancy lighting, just a single spotlight on a tall stool in the center of the stage, but it's the most compelling performance of the night. The applause is deafening when she's done.

"Thank you. I have one more song for you before I let you all get out of here to get into whatever naughty plans you have for tonight. But first, I'd like to say a special thank you to Hale Cosmetics for sending over swag bags full of fabulous cosmetics for every single performer you've seen tonight. We love you and appreciate your support for our community."

My gaze cuts sharply to Helix, whose cheeks turn slightly pink in the dim light as the crowd claps. He finally gives me his eyes and explains, "I sent over a box earlier this morning. Thought it would be nice."

Without realizing it, I lean into him and press a soft kiss to his lips. His arm tightens around my shoulder, and he hauls me closer until I'm so close I'm practically in his lap. I lean my cheek on his chest and turn my attention back to the stage. It's nice being held like this, and I can feel the release and flow of oxytocin into my system. My affection and attraction for this man grows by leaps and bounds, and I realize, there's nothing sexier to me than kindness.

Dolly's next song surprises me. It's slower than the first one but no less spellbinding. The iconic song "I Will Always Love You" floats through the room in her sweet, passionate voice, and I don't think anyone in the room moves a muscle until the last note is done.

There's silence for five long beats, as if the lyrics have mesmerized every soul into a stupor, and then the room explodes. Everyone is on their feet, cheering and whooping as Dolly drops her head and absorbs the well-deserved love she's getting from the audience.

Someone tosses a bouquet of pink roses onto the stage, and she stands to pick them up, taking a long sniff before blowing kisses at the crowd on her way offstage.

When we make our way out of the theater, Helix keeps me tucked against his side, his big hand firm on my waist. I'm quietly attempting to rein in my emotions. I know he's about to take me home, but the problem is...

I don't want him to leave.

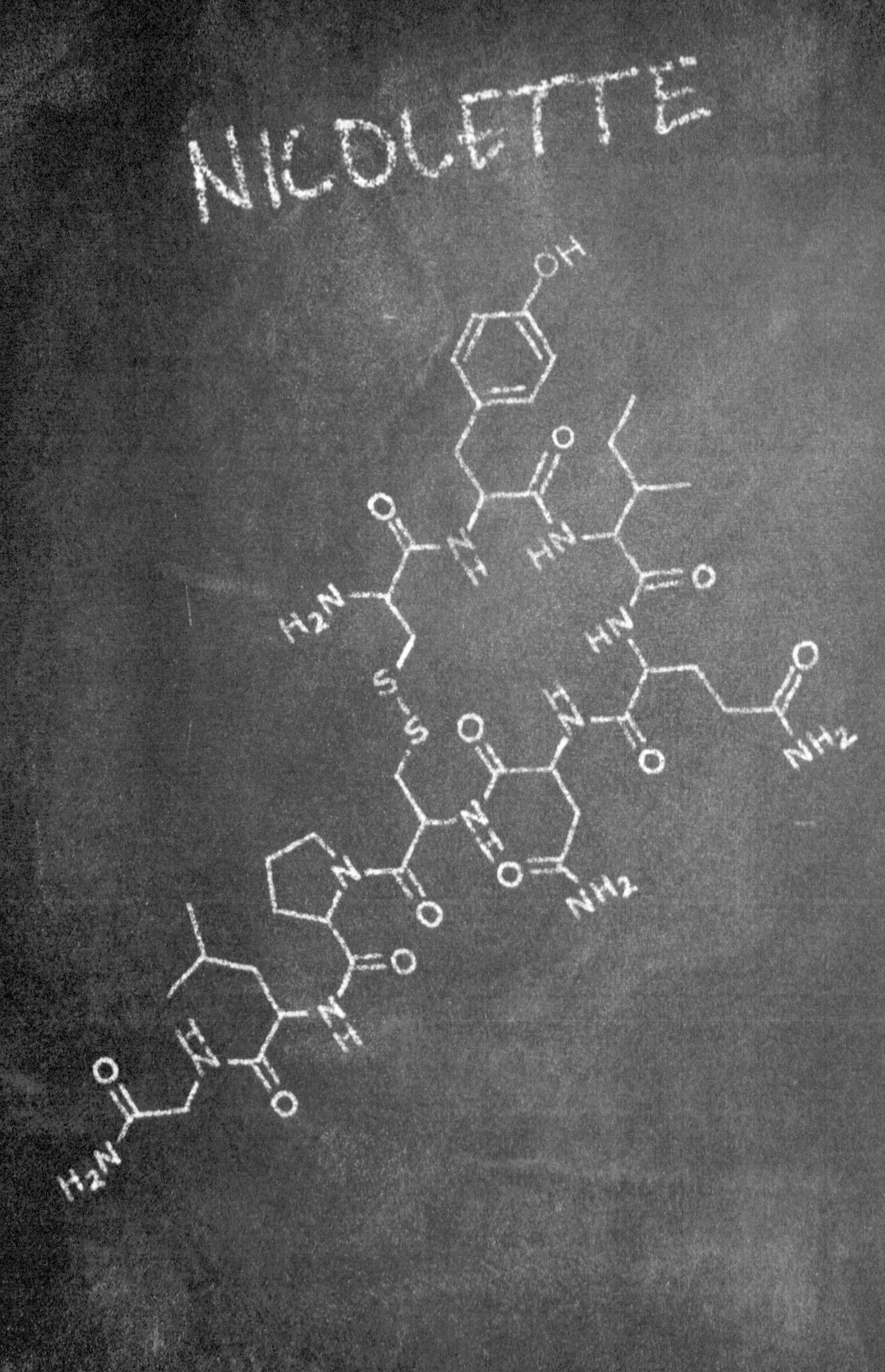

NICOLETTE

Chapter Twenty-Four

I'M GOING TO HAVE YOU TESTED BECAUSE YOU CAN'T BE HUMAN

We crash into my townhome with my legs wrapped around Helix's waist and our mouths fused like someone welded us together. Apparently, he didn't want to leave either.

"Please tell me you have condoms," he mumbles into my mouth.

My frantic words come out in pants as he strides through my kitchen like he's not carrying a fully grown human. He's so fucking powerful, and I'm dripping with need.

"In my nightstand. My room is on the third floor."

"I remember."

"Oh god. The sangria incident," I groan as he jogs up the first flight of stairs. "I'm so sorry about—"

"Shut up," he growls, turning to head up the next flight. "The only words I want to hear from your mouth are *fuck* and *me*."

"Fuck. Me," I say, and desire flares in his blue eyes. His mouth crashes over mine again, and we bump into the wall before he shifts course to get us safely to the third floor.

Once in my room, Helix tosses me on the bed and immediately shucks his suspenders from his wide shoulders. "Take off everything except the fishnets and heels," he orders, starting on his shirt buttons. "And hurry up."

Removing my belt, I roll my eyes and mutter, "Okay, okay. Hold your horses, bossy-butt."

His eyes narrow. "Keep giving me attitude, and you'll find yourself tied to that bed."

That doesn't sound like such a bad idea, so I retort, "Then I guess I'll just keep giving you attitude."

Helix's head jerks up, and he pierces me with an assessing gaze. I return it and give him a tiny nod of consent.

"Goddamn," he groans, shoving his pants down to reveal gray boxer briefs that are distorted by the huge bulge that's evident. "You have two seconds to get that dress off before I rip it from your luscious body."

"No," I say, quickly, undoing enough of my dress buttons to slide it off my torso and down my legs. "Don't rip it. It was a gift."

I toss the garment, and he catches it in mid-air before checking the label. Then his angry eyes meet mine.

"This is a Bouvier dress. Who the hell bought you such an expensive gift?"

I sit up wearing only my lingerie, earrings, and heels, fisting a hand on my hip. "Not that it's any of your business, but it was a birthday present from Gianna and Auburn."

That gets his attention. "You know the Bouviers?"

"I do," I say indignantly. "Lehra works there, and she introduced us. Gianna is a good friend of mine."

To my surprise, Helix laughs. "I should rip that dress into shreds and send a picture of it to Auburn."

My forehead furrows. "You don't like him?"

Helix bends and unhooks his suspenders from his pants, still chuckling. "No, I actually like the grumpy bastard a lot, but it would be fun to fuck with him. He's so sensitive about his fashions."

He drops the dress on the heap of his own clothes, and there's something innately intimate about seeing our clothes tangled together.

Striding slowly toward me, he tosses the suspenders on the bed and presses one knee into the mattress beside me. With two fingers, he gently lifts my chin. "I would never destroy anything that's important to you, Nicolette."

What about my heart? I want to ask, imagining the organ on the floor in tatters beside our clothes.

With a suggestive smile, I lie back and say, "I don't really care for these panties all that much. They tend to ride up my butt crack."

His lips twitch and his fingers leave trickles of warmth as he eases them down my body and to the forest-green string at my hip. A second later, a ripping snap cracks through the room, and my panties are a thing of the past.

Helix exposes the crotch and rubs it over his lips, eyes closed in apparent ecstasy. "You're wet, queenie."

"And you're hard," I note, glancing down at his crotch. "Sometimes there's a direct correlation between the two."

He laughs softly and then bends to kiss my lips, giving me a taste of my own desire. "You're going to need a safe word for the things I'm about to do to you, Nicolette. Do you have one?"

"No, but what about *safe word*?"

He frowns. "That's what I said. You need a safe word."

"I know. I want my safe word to be *safe word*," I explain. "It seems like that would be the easiest one to remember."

Helix shakes his head, lips curling in amusement. "Sometimes I forget what a genius you are."

"Well, it would do you well to remember," I say tartly as both his hands go to my right ear. He carefully removes one earring and then the other, setting them on the nightstand, and I suck in a breath at the sweetness of it. Then he removes my bra, leaving me bare to his gaze.

And he definitely gazes, his blue irises seeming to light from behind with appreciation. "I can't stop thinking about how beautiful your body is," he murmurs, dragging a fingertip around one nipple, sliding it across my body, and doing the same with the other, over and over in a sensual figure-eight motion. "I thought I could fuck you out of my system, but it only made me want you more."

"Maybe tonight will help," I say, trying to infuse false hope into my tone. Because I actually hope the opposite is true and that he wants more of me. I like the way Helix touches me, and I've never had a sexual encounter as fulfilling as our one time together. We enjoy hanging out together, so why shouldn't that extend to more... naked activities?

"We'll see," he tells me, standing and walking to the foot of the bed. "Now grab onto the headboard." I do, and he adjusts me, tugging me by the ankles until my arms are straight but not uncomfortably so. Then he grabs the suspenders and climbs over me until he's straddling my torso.

Helix's balls are heavy against my stomach, and I have the perfect view of the wet spot turning his underwear a couple shades darker where the tip of his big cock sits. My breaths come sporadically as he expertly ties my hands to the slats of the headboard.

"You okay, baby?" he asks, eyebrows pinching in concern.

"I'm excited," I admit. "I've never been tied up before."

His hands press into the pillow on either side of my head, and he leans so close I can smell the cherry and vodka on his breath from our drinks.

"I like having you at my mercy, Nicolette. I want to be able to touch and lick you wherever I want. Have no doubt, I will fuck you exactly how I want and use your body for my pleasure." A smirk forms on his full lips. "And I think you'll enjoy every second of it. If not, you will use your safe word immediately, understood?"

Outside the bedroom, Helix grants me free will. He gives me strength and confidence in myself I didn't know I possessed. Maybe it's always been there, hidden beneath the surface, waiting for someone to peel back the layers. But as soon as the clothes come off, he takes that will and makes it his own. And I'm not ashamed to admit I enjoy ceding control. I love every deep command he utters.

I also understand that my safe phrase gives me complete control over him. I can shift the balance of power with two simple words.

"Yes, I understand."

"Good girl," he rasps, and I can feel the evidence of his approval throbbing against my stomach. Scooting down, Helix kneels between my legs and runs his hands up and down my thigh-high fishnet stockings, stopping to trace the delicate lace at the top. "I approve of these. Did you wear them for me?"

"I wore them because they look good with the dress," I hedge.

His eyebrows shift inward. "Did. You. Wear. Them. For. Me?"

"I, um..." My gaze shifts away from those intense blue orbs, and he immediately rolls my legs toward my chest, holding them there with one strong forearm. Then he spanks my right ass cheek. Hard.

"Did you wear these sexy fucking stockings to turn me on?"

"Yes!" I cry, and he spanks me again, this time on the left side.

"Were you trying to make my cock so fucking hard I couldn't resist you?" he barks, eliciting the truth from me with his imposing tone.

My voice ekes out in a whimper. "Yes."

He smacks the right side. "Because you have a slutty little cunt that's been craving my cock since the last time I fucked you?"

I clamp my lips shut, knowing my refusal to answer will reward me with more of his beautiful punishment. It comes a second later, and I think my pussy is going to spontaneously combust with the slap.

"Yes! God, Helix, I'm about to come."

"Don't you fucking dare," he growls, spreading my legs wide and staring at my exposed vagina. "You have three choices where to come: on my fingers, on my mouth, or on my cock. You do not come around thin air when I'm here to give your body what it needs."

"I can't... help it," I pant. His dirty words aren't helping a bit, and I can feel the orgasm spreading through me, the clenching and leaking between my legs.

Helix watches with fascination etched on his handsome features. "Fucking hell, you're really coming," he grumbles a split second before he spanks my pussy.

And that does it. My hips buck and my back arches off the bed as a scream rips up my throat. I'm flying, only vaguely aware that Helix's mouth is now attached to my pussy like a leech, sucking up every drop of me. My body floats on a soft cloud, lower and lower until I'm back on my bed, sweaty and spent with a large, dominant man between my legs.

He unlatches and lifts his head, allowing me to see my release dripping from his chin. Swiping it with the side of his finger, he sucks it off, causing one more tremor to vibrate through me.

"You're a very bad girl, queenie."

"I'm sorry," I lie, and I think my sated smile gives away the fact I don't give a fuck.

Helix inspects my ass cheeks and then licks the handprints he put there, leaving a coat of saliva before blowing on them. It cools my heated skin, and I sigh.

"I think the punishment should continue," he remarks.

My body doesn't know whether to revolt or rejoice. I enjoyed the last spanking, but my ass is pretty sore. "What kind of punishment?" I ask warily, and his grin turns wicked as he sits up on his knees.

"I would normally finger-fuck you and stretch you out for me, but..." He cocks his head to the side. "I think I'll make you take me without any warm-up."

I glance down to see the front of his underwear pulled down and his cock in his hand. If a penis had emotions, his would be furious. Helix was big last time we were together, but the head looks swollen to twice its normal size right now. Every cell of his blood seems to be pooled in that magnificent organ, turning it a deep shade of red, and the engorged veins running along the underside only add to the impression that his dick is quite angry with me.

Bring it on.

"If that's what you think you need to do," I say coyly, and he bites his bottom lip to fight the smile I can see threatening to take over.

Helix reaches for the box of condoms in the drawer and immediately checks the bottom, no doubt looking at the expiration date. He glances up, catching me watching, and gives me a chagrined half-smile. "Sorry, it's something my dad taught us when he had *the talk*."

I'm pretty sure Haywood Hale most likely had an addendum to that lesson, one that all fathers of rich young men should teach. "It's a brand new box," I tell him quickly. "You can check the seal."

He frowns when he realizes why I brought it up. "You don't have to say that, Nicolette. I trust you." Helix's lower jaw drops a few millimeters, and his eyes seem to defocus as he repeats his declaration. "I trust you." Somehow, I get the feeling the second time he said it wasn't for me.

Opening the box, he pulls out three foil packets before replacing the box in the drawer.

"Awfully ambitious, aren't we?" I tease, and he gives me an imperious eyebrow.

"You insulted my rebound time last time, Dr. Bell, and I feel I have something to prove."

I grin, happy I goaded him because now he's going to take it out on me in the very best way. Once he's sheathed, Helix kneels between my legs and drags the head of his erection up and down my slit a few times, bumping it against my clit.

"Fill me. Please," I beg because I know he loves it.

Sure enough, he groans deep and low as he slides the head inside me, the crown doing its designed job to open me up. "Hell yes, baby. Beg for this cock. Give me all the thoughts in that beautiful, filthy mind of yours."

"I want you to use that thick cock of yours to stretch my cunt open wide. Get yourself off with my body, Helix."

His jaw clenches, and he pushes in another couple inches. It's pleasure laced with pain because *mother of science*, he's big.

"Like this, my pretty queen? This how you want your pussy used?"

I strain against my bindings, my back arching off the mattress as my sex attempts to accommodate his intrusion. "Yes, like that. I want to squeeze every bit of cum from your dick until you're so weak you can't even stand up."

"Fuuuuck," he growls. "You're better at this than me."

I wasn't sure about that, but the compliment was like champagne bubbles in my mind, leaving me feeling high and uninhibited.

"I can take it," I say. "Give me all of you."

Helix leans forward and kisses me, his dick inching in a bit more with the movement. "That's what I'm afraid of," he murmurs quietly against my lips. Before I can process that comment, he plunges his tongue into my mouth and distracts me. The man is a damn good kisser, his pacing and rhythm unmatched, at least in my experience.

I've dealt with all the bad kissers in my life. I even have special names for them. The snake, who rapidly flickers his tongue in and out. The goalie, who rams his tongue down your throat to play tonsil hockey. The slug, whose tongue just sits in your mouth and expects you to do all the work. Then there's saliva waterfall guy; I think that one's pretty self-explanatory.

But Helix Hale is none of those guys. He understands the assignment and kisses a woman properly. To me, a kiss is like a dance between two people. Sometimes the motion is back and forth; sometimes it's circular; at other times it's frenzied. But it's always dependent on both participants.

Right now, our tongues are waltzing in slow, rhythmic circles. They wrap and twist like two lovers who only exist for each other, the rest of the world be damned. My body opens fully for him, and we both make noises of approval as his cock sinks deep.

"You're like warm butter," he tells me, ending the immersive kiss to pepper little pecks along my jawline. "Melting for me."

He nuzzles my ear before rising back up above me and sliding his hands up my thighs. His fingers dance in the wide holes of the fishnet and ignite my skin. Then he reaches beneath me and grabs my bare ass, hoisting me easily until my lower back is off the bed.

I look up at him from where I'm trussed on my bed. He's a beautiful specimen of man, his shoulders and chest seemingly taking up all the space in the room. His torso tapers at the waist, giving way to a rock-hard eight-pack that's currently quivering with the obvious effort of holding back. He has a little body hair, but it's well-maintained and not even close to bushman levels.

And the arms? They are the kinds of arms women dream about having around them. Thick, strong biceps and muscular forearms with veins that bulge when he flexes. Not to mention the sexy ink that means "Pursuit of happiness."

Our eyes meet, and I can read the desire in his dark pupils. "You're a very bad girl, Nicolette, but you're about to take me like a good fucking girl."

"Make me," I challenge, and his resulting smile is nothing less than triumphant. I asked for it, and he's about to deliver.

Helix's hips pull back, and I watch his cock slide out of me, swollen and dripping wet from being inside me. Then he slams into me so hard, I'm forced up the bed a few inches.

"Fuck!" I cry as he slides me back down and folds me almost in half with my knees near my shoulders.

Then he rides me like he owns me, his pace punishing. He leans forward and props his hands on the wall over the headboard, changing the angle to one that has my eyes rolling back in my head. The thick ridge of his penis slides over my G-spot with every deep thrust.

Helix uses his entire body to fuck, not merely a back and forth hip motion like most. There's rolling and circling, a bowed back, and bunching muscles. It's like my body is some kind of advanced workout machine that he uses to exercise every muscle group in his body at the same time.

He goes deeper than I ever imagined possible and holds there, grinding his pubic bone against my clit, giving me stimulation from the inside and outside. My vagina clamps around him like she's found what she's been looking for all these years, and she's determined to keep him.

"Fuck yeah. I love when my bad girl is good for me," he groans, finding a new rhythm that's exactly what I need. *In and out. Hard grind. In and out. Hard grind.*

I'm making unintelligible noises, and he reads them like a book, taking full advantage of my bliss. Helix is relentless, pushing against the wall for leverage as his body pounds into mine. He's taking what he wants while at the same time he's making sure I get what I need.

The bedsprings squeak and the headboard bangs against the wall so hard I probably won't get my security deposit back. I don't give a rat's ass right now. Helix could fuck the house down and I wouldn't care.

I need to come. Immediately.

"Helix, please," I whimper. I look up at his handsome face, pinched with exertion and dripping sweat onto the pillow and my face. A droplet lands on my lips, and I greedily lick it, tasting the salt of him. "Please let me come, Dr. Hale."

His reply is a guttural rasp. "Goddamn, baby." He pushes forward until his hips rest against my ass and he grinds. His cock is so deep, and the friction of his leg hair abrades my tender flesh, pushing me over the edge in a split second.

I scream. He grunts. We come.

It's the most perfect orgasm I've ever experienced. We buck against each other, taking and giving until we're both spent.

Helix has my hands untied a few seconds later, and then he collapses on top of me, our sweat mingling together.

"We're so good together," he pants, nuzzling into my neck. His weight is heavy, but not overwhelming because he keeps himself propped on one forearm, using the other hand to stroke up and down the outside of my leg. "Why do I keep trying to deny it?"

"I don't know," I say softly, looping my arms around his neck and brushing my fingers through his dark hair. Helix kisses the side of my face and slowly pulls himself from my body. I make a small sound of protest, and he moves to lie beside me.

"What do you want me to do now?" he asks, his voice so quiet it's almost inaudible.

"What do you mean?"

"Do you want me to go?"

I glance at the bedside clock. "It's really late. You can stay if you want." Then I realize that sounded a bit cold and amend my statement. "I *want* you to stay," I tell him, emphasizing the second word.

His dimple pops gently with his smile. "Okay, baby, just give me a second to take care of the condom, and I'll be back."

We just finished round two, this time a hard fuck from behind. Helix wasn't exaggerating at all about his outstanding rebound time. He positioned me up on my knees and once again had my hands bound to the headboard with his suspenders. I knew there was a reason I was turned on by those damn things.

While my hands were rendered useless, Helix's had free rein of my body, alternating between rubbing my clit and pinching my nipples. All the while his mouth was on me, licking up my spine, biting my shoulders, sucking on my neck. It was sensation overload and just as explosive as the first time tonight.

We didn't shower after either romp. I loved the scent of hard sex that permeated the room, and since he didn't mention cleaning up, I assume he did as well.

Or maybe the poor man was simply exhausted. He'd put in some serious work tonight, taking us both to soaring heights. We did take time to remove our contact lenses. I always keep an extra case, and we stood beside each other at the double sink and bared our eyeballs, our blurry gazes meeting in the mirror. It felt like a very couple-y thing to do and I liked it way more than I probably should have.

Now we're facing each other on the bed, our legs tangled together and our hands roaming.

"What are we doing?" Helix whispers into the darkness as his fingers draw lazy circles on my hip.

I open my eyelids. His face is inches from mine, and since my eyes have dark-adjusted, I can make out some of his features. His dark brows are pinched together.

"I thought we were going to sleep. Swear to god, if you want to fuck again already, I'm going to have you tested because you can't be human."

He barely cracks a grin. "No, I mean what are we doing, as in... us? Are we dating? Fuck buddies? Friend with benefits?"

I lean up on my elbow and squint at the bedside clock over his shoulder. "You really want to discuss labels at 2:37 in the morning?"

His self-deprecating chuckle rumbles his chest beneath my hand. "Sorry, baby. You're right. We can talk about this tomorrow."

He pulls me closer, and my leg slips between his. Against my belly, I can feel his cock, which is still sizable though not hard at the moment.

"Good, now shut your sexy pie hole and let me sleep. Some maniac took over my bed and defiled me tonight."

"What a bastard," he says, kissing my forehead sweetly. "You want me to kick his ass?"

I'm so content and sleepy right now and nuzzle my nose into his chest. "No, just hold me like this. I miss being hugged."

HELIX
NH₂
HO
N
H

Chapter Twenty-Five

I'M A MAN OF MY WORD

I pause at her words. I know she's tired, but I can't just let a statement like that go.

"What do you mean you miss hugs? Do you not get hugs a lot?"

She hums, her eyes closed. "Yeah, from my friends sometimes."

"What about your family?" When we were in New Jersey, I noticed the brief embrace with her dad seemed forced and awkward, and her mom and sister hadn't hugged her at all. Though I didn't think too much of it at the time, assuming they just weren't a very affectionate family.

"No," she mumbles. "They don't hug me."

My hand smooths up her back into her hair, running my fingers through the curls. "Why not?"

"My mother," Nicolette sighs.

I should really let this go. It's none of my business, but I can't. "Your mother?"

"Mmhmm. When I was a kid, I noticed she always hugged Angelica and not me so I told her I wanted hugs too. So she started hugging me, but I noticed her hugs were different from my dad's. They hurt."

I have to make an effort not to jolt, and I look down at her closed eyes. I'm not even sure if she's fully conscious. "What do you mean they hurt?"

Nicolette's face scrunches up. "Ma hugged me really tight and sometimes she would pinch my side. It just... hurt. I didn't like it."

Her voice sounds higher, almost childlike, and my heart is about to beat out of my chest. I thought Nicolette's mother was just a bitch, someone who clearly favored one child over the other, but it's more than that. She's fucking evil.

"What about the rest of your family?" I ask.

She hums again. "After I told Ma I didn't want her to hug me anymore, she told everyone else not to hug me either because I didn't like it, but I do. Hugs feel good when they don't hurt." Nicolette lets out a sigh. "I miss Pop hugging me."

Now I understand her tattoo a lot better since oxytocin is known as the hugging hormone or the love hormone. Affection was something she was denied as a child, so she had the molecule permanently imprinted on her skin. The tat is on the back of her shoulder and I can't reach it with my mouth right now, so I kiss my fingertips and rub them against the ink.

Tears well in my eyes and I pull her just a little bit closer, burying my nose in her curls as I whisper, "I've got you, baby girl. I'll be your hug."

I awaken with a warm, gorgeous body draped over mine, and I'm a little confused at first. I haven't had a sleepover with a woman in years.

When my mind wakes up enough, I remember last night and smile. It was an amazing night... until what she said in her sleepy confession. Wanting to hold her closer, I haul Nicolette all the way onto my body.

She shifts, and her pussy finds my morning wood like it knows where it belongs. After a couple rocks of her hips, she slowly opens her eyes and smiles down at me, her face all drowsy and beautiful.

"Am I attacking you in your sleep?"

I laugh, the sound dusky in the dimness of pre-dawn. "Yes, and please continue."

Her legs are straddling my hips, putting her in the perfect position to feel how hard I am, and her pussy weeps in response.

"You just had to prove you needed all three of those condoms, didn't you?" she teases.

"I'm a man of my word."

It only takes another minute of her dragging that juicy pussy up and down my dick before I'm rolling on the rubber and settling her on top of me. This time, the sex isn't hard and frenetic like our previous times. Instead of Nicolette sitting up and riding me like a cowgirl, I hold her close to my body and rock up into her.

We move in perfect synch, a melding of bodies in a slow and sensual dance. Our lips are connected the entire time, and I feel something inside me loosen, like a tightly-bound ball of string that's being unraveled with every move of her soft body over mine.

I want more with her. That realization slaps me in the face when we come at the same time, swallowing each other's euphoria.

I'm still thinking about it after we nap for another two hours, and it's still at the forefront of my mind while we shower together, along with something else I told her last night.

I trust Nicolette Bell. And that scares the shit out of me. My natural fight or flight instincts tell me to end this before I get in too deep, but another part of me—a significant part I can't quite define—craves the connection we're building.

She's ensnared me with her brain, her body, and especially with her heart.

"You're quiet," she notes as I rinse the conditioner from her long hair.

"Just thinking," I say absently, trying to sort through those dreaded things called feelings.

Nicolette kisses her way down my body, her tongue flicking my nipple before sliding over my abs. "I'm sore, but maybe I can take your mind off things in another way."

I snap out of my reverie and hook her beneath the armpits before she can sink to her knees. *Am I really turning down a blow job? Who even am I right now?*

"Maybe another time," I tell her, softening the rejection by pressing her against the tiles of her shower and kissing the hell out of her. When I pull back, I give her one more soft peck. "Why don't we go to brunch and talk about those labels?"

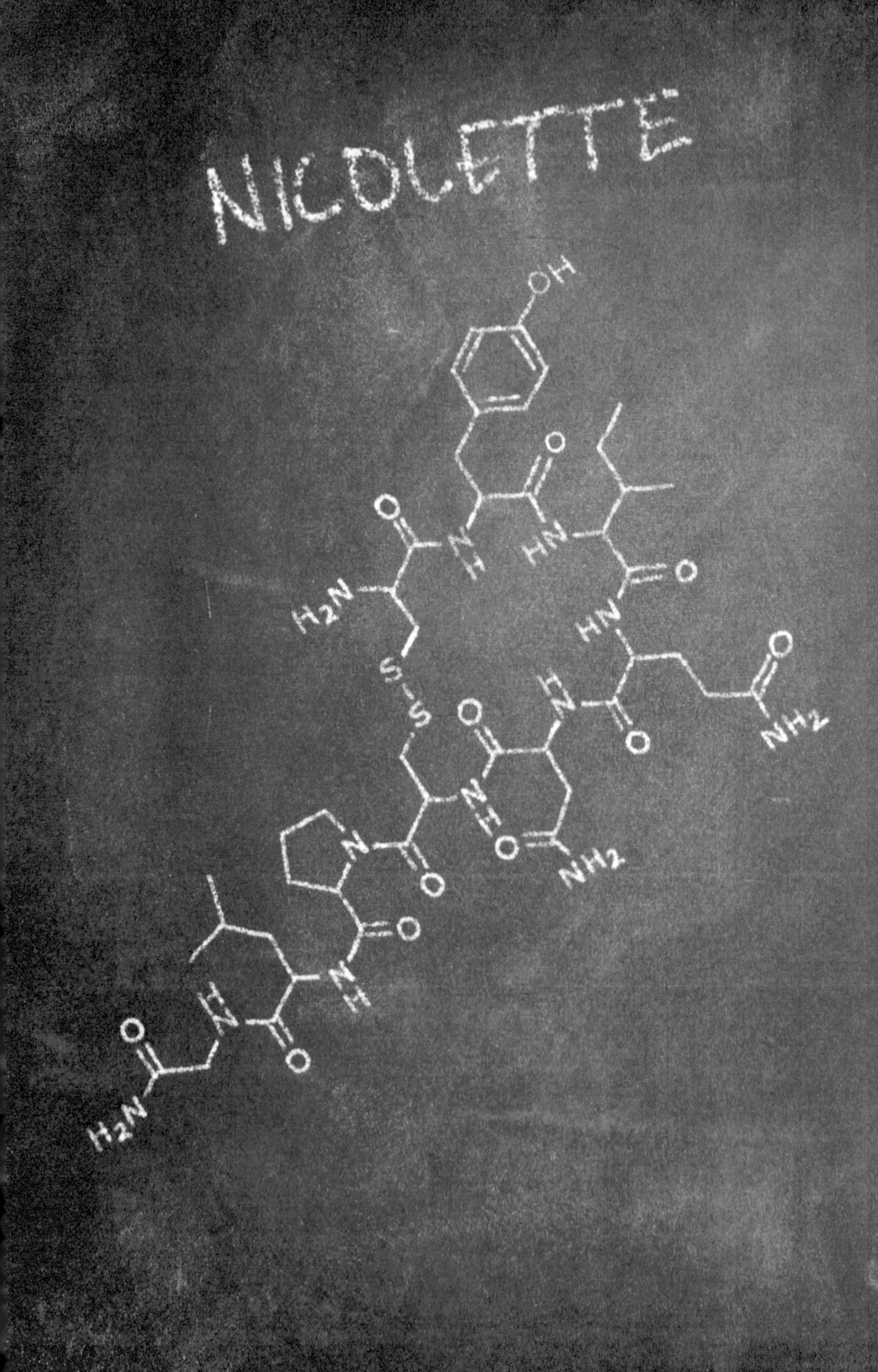

NICOLETTE

Chapter Twenty-Six

THE STATE OF MY ASSHOLE

Helix Hale lives in a palace. I'm aware the entire Hale family is loaded. After all, the cosmetics industry is highly lucrative, but holy shitballs. This is like *rich* rich.

"You can wait in the living room or the solarium," he tells me as we traverse the beautifully outfitted kitchen, where we entered from the six-car garage.

"No parlor?" I ask because I'm a smartass.

His lips hike up at the corners. "It's on the other side of the house. I'll be changed before you can walk there."

I sigh dramatically. "Perhaps you should provide indoor golf carts so your guests won't be inconvenienced when they want to have a mint julep and tea cakes in the parlor," I tell him in my best southern belle voice.

He swats my ass. "It's this kind of attitude that's going to get you turned over my knee." *Um, yes please!* Helix kisses my forehead and instructs, "Go wait in the living room. It's the most comfortable."

We exit the kitchen, pass through a short hallway, where I can see the arched opening to a formal dining room on the left, and enter the marble foyer. "It's right through there."

He points and then heads up the curving staircase. I find the living room—honestly, it would be hard to miss because it's the size of a car dealership—and am pleasantly surprised by how cozy the large space feels.

The base colors are black, white, and gray, though there are pretty splashes of color added in the throw pillows, rugs, soft blankets draped over black leather furniture, and modern artwork. The floor is shiny gray wood, and the walls are painted a stark white with crown molding. Arched windows allow morning sunlight into the room, and I don't see a speck of dust anywhere, though there is one corner with a small cluttering of toys, including a pink tent I assume is Reece's.

I've barely made one round around the space before I become aware I'm not alone. Turning, I see Helix standing beneath the high arch, casually leaning a shoulder on one of the columns that's wider than the big man watching me. He's wearing navy shorts, boat shoes, and a baby-blue V-neck tee that molds to every one of his muscles. He's totally pulling off the preppy-but-athletic vibe.

"Does it meet with your approval?" he asks with a sardonic grin.

"It's absolutely beautiful." My eyes go back to the piece I was admiring on the wall. It's abstract, but the longer I look at it, the more I can make out faces within the mishmash of colors. "I love this one."

He strides over and stands beside me, his hands in his pockets as he gazes up at it. "The style is called ink wash. It was done by a local artist who reportedly has the same kind of synesthesia as me. I saw it at a gallery, and it felt like it wanted to come home with me."

"Did you pick out everything in here?" I'm a bit surprised because it looks professionally done.

He chuckles. "I picked out all the black-and-white stuff when I bought this place. I thought it would be functional, you know? Reece was two, and when Phoenix brought her over for the first time, she told me, and I quote, 'It's not very pitty, Uncle Helix.' She just looked so serious and a little sad for me."

I can't help but laugh. "So you hired someone to make it prettier?"

He rubs the back of his neck. "Actually, I took Reece with me to an interior design studio where you can choose your own items. Kind of a fancier version of Home Goods."

My heart is smiling so hard right now. "You let your toddler niece be your interior designer?"

"I mean..." He shrugs. "They have consultants there to guide you, so it's not like I just let her run around grabbing everything in sight. The guy thought it was adorable and gave her choices, kinda like *do you like this painting or this one to go over the fireplace?* The kid's got a pretty good eye."

"She does." I look back at the ink wash art. "This is my favorite though. I can feel you in this painting." When I look back at him, his gaze is intent on my face. Then he pulls me to him by my hips and kisses me hard on the lips.

"You ready to go eat? I promise I'll bring you back for a full tour some time, but I'm starving right now."

I pat his chest. "Well, we did work up quite an appetite last night."

"I've never brought a woman to my house." He drops that little bombshell on me and then hops out of his vehicle, this one a black Range Rover, and comes around to open my door.

"Why?" I ask.

"I don't date," he says. "And I won't bring anyone into my home if I'm not dating them. It's my personal space."

I'm equal parts flabbergasted and confused. He doesn't date. He doesn't bring women to his home. And yet he brought me today. Was it just for convenience's sake so he could change clothes for brunch? Or are we dating now? I have no idea what to think or if I even want to date Helix.

You do, my brain and heart say at the same time. My vagina chimes in with a very tired thumbs up of agreement. Poor old girl has been put through the wringer in the past few days.

I need clarity and maybe a second opinion from someone that hasn't been fucked by Helix Hale because all my body parts are completely enamored. So I excuse myself to the restroom when we get inside the restaurant, which is called The Good Egg.

Punching Lehra's name on my phone, I wait for her to pick up, but it goes straight to voicemail. *Dammit.* On a whim, I decide to leave her a message, so I blurt out the whole thing, my words coming rapidly.

"Hey, girl, it's me, and I'm in the bathroom of a restaurant. I. Need. Advice. ASAP, so I'm leaving you this message. If you get it in the next few minutes, call me back. Otherwise, shoot me a text because I'm going to sit down for brunch."

I take a deep breath and begin to pace around the lounge area of the bathroom.

"So, long story short, we finally had sex last week. And girl! It was... Jesus, I can't even tell you how good it was. He has this enormous dick, and the man knows how to use it. And his tongue? It should be declared a weapon of mass satisfaction. To put it bluntly, he ate me out, bent me over, and fucked my damn brains out. I'm pretty sure he bruised my cervix, but I liked it.

"We decided it was going to be a one-time thing, like a *fuck you out of my system and move on* type of deal. He said he doesn't do relationships so that was all he was after, and I agreed, right?"

I flop onto the velvet settee and lean back, one wrist over my eyes.

"Okay, so we went out last night, like we always do on Friday nights. I told you about that, right? Anyhoo, we already discussed it beforehand. We were going to ride together for the environment or something, and then he'd take me straight home. So we went to an amazing show— tell Artie he would have loved this show, like, for real—and on the way home, his hand brushed against my thigh. I was wearing those black fishnets I got last time we went shopping, remember? The super soft ones? Oh, I was also wearing that black blazer dress, and girl! If I do say so myself, I was looking fierce."

Pulling my feet onto the little sofa like I'm at a therapist's office, I cross them at the ankles and speak even faster.

"But back to the story. A minute later, he ran the backs of his fingers over the fishnets again and asked if they were thigh-highs. I told him there was only one way to find out. Eeee! Can you believe I fucking said that? He got this look in his eye, and the next thing you know, his fingers are in my panties, and he made me come... *while he's driving down the damn road!*

"When we get to my house, I'm about to ask him if he wants me to return the favor, but then he pulls me out of the car and picks me up like I don't weigh a thing. Is there anything hotter than that? Dear god, you have no idea! Well, I guess you do because Cruz is a big ole boy, and I know he likes to toss you around."

The phone beeps a notification that the voicemail has ended, and I push off the settee, needing to walk off some of this frantic energy. I redial and jump straight back into my tale.

"Sorry, it cut me off. So the man tied me up and completely disrespected every inch of my body. It was full-on bougie sex, girl, nothing vanilla about this guy. He's completely depraved. We went at it like rabbits three times, Lehra. Three! Never in my life have I witnessed such a thing. That one dude I dated, Carl? You remember that fool? He needed a two-day turnaround before he could have sex again. The dipshit tried to tell me that was just how biology works, like I don't have more than one fucking biochem degree.

"Shit, I'm getting off-topic. Where was I? Oh yeah, he fucked me so good it makes my asshole clench up just thinking about it. Etcetera, etcetera. So on to today... he said we should go to brunch and talk about labels. We stopped by his house so he could change clothes, and when we got to the restaurant, he just casually mentioned he'd never taken a woman to his house before and that it was his private personal space, and he'd only ever take a woman if he was dating her."

I stare at a wide circular pattern on the carpet and begin walking its perimeter, wringing my free hand nervously.

"What do you think that means? Before we were seated, I said I had to go pee, and I've been in here so long, he's going to think I have some kind of malfunctioning bladder or that I really came in here to poop. But I just needed to know how to decipher what he said so I know what I'm walking into before we talk. Because I'm starting to like him a lot. I mean, I was encouraged by what he said, like maybe I'm special or something, but that's unlikely, right? He doesn't date. He's not looking for anything. He told me that with his very own sexy mouth."

Blowing out a breath, I reverse my circle because I'm getting dizzy going the other way.

"Okay, you're right. I shouldn't get my hopes up for anything more.

I know you didn't actually say that, but I can literally hear you right now inside my head. I should woman up, go out there, and have a rational conversation with him. I just really, really like him, Lehra. More than I've ever liked anyone. We get along and have so much in common. And did I mention his mega-dick? Pretty sure I did.

"All right, babe. I've been in here so long, I really do have to pee now. Thanks for talking me off the ledge, even though you did absolutely zero talking. You're the best. Love you."

Hanging up, I push out a sigh. I feel better after saying all that out loud and getting it off my chest. Until I look up.

A woman is standing at the sink in the main part of the restroom. She appears to be about my height, so about five-seven, though she's wearing modest pumps that perfectly match her periwinkle suit. It looks designer, the classic cut draping perfectly on her slender frame.

Her hair is dark with a few tendrils of gray at the temples. Weirdly, that makes me like her a lot. She obviously comes from money, but she's the picture of aging gracefully. I would put her probably in her late fifties.

As she stands there with her arms crossed over her chest, she meets my eyes and smiles a knowing smile.

Fucking fuck a duck. How long has she been there? I've been in the anteroom and there's only one entrance to this restroom, which is behind me. Even though I was distracted, I would have seen her if she'd come in since she would have walked right by me, so I'm assuming she's been in here the entire time.

Which means she most likely heard *everything*. I stare at her, scrolling through the one-sided conversation in my mind.

The enormous dick, getting eaten out, the potential bruising of my cervix, the vehicular finger-banging, getting tied up... Oh. My. God... I talked about my asshole clenching! And she most likely heard it all.

"I am so sorry," I begin. "I didn't know anyone else was in here."

"Obviously," the woman says, her grin widening. Her lips are beautiful, coated with a lovely pink color that looks a lot like Hale's *Perfect Peony* shade.

It hits me then, and I scramble back into my brain to see if I mentioned Helix's name at any point in my long-winded monologue.

That could be a freaking public relations nightmare for the company if personal information of a sexual nature came out about a core member of the very high-profile Hale family. Especially things that are a little on the kinky side.

I'm ninety-nine percent sure I didn't mention his name because I didn't need to. I'd talked to Lehra about my crush on Helix before, so she would be aware of exactly whom I was speaking of.

Sucking in a deep breath, I say, "Again, I apologize for..." I wave my hand vaguely. "All that. I'm normally a very calm and private person, but I was having a bit of a, um, personal internal crisis."

Her smile fades into an expression of polite neutrality. "We all do from time to time, dear, and I'm afraid I'm the one who should apologize. I should have made my presence known, but you really seemed to be on a roll, and I felt bad interrupting."

A giggle escapes my lips, and she laughs too, the sound light and pleasing to the ears. "I don't blame you," I say. "I definitely would have eavesdropped if I'd heard someone rambling about those kinds of things."

She tosses the hand towel I hadn't realized she was holding into the hamper and walks toward me, her heels clacking on the intricate mauve tiles before they're silenced by the thick carpet.

"I know it's none of my business, dear, but if I may be so bold as to offer a word of advice?"

"Of c-course," I stammer, not knowing what the hell else to say. I'd just subjected this poor woman to the dirty details of my sex life. Surely I could hear her out.

"First of all, whether or not you're special doesn't depend on what another person thinks. That has to come from inside. You seem like an intelligent young woman, and you're obviously quite confident in your sexuality." Her lips turn down a hint at the edges. "To be honest, that's something I wish I had."

She looks sad, so I reach out and squeeze her arm. "You are stunningly beautiful..." I pause for her name.

"Ophelia."

"You are drop-dead gorgeous, Ophelia. There's no reason you shouldn't have all the confidence in the world."

"Oh, honey," she laughs. "I'm way past my prime."

Releasing her, I cross my arms over my chest. "Says who?"

Her perfect eyebrows wing upward. "Society."

"Fuck society. Age is just a number, and no one gets to decide what you do with your body except for you."

Ophelia laughs. "Oh my, you are refreshing, er... Sorry, I know a lot of things about you but not your name."

"Nicolette," I answer, feeling a blush creep up my neck when I think about all the things this woman overheard. She literally knows the state of my asshole when I'm thinking about getting fucked.

"Thank you, Nicolette. I needed that pep talk." She dusts off her manicured hands. "Nothing like a little bit of shared girl power in the restroom to get the day started."

"Amen."

She blinks her pretty brown eyes and regards me. "Are you going to be okay, Nicolette?"

"Oh, sure. Just a momentary freak-out. I'm fine."

Ophelia nods. "Good. Just be careful with your young man, Nicolette. Commitment-phobes are difficult to change. Many a woman has tried and failed. Protect your heart at all costs." Her smile is back, this time looking mischievous. "To paraphrase Johnny Cochran, if he doesn't commit, you must quit. Honey, if he doesn't see your worth, then fuck him. Pardon my French."

I can't help my giggle at this elegant woman dropping the f-bomb. "Oh, you don't even need to apologize for that, given the things you heard me say. I spoke French and then some. I was practically multilingual."

"That's all right, dear. I raised boys, so there's not much I haven't heard before." She rolls her eyes. "Good lord, those three. The trouble they got into when they were younger. Remington was wild as a march hare in high school but calmed down in college and got serious."

Did she say Remington? And three sons? A pit begins to open up in my stomach as Ophelia continues her reminiscing.

"Phoenix was mostly the instigator, and I'm not being unkind by saying that. He'll tell you himself. I was always happening upon some booby trap or other after he and his twin watched *Home Alone*. It was a complete madhouse at times."

Phoenix? Twin? This has to be a coincidence. Surely...

"And what is his twin's name?" I croak out, bracing myself for the answer.

"Helix. Ah, he's such a sweet and smart young man. Now he's the kind of man you need to be looking for. So polite and unassuming." Ophelia straightens her jacket and pats her perfectly coiffed dark hair as I attempt to not throw up. "It was so nice to meet you, Nicolette, but I'm headed home. Good luck with everything today. I hope you get everything you wish for."

And she's gone in a puff of flowery perfume, leaving me standing in the restroom with my mouth on the floor.

I'm going to have to leave the country, I decide. Or better yet, the planet. I could probably qualify for one of those civilian space flights. I could study the effects of space on my brain as I contemplate my life choices.

But that would probably take a while to get set up. No, I need something more immediate. Perhaps I could sneak into the kitchen and stick my head in the oven. Asphyxiation generally takes less than five minutes. Restaurant kitchens are chaotic places, and no one would notice a convulsing woman with her head in an oven, right?

Fuck me with an Erlenmeyer flask. This is a nightmare.

I take a cleansing breath and try to think of a solution besides imminent death or launching myself into space. Okay. All right. I'll just remain calm and go out there and tell Helix I'm not feeling well and would like to go home. Then I'll just let this thing between us fizzle and die.

Because if we date, it's inevitable that he'll want to introduce me to his mother. I've already met most of the rest of his family, so that would be the next logical step. But I can never face that woman again. I discussed her son's big cock and called him depraved, for fuck's sake.

Polite and unassuming young man, my ass.

Ophelia said she was leaving, so I'll give it another minute and then put this hastily formed plan into place.

And I'll never have to see Helix's mother again.

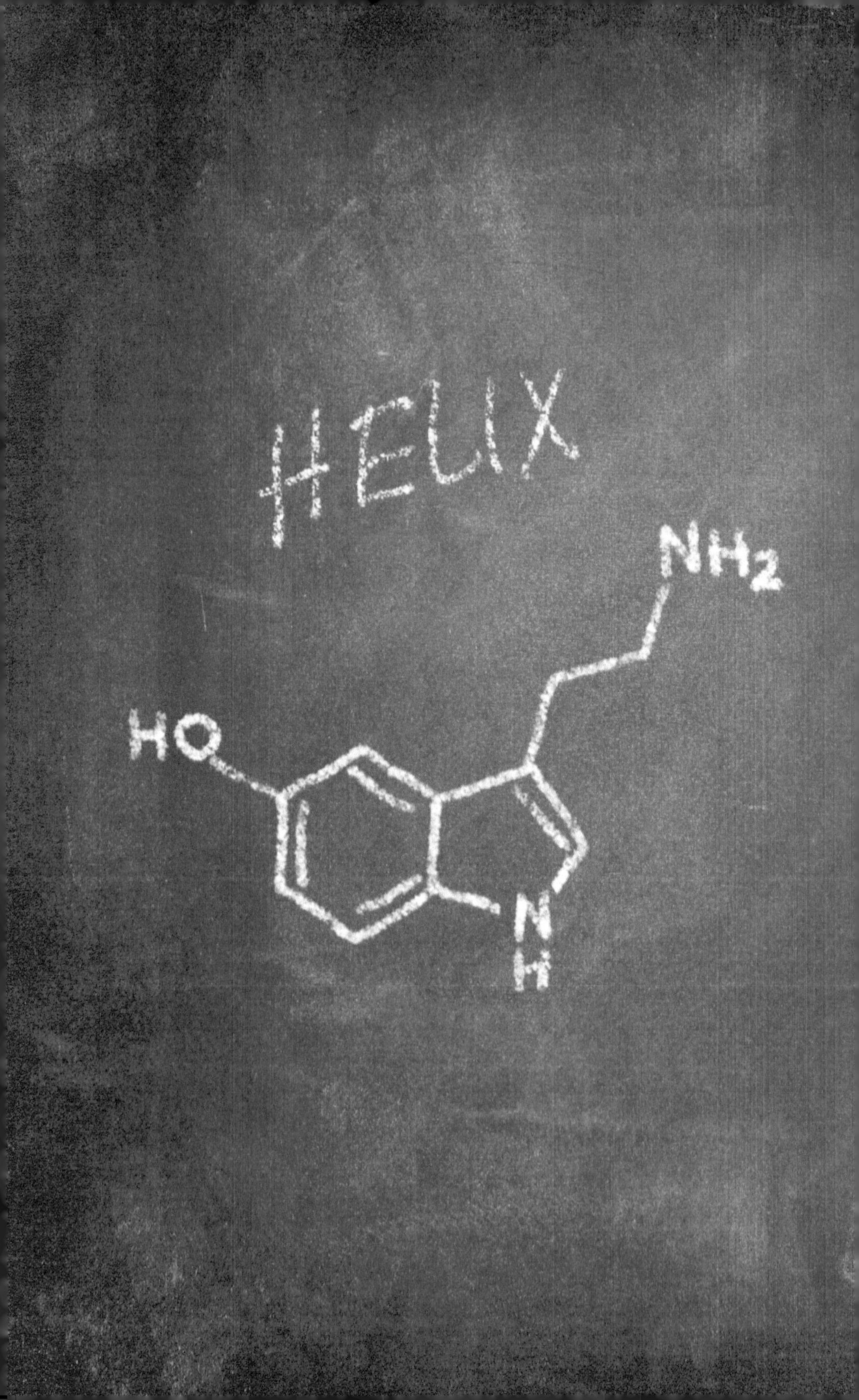

HEUX

Chapter Twenty-Seven

THE DREADED GERANIUM STORY

I glance around the restaurant for the millionth time and then check my phone. Nicolette has been in the restroom for a long time, and I'm starting to get worried.

Maybe she's sick. Oh, or maybe she started her period and doesn't have any supplies with her. I should probably text her. If it's her time of the month, I can dart out right quick and grab her whatever she needs from the 7-11 down the block. Come to think of it, she was wearing white shorts, so I might need to grab her a new pair if that's the problem. I'm sure I could find something in one of the boutiques around here.

I lift my phone to text her when a flash of familiar dark hair catches my eye. "Mom?"

My mother turns around, and her face lights up. "Helix!" I stand and bend to kiss her cheek when she walks over.

"Mom, you look so pretty today," I tell her, running a hand down the sleeve of her Chanel suit. "Did you already eat?"

"Thank you, sweetheart, and yes. I dined with Grace this morning, but she's already gone. Had to pick up her grandson."

I pull out one of the chairs for her and gesture for her to take a seat. "Can I get you a mimosa or something?"

She sits, and her eyes light on the table, draped with a white linen cloth and displaying two mimosa glasses. "Oh, are you here with someone?"

My grin stretches across my face at the thought of Nicolette. "I'm here with my lab manager, the one we talked about before."

"Ahhh, the 'lab manager,'" she says, actually doing quotation marks in the air. My mother's brown eyes twinkle. "What is her name again?"

"Nicolette." I straighten my napkin in my lap. "She is... god, she's so amazing. I really think—" I cut off when I notice the expression on my mom's face has transformed from one of delight to one of... horror? "What's wrong?"

"Oh. What's wrong? Nothing's wrong. Nothing at all," she says, her words tumbling over each other as her eyes dart nervously around the room. "I really should be going."

She moves to stand, but I place my hand on the back of her chair. "I'd really like you to stay and meet Nicolette. Just for a minute. It's really important to me."

Mom sags back into her chair, her face softening. "It is?"

I nod with conviction. "I think I'm ready to start dating again." My teeth sink into my bottom lip. "For the first time since everything went down five years ago."

Her face seems to melt into acquiescence, and she reaches up to lay her hand on my cheek. "Oh, Helix, honey. That makes me so happy. I worry about you all the time."

A sigh escapes from deep in my lungs. I hate that what happened to me still affects her. "I'm sorry, Mom, but you don't have to worry. Nicolette is a wonderful woman. She's the smartest person I know, and she has the best heart." I swallow hard. "I can't tell you much because it's not my story to tell, and I would never betray her confidence, but she didn't grow up with the kind of love we had as kids. I think she could really use a mother figure like you in her life."

My mother is a marshmallow in Chanel right now. If there's one thing she's a pro at, it's caring for children, and she abhors the thought of a kid being mistreated. Even when she was scolding us—and rightly so in all cases—we never felt anything less than loved.

"Oh dear," she says, pressing her fingertips against her pink lips as tears well in her eyes. "Of course I'll stay and meet your friend."

I glance around and see her. *Finally*. Nicolette looks amazing in a pretty mint-green floral top and long white walking shorts. I stand and take two long strides to greet her.

"Hey, are you okay? I was beginning to get worried." I link my fingers through hers.

"I'm fine. I was just... washing my hands."

I laugh. "Well they should be plenty clean by now." We take two steps, and she freezes in her tracks, her gaze trained on the back of my mother's head. With her eyes popped wide, she emits a squeaky sound.

Wait, does she think I invited some random woman to sit at our table or something? "It's okay. It's just my mom," I explain. "She happened to be walking by, and I spotted her. Come on and I'll introduce you."

"I... uh... your mother?"

"Yes, the woman who birthed me," I clarify with a laugh. "You're both acting really weird."

"We are?" she asks, her voice way higher-pitched than normal.

I step in front of her to catch her agitated eyes, pretty sure I understand what's going on here. Meeting someone's family can be nerve-racking, and while I don't think my mother is intimidating, I can see where some may think so because she's wealthy and always perfectly put-together.

"I promise this was not some kind of ambush or anything. My mother being here is completely by coincidence, though not completely unusual. She and her friend Grace come here a couple times a month." My fingers brush along her tense jawline. "I'm sorry, baby. I didn't even think that this might be awkward for you. I didn't mean to be pushy. I can tell her we'll catch up with her another time."

Nicolette's shoulders deflate, and she shakes her head, making her curls bounce. "No, that would be rude. I'm sorry. I was just... startled." She smiles but still looks nervous. "I'd love to meet her."

"Mom," I say, touching her shoulder lightly while still holding onto Nicolette's hand. I don't want her to be apprehensive around my mother. She really is a sweetheart. "I'd like to introduce you to Dr. Nicolette Bell."

My mother stands and turns with a big smile on her face. "Nicolette," she purrs, "how lovely to meet you. I'm Ophelia Oakley-Hale, and I've heard only good things about you. Please call me Ophelia. Or Mom."

Okay, well, that might be laying it on a little thick with the *call me Mom* thing, but whatever. I release Nicolette's hand when my mother pulls her close and kisses both her cheeks. And it looks like she whispers something, though I can't imagine what. They've never even met before.

"Ophelia, it's nice to meet you as well. You've raised such a wonderful son, and I know you're proud of him."

"I'm glad you've been enjoying him," my mom says, and Nicolette lets out a high-pitched giggle that's completely uncharacteristic of her. My mother joins in, and I feel like I'm missing something. "Please, sit down. I promise I won't stay and interrupt your date for long."

Nicolette rounds the table and sits in the chair to my right, while Mom is on my left. I place a reassuring hand on Nicolette's knee because she's still acting a bit sketchy.

"I apologize for taking so long in the restroom."

My mother waves a hand and shakes her head. "Don't think a thing of it. Sometimes it takes us women a while, and you never know what kind of interesting people you're going to meet in a public restroom." The women share a smile while I eyeball them both suspiciously. "Now, tell me every little thing about you."

Nicolette details her educational and work highlights, which are impressive to say the least. "Brilliant!" Mom trills. "That makes me so happy. I love seeing women being successful in STEM careers."

"Nicolette was also the keynote speaker at the American Academy of Clinical Biochemistry conference in L.A. earlier this year," I brag.

Mom reaches across the table and pats Nicolette's hand. My girl is slowly relaxing, which makes me relax as well.

"That is so impressive. What do your parents do, dear?"

Nicolette glances at me, and I give her a soft smile. Maybe she's nervous about coming from a blue-collar background, but honestly,

Mom doesn't care about stuff like that. Yes, she has a lot of high-society acquaintances, but some of her closest friends are blue-collar.

"My pop runs a hardware store, and my mother helps him."

Mom beams. "A family-run business. I love that, and I bet it's wonderful having a father who is good around the house. I'm not particularly handy with household repairs, but I can use a screwdriver like a boss."

We all laugh, and I add, "Mom has been very impressed with herself since she replaced all the light-switch covers in her house without help from anyone."

"And the electrical plug covers," she adds, giving me a playful glare for teasing her.

"Ophelia, tell me all of Helix's most embarrassing childhood stories," Nicolette requests, and Mom brightens.

"Oh, where to begin?"

I groan, but they both ignore me as my mother begins spilling the tea.

An hour and a half later, I've pretty much been relegated to simply an accessory at this table. My mother and my girl are laughing their asses off, most of it at my expense, but I'm not mad about it. They're getting along swimmingly.

We shared The Good Egg's famous bacon flight, and then Nicolette and I ordered our meals since Mom had already eaten. Nicolette had one mimosa before switching to bloody marys due to her propensity for falling asleep after too much wine, and my mother drank three mimosas. Both of them are adorably tipsy.

At one point, Nicolette invited my mother to go to something called Cowboy Yoga, which I'm assuming is yoga done on horseback or something? I have no idea, but Mom had heard about it before and seems excited to go with Nicolette. I tune back into the conversation.

"So there I am in the garden section trying to pick out some new flowers with two rambunctious four-year-olds."

Christ on a cracker. I hope to god she's not going to tell the dreaded geranium story. But my hopes are dashed with her next sentence.

"And I look down to find Helix peeing in a pot of geraniums."

I shake my head as they howl. "No, he didn't," Nicolette wheezes, pulling a stalk of celery from her most recent drink and nibbling on the end of it. "What did you do?"

Mom shakes her head. "I had to buy them of course. Planted them in the front yard, and let me tell you, that plant grew bigger than any of the other ones that year."

"My urine has magical powers," I say dryly, sending them into another fit of giggles.

My mother smacks my arm. "I swear, raising boys should come with an instruction manual, including an entire chapter on their fascination with their penises."

"Moooom," I groan, covering my eyes with my hand.

She smacks me again. "If Helix and Phoenix were outside, they were whipping them out and peeing on something. I was so afraid they were both going to end up having that fetish when they grew up. What's it called, dear? A golden sprinkler?" She looks at me with guileless eyes.

For fuck's sake.

"The term is golden shower, Mom, and I think we're done here." I wave frantically at the server. "Check, please!"

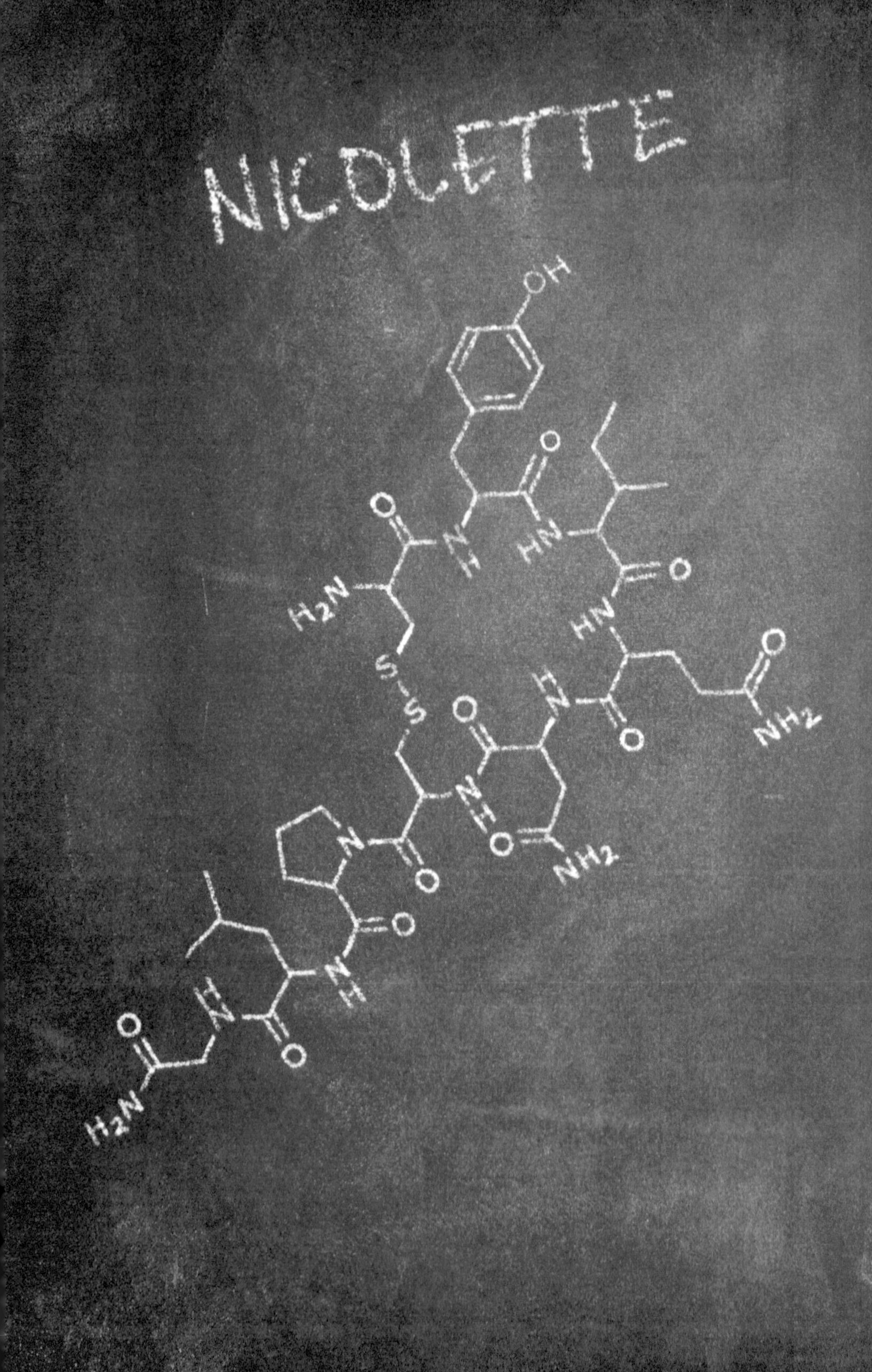
NICOLETTE
OH
H2N
S
S
O
O
N
HN
HN
HN
N
H
O
O
O
O
O
O
NH2
NH2
NH2

Chapter Twenty-Eight

IS THAT A DILDO?

I glance over at Helix, doing my level best not to drool. He's been poring over paperwork for the past two hours, and his hair is sticking up in places from where he ran his fingers through it. His shirt is halfway untucked, and he's completely, delightfully mussed.

He's currently using the centrifuge while some of the lab assistants sort samples. Looking over and catching me staring, he gives me a subtle wink.

"Hey, you guys can go ahead and knock off early for lunch," he tells the assistants.

They don't argue for a second, cleaning their areas and heading downstairs. Which leaves me alone in the lab with Helix. As soon as they're gone, he locks the door and saunters over.

"Dr. Bell, why aren't you working?" he asks sternly.

I brush his crotch with a teasing drift of my hand. "Because I'm distracted by this big... sample."

He laughs and pins me against the lab table with his hips. "I want to have my wicked way with you on this table, but first I wanted to talk to you. I planned to during brunch last weekend, but you and my mother were too busy talking shit about me."

I roll my bottom lip out. "Aww, poor little Helix got his feelings hurt? Maybe you should punish me." He lifts an eyebrow at the hopefulness in my voice.

"Oh, I fully intend to, but that will be later when you're least expecting it."

"For the record, golden sprinklers as a punishment is a hard limit for me."

Helix's expression goes flat. "I don't like you very much right now."

My hips press forward against his growing erection. "Your big sample says otherwise."

His only response is a slow, deep kiss that makes my toes tingle in my loafers. "I do like you, Nicolette," he says, pulling away and making eye contact. "I want to date you. I've had trust issues in the past, but I want to try and make this work if that's something you want too. You'll just have to be patient with me while I work through how to be in a healthy relationship."

The organ inside my chest constricts at his words. "That's exactly what I want. And I can be patient. Everyone has past hurts, and that's okay. We can work through them together."

His blue eyes are so soft as he searches my face. "I think I'm falling for you, and it scares the shit out of me."

Before I can respond, his phone rings and he curses before pulling it from his pocket and frowning at the display. "It's Reecie's pre-school. Phoenix is out of town, and she's staying with me for two days, so I need to take this."

"Of course," I say, rubbing my hand up and down his bicep as he answers with a clipped hello.

He listens for about a minute before responding with, "I'll be right there."

"What's wrong?" I ask, watching him pocket his phone and shrug off his lab jacket.

"Reece is sick. It's just a sore throat so probably nothing serious, but I need to take her to the pediatrician because she might need antibiotics."

"Go," I say, taking the jacket from him. "I'll handle the lab and call Phoenix for you. He'll need to call the doctor's office and give you permission to bring Reecie in for treatment."

Helix shakes his head. "You don't have to call him. I have power of attorney for her when he's out of town or in case anything ever happens to him. We had the paperwork drawn up the day after she was born." He grabs my face and kisses me hard. "Thank you, baby."

And then he's out the door, leaving me flabbergasted in his wake. I can't even imagine being so close to another person that you'd put that kind of trust in them. I certainly don't have that kind of relationship with Angelica. I wouldn't trust her to look after a house plant.

But the Hale family is different. They have a mutual bond and respect for each other that I'm not sure I've ever experienced. To be honest, I'm a little jealous, but then I remember how open and welcoming they all were to me. His mother included, despite the embarrassing freak-out scene she witnessed in that restroom.

After our initial awkwardness at seeing each other at the brunch table with Helix, all those walls seemed to fade away. Might have been the mimosas and bloody marys lending their boozy support to the situation, but it's more likely because she's a genuinely nice person.

I took Ophelia to Cowboy Yoga on Monday evening, and thankfully I had no more gaseous interruptions. She absolutely loved it, though she blushed through the entire class.

Taking a seat on one of the padded stools, I get to work on some of the fragrance additives we were working on and wait for word from Helix about his niece.

Two hours later, I'm alone in the lab. I'd sent the assistants down to the microbiology lab to do some cultures on our next mascara. Mascara tubes are notorious places for bacteria to reside, so it's a struggle to find a formula that's as antimicrobial as possible while also being gentle enough for the sensitive eye areas.

The door creaks open, and I swivel around in my chair to find Helix with Reece on his hip. She has a ring of what looks like chocolate ice cream around her mouth, and she's holding a giant teddy bear.

"Hi, Nicolette," she says, her little voice raspy. "I got a shot, so

Uncle Helix got me ice cream and a teddy bear and new shoes." I notice a bag from the Nike store hanging off Helix's arm.

"New shoes make pretty much anything better," I tell the cutie pie, standing and walking toward them.

Helix backs up a step into the hallway. "It's strep throat, so she's contagious. You might not want to get too close."

Chuckling, I say, "I did a rotation in emergency medicine. I'm pretty much immune to everything except the bubonic plague." I reach forward and press my hand against Reece's forehead. She's pretty hot but not dangerously so. "How are you feeling, sweet girl?"

Her face is a precious pout. "Pretty icky, but Uncle Helix said I could sit in his office and draw. That way I don't spread germs to all the lab people."

Her uncle kisses her forehead. "I think we have some popsicles in the refrigerator if you want one later. Let's get you settled. I'll leave you my phone because your daddy said he would call you again in about an hour to check on you." He turns around, and I giggle at the sparkly dragon backpack slung over his shoulder.

I'm still laughing when Helix returns a few minutes later. "What's so funny?" he asks, washing his hands and forearms at the sink.

"You look cute with a glittery backpack."

He cuts me a glare. "Keep on pushing me, woman."

I bite into my bottom lip and wait for him to join me. "I think I solved the issue with the new fragrance," I tell him, trying to contain my excitement. "Well, *we* solved it because I used what you came up with." I flip through my notebook and hold up a page of his scrawled writing.

He takes it from me and scowls. "I thought this one didn't work."

"It didn't by itself but flip to the last six pages. That's what I've been working on while you were gone."

He does and I watch as his face changes. Lowered brows, raised brows, lips twisted to one side and then the other before rolling in between his teeth. Finally, his lips part, and his eyes widen. He flips through the pages again, and a smile broadens across his face.

"Dammit, Nic, this is fucking brilliant." His eyes meet mine. "*You're* brilliant."

"You are too. It was your original idea that spurred my own."

He shakes his head in awe. "But your brain is at another level. I never would have thought of this in a million years," he tells me, flapping the notebook in my face.

"It was a team effort, and I think we should apply for a patent together."

"This was your baby though. You thought of the idea for it before you ever even came here."

"And you gave me the resources to make it happen." I bite my cheek, feeling a little emotional. "Including your confidence in me. I probably wouldn't have pursued it if not for you."

Helix picks me up around the waist and spins me in a circle, his eyes sparkling with happiness. "You really want us to apply for the patent together?"

"I really do," I laugh, cupping his face with my hands and kissing him. "There's no one I'd rather share it with."

He puts me down and begins pacing, his fingers tapping against his lips. This is what he does when he's deep in thought. "We'll have to do some testing first."

"And clinical trials, of course," I add.

"Yes. We should have the patent ready to be filed by spring of next year."

"Your birthday is in March. What if we file it then?"

I can tell he's touched by the suggestion because he binds his lips together and nods tightly. "Okay."

"I know you're dying to run some analyses on it, so go ahead. I sent everyone else to the micro lab to work on mascara so we could have the place to ourselves." I hand him a small vial of clear liquid.

"I also want to see if I can replicate it. It seems like it would be pretty easy to mass produce."

"It is. Production wouldn't need to buy any new equipment, so it's definitely cost-effective."

He nods knowingly. "And that's the thing. So many good ideas end up on the drawing room floor because the product would cost more to make than the market allows."

I don't hover while he gets to work, instead busying myself around the lab. I went to check on Reece a couple times, and last time I did, she was curled up in Helix's big leather chair fast asleep. I removed my jacket and balled it up beneath her head as a makeshift pillow.

Now I'm beside Helix as his hands work beneath the ventilation hood, my head level with his shoulder. I catch the scent of chlorine and ask, "Do you swim?"

He glances down at me. "Every day. Why?"

"I can smell chlorine on you sometimes."

"I have a saltwater pool, but of course it has a chlorine generator."

"Right, the chlorine is separated from the salt through electrolysis." I eye him up and down. "You have a perfect swimmer's body. Did you ever swim competitively?"

His hands freeze for a long moment before he answers, and I wonder if I said something wrong. "I did when I was younger, but now I just do it for exercise."

We're interrupted by a squawking sound and then a little voice. "Dr. Uncle Helix, come in, please."

He grins and motions toward his hip. "Will you grab the walkie-talkie out of my pocket?" I pull out a Hello Kitty device and depress the button, holding it close to his mouth. "Go for Dr. Uncle Helix."

"This is Doodlebug. I believe you said something about popsicles earlier? Over."

He chuckles, and I push the button again so he can talk. "Of course. What kind would you like? Over."

"I'm not picky. As long as it's red or pink. Over."

"Give me just a second, Doodle. I need to get my gloves off and wash up. Over."

"I can get her a popsicle," I offer. "You're right in the middle of this. If it sits too long, you'll have to start over."

"Are you sure?" he asks, brows lowering over his bright blue eyes.

I pat his ass. "Positive. The sooner you can get done, the sooner you can take Miss Priss home."

He scratches his nose on his shoulder. "Okay, thanks. I hated to bring her with me, but when I called the nanny, she has strep too. It's apparently going around, and she said she feels like crap."

"Aw, poor lady. Strep can knock an adult on their ass, while kids bounce back a little easier. Reecie should feel better tomorrow after the shot, but if you want to stay home with her, I'll keep things afloat here."

"Thanks," he says gratefully. "Though I'm pretty sure Phoenix is going to show up back in Houston tonight. He almost had a conniption fit when I told him she wasn't feeling good. I assured him I could handle it, but I understand where he's coming from. She's his world."

"He seems like such a good dad," I say, heading to the door and calling over my shoulder. "Be back in a few."

I enter Helix's office holding a cherry popsicle, one of those long ones in a plastic tube. I've already snipped off the top and squished it with my fingers so it would be soft for Reece. I find her at the desk, drawing away on a small sketch pad, her tongue poking out one corner of her mouth.

She looks up and motions to me with a pencil. "Come on in and have a seat," she offers, sounding like a pint-sized CEO. She is truly freaking adorable.

"Your red popsicle, Madam Doodlebug," I tell her in a formal voice as I hand over the treat wrapped in a paper napkin.

She takes a long slurp, and her eyes widen. "Mmm, cherry." She licks her lips and asks, "Is Uncle Helix your boyfriend?"

Well. Uhhhh.

"We're dating each other," I say evasively.

"Okay," she says easily, taking another suck of her popsicle. "I'll call you Auntie Nicolette then."

My heart melts like an ice cube on a Houston sidewalk. "Whatever you want to call me is fine," I tell her.

"I don't have a mom," she informs me, very matter-of-factly. "Do you have a mom?"

"I do."

"Is she nice?"

That's a loaded question, kiddo.

I'm not sure how to answer without lying, so I keep it neutral. "She's not the nicest mom in the world, but she's not the worst either."

"Okay," she says, holding the popsicle in her mouth with one hand and picking up her pencil with the other. I sit in the chair across from her and watch her draw two stick figures, one taller than the other, as she intermittently sucks on the frozen treat.

She works diligently, adding curls to the shorter figure, and then she gives us both glasses. I think I know where she's going with this.

"Is that Uncle Helix and me?" I ask, and she nods before adding two circles to my body.

"Those are your boobs," she informs me before sticking the popsicle back in her mouth and adding a lot more hair to my head. I have to turn my head and stare at the wall for a long moment to hide my laughter.

When I look at her drawing again, Helix is holding something long and... *Sweet Jesus! Is that a dildo?*

"What is your uncle holding?" I ask tentatively, almost afraid to hear the answer.

"A test tube," she tells me, in her best *duh* voice before handing me the popsicle. "Here, hold this."

I diligently do as I'm asked, relieved that the drawing is still relatively PG rated. Reece tears out the picture with the utmost care and smiles with red-stained teeth as she holds it out.

"You can have it."

"Thank you," I tell her, switching the popsicle for the sweet drawing. "I'll put it on my refrigerator at home."

"Really?" She seems pleased by this. "You want to see some of my other work?"

"I would love to."

She flips through her sketch pad and shows me various drawings she's done, mostly of her family, including her dad, aunt, uncles, and grandparents.

"Who is that one?" I ask, pointing at a stick figure with boobs and a huge bubble head.

"That's Jordie. She's wearing her helmet." Reece looks up at me with intent seriousness. "I think Jordie is so pretty. Do you think my daddy thinks she's pretty?"

Yikes! Not sure where to go with that one, so I go for diplomatic.

"I think everyone thinks Jordie is pretty."

Helix's phone rings and Reece checks the display. "That's my dad. Again." She answers and puts it on speakerphone. "Hi, Daddy."

"Baby." His voice sounds frantic. "How are you feeling?"

"I'm good. Auntie Nicolette brought me a cherry popsicle, and it feels nice on my throat."

I cringe, hoping Phoenix doesn't think I prompted her to say call me that. "Hi, Phoenix," I say sheepishly.

"Nicolette, thank god you're there," he gushes, sounding relieved and panicked at the same time. "How is she? You're a medical doctor, right? Do you think my Reecie is okay?"

I press my hand to her forehead again and notice she seems marginally cooler than a few hours ago. "I think the shot helped. Her temp is lower than earlier, and the pharmacy just delivered some meds for her. I'll make sure she takes it."

Phoenix's voice calms a bit. "Okay, thank you. I'm trying to get home, but there's a storm here, and they won't let the plane take off."

"You're being fussy, Daddy," Reece pipes up. "Uncle Helix said we're going to chillax and watch movies. Oh, and Dr. Clark said I can swim when the sun goes down because the cool water will feel nice."

"Okay, baby, but don't overdo it. I'm so sorry I'm not there. Daddy is trying so hard to get back. I promise." His voice sounds full, like he's holding back tears.

"Fussy, Daddy," she sings in a playful but scolding tone, and I can hear him chuckle on the other end.

"Sorry, Reecie."

"Okay, I'm gonna let you go," she says in her grown-up voice, drumming her fingers on the desktop. "I have a lot of work to do here."

"Okay, baby girl. I love you so much."

"I love you so mucher," she replies sweetly and then hangs up the phone. "That was my daddy. He can be so dramatic sometimes."

I stand and kiss the top of her head. "It's just because he loves you so much. You're very lucky to have a daddy like him. I'm going to get your medicine. I'll be back in a few minutes."

"Okey dokey," she says, tipping up the tube holding the popsicle and draining it. "I hope it's not the bubble gum flavored medicine. That one is gross."

After I'm done, I report back in to Helix. "Gave Reece her medicine and put a sticky note on it with the time so you'll know when to give her next dose. Warning, it's the bubble gum flavor and she doesn't like it, but I got her a Sprite from the vending machine to wash it down. I hope that was okay."

He takes his gloves off and tosses them in the trash before kissing my forehead. "It's fine. Phoenix lets her have clear sodas sometimes, and I say anything that gets her to take the medicine is okay."

"Good because I gave her a vodka chaser afterward."

He rolls his eyes at my ridiculousness and goes to the sink to wash up. "I'll go check on her."

"Phoenix called while I was in there, and she totally handled him like a champ."

"She's good at that," Helix says, scrubbing his hands with the precision of a surgeon.

"And she drew me a picture of us." I hold up the masterpiece for his viewing.

"Your boobs look great. Thank god she didn't decide to draw me anatomically correctly." He leans over and inspects it more closely. "Wait, am I holding a dildo?"

"It's a test tube," I inform him. "Also, she started calling me Auntie Nicolette. I didn't tell her to."

His smile is soft on my face. "It's okay. Maybe it will be true one day."

And with that, he dries his hands and walks out of the lab, leaving me stunned by his last sentence.

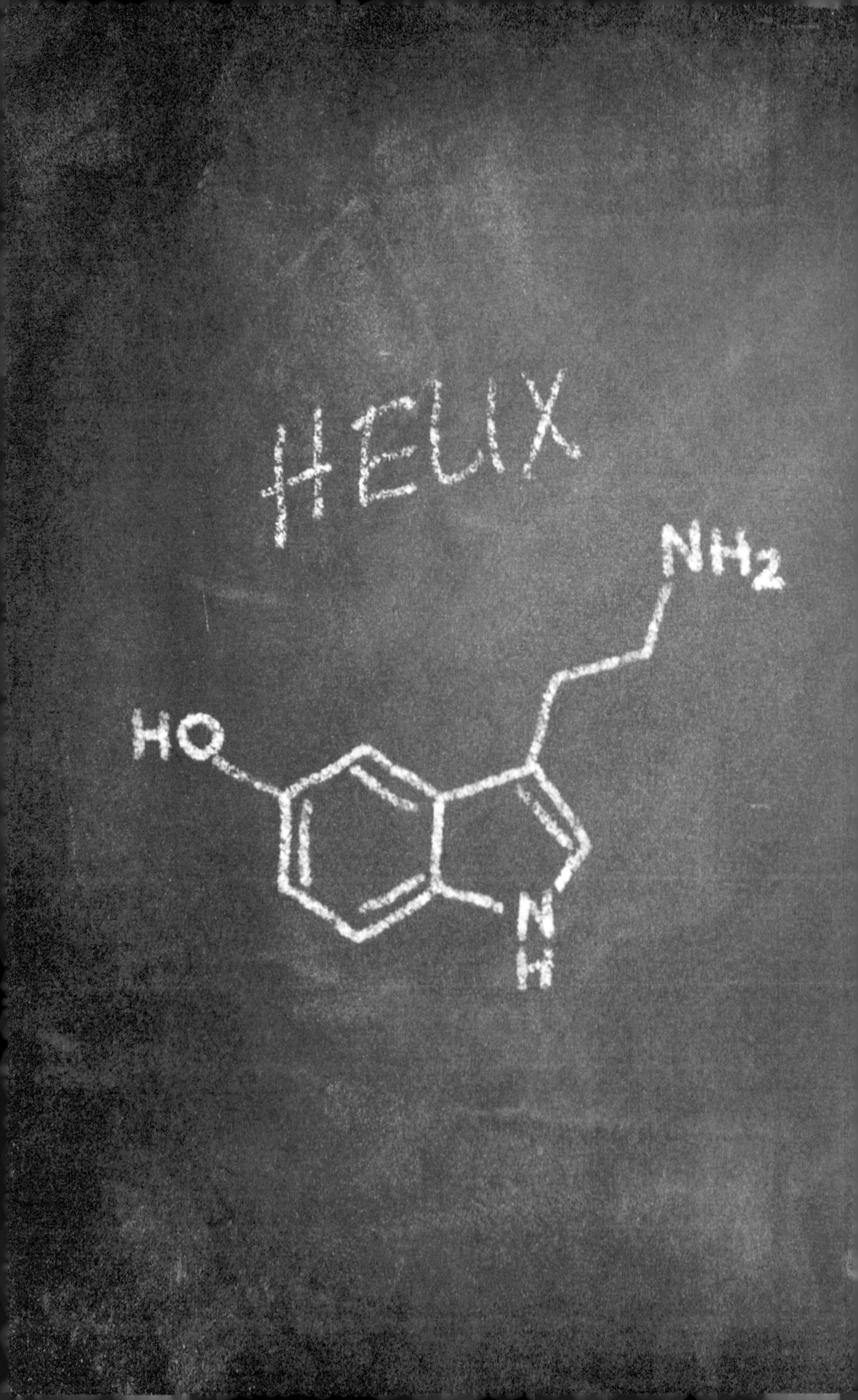

HELIX
NH2
HO
N
H

Chapter Twenty-Nine

THE BALL-TICKLING BRAT

It's been a month since Nicolette and I began dating out in the open. I told my father first since he's the CEO, and then I spoke with HR to inform them that we're in a relationship.

Relationship. That's a word I never again thought I would use about myself, but here we are. And it's been easier than expected. Because of her.

Nicolette isn't pushy or clingy. I never feel pressured by her to spend time together, and that makes me want to be with her all the time. She is absolutely my dream girl, and I'm crazy about her.

We go together to the NICU each week, and I'm so grateful to her for introducing me to the baby cuddling program. Is it hard? Yeah, some days it's really fucking hard, but it fulfills something inside me when I'm able to calm an infant who just need someone to love it.

I feel like I'm a thousand pounds lighter now that I'm in a happy and healthy relationship. Our sex life is amazing, and that definitely contributes to my good mood. The oxytocin and serotonin float freely through my brain in an almost constant flow.

On the work front, the new fragrance development is going better than expected. We've run some preliminary trials to get a feel for how it affects various individuals, and the results have been more than encouraging. They've been blind studies, so we don't tell the participants what the expected effects are because that could skew the results. We simply give them a blank spreadsheet with times listed down the side and ask them to write down how they feel during the day while wearing the fragrance, as well as a blank space at the bottom for comments.

Of course, the results are better first thing in the morning, right after they apply it, but the effects seem to last a full twelve hours. Nicolette and I spend our mornings poring over the results from the previous day, both of us practically giddy when we see the words we're hoping for.

I feel so good while wearing this.

My soul feels warm, like someone just gave me a big hug.

This is liquid comfort.

Can I have a gallon of this stuff?

It's like that feeling I get when my husband hugs me.

I stack yesterday's reports and place them in a manila folder before dating it and placing it on the corner of my desk. Then I press the button on my intercom that goes directly to her office phone.

"Hey, can you come in here?"

Our offices are right next to each other with a connecting door in between. I don't think I've ever even unlocked it before I started dating Nicolette, but now it remains open all the time. She comes through a second later.

"Why didn't you just holler?" she asks, setting a fist on her hip. "I'm right next door, so there was no need to use the damn intercom."

I lean back in my chair and rest my elbow on the arm of it, brushing my thumb along my bottom lip. "I wanted you to feel summoned."

Understanding dawns on her face, and her smile turns coquettish as she closes the door behind her. "Oh, did you? And why did you summon me, Dr. Hale?"

My eyes rake up and down her body, letting her feel the heat of my gaze. The skirt she's wearing is completely work-appropriate, as are her closed-toe flats. Her blouse is a rosy pink that matches the blush rising up her cheeks right now. She looks sexy as fuck, even in her prim clothing.

"What kind of panties are you wearing, Dr. Bell?"

She dips her chin, feigning shyness, and says, "White lacy ones, sir."

I waggle my fingers in a come-hither gesture. "Give them to me."

Without hesitation, she leans against my desk and pulls off the smallest panties I've ever seen, handing them over to me. I hold them up and glare at her.

"This little scrap of lace is not compliant with the company dress code," I inform her, putting a distinct chill in my voice.

Nicolette bows her head. "I'm sorry, Dr. Hale. I didn't think you would find out."

"Well, I did, and now you're in big fucking trouble." I jerk my chin upward. "Come stand between my legs while I try to figure out what to do with you."

She moves quickly with a pep in her step. She likes this little game, and fuck if I don't too. I spread my knees wide, and Nicolette stands between them, watching as I lift her underwear to my nose. I growl at the delicious scent of her.

"It smells like you're aroused. Do you think that sounds like professional work behavior?"

"No, sir, but it's hard to control myself around—"

I lift one brow when she cuts herself off. "Around whom?"

Her cherry-red lips form a whisper. "You."

"Is that so?" She nods, and I stare at her for a long moment as she squirms. "The way I see it, there are only two options."

"I'd be happy to hear any suggestions you may have, Dr. Hale."

Fuck, she's good at this role-playing thing.

I recline in my chair and rest my hand on my dick. "Number one, I can jack myself off with these slutty panties of yours and cover them with my cum. Then I will stuff your cum-soaked panties in your mouth to keep you quiet while I bend you over my desk and fuck you stupid."

"And number two?" she asks.

"Number two, you can get on your goddamn knees before me and suck my cock until I come down your throat." I lift one finger when she starts to speak. "And then I'll stuff your panties in your mouth while I bend you over my desk and fuck you stupid. Your choice."

Nicolette taps two fingers against her lips and hums. "Hmmm, it's a hard choice. To be honest, I haven't had my throat fucked in a while, so I'm leaning toward option two."

My face hurts from trying not to smile, but I maintain my stern demeanor. "Option two it is." I slide a hand up the back of her skirt and give her ass a firm squeeze. "Get on your knees for me, Dr. Bell."

She does, and it's the most beautiful sight I've ever seen. We've done a lot of sexy stuff since we started our relationship, including Nicolette wrapping that pretty mouth around my dick, but I always stop her before I come in her mouth because I'm too anxious to get inside her hot little pussy.

But this afternoon, all my fantasies are about to come true.

I nod at my crotch. "Take my dick out and stroke it." She licks her lips and unfastens my pants, pulling the waistband of my boxer briefs down enough to pull out my turgid erection. Her hand wraps around me, and I groan, "That's a good girl."

My fucking cock is dripping, leaking pre-cum down the side of my shaft. Her small hand finds it and uses my natural lubrication to ease the slide of her hand up and down.

"May I lick it?" she asks, looking up at me from beneath long lashes. She's so damn pretty.

I remove her glasses and set them on the desk before dusting the backs of my fingers down her cheek. "You may," I tell her quietly.

The first swipe of her tongue has me clenching the arms of my chair with enough force to break it. "Yeah, just like that, baby." She rolls her tongue around the ridge of my crown and moans her approval. "Do you like how I taste, Dr. Bell?"

She lifts her head only long enough to say, "Yes, sir," and then she's back at it, cleaning me up as quickly as another drop spills from my tip.

I press my head back against the chair and bring her panties to my nose. "Christ," I say on a deep inhale. "Wrap those cherry lips around me and let me fuck up your lipstick."

"I'm wearing Hale's smudge-proof," she says with a smirk.

"Challenge accepted, Dr. Bell," I retort with just as much cockiness. "Now suck my dick."

She does, taking me about halfway before dragging those gorgeous lips up my shaft. On the next downstroke, she goes even deeper, making herself gag.

"Fuck, yes," I pant. "I love hearing you gag on my cock, Dr. Bell."

Nicolette does it again, and I grab her bun with one hand and hold her down. "Take it, baby. Open that throat up for me." She relaxes her throat muscles, letting me slide home. She's hot and tight around my dick, and saliva pools at the corners of her lips.

My hips lift from the seat, fucking her mouth as she sets a quick pace, her head bobbing up and down as I fight for my life to keep from coming already.

I realize we forgot to lock the door, but I'm not too worried about it. None of my employees would dare open my office door without knocking.

However, the CEO of Hale Cosmetics has no such qualms.

"Helix?" my dad says, pushing open the door a little. I freeze with my dick in my girlfriend's mouth and snap my gaze to the door. Luckily, my father pauses, and I hear him say, "Oh, hello, Isla. Yes, I'm just coming to say a quick hello to my son."

"Under the desk," I hissed at Nicolette, and she releases me from her mouth and moves back into the foot space. I glance down to see her wide green eyes staring back at me.

"Great to see you as well," Dad is saying. "Tell your mother hello from me."

I don't have time to button up, so I do the only thing I can do. I slide my chair beneath the desk and hope like hell my father doesn't ask me to stand for some reason.

"Hey, son," he says, and I realize with horror that I'm still holding Nicolette's panties in my hand, so I quickly open a drawer and stuff them inside.

"Hi, Dad. To what do I owe the pleasure?" I say, praying he doesn't notice the strained tenor of my voice.

"Just wanted to check in," he says, taking the seat across from me. *Goddammit.*

I swipe away a layer of sweat from my brow and fold my hands on the top of my desk, attempting to look natural. "Everything is going well here," I tell him.

Dad settles in, and I inwardly curse. *Please leave now so I can continue getting my dick sucked. At work.*

"I can't tell you how pleased I am at the work you've been doing. I just wanted to let you know in person."

I feel a hand slide up my thigh and have to force a smile. "That's really nice, but you could have sent an email," I say, and my father chuckles. My toes curl into my shoes when Nicolette takes my dick in her hand and stuffs it into her mouth.

What the fuck are you doing, queenie? Cut it out.

"I thought this conversation needed a personal touch."

Oh, I'm getting a personal touch right now, Haywood, and it's not from you.

"I appreciate that. I'm guessing you got the latest reports on the fragrance additive?" Maybe if I just chat for a second, he'll leave, and I can turn Nicolette over my knee and paint her ass red, the little shit.

Dad rubs his hands together in glee. "This is so exciting. You and Nicolette really do make a wonderfully innovative team."

The woman in question sucks me so hard, I go cross-eyed, seeing two of my father sitting in front of me.

"I hope we're paying her enough," he continues. "Do you think we should give her a raise?"

This is so fucked up. We're sitting here discussing giving Nicolette an increase in pay while my goddamn cock is in her mouth.

"I think... whatever you think is best," I rasp as she tickles my balls, and *good god almighty! She knows what that does to me.* Women always like to fondle my testicles, rolling them between their fingers or squeezing them, but that does nothing for me. Nicolette is the only one who has ever given me the light touch I need, and it drives me wild.

"Good," Dad says, pleased. "I'll secure that with payroll tomorrow. We definitely want to keep Dr. Bell."

"Agreed," I say because it's the god's honest truth. I can't imagine ever letting this little ball-tickling brat go.

Needing to get my dad out of here, I subtly unlock my phone and send Phoenix a 9-1-1 text. That's the signal we use if one of us needs the other to call with an interruption, though my twin is usually the one summoning me to call so I can get him out of a boring meeting that's droned on too long. Well, he fucking owes me.

A second later, my phone rings, and it's the most glorious sound I've ever heard. Putting on my best apologetic smile, I waggle my phone at my father. "Sorry, Dad. That's Phoenix. We're supposed to have a, uh, a phone meeting about the packaging ideas for the men's skin care line."

"Ah, yes! Another brilliant idea. I'll just get out of your hair." He stands, and I stay seated but reach across the desk to shake his hand, which causes my dick to go deeper into Nicolette's mouth. I hear a little gagging noise, and clear my throat, hoping Dad didn't notice it.

"I'll talk to you tomorrow," I tell him.

"Okay, son." I think he's about to walk out the door, but he turns back. "I'm really happy for you and Nicolette. I think she's a lovely young woman, and you deserve to be happy."

The *lovely young woman* tickles my balls again, and I swear on my life, I'm going to strangle her.

My phone is still ringing so I answer it, saying a quick, "Thanks, Dad. Gotta get this," followed by a "Hey, Phoenix. Thanks for calling."

A chuckle sounds in my ear as my father exits and thankfully closes the door behind him. "Got stuck talking to the old man, huh?" my twin says at the same time Nicolette shoves her mouth down my shaft and does some kind of magical shit with her tongue.

"Goddamn, I'm coming," I groan, grabbing Nicolette's hair and fucking roughly up into her mouth as my head drops back. "That's it, baby. Take it all."

"Holy fucking shit, are you getting a blowie right now?" Phoenix blurts before yelling, "You go, Nicolette!" And then quieter, "Hey, dude, can you put me on speaker?"

"Fuck off," I say, tapping my thumb against the screen to disconnect the call as I spill down Nicolette's slim throat. "God, you're such a bad fucking girl."

"I'm still here," Phoenix chimes in, and I realize I must have missed the button with my thumb. "I think you're supposed to call her a good girl, bro."

I do my best to focus on my phone—*because I'm still fucking coming*

—and disconnect for real this time, relaxing back in the chair while my girl sucks my soul from my body.

When I'm completely dry with my head lolling to the side, Nicolette finally pulls off me and grins from beneath the desk.

"How's my lipstick?"

I look at the smudges around the outside of her mouth and grin. "We might need to work on a blow-job-proof formula."

She kisses my tip and says, "I'll put that on the schedule for next year."

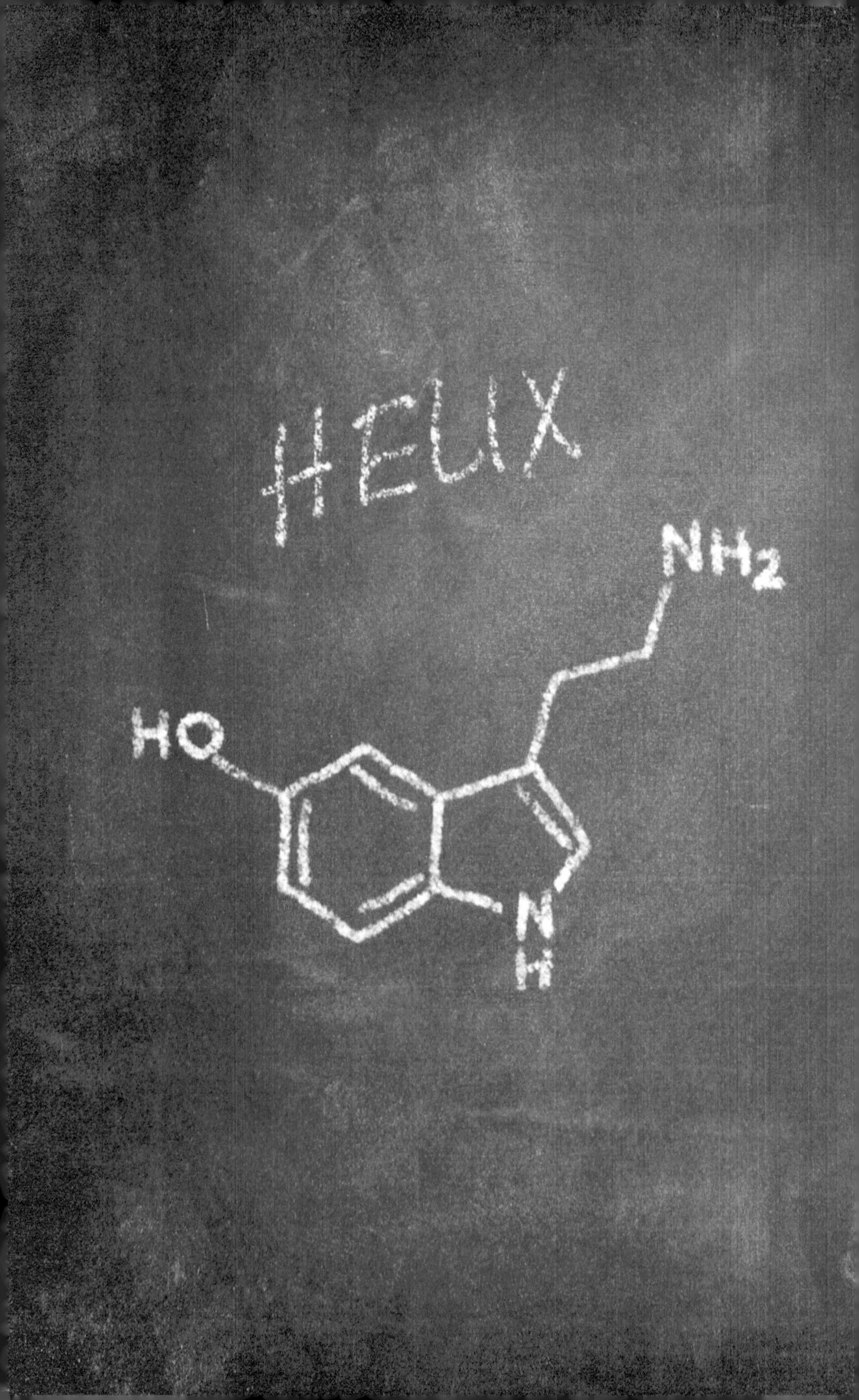

HELIX
HO
NH2
N
H

Chapter Thirty

THE PUSSY SPOON INCIDENT

Now that I've regained the use of my legs, I begin to right my clothes while Nicolette grins smugly at me. "You're coming home with me tonight," I tell her. "I was going to fuck you on my desk, but I think we need more privacy."

A delighted shudder dances through her body, and I smile at her reaction.

"Whatever you say, boss."

Checking over my desk, I see the manila envelope sitting there. "Can you initial those results and then put them in the safe?"

Nicolette grabs a pen and scrawls her initials on the envelope before lifting it. "You want to unlock it for me?"

I nod to my computer. "Use the app on my laptop. The code is seven-nine-four-six-six-four-six-four."

She laughs as she flips open my laptop and gets to work. I can't stop staring at the smudge of her lipstick around her mouth. Not sure I've ever seen anything sexier.

"How did you come up with that number? Is it a combination of birthdays or something?"

"Nope, it spells swimming on a telephone keypad. I've used that combination of numbers for years for secret stuff because it seems random to anyone else. I think Phoenix is the only person I've told about it."

The lockbox door on the wall pops open, and Nicolette slides the envelope inside. "So this is where you keep all the secret formulas?" she asks before closing the door and making sure it's secure.

"Yes, my dad is the only other one with access to the safe, and he has his own code to get in." I stride toward her and grasp her hips. "Let's go home. I have some spanking to get to."

Nicolette is bent over my legs with her ass in the air. I'd planned to do this in my bedroom, but I couldn't seem to wait once we were alone in my home, so we didn't make it farther than the breakfast nook of my kitchen.

"Are you going to tickle my balls again?" I ask, eliciting a giggle from her.

"You know you like it."

I swat her ass again, adding a bit more color to the already red shade. "In front of my father?" I ask.

"Okay, maybe that was a bit much. I promise I won't do that again."

"Good girl," I purr, rubbing her butt softly. My woman seems to love receiving spankings as much as I love giving them to her. Her pussy is dripping wet. Picking up the wooden spoon I grabbed earlier, I show it to her. "Can I use this on you? I promise I won't leave a mark on your perfect skin."

Nicolette twists her head to look up at me. "I trust you."

Her words are simple, but god, they hit me directly in the chest. Because I trust her too, and my trust is a really fucking hard thing to earn.

I lean down and kiss her before gently turning her head to face down at the floor. "Spread your legs wider for me, baby."

She does, putting that pretty cunt on full display for me. I rub the spoon between her legs, letting her feel the smooth surface before I slap her pussy with it.

"Oh!" She jolts, and I rest my forearm along her back to steady her.

"Do you need your safe word?" I ask, my voice gruff with need because I'm so damn turned on right now.

"No, do it again," she breathes.

I clench my jaw and grit my teeth at the perfection of this woman. Three more spoon spanks leave her cunt red and dripping, and I'm about to burst from my pants.

Helping her to stand, I turn her to face away from me and softly kiss her ass cheeks. I have some arnica cream upstairs that I'll smooth on for her later. But for now...

Nicolette is already naked. I'd stripped her as soon as we entered, but I quickly remove my own clothes before hoisting her legs around my waist. Her sex is bare against mine, and she swivels her hips, coating me with her wetness.

"I have condoms upstairs," I tell her, searching her face for a reaction. "Or you could let me take you raw against the wall."

Her breath catches and her eyes widen as we stare at each other for a long moment. Instead of answering with words, she places her hands on my shoulders and lifts herself a few inches before notching her opening over my tip.

"I've never done this without protection," she tells me.

"Me neither," I assure her, and then she's sliding down, using gravity and her desire to sink onto my cock. I have to close my eyes at the sensation. It's like nothing I've ever experienced before. The slickness and heat of her surrounding me is almost too much.

I open my eyes and walk us across the nook to the wall, where I press Nicolette's back. "You feel so fucking good wrapped around me like this."

She grabs the back of my head and slams her mouth to mine as I slide all the way home inside her until our groins are flush. We both moan into the kiss and begin to move. It's slow, each of us taking in these new sensations of pleasure like we've never experienced.

Her inner walls are tight and grip me like a fist. I thought her mouth on me earlier was the ultimate, but this feeling surpasses it a thousand-fold. I break the kiss and watch as she tilts her head against the wall and closes her eyes. I want to demand that she open her eyes and look at me, but she's too damn beautiful like this, lost in her own euphoria. And I'm lost in her.

My hands grip her ass and pull her down onto me as I thrust upward, our bodies meeting with soft slaps of flesh. I adjust my angle a little until I find the spot that has her fingers clenching in my hair.

"Oh god. Right there, Helix. Don't stop, baby."

"Not stopping," I grunt. A team of highly trained Navy SEALs could burst through the door right now, and they wouldn't be able to pull me off my woman.

Mine. Mine, mine, mine. It's a mantra running through my head, and I test the word on my tongue and give it my voice.

"Mine."

Nicolette's eyes pop open, and she stares at me, wide-eyed before her face relaxes into a soft smile. "Yes, I'm yours."

Have there ever been three words as beautiful as those? Screw poetry. Nicolette saying she's mine is my poetry, and I want to give her the same gift.

"And I'm yours." It comes out more easily than I would have expected, but it feels good. My soul feels lighter somehow after saying it.

I push forward with a particularly deep thrust, and Nicolette moans, her hands tugging my hair so hard I may have a bald spot. I don't give a fuck. I do it again and again until she's coming around me with my name on her lips. I don't stop until I feel her fingers loosen and her hands drop to my shoulders as her breaths come out in harsh pants.

But I'm a greedy bastard, and I want more.

Dipping my head, I take one of her nipples into my mouth, and she gasps. I suck her hard, giving her a scrape of my teeth across the tender bud, and she moans, "Oh god, that feels so good."

"Give me another one," I demand, moving to the other breast to give it the same treatment.

"I don't think I can."

I kiss up her chest and neck until we're eye to eye. "You can and you will. Put your hands above your head." She hesitates until I narrow my eyes at her, and then she complies.

Taking both her wrists in one of my hands, I use the other to hold her up while I pull back my hips and give her a long, slow stroke. "Feel that, baby?" I ask. "That's all for you. My cock belongs to only you."

She quivers around my throbbing erection, and I have to hold back my own orgasm until I get another from her. I don't just want it. I *need* her pleasure like I need air.

A dozen more thrusts have us right on the edge, and my entire body tenses as it prepares for the impending orgasm. "I can't hold back. Come for me, my queen."

My words tip her over, and I follow a second later, holding myself deep inside her perfect pussy and letting go. I watch the grimace of ecstasy on Nicolette's face, the way she bares her teeth and squishes her eyes closed. And I fall into the abyss of something I never imagined.

Releasing her hands, I press my forehead against the wall beside her head and inhale the sweat from her skin as a few of her escaped curls tickle the side of my face. I continue to pump gently into her, my release mixing with hers.

I don't know what to do with all these feelings. I don't know how to handle this aching sweetness in my heart. Because...

I think I'm falling in love with this woman.

"Enjoy your bath, queenie," I tell her, brushing my hand across the top of her messy head. "I'll get dinner started, but text me when you're getting out so I can put arnica cream on your butt."

She looks up at me with fire and adoration in her green eyes. "I can put cream on my rear by myself."

I bend and kiss her before capturing her eyes with my own. "I know you can, Nicolette. You are a strong, capable elephant, but I want to take care of you. It's important to me."

Her face softens, and she gives me a nod.

Downstairs, I start making a nice sauce I'll serve over pasta. I have a chef that comes in and meal preps for me once a week, but I want to do this all by myself. For Nicolette.

My mother is of Italian descent, so I use her recipe, adding in all the spices she taught me about when I was little. I liked cooking with my mom, while Phoenix wasn't patient enough to sit still long enough to learn. Being with Mom in her kitchen brings back some of my best memories.

My eyes fall on the breakfast nook, and I see the wooden spoon I'd used to spank Nicolette's pussy. Walking over, I pick it up and rub it against my lips. Then, I go back to the stove and use that spoon to stir the sauce with a big grin on my face.

When Nicolette texts me that she's getting out of the sunken tub, I turn the sauce on low and rest the pussy spoon on the spoonrest before hauling ass upstairs. I find her wrapped in one of my fluffy white towels, the loose curls at her nape damp from the hot bath.

"Okay, can I just say that I love your bathtub? It has spoiled me for baths now."

I lead her to the counter and unwrap the towel. "You are welcome to come bathe at my house any time, baby. Now lean forward." Snagging the arnica cream from the cabinet, I smooth a generous amount over her ass cheeks. The redness is no longer visible, masked by the pretty flush from her time in my luxurious bathtub.

When I'm done, I turn her around and kiss her thoroughly. "Thank you for taking care of me," she says, her voice sweet and vulnerable. I like that she shows me this side of her, so I kiss her again.

"I have sauce on the stove. Come down when you're ready."

Winding my way down the stairs, I hear a noise from my kitchen, but I'm not worried. I know who it is before I even turn the corner. I recognize my twin immediately, even though he's got his back to me.

Phoenix senses me before I say anything—it's a twin thing—and says, "This sauce smells fucking good."

Holy fucking hell. He's holding the pussy spoon and lifting it to his lips.

"Stop!" I yell, rushing over and snatching the spoon from his hand and splattering sauce all over. "Don't eat that."

"Whoa, okay," he says, lifting both hands in surrender. "I didn't know you were so sensitive about sharing food with your brother."

"I'm not sensitive," I tell him indignantly as I set the spoon down and start cleaning up the mess. "You just can't eat *this* sauce."

Phoenix's face morphs into one of horror, and he retches. "Oh my god," he gasps, making another gagging sound. "Did you jizz in it?"

I burst out laughing and smack him upside his stupid head. "No, you moron, but..." I pick up the spoon and give it a long lick while giving him a pointed look.

He seems to get the picture, somewhat anyway, and finally stops making puke noises. Again, the twin brain thing.

"I'll be damned. You kinky motherfucker. What exactly did you do with that spoon?"

"None of your business," I tell him, spotting a blob of sauce I missed and quickly swiping it away. I have a housekeeper that cleans twice a week, but I'm very conscious of cleaning up after myself. I'm a grown-ass man and not some frat boy punk who expects someone else to pick up my messes.

"Phoenix, hey!" We both turn to see Nicolette entering the kitchen barefoot and wearing my navy-blue bathrobe. It swallows her, and she looks adorable in it.

"Hey, shorty," he says, crossing to her and curling an arm around her neck to give her a kiss on the top of her head. A possessive feeling creeps up my spine, but it's not exactly jealousy. Not where my twin is concerned. I trust him more than anything.

Phoenix has always been my person, but watching them together, I can see there's room for Nicolette to situate herself beside him in our circle of trust. I like the thought of that, having *two* people.

"I'm not short," Nicolette protests. "You two are just freakishly tall."

My twin widens his eyes, placing a hand over his heart. "How did you know I was a freak? I mean, I know you're aware of how this guy operates." He glances at the spoon and then at me, and I give him a murderous glare.

Nicolette shoves him playfully and laughs. "You are so crazy. Are you staying for dinner?"

"No!" Phoenix and I say together.

We lay in my bed facing each other late that evening. One of Nicolette's legs is between mine, and she's wearing one of my T-shirts. I never knew how much I would like that. She traces the lines of my shoulder and arm before leaning in to kiss the scar on my shoulder.

"What happened here? Did you have surgery?"

My eyes dart down to the ugly scar with her pretty lips against it. "I did. Five years ago."

She nuzzles her head beneath my chin. "Is that why you stopped swimming competitively?"

I hesitate before answering. "Yes. It ended my career."

"I'm sorry. I know that must have been hard." She lays a soft kiss on my neck. "You can talk to me about it if you want."

Pulling her closer, I absorb the warmth of her body against mine and feel the need to tell her everything. But I don't.

"It's okay," I say. "I'm over it." And for the first time, I think that might actually be true.

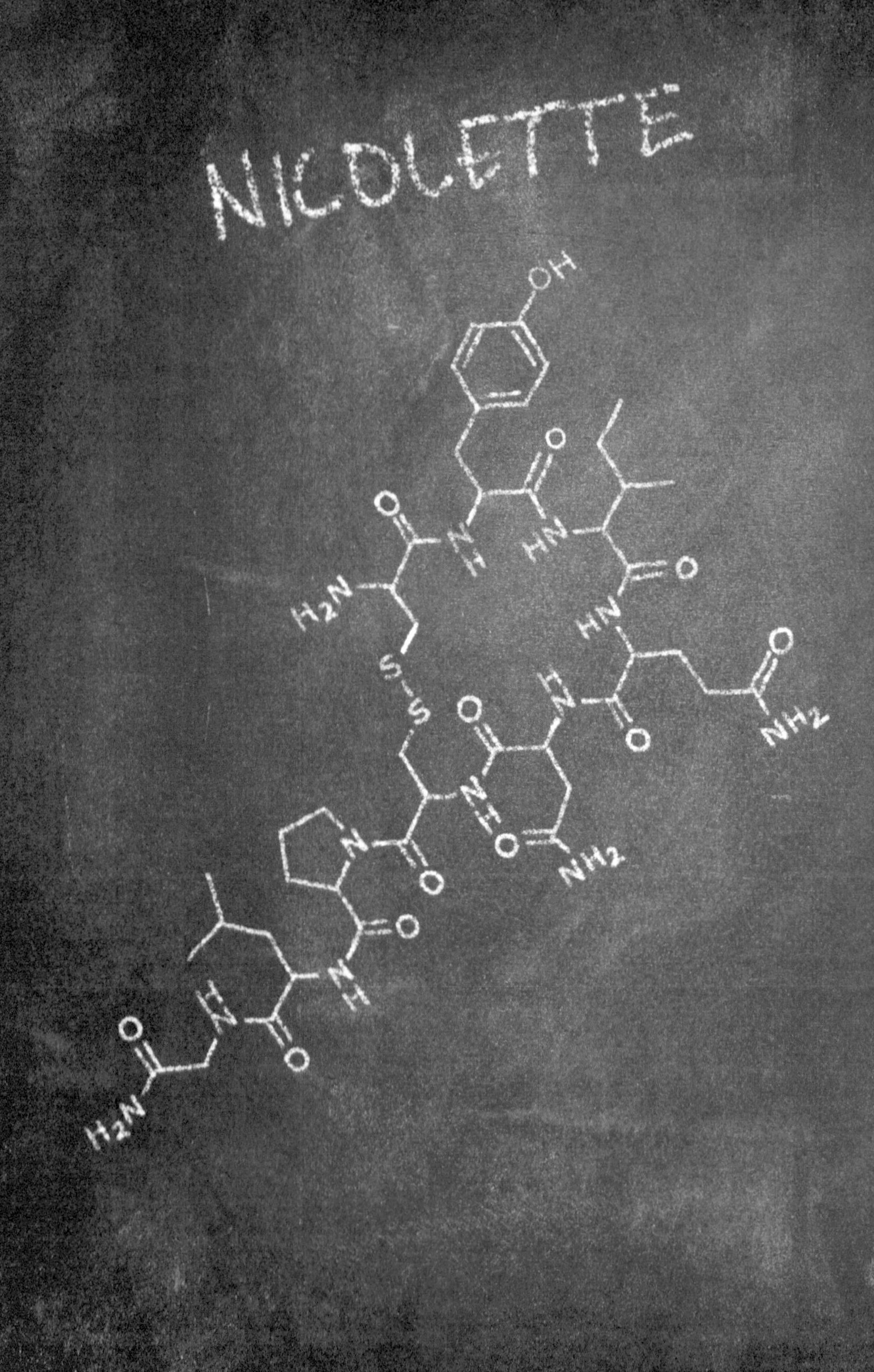

NICOLETTE

Chapter Thirty-One

THE PROCLAMATION

October fades into November, and it's still fucking hot in Texas. At least it's not in the nineties or hundreds anymore, but eighty-eight is still extremely warm.

My eyes follow Helix as his large body slices through the water. He is always attractive to me, but he's downright stunning while he's swimming. The sun glistens off the surface of his wet body when he stands and shakes his head, sending droplets flying.

Then his eyes meet mine as I sit in one of the cushy lounge chairs, and he grins. It is devastating.

"Hey, beautiful. Want to come in?"

"Not today," I say. "I'm enjoying the show."

My man swipes his hair back and winks. "Okay, baby. But don't worry; I'll get you wet later." And I know he's not talking about in the pool.

His pool area would be right at home in some fancy tropical resort with a stone waterfall at one end and palm trees scattered between colorful flowers.

A buzzing against my hip has me reaching for my phone, and I see it's Helix's mom calling. Probably wants to ask when we're going back to Cowboy Yoga. I swear, the woman is obsessed.

"Hey, Ophelia," I answer with a smile in my voice. I really like this woman. She's warm and funny, and she's welcomed me into her family with open arms. I often wonder what it would be like if I'd had her as a mother growing up instead of my own.

"Nicolette! It's so nice to hear your voice. Listen, I was wondering if you'd like to come over to my house today. Just you without my son."

I'm taken aback and a little worried. What if she thinks I'm too much of a freak after thinking more about my bathroom rant the first day we met? "Sure. What's going on?"

"Well, I hope you won't take offense because that's not how I mean it all, but I was hoping to share some of my family recipes with you." She rushes to add. "I'm not saying you can't cook or anything. I'm sure you can because you're a very smart woman, but I thought... Oh dear, am I making a mess of things?"

I can't help but laugh. "Not at all. I would love to."

"Great! I always dreamed of having a daughter who would become my best friend when she was all grown up. Someone who would come over and hang out in my kitchen while we cooked, but I just had three stinky boys." There's affection for her sons in her words, despite the mild insult.

"What time would you like me to come?"

"In about an hour, if that gives you enough time."

"I'll be there."

"I can't wait. You're very important to my son, and I want to get to know you better."

The excitement in her voice thrills me. Is this what having a real mom is like?

She sends me the address by text once we're off the phone, and I walk over to the edge of the pool. Helix swims over like a damn dolphin and props his chin on his folded arms on the side.

"What's up, buttercup?"

"I'm going over to your mom's house."

He wipes some water off his tanned face with a big hand. "Okay, I'll need to take a shower before we go. Did she say what time?"

"In an hour... and you're not invited," I tell him, nudging his thick forearm with my bare toe.

Helix appears to be insulted. "But why?"

I squat and run my fingers through his wet strands. "Because we're having girl time, and you're not a girl."

"Thanks for noticing," he mutters.

"There you go. That looks perfect," Ophelia says, holding up a strand of linguini and inspecting it.

"About time. I ruined two batches already," I grump, wiping off my hands on a dish towel.

"You did fine. Helix does a great job with my sauce, but he sucks at making pasta. I think he just uses store bought." Ophelia shudders delicately.

"He made spaghetti for me last month. He said the sauce was your recipe."

She appears delighted by this news. "Did he?" Lowering her voice like she's telling a secret, she asks, "How was the pasta?"

"It was actually good. He bought it freshly made from some store."

"Okay, I guess it's better than that boxed mess," she sighs. "I tried to teach him, Nicolette. I really did."

I laugh at her dramatics. "Thank you so much for teaching me, Ophelia. It really means a lot."

Pride is evident on her pretty face. "Your sauce turned out beautifully. Let's call Helix and Phoenix over for lunch. I do wish Remington lived closer." Her smile turns wistful. "But that's what happens when your little birds grow up. They leave the nest and fly."

I dial my father's number later that evening and am surprised when Ma answers. "Hello?"

"Hey, Ma. It's me. How are you doing?"

"Oh, I'm all right, I guess. My knee has been bothering me a little."

"I'm sorry. Have you had it checked?"

"No, your father insists I should, but I think he's overreacting."

"You're a little young to need knee replacement, but it's still a good idea to get it looked at. Let me know if you need me to help you find a good ortho, okay?"

"I'm sure it will be fine."

I wait for her to ask me how I am or anything about myself, but when she doesn't, I ask, "Where's Pop?"

"He's in the bathroom. I told him not to have that second bowl of chili, but you know how he is. He never listens."

Laughing, I say, "Okay, well tell him I hope he feels better. I was just calling about the holidays."

"Rory invited us to have Thanksgiving with his family. Isn't that nice?"

Ugh. No. I'm not going over there, so I make the quick decision to stay in Texas. "That is nice, Ma. I think I'm going to stay here for turkey day, but I'll see you at Christmas."

"Oh. Well. I thought I told you, Nicolette. We're not going to be here then. We're going on an eight-day cruise over Christmas and New Year's."

"No, you didn't tell me. Just you and Pop?"

"Rory and Angelica are coming too, of course. It's like a family vacation."

I should probably be insulted that I wasn't invited on this *family* trip, but to be honest, eight days on a boat with them sounds like a nightmare.

Maybe I'll go to New York. Lehra and Cruz will probably be spending the holidays with their families, but maybe we could at least have lunch on Christmas Eve.

"Did you have fun with my mother yesterday?" Helix asks as we walk down the beach, hand in hand. The moon is full overhead, and the stars reflect tiny sparkles on the gently rolling water.

Helix brought me to Galveston tonight for dinner. It's an island less than an hour south of Houston. Our meal was amazing, a seafood feast in an elegant restaurant with white linens and flickering candles on each table. The mood was soft and romantic, and Helix touched me every chance he got.

Afterward, he suggested a moonlit walk, and here we are with sand between our toes.

"I did. It was really nice of her to invite me."

"She knows how special you are to me." Helix stops walking and turns us to face each other. "Do *you* know how special you are to me?"

Unsure how to answer, I say, "I guess. You're really good to me, and we seem to enjoy being together. At least I do."

The wind whips my hair across my face, and Helix pulls the band from my wrist and fashions what feels like a very messy bun. "How does it look?" I ask, and he chuckles.

"Pretty terrible. I'm definitely not quitting my day job to do hair." He steps closer, his warmth infusing itself in my skin. "And for the record, you are very special to me, Nicolette."

I swallow hard. "You're special to me too." I've never seen his eyes this blue. Maybe it's because of the moonlight.

His hand cups my chin as his eyes flit over my face. "I love you, Nicolette."

My heart takes flight, fluttering like it has wings. "Helix…"

"You don't have to say it back. I know I only met you a little less than five months ago, but I can't imagine not having you in my life."

I climb the man like a damn tree, and he laughs, holding me beneath my butt. "I love you too," I tell him. "And you don't have to imagine me not in your life because you're not getting rid of me now."

He kisses me then, and it's tender and poignant, an impeccable proclamation of love kiss, if that's even a thing. The lapping of the waves is the perfect soundtrack to the perfect moment.

When we break apart, Helix rests his forehead against mine. "I'm just warning you that I've never been in love, so I probably won't be very good at this. But I want you to call me out if I ever make you feel like you're not the most important thing in my life. Because you are."

Who the hell kidnapped my dirty-talking man and replaced him with this sweet impostor? I don't know, but I love both sides of him.

"I feel it," I tell him, looking out at the water. "I've always felt like I've been written in the margins by pretty much everyone." I bring my eyes back to him as emotion thickens my words. "But you make me feel like I'm written on the very center of the page. And I hope I make you feel the same."

"You do," he whispers before kissing me again.

As he holds me tight, I try to figure out what I did to get so lucky. Because I'm in love with Helix Hale...

And he loves me right back.

NICOLETTE

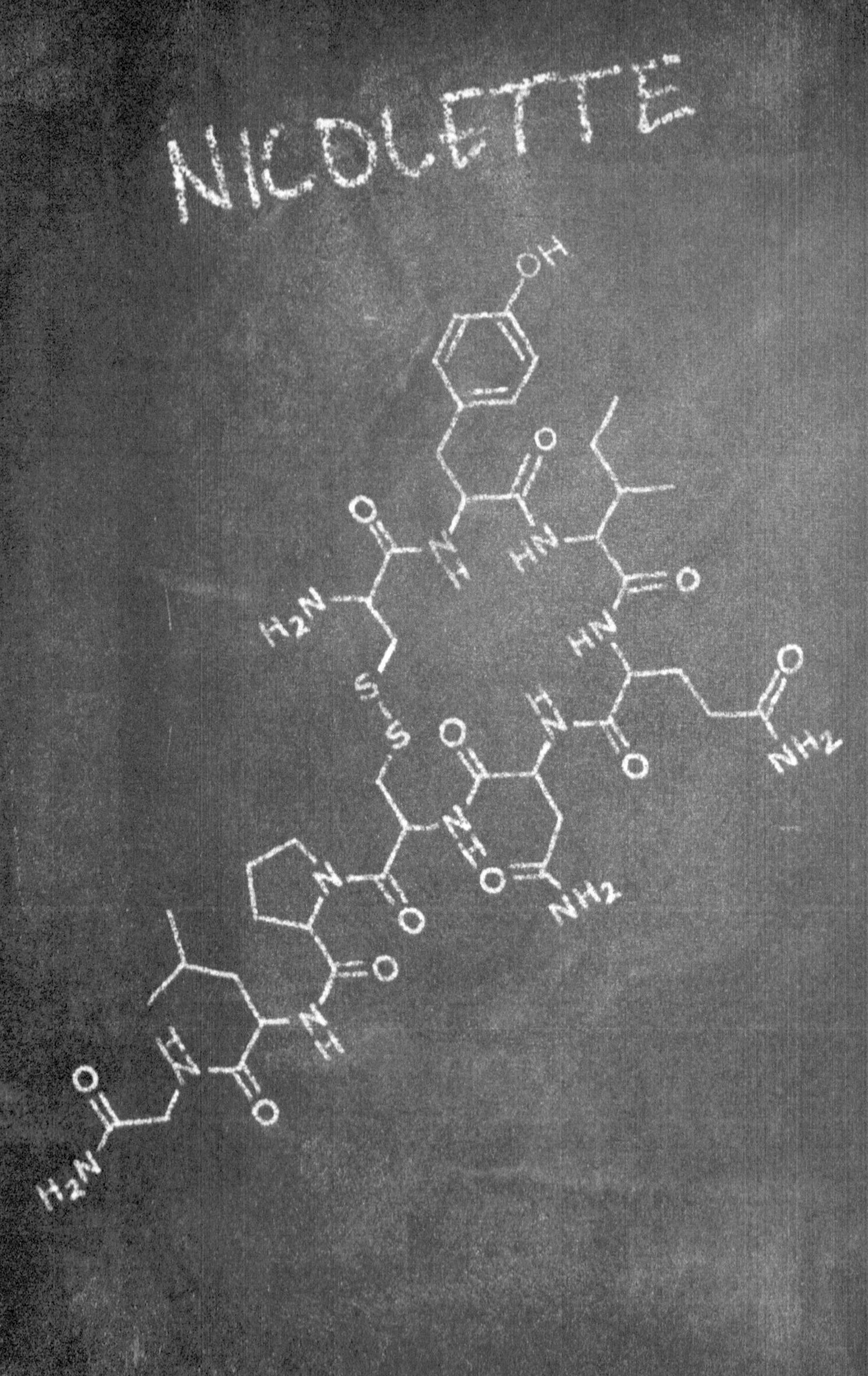

Chapter Thirty-Two

A VERY ANAL CHRISTMAS

When Helix found out my family was going out of town for the holidays, he invited me to celebrate with the Hales. Actually, it was less inviting and more insisting. I believe his exact words were, "You're fucking coming if I have to hog tie you and drag you there."

I was a little apprehensive about what exactly hog tying entailed, so I said I'd go.

Thanksgiving was great. The entire family gathered at Helix's house, including his mother, father, and stepmom. Rebecca and Ophelia avoided each other like the plague, and it was all very civilized.

Christmas Eve was last night, and we went to Haywood and Rebecca's mansion. Everything in their home looked like it belonged in a museum, but the atmosphere in the family room and kitchen was surprisingly casual with everyone talking and laughing while kids ran around.

Today we're at Ophelia's and things are a bit calmer though still festive. It's only Ophelia's sons, and of course, Reece and me. Reece looks like a little doll with her red-and-white striped tights and a bright green top with sequin candy canes on the front.

"That outfit is adorable," I tell Phoenix as we watch his daughter clip a red bow into Remi's jet-black hair. Phoenix and I are already sporting hairbows because Reece informed us everyone had to match because it's Christmas. I love that the whole family indulges her sweet ideas.

"I got that at a kids' boutique in The Galleria. I was clueless about little girl stuff at first, but my mom helped, and now I know all the hot spots." He laughs and runs a hand over the back of his neck. "I still feel like I'm winging this dad thing on a daily basis. New things pop up and I wonder what in the hell I'm doing."

I bump him with my shoulder. "You're doing great. Reecie is a great kid."

His smile is pure proud dad as his eyes stay trained on his daughter, who is now bedecking Helix with a red bow directly on top of his head. He looks ridiculous, but it only makes him hotter. Especially when he catches me looking and mouths, "I love you."

My heart performs a gymnastics routine in my chest like it does every time he says it. I still can't believe this incredible man is mine, but every single day he makes me feel like I'm worthy of his love.

"I love you too," I mouth back, and Phoenix snickers. I bump him hard with my hip. "Shut up, buttface."

"Buttface? Wow. I feel like you're my sister already." He bobs his eyebrows. "You know that's where this is headed, right?"

"We'll see," I say vaguely, though a smile teases my lips. The truth is, last night when we were in bed and I was halfway asleep, I heard Helix whisper a single word against the back of my neck. *Wife.*

I feel like a glass that's already full to the brim with happiness, but someone keeps pouring more good stuff into it until I'm overflowing. The only problem is, I can't help but worry that one day the glass is going to crack and break into pieces.

"That is not a thing," I say, tilting my head and giving Helix a *you're ridiculous* look.

"Christmas anal is totally a thing."

We're sitting in Ophelia's backyard having cocktails after Christmas dinner. Helix and I are alone right now because Phoenix went inside to say good night to Reece, and Remi is refilling our drinks. Ophelia has happily taken over Nana duty. Helix is trying to tell me that having anal sex on Christmas Day is some kind of tradition.

"You just want in my ass again," I argue, and he shrugs.

"Of course I do. Your tight ass is amazing, but that doesn't mean it's not a real thing, kind of like an adjunct holiday."

"You guys talking about Christmas anal?" Phoenix asks, sitting down in the cushioned rattan chair across from us.

I groan. "Not you too. How did he get you to agree with this insane idea, Phe?"

"I didn't have to. It's just a thing. You can ask Remi."

"Ask Remi what?" the oldest Hale brother asks, arriving with a tray of drinks and passing them out.

"Christmas anal," Helix says.

Remington grins and holds up his glass in a toast. "Best fucking holiday ever."

I shake my head, half in amazement and half in amusement at these three unfairly handsome men. Seriously, the genetics fairy must have sprinkled their parents during the act of conception. But the idea of this is ludicrous.

Bringing my glass to my lips, I lap a little salt from the rim and take a drink of my tangy margarita. "What if your partner doesn't want to?"

"Then you don't do it, of course," Remi says adamantly. "There have been years where one of us was unable to fulfill the terms of the Christmas anal festivity."

I snort at festivity and challenge, "Why have I never heard of this?"

"It's a family tradition," Phoenix explains.

"So your mom knows about it? Does she also observe this holiday?"

A collective shudder runs through the brothers. "Hell no, our mom doesn't know. In fact, she's only had sex twice in her life as far as we're concerned," Helix tells me. "Maybe we should have said it's more of a *brotherly* tradition."

Remington swirls his cocktail in his hand. "It started kind of by coincidence when I was twenty, and I overheard Phe and Helix talking about their, um, dates from the night before. It so happens that I had gotten lucky in the same way, and since then, at least one of us has participated each year."

Phoenix crosses one ankle over his knee. "I'm abstaining this year. I'm not dating anyone right now."

Remi frowns into his glass. "Things aren't looking good for me at this point either, so I guess it's up to Helix this year." His eyes shift to my boyfriend who picks up my hand and kisses it.

"It's up to my girl, of course. If she's not in the mood, I guess the butt gods will frown upon the Hale brothers this Christmas season."

"I think you're all absurd," I say, taking another swig of my drink. But I'll be damned if I'm not thinking about taking Helix's big dick up my back hole now.

"That's it, baby. You have such a sweet little ass."

I tilt my head back, letting my hair fall down my back as I ride Helix reverse cowgirl style. And yes, we're having Christmas anal. Don't judge... it's a tradition.

"I love when you fuck my ass," I groan, sinking down a little more while he wraps my hair around one hand and uses the other to slowly circle my clit.

I've never been a fan of butt stuff. My only prior experience was when I was in grad school and dating a guy who loved anal. In fact, it's the only way he liked having sex, but it wasn't enjoyable for me because he didn't even offer a courtesy reach-around. Our relationship didn't last long at all.

Helix, on the other hand, always makes sure I'm properly prepped and keeps his fingers between my legs until I come at least once. Since he showed me how a real man takes his woman's back entrance, I freaking love it.

"You are so fucking wet, queenie," he says, slipping a finger inside my pussy and using my arousal to slick across my sensitive little button.

Using my thigh muscles, I raise and lower myself, loving the fullness this position provides. My hips roll and pick up speed, and when Helix pulls my hair to arch my neck back, my entire body shivers. "I'm so close," I call out to the ceiling of his bedroom.

"Good girl," he growls, pushing two fingers into my pussy so I'm completely stuffed with him. "Fuck me until you come on my cock and my fingers like I taught you."

I lean back with my hands on the mattress beside his body and ride him for all I'm worth. The orgasm slams hard into me, spots dancing around the edges of my vision. There's something about these climaxes that hit me with so much intensity I feel it from my head to my toes and everywhere in between.

"God, that was good," I pant. "So happy to be part of your family's tradition."

He chuckles and pushes me forward until my hands meet the mattress between his knees. Then he takes time to add more lube to his cock before positioning himself behind me and swiping my hair over one shoulder so he can kiss my neck.

"I love you, Nicolette. So goddamn much."

"I love you so goddamn much too," I tell him, turning my face so we can kiss. His tongue strokes against mine as he slowly enters me from behind and fucks my ass with long, measured strokes.

His chest is flush with my back, and we're both sweating from the exertion. Helix kisses across my cheek and to my ear. "Are you ready, baby?"

My body trembles in anticipation. "I'm ready."

"What's your safe word?"

"Safe word," I say dutifully, and he kisses my cheek before raising his body and placing his hand on the back of my head.

"Head down, Nic. You know how I like it," he tells me, and I grin to myself.

"Make me."

That never fails to bring out the darker side of him. Shoving my head roughly so my cheek rests on the mattress, he slaps my ass. Hard.

"Why do you insist on acting like a fucking brat?" He pushes deep, his hips clapping against my cheeks before withdrawing to the tip. "Why do you like pushing my buttons?" Another deep thrust. And another.

My fingers curl into the sheets, and I arch my back for him, taking each one of his punishing movements as he propels himself into me time and time again. It's hard, and it's dirty, and I fucking relish every second of it.

"Because it makes you lose control and fuck me exactly how you need it," I pant.

His cock is rock hard, filling me up so tightly I can feel every ridge and vein on the slick surface. My face is turned toward the dresser mirror to the left of us, so I can see the profile of Helix's perfect, toned body. Sweat drips off him as he clenches and releases his muscular butt muscles. The man has got some serious cake back there.

His eyes are downcast, looking at the spot where we're joined while he pounds into me with furious thrusts. "Your tight little asshole looks so pretty when she stretches for my cock. Use your vibe on your clit, baby. You're coming with me."

I'd forgotten he slipped a small finger vibrator on my middle finger earlier, telling me he'd let me know when to use it. He reaches down and presses a button on the back of it twice before guiding my hand between my legs. Finding the right spot in about a second, I feel my entire body light up with the buzzing stimulation.

I watch as Helix's lips part, and I can hear his breaths coming out in pants punctuated by grunts. That's how I know he's close. His head tips up to the sky, and he leans back slightly, letting his strong back and narrow hips do all the work as I clench around him.

My body is so attuned to him that his orgasms and mine often blend together. I can feel that happening now. As soon as his thickness begins to throb with his release, I find my own.

And we soar together.

"Do you love me more than my shower?"

This is a silly little game we've been playing the past couple of weeks. We ask the other if they love them more than some random thing.

Do you love me or pizza more?

You.

What do you love more? Me or Grey's Anatomy?

Always you. Especially since they killed off McSteamy and McDreamy.

Do you love me more than science?

Infinitely more.

But tonight, I decide to tease him a little.

"Well," I draw out, "you're pretty great, but you don't have a skylight with rainwater jets."

He laughs and holds me closer, burying his face in my neck. "That's true, but I did pick out this shower."

I press my slick body against his big one and look up at the skylight in the ceiling of his shower. Small jets line the perimeter, casting soft streams down on us. It's dark, so I can see the stars twinkling in the night sky, giving the moment an almost dream-like feel.

"Okay then, I love you more than your amazing shower."

"Good." He lifts his head, his eyes hazed with satiation and love as they turn serious. "I want all of you, Nicolette."

My hand rubs the stubble forming on his jaw, and I frown. "You have all of me."

He lifts my left hand and kisses the spot on my third finger where a very specific ring might sit. My heart forgets how to beat. "What if I want this?"

I stare at him for a long moment, wondering if he's really talking about what I think he's talking about.

"Then you can have it."

Resting my cheek against his chest, I close my eyes as the steam from the hot shower billows around us.

I know in my heart I would give this man anything he asked for... including myself.

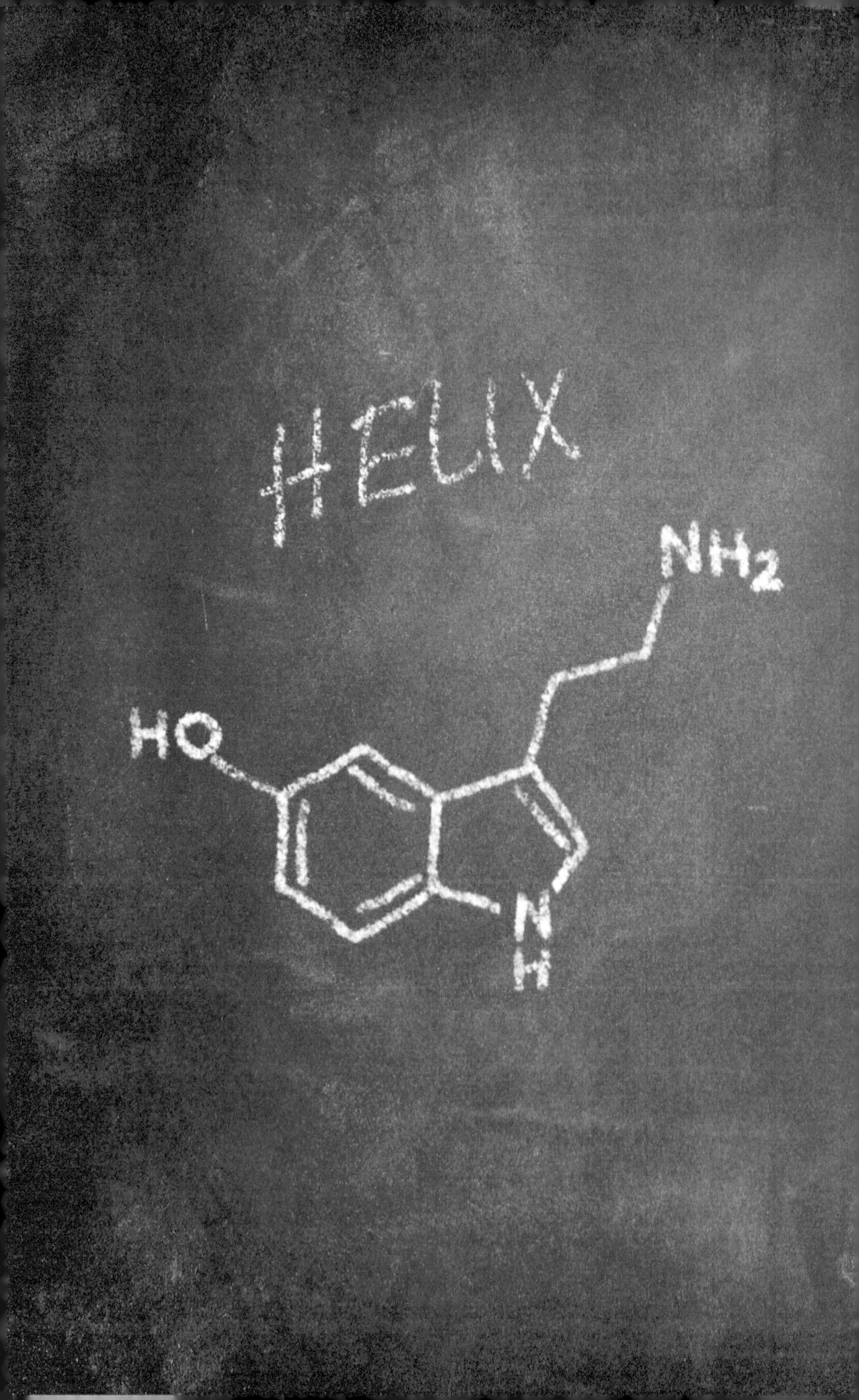

HELIX
NH2
HO
N
H

Chapter Thirty-Three

ESPIONAGE AND A FLY

Staring down at the box in my hand, I smile. This is something I never thought I would do, but when I flick up the lid and see the light catch the enormous solitaire diamond, I know I'm making the right decision.

I am going to propose to Nicolette.

I considered doing it on Valentine's Day, which is in two weeks, but her sister is getting married that weekend, and I want this proposal to be special and not overshadowed by anything else. And besides, I have very romantic plans to ask Nicolette to be my wife.

For Christmas, I gave her a week-long vacation in Aspen, and the date we scheduled is coming up in March. A secluded cabin. The mountains as a backdrop. A cozy fire in the fireplace. It's going to be perfect.

When the door to my office opens, I quickly close the box and pocket it, mildly panicking that it's my future fiancée, though I know it's not. She's off work for the rest of the day to get her birth control shot.

"Hey, Dad," I say, relieved to see him striding purposefully inside and closing the door. Until I get a glimpse of his face. "What's wrong?"

He slams a sheaf of papers down on my desk, and I notice the pallor of his face. "What is this?" he demands.

Looking down at the paper, I inspect the formula with detailed notes below it. "This is our formula for the additive for the new fragrance line."

"I know," he says sharply, and I shake my head.

"Is there some kind of problem with it? We've tested and re-tested it a million times, so I don't—"

He cuts me off. "Look at the next page."

"Okaaaay," I draw out, turning to the next sheet of paper as my father begins to pace. That's when my blood runs cold. "What the fuck is this?"

He stops his pacing and jabs a finger onto the paper. "That," he snaps, "is a patent application that was just filed today by Aquarius Cosmetics in New York."

"But... no." Dread seeps into my system, and I shake my head back and forth like I'm trying to shake the idea of this from my brain. "How did they get hold of our formula?"

"That's what the hell I'd like to know," Dad roars, bracing himself with both hands on the desk. He doesn't look well, and I don't blame him. I feel pretty shitty myself.

Rounding my desk, I take my father by the arm and guide him into one of the leather chairs across from my desk. "Just calm down," I tell him. "Let me get you some water."

"I don't need fucking water. I need to know how Aquarius Cosmetics got our goddamn formula." Despite his protests, he accepts the bottle I hand him from the small fridge in my office. "There's been a leak."

"Obviously," I fume, resting my butt on the edge of the desk so I can grab Dad if he topples over. "Have you told anyone about this?"

He guzzles half the bottle and wipes the back of his hand across his mouth. "Not about that." He waves his hand at the offending paperwork, a look of disgust pinching his face into a grimace. "As we agreed, we've leaked rumors of a groundbreaking new fragrance. You know, just to get some excitement generated in the industry."

"But you didn't release the actual formula." I state it rather than ask it because I already know. He and I worked with Phoenix on the exact wording of the rumors.

Dad just stares at me like I'm insane for even entertaining such an idea. "I would never release an actual formula. That would be pure ignorance, and I didn't get into my position by being ignorant. Who else knows this information?"

"I do, of course, and Nicolette. We produced small batches of it ourselves for testing purposes so not even the production line has seen it. We've kept it top secret, and other than the copy we gave to you, all our paperwork stays locked in my safe."

My father nods and takes another drink. "Dammit, I need something stronger than this."

"Me too," I mutter, digging around in the cabinet along the far wall and coming up with a dusty bottle of bourbon Remi gave to me last year. I used to drink a small glass when I was working late to take the edge off, but I haven't touched it in months. Nicolette has been taking care of my edges.

I pour us each a healthy portion into two coffee mugs. My father would normally complain that it's a crime to pour fine bourbon into simple mugs, but he doesn't utter a word, simply taking a long sip. I do the same, feeling the warm burn down my throat.

"First of all, let me check this against the one in the safe," I say, rapping a knuckle against the patent application. It's kind of silly to do because I could reproduce this formula in my sleep, but I'll feel better if I can lay them side by side and compare every single element listed.

When I open the safe, the envelope that should be right on top is gone. I feel like I'm going to puke. I rummage through the meager contents, certain my eyes must be missing the hundreds of pages of notes and test results.

"It's not here," I finally croak out.

"Okay," he puffs out on a long sigh. "Who has access to your safe?"

"Phoenix knows my password," I say before remembering something. "Oh, and Nicolette." My father's eyes widen, and I shake my head. "She's very cautious, Dad, and she would never remove the formula and just leave it lying around where anyone could find it. She's not stupid."

"I know that, son, but we need to talk to her and Phoenix to see if there was some kind of inadvertent... whatever. I don't even know." He drains his drink, and I do the same.

"Nicolette is out of the office today for a doctor's appointment, but let's head over and talk to Phoenix. I'll tell him to meet us in your office."

"I have no clue," my twin says, looking as disturbed as Dad and I feel. "I know the password because you told me years ago, but I've never even opened your safe."

"Dammit to hell," I curse, checking the time. "Nicolette's appointment time is happening right now. She's going to freak the hell out when I tell her about this."

"When was the last time you saw the envelope?" Phoenix asks.

Running my fingers through my hair, I reply, "Day before yesterday at the end of the day. It was in the safe."

"You're sure?" Dad asks, and I frown at him, though this isn't his fault. We already checked, and his copy of the paperwork was sitting securely in his office safe. Only my and Nicolette's copy is missing, obviously stolen.

"I'm positive. Let's get over to security and have them check the cameras from the past two nights." A sense of unease settles heavily on my shoulders as we take the skybridge over to the main building.

Bernadette Starrett is our head of security. A former officer in the United States Army, she's no-nonsense down to her core. As soon as she sees the CEO and his two sons being let into the security room, she knows something is up and marches from her office to greet us.

After filling her in, we're invited into the control room, where a wall of screens shows views of the executive office building and the laboratory building. Bernadette is stone-faced. She knows this is serious.

Three hours later, we've found jack shit. Bernadette has fast-forwarded through all the camera feeds in the lab building, finding not one hint of a person in the hallways the past two nights. Isla was the last person to leave yesterday, which isn't unusual. She often stays to catch up on emails once everyone is gone for the day. Her office is down the hall from mine, and she never even approached that end of the hallway.

No one else was seen until Nicolette and I arrived first each morning, as usual.

"Shit, let's watch it again," I say, frustrated beyond belief. "Maybe slower this time."

"I need to go pick up my kiddo," Phoenix murmurs. "Do you want me to get Mom to pick her up so I can stay with you?"

"No, you're fine." I glance at my dad, whose face looks haggard and still a bit pale. "Why don't you drop Dad off at his house since he's in the same neighborhood as us?"

"I can stay," our father protests.

Bernadette takes over, obviously picking up my cues that Dad needs some rest. "Mr. Hale, let me do my job. Dr. Hale will stay with me as an extra set of eyes, but there's no need for you to watch all this again. If we see anyone, I'll call you straight away, but I'm not hopeful. There's simply no one there."

Dad's body sags a little. "So you're telling me a damn ghost sneaked in and stole that information?"

"I have no idea, sir, but I'll get to the bottom of it. I doubt anyone would steal it during the day because there are so many people around, but we will check the hallway feeds throughout both workdays just to make sure no unauthorized person went into Dr. Hale's office."

Finally relenting, my father allows Phoenix to drive him home, and Bernadette and I get back to work.

We watch the two days on fast-forward, only slowing down when someone passes my office door. The only person who didn't simply walk by was Isla, and the camera clearly showed her sticking my messages in the box affixed to my door and immediately going back to her own office. No one went inside except for Nicolette and me, and we were always together.

I check my phone for the time and notice a text message from my girlfriend.

Nicolette: Hey, want to grab dinner?

Hesitating, I decide not to fill her in on the situation by text. She's understandably going to be upset, and I want to be there to comfort her when she finds out the news that our work has been stolen.

Helix: Not tonight. I'm worn out.

It's the truth. This whole thing has me exhausted.

Nicolette: Ok, see you tomorrow. Love you.

Helix: Love you too, baby.

"What time do you get off work?" I ask Bernadette when I pocket my phone. It's after seven in the evening.

"My shift ends at midnight, but I'll stay as long as you need me. Let's watch the nighttime videos again, as my guess is that's when the information was stolen."

"Do you want me to order you some food?" I ask, and she shakes her head.

"I brought my dinner, but you can order something for yourself."

My nose crinkles at the thought of eating. I'm sick to my stomach over this. "I'm okay, but you go ahead and take a break if you need to."

Instead, she brings her sandwich to the control room, and we begin watching the footage once again, not at regular speed but definitely slower than the first time.

When we get to 11:08 p.m. on the first night, Bernadette freezes the feed, rewinds it to 11:04, and turns it back on. My eyes search the screen, but I see nothing except for a fly buzzing by the camera.

"Well, I'll be damned," she says.

I lean closer, wondering what the hell she's seeing that I'm not. "What is it?"

"Watch the fly," she says, rewinding again and slowing the feed to regular speed.

The insect flies in a circle in front of the camera and then zooms off to the right of the screen.

"Okay, so you think the fly is a thief in disguise?" I ask, unable to hold back my sarcasm.

"Keep watching," she says. Four minutes later, the fly is back. He circles once and then exits the view to the right, just like before. We continue watching, and the exact same thing happens again. Bernadette's voice is hard when she explains. "This part of the video is on a loop."

My blood freezes in my veins, and my voice comes out strained. "But... how could that be?" My brain knows exactly how, but my heart refuses to believe it.

Her mouth is a tight line. "Someone fucking hacked my system." Her fingers fly over the keys. "I have no idea how this happened. This system is state-of-the-art. It would take a damn genius to be able to hack in and put this on a loop for around twelve minutes."

I happen to know a genius who has done exactly that, and bile rises in my throat. "I need to run to the bathroom. I'll be right back," I croak out, almost knocking my chair over when I stand.

"You all right, Dr. Hale?"

My head bobs up and down in a silent yes on my way out, because if I open my mouth right now, I'm going to lose the meager contents of my stomach on the floor.

I shove open the bathroom door and check beneath the stalls for feet. I'm alone.

"Fuck," I whisper, dropping my forearms on the formica countertop and slamming my fingers into my hair. "Fuck, this can't be happening." My eyes stare unseeingly into the sink basin as my guts threaten to upend themselves.

Finally, I look up and don't recognize the man in the mirror, the man who's found his happiness in a woman he thought he could trust. But the man looking back at me isn't happy at all. He's fucking broken.

You can trust her. My heart speaks louder than my brain before my brain shouts back. *But she does have the capability. You watched her do it.*

Logic and love battle for supremacy, and I have no idea who is going to win when I splash cold water onto my face and the back of my neck. The collar of my dress shirt is damp when I return to the control room, and I still don't know who will be the victor.

Bernadette's cool gray eyes meet mine when I walk in. Her arms are crossed over her chest as she watches me sit in the chair beside her.

"You know who did it, don't you?"

The question is both an accusation and a plea.

"I..." God, these are the hardest words I've ever tried to say. "I have an idea."

The story tumbles from my lips. How Nicolette and I had a sexual encounter in the lab. The way she put the cameras on a loop for a few minutes to dart unseen into my office for my shirt before going into the restroom to straighten herself up. How I knew there was a weakness in the security system, but I said nothing because I trusted her, and it seemed harmless at the time.

Bernadette listens, occasionally running a hand through her cropped salt-and-pepper hair. When I'm done, she stares at me for a long moment, and I can feel the judgement radiating off her at my stupidity.

But when she finally speaks, her words hold a hint of kindness. "That was a reckless thing to do, Dr. Hale. I should have been notified the instant you found out our system could be breached like that."

"I know," I say, feeling miserable about lying by omission. "But I really don't think she did this. Nicolette has no reason to betray us like this."

The slight shake of her head lets me know she thinks I'm being a lovesick dumbass. "Money can make good people do bad things, Dr. Hale. Industrial espionage is a lucrative business. And I understand Dr. Bell previously worked at Aquarius?" I nod dumbly, my head feeling like it weighs a thousand pounds. "It seems like an awfully big coincidence that the one person that's been known to hack into our system left the company that stole your work less than a year ago."

What she's saying makes perfect sense from a logical standpoint, but my heart doesn't want to be logical. It just wants Nicolette.

"Can you let me tell my dad about this? Tomorrow?"

Bernadette's eyes check the clock over my shoulder. "It's late, so Mr. Hale is probably in bed. I think waiting until tomorrow would be fine. There's nothing we can do about it tonight anyway."

"Thank you," I say gratefully. "I also want to speak with Nicolette personally. Maybe there's a reasonable explanation."

Our head of security eyes me skeptically. "I don't think that's a good idea, Dr. Hale. A cornered animal can be dangerous."

I grit my teeth. "She's not an animal, and she's not dangerous. Nicolette wouldn't hurt me."

A memory pops unbidden into my head, and I shake it away. *This isn't the same thing.*

Bernadette grits her teeth. "I obviously can't stop you, but I would caution against it."

"Noted," I say tightly.

"And I'll have to notify the police about the break-in tomorrow. I'll also get the company that designed and installed the security camera system on the job. Sometimes the actual footage can be recovered, but to be honest, that's not my forte. I'll leave that up to the professionals."

"Can we wait to see what they find before you call the police? That will give us the evidence we need, and they can deal with it then." My voice sounds overly hopeful, but she shakes her head.

"I'm sorry, but I'm afraid not, Dr. Hale."

My jaw clenches in anger, but I know she's just doing her job. "I understand."

And with a heart full of dread, I walk out of the security office and straight to my car. The ring in my pocket seems like a heavy boulder, reminding me what I stand to lose. I love Nicolette, and I know she loves me too, but I need to talk to her in person about this.

It's not a conversation I'm looking forward to having.

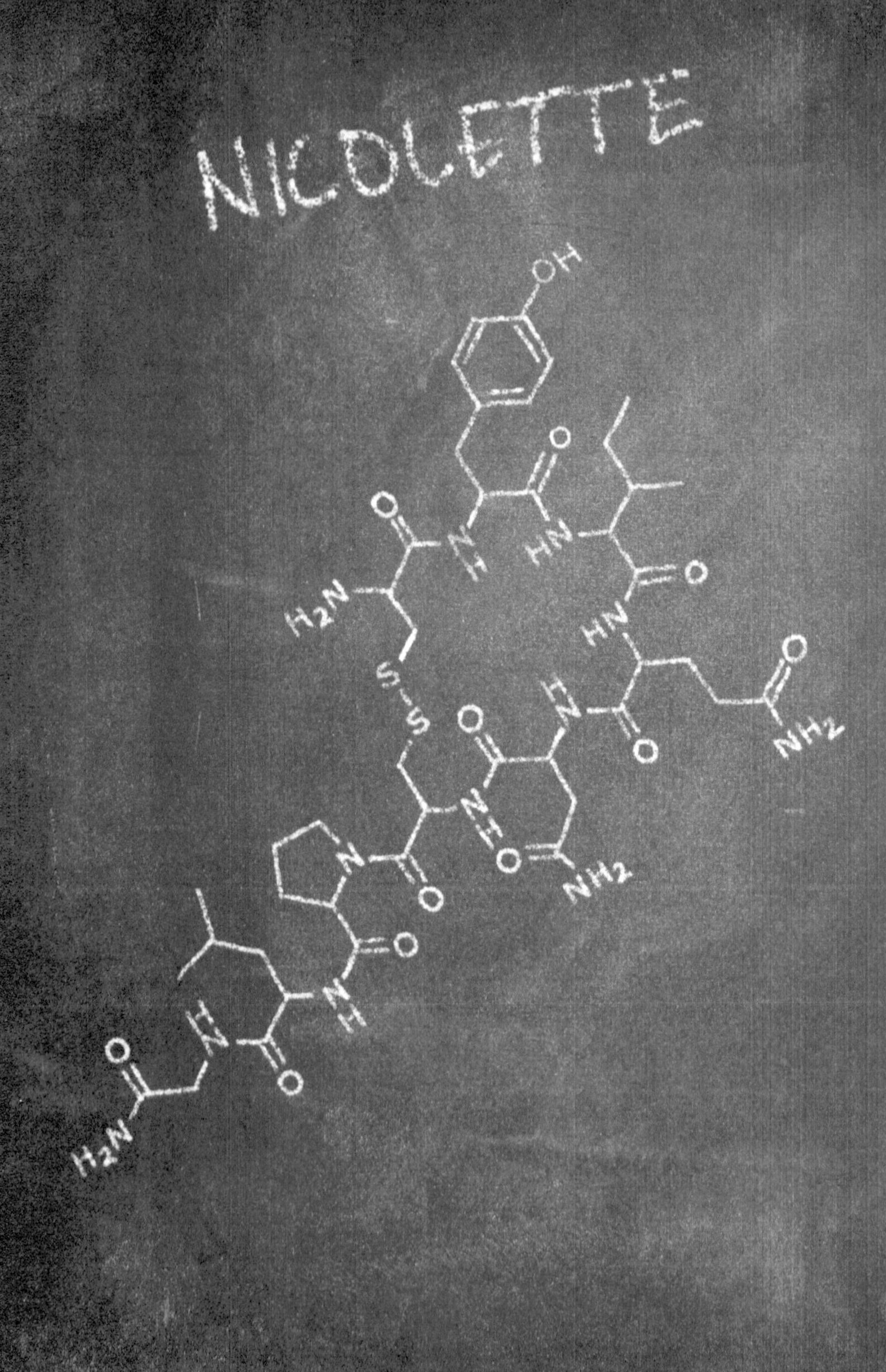

NICOLETTE

Chapter Thirty-Four

IT'S OVER

The security system in my townhome beeps, and I roll over in my bed to check my phone to see it's almost midnight. *What the hell?*

I just laid down a couple minutes ago, so I'm still fully awake as I creep from bed and notice the panel on the wall says the alarm has been disarmed. Must be Helix since he has a key and the code.

I smile to myself as I stick my head out and call down the stairs, "Did you miss me?"

"Can you come down?" he calls back, and I frown, wondering why he doesn't just come up and get in bed.

Working my way down the stairs, I see my sexy man sitting on the couch in the dark, his elbows on his knees and hands wrapped around the back of his neck. When I first realized he was here, I thought he wanted some sexy couch time, but his posture tells me something is wrong.

With my hand on his shoulder, I sit beside him. "Are you okay?"

He shakes his head, and I begin to get worried. "Is someone sick?"

"No," he finally says before straightening and clicking on the lamp, draping the room in a soft glow. When his eyes meet mine, my concern ramps up to a thousand. Before I can ask anything else, he says something that knocks me for a loop. "Aquarius filed a patent today for a formula that's an exact replica of ours."

I'm stunned silent for a full minute. "That's impossible."

"Apparently it's not because I saw the fucking paperwork," he snaps.

I ignore his sharp tone because I'm just as pissed as he is. And confused. My mind tries to work through what the hell he's saying. "There's no way they came up with the exact same formula. It's too complicated for that to be a coincidence. Shit, I've been working on it for two years."

"There's no coincidence. The paperwork was stolen from my safe. They copied it, put their name on it, and are now trying to patent it as their own."

My head cranes so far forward my neck cracks. "They literally stole it?" I shout. "But... how did they get into the building and then into your office safe?"

Instead of answering, he stares at me, his eyes rimmed with red. The silence becomes uncomfortable, so I speak again. "Have you contacted security?"

"Yes. We went immediately to Bernadette when we discovered the theft." His blue eyes have gone dark and intense, as if he's waiting for something from me.

Standing, I begin pacing. "We put it in there Wednesday before we left the office. Have you taken it out since then?"

"No."

I nod, walking from one side of my living room to the other as Helix's eyes track me. "Okay, so they need to watch the camera footage for the past two nights. I'm assuming that's when it happened since I don't think anyone is stupid enough to try and pull that off while everyone is in the building." My finger taps a rapid, nervous beat against my bottom lip. "There are cameras all over the place, but security can focus on the third floor hallway where your office is located, and they should be able to see whoever entered."

Helix says nothing, so I continue to narrate my stream of thought as my mind works overtime. "Hopefully, the cameras are able to get a good enough view to make an identification with facial recognition software. There are some really good ones out there."

Still, he doesn't speak, and I fill the silence. "We should file a cease and desist on them. We have proof of every step of our work, and they'll never be able to get away with this." I stop in front of Helix and prop my hands on my hips, growing angrier by the second. "Whose name was on the patent? I know you said Aquarius, but who was the scientist who *supposedly* developed it?"

"Will Wilhelm," he finally says.

I snort out a furious scoff. "The guy they hired to replace me? That's fucking bullshit. He was a grad student at Aquarius while I worked there, and trust me, the guy couldn't formulate a breath mint. Plus, he just finished grad school last year." Jabbing my finger in Helix's general direction, I rant, "There's no fucking way anyone would believe he came up with that work of art we developed once we tell our side. No. Way."

"We will definitely be stopping this."

"How did you find out?" I ask, and his eyes narrow. I have no idea why he's acting so weird and quiet. Maybe this is just how he processes during a crisis.

"Someone in the patent office knows my dad. That person heard rumors we were working on something similar and thought it was too much of a coincidence. They will probably lose their job if anyone finds out who it was."

"I would give him or her a medal," I mutter. "What about the security cameras? When are they going through the footage? Should we be there to help? If it was actually Wilhelm who broke in, I can identify him in about two seconds. He walks like Shaggy from *Scooby-Doo*."

Helix licks his lips. "We already looked at the footage." His eyes bore into me, and I throw up my hands.

"Why didn't you say that while I was blabbering about it earlier?" I ask, tossing my hands up and letting them fall in frustration. "What did you find?"

"Nothing."

I stare at him, waiting for him to elaborate. Rolling my hand, I say, "You're going to have to give me more than that. The cameras had to have picked up someone."

"Not if they were set on a loop for several minutes," Helix replies, lifting one eyebrow as if waiting for me to explain this.

My hand goes to my mouth in horror as I flop onto the chair across from him. "Someone put the camera on a loop?" He nods once, and my mind goes into overdrive. "Oh my god! That means someone in the security office is in on this. They must have looped the feed so the thief could break in undetected."

This is even worse than I thought. Some stranger didn't just break in. Someone who the company trusts to keep them safe betrayed them.

"Or..." Helix starts, standing and retracing my steps back and forth across the wood floor. "Someone hacked into the system and then went in and stole the formula. Someone who is very good with computers and who knows my passcode to the safe."

He stops, and with his back to me, asks, "Do you know anyone like that Nicolette?"

That's when it hits me. He's talking about... me.

"Helix." I rise from the chair with acid churning in my stomach and take a step toward him. "Helix, look at me."

When he does, I stumble backward at the cold accusation in his eyes. "Tell me you don't think I did this," I croak.

His jaw works back and forth. "What other explanation is there?"

I gape at the man I thought loved me. "You didn't answer me. Do. You. Think. I. Did. This?" Each word is clipped and filled with all the anger and pain that I'm feeling.

He averts his eyes, and my heart drops to the floor. "I don't want to believe it, baby."

"Don't call me that," I yell, startling his eyes back to me. "Don't you dare stand there and accuse me of stealing and lying while calling me baby in the next breath. I've never been so fucking insulted in my life."

And hurt. So damned hurt I can barely stay on my feet.

"Do you think this is easy for me?" he barks. "Do you really think I want to consider that the woman I plan to marry could have betrayed me?"

They say when you die, your life flashes before your eyes, so I wonder if I'm actually dead when everything I care about blurs through my vision. The career I've worked so hard for. My relationship with

Helix. The entire Hale family that opened their collective arms and welcomed me more than my own family ever has.

All of it is gone in a snap, and suddenly, my legs can no longer support my weight. I drop to my knees as tears haze my eyes. I haven't cried since I was twelve years old. It's not that I don't feel emotions. I definitely do, but I haven't allowed the physical representation of those emotions in the form of tears in over two decades. I've often thought that maybe my lacrimal glands were somehow defective.

But as twin waterfalls stream down my cheeks, I know I was wrong. My glands were simply saving up the torrent until I got drop-kicked in the heart and lost everything good in my life.

"Nicolette," Helix says, dropping down beside me and trying to pull me into a hug.

I fight him off, shoving against his chest as I attempt to catch my breath enough to hiss, "Don't touch me."

He holds up both hands at my demon voice. "I won't touch you, but I need you to talk to me. Tell me what happened, and I'll help you."

"You'll help me?" I shriek. "How exactly are you going to *help me*? My career is over. The only good relationship I've ever had is over. So tell me what the fuck you think you can do for me."

His face goes soft with so much sincerity, and that stabs me in the chest deeper than anything. "I love you, bab— Nicolette. I would do anything for you."

"Except believe me," I say quietly, and he looks away, blinking as his own tears begin to fall. That just pisses me off. "I want you to leave."

I thought I was entirely broken a few seconds ago, but the stricken look on Helix's face feels like it's going to snap my spine in two. "Please let me help you. I want to."

I shake my head, slinging tears from my eyes. "No. Go." The words are so raspy, they sound like I've inhaled a gallon of sand.

The muscles of his jaw look like they're going to snap from the pressure. "I don't want to leave you. I'll sleep on the couch or in the guest room downstairs."

Lifting my chin, I put on my best brave front, though I know my face is blotchy and my eyes are swollen. "I don't want you here. I'd rather be alone than look at your face right now."

To his credit, he only winces a little. "I can't leave you like this. Please let me stay, Nicolette. We can figure out what to do tomorrow after we've both had some rest."

I think that might hurt the worst... him offering to help me even though he thinks the worst of me. A stupider person might think that means he still has some love in his heart for me, but I can't allow myself to even fathom that. No. Absolutely not. That would be a betrayal of my own heart.

"Go or I'll call the police." I purposely harden my voice. "Or did you bring them with you to arrest me?"

Helix cringes and shakes his head. "That's not what I want. I tried to talk Bernadette into holding off on contacting the authorities until we get this straightened out. Because deep down inside, I can't let myself believe you did this." He reaches for me and then thinks better of it, letting his hand fall limply to his side. "I've never seen you cry before."

I let out a half laugh. "Well, congratulations. You've done what others have tried to do and failed." Swallowing hard, I say, "If you have any shred of feelings left for me, you'll leave me alone. You are hurting me by being here right now, Helix."

Staring at the floor, I silently will him to go. I sense him rise to his feet and notice his shoes only a few inches from me for a long while. His big body hovering over me pulls like a magnet, and it takes every ounce of my power to resist it. Then he brushes a hand across the top of my head before his footsteps retreat. I don't allow myself a breath until I hear the beeps of the security system being engaged and the soft click of the back door.

Only then do I bend at the waist and press my forehead to the floor as a fresh wave of sorrow pools in a puddle of salty tears beneath my face.

I awaken on the floor of my living room with sunlight pouring through the thin drapes. It takes me all of thirty seconds before the disaster of last night floods back into me.

My entire body aches as I drag myself from the floor and go upstairs. But that ache is nothing compared to the utter devastation in my heart. It's in a million pieces. I've lost everything important to me.

After showering, I slump onto the floor, the tiles cold against my bare ass as I stare at the wall for an interminable amount of time. I push the pain away and allow the anger to take over. Someone has royally fucked with my life, and I'm not going to sit here and take it.

With a renewed sense of purpose, I dress and head downstairs. My hair is still wet, but I don't bother with it. Grabbing a glass of water from the filtered jug in my refrigerator, I down the entire thing in one go before pouring another and drinking it more slowly. I'm pretty sure I cried out all the liquid in my body last night, and I need to replenish.

A knock sounds at my front door, and my hair whips around, the wet strands slapping me in the face. I have the stupid wish that it would be Helix, coming to apologize and tell me it was all a big mistake. Or maybe an elaborate prank.

But it's not. It's the police.

"Dr. Nicolette Bell?" a portly officer with a round face asks. If I was meeting him under any other circumstances, I'd think he looked sweet.

"Yes."

"Would you mind coming down to the station with us? We have some questions for you."

Four hours later, the officers drop me back at my townhome. They were frustrated that I hadn't said a single word except to inform them I wouldn't answer any questions without a lawyer present. Over and over, no matter what they asked me, I repeated the same line until they grew weary of me.

As soon as I get home, I place a call to Gianna Bouvier's sister-in-law, Kassie. She's a bad-ass criminal lawyer in New York, and after I give her a detailed rundown of what I'm facing, she gives me the name of two attorneys in Houston that she trusts.

I open my computer and research both of them before deciding on Lina Davidson, a woman with the reputation of being a shark, and I set up an appointment for two days from now, the soonest they had available. The paralegal I talked to told me to give Lina's name if the police contacted me in the meantime and to say nothing else.

Then I get to work. I'm not waiting around for someone else to save me, so I do the absolute last thing I should probably be doing. I hack back into the Hale Cosmetics security system.

I know how to do it cautiously so I remain undetected, but it's going to take me a while to find what I'm looking for. I turn on Limp Bizkit's "Break Stuff" and let the hard beat and lyrics inspire me.

Eighteen hours. That's how long it takes before I finally relax back in my chair with a sigh. I'd taken bathroom breaks when I needed to, ordered two pizzas, which I ate with one hand, and took two catnaps on the couch. I also listened to a shitload of gangster rap and thrash metal. Other than that, I was digging, searching for the one thing that would exonerate me.

And I fucking found it. I may not have my job, and I may not have my man, but I do have one thing...

Validation.

Opening an encrypted and untraceable email account, I attach the file and enter Helix Hale's email address. I'm not signing my name, but he'll know it's from me by my made-up address and the four words I type at the bottom.

Then I press *send*.

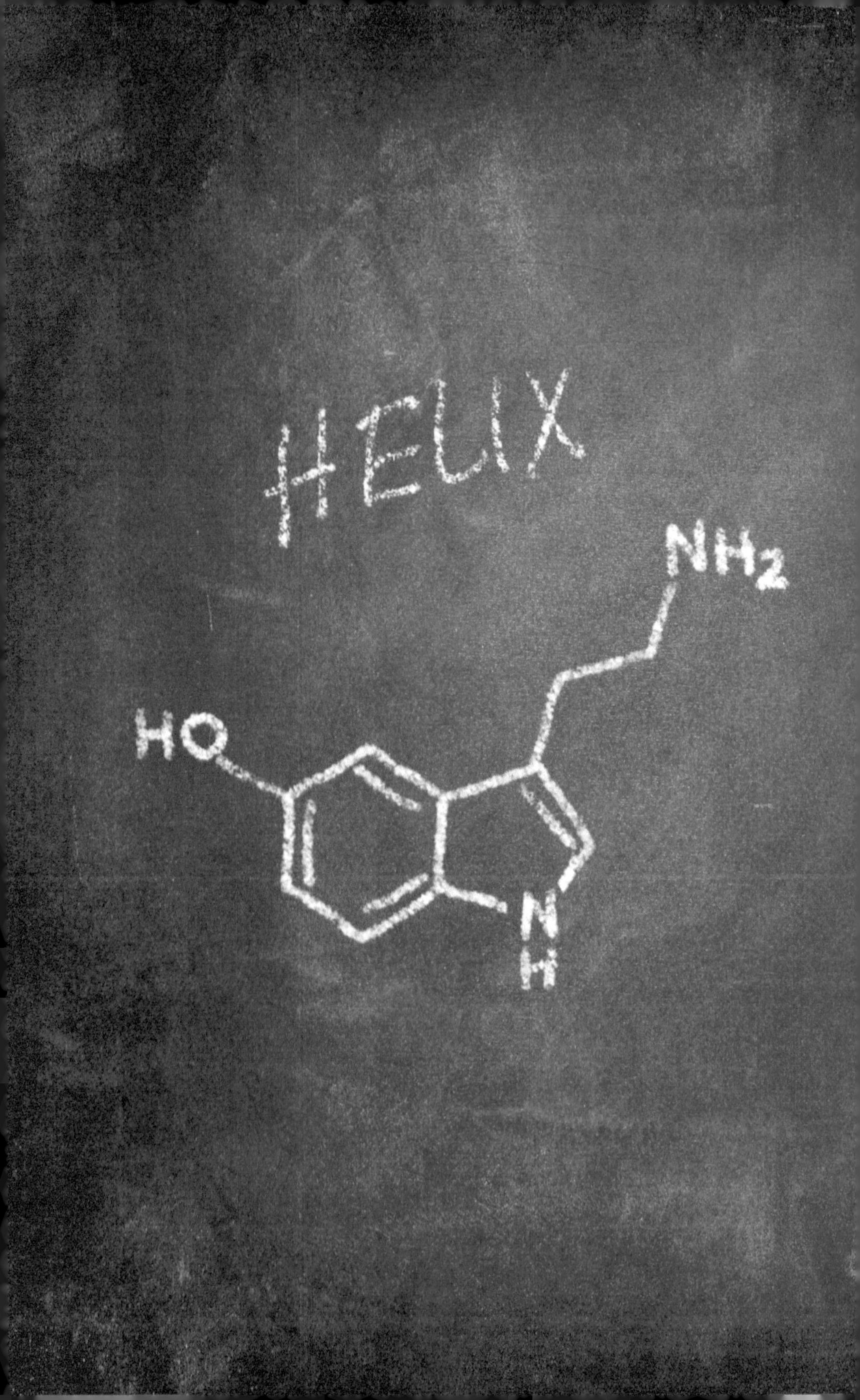

HELIX
NH2
HO
N
H

Chapter Thirty-Five

I NEED A PLAN

I have a million cuts all over my body. Not literal cuts but they hurt all the same. Each one of Nicolette's tears sliced ribbons from my soul.

The number of times I've driven by her home the past couple days would probably get me put in jail or a mental health facility.

You are hurting me by being here right now, Helix.

Those words she spoke to me are the only thing holding me back from marching up to her door, kidnapping her, and running away to some remote island where no one knows us.

I'm more convinced than ever that Nicolette had nothing to do with the theft and betrayal. Even with all the signs pointing her way, I know in my bones that she's innocent. The utter shock and devastation on her face made that perfectly clear.

I also know I screwed up by doubting her for even a second, and that all comes down to my trust issues stemming from my fucked up past. Not that I'm using that as an excuse because there is no excuse for doubting her and making her feel the way I did.

And now I've lost her.

When I pull into the garage of my house and see Phoenix's car in the bay next to where I park my SUV, I'm not sure if I'm glad or annoyed that he's here. Walking inside, I see him on the couch with his feet on the coffee table, and something relaxes inside me, though I gripe at him anyway.

"Do you have to put your stinky feet on my furniture?"

"I washed them this morning," he replies, wiggling his toes before jerking his head toward the seat next to him. "Sit."

"You're awfully bossy for someone who doesn't live here," I grump, though I fall onto the couch beside him and take off my shoes.

When I prop my feet up beside his, he bumps me with his pinky toe. "My feet are prettier than yours."

"We're identical twins. Our feet are literally the same." This inane banter distracts me a little bit. Phoenix is good at that.

We sit for a long while looking at our feet like a couple idiots before my brother speaks. "You drove by her place again?"

"Yeah."

"Anything new?"

"Nope. The light in her dining room is still on."

"She probably just forgot to turn it off."

"Nicolette always turns off lights when she leaves the room. She must be in there."

I feel Phoenix's eyes on the side of my face. "Does it make you feel better knowing where she is in the house?"

With a shrug, I say, "Maybe a little." We're quiet for another moment before I add, "Thanks for not judging me."

"You're going through enough without my judgment. You're being pretty hard on yourself."

"Rightly so. I was a dick. The police detective said they took her down to the station yesterday." My eyeballs throb, and my voice goes thick. "They had her in the fucking police station like a criminal. She must have been scared."

"I'm sure she handled herself well. Nicolette is a smart lady. She's probably more scared of losing her job and being blacklisted from the industry."

"Thanks," I say with flat sarcasm. "I hadn't even thought of that." *Not more than fifty times anyway.*

"Did the detective say anything?"

"Just that she refused to answer anything without an attorney present."

"See? She's smart."

"I'm going to hire her a lawyer."

Phoenix releases what I recognize as his *oh for fuck's sake* sigh. "No. You're not. She's being investigated for a crime against our family's company. It would be a conflict of interest for you to hire an attorney for her." He pats my hand. "But I can recommend someone for her."

I turn my head to look at my brother. "Sometimes I forget you're a lawyer."

He rolls his eyes. "Appreciate that, bro. Makes those seven years I spent in college totally worth it."

"Sorry," I mumble. "I just don't see you doing lawyer shit very often. Who is the best in Houston? Actually, who's the best in the state?"

Phoenix thinks for a minute. "If it were me, I'd pick Lina Davidson. She eats opposing counsel for lunch. She was a year ahead of me in law school, and she was top of her class."

"That's who I want."

My twin shakes his head. "You know it's not your decision, right? Has Nicolette even answered any of your texts?"

"No," I grumble. "She hasn't even read them."

"Probably has you blocked."

"You're not helping," I snap before softening my tone. "Would you text her and give her Lina's name?"

"I'm not sure that's the best idea since I'm also employed by the company, but I could get Mom to pass along the name."

I frown. "I was really hoping to not tell Mom about this. She adores Nic."

"She does," he agrees. "Mom is going to kick your ass."

Rolling my head to the left, I give him my best glare. "Don't you have somewhere to be?"

"Actually, no. I just dropped off Reecie at Perri's new place for a sheepover, so I'm free."

"A... *sheep*over?"

"Yep, it's like a sleepover, but they wear sheep pajamas and eat sheep, which is really just cotton candy with raisins for eyes."

A small smile tests itself on my lips for a brief second. "That's cute."

Phoenix stands and ruffles a hand through my dirty hair. "If you promise to take a shower, I'll come stay with you tonight. We can have our own sheepover. What color cotton candy do you want?"

I'm touched by the gesture, but I don't want to be around anyone right now, not even my twin. I simply want to sit in the dark and be miserable, like I deserve.

"Thanks, brother, but I don't feel like having company tonight."

"Just want to wallow in wretchedness and your own rancid smell?"

I sniff an armpit. "I'm not that bad."

"You're not that good either. Go shower. With soap."

I'm a little ashamed to be a grown man whose brother has to tell him how to shower like I'm a seven-year-old boy, so as soon as he leaves, I go upstairs and take a shower. With soap.

When I'm done, I have to admit I feel better, on the outside anyway. After dressing in a pair of black-and-white athletic shorts, I go to my study and check my emails, finding one from an address I don't recognize, but it makes my face break into a genuine smile for the first time since Friday. The domain name is one I've never heard of, but I know this is Nicolette by the username portion: TheSleepySangriaQueen.

I've never clicked on an email so quickly in my life. My chest deflates when I see the words typed in the body of the e-mail.

Fuck you, Dr. Hale.

Did she make up a whole new email just to insult me? She could have done that by text, or better yet, in person. I'd even let her punch me or kick me. Whatever, as long as I could be near her.

That's when I see there's an MP4 attachment. Without a second thought, I click on it, and after a few seconds I recognize it as the corridor outside my office. Checking the date and time stamp, I see it's from Wednesday evening, the night the formula was allegedly stolen.

Is this the raw, unlooped footage from that night? Did Nicolette hack into our security system today to prove she didn't hack into the system on Wednesday?

I can't help but laugh. She's got some fucking balls on her.

Fast-forwarding to around eleven, I see the fly do his thing, so I slow the video, and it doesn't take long before a lone figure enters the frame. I'm so shocked to see an actual person, I suck in a sharp breath and hold it.

The person is dressed in black from head to toe, including a black ball cap with the hood of a sweatshirt pulled up over it. The intruder is walking toward me, and based on their gait and body, appears to be a woman.

Though I was already convinced it wasn't Nicolette, I let out my breath and do a fist pump when I see it's definitely not her. This woman is very petite and at least a few inches shorter. The camera is at a high angle, and the intruder keeps her head down so her face isn't visible as she uses a handheld device to unlock the door to my office.

I lose sight of her when she goes inside, but when she returns seven minutes later, she's stuffing the envelope beneath her sweatshirt. The hood slips a little, revealing a flash of blonde hair, but she covers it quickly as she jogs toward the exit at the end of the hallway.

After watching the moments around the theft three more times, I send the video to the detective in charge of the case. The security company has been working to recover this piece of the puzzle, but my brilliant woman took care of it her damn self, and I'm so proud of her.

Then I hit *reply* on the email and tap out a quick note.

Nicolette,

I know you didn't do any of this. Deep down inside, I knew before I even watched the footage. My trust in you is strong, and I apologize I let that slip for even a second.

I love you, my queenie, and I know I betrayed you and hurt you, but I will spend my life making it better. Please talk to me and let me apologize in person. I'm under no assumption that you'll ever take me back, but you deserve to hear me say the words out loud to you. I have a lot to explain.

All my love,
  Helix

P.S. I sent the video to the detective. This should be enough to completely exonerate you with the police.

But when I hit *send*, it bounces back as *undeliverable*.

Trying again, I get the same response. An undeniable itch starts beneath my skin, a sensation I don't think I could scratch with a thousand fingernails. No, this particular itch can only be relieved one way...

With the truth.

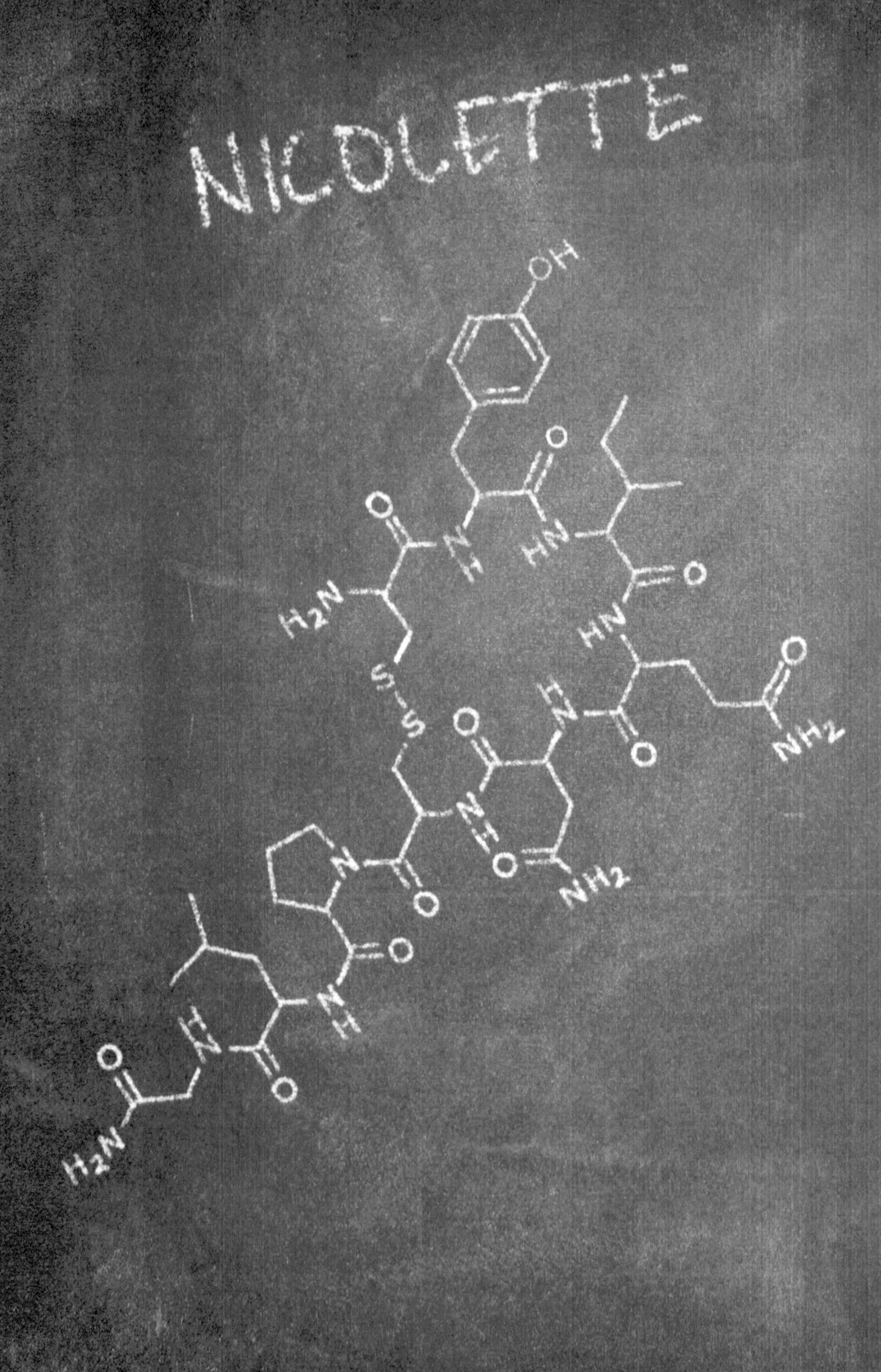

NICOLETTE

Chapter Thirty-Six

HE WHO SHALL NOT BE NAMED BUT IT RHYMES WITH FELIX

"Nicci!" my father calls, waving wildly as I exit the Newark Liberty International Airport on a Friday afternoon. I smile and release my suitcase, walking directly into his outstretched arms.

It's so good to feel and smell Pop's warmth, not awkward in the least, and I'm happy we're getting to the point of normalizing hugs again.

Tears threaten, but I hold them back with a bite to my inner cheek. Not sure what's wrong with me lately, but the tears I've held back for years now slide down my cheeks at the drop of the hat. It's like my tear repressor has finally grown weary of repressing and gone on vacation.

"Good to see you, Pop."

"You too. Where's Helix?"

His name is a punch to the gut, and I have to work hard not to physically react.

No, I haven't told my family about the breakup and all the other bullshit going on in my life the past couple weeks. I kept meaning to come up with an excuse to explain his absence at Angelica's wedding festivities, but my mouth wouldn't say the words out loud.

So, I paste on an apologetic smile for my father. "He said he sends his regrets, but an important family matter came up that he couldn't avoid."

"Awww, I hate that," Pop says, taking my bag from and leading me to his parked car in the lot. "I really like him, honey."

Me too, a tiny voice says, but I swat it away.

The past couple weeks have been eventful, to say the least. The woman who broke into Helix's office at the lab has been identified, and charges have been brought for breaking and entering, corporate espionage, and a laundry list of other crimes. The detectives called to let me know I've been completely exonerated, though they did ask if I knew anything about the video "an anonymous source" sent to Helix. Apparently, he didn't rat me out and tell the cops it was me, which I guess gives him half a point in his favor. He's still about minus five-thousand though, by my estimation.

Charges are also pending against Joyce, my ex-boss at Aquarius, and Dr. Wilhelm, which makes me happy. Well, happy is a relative term at this point. I'm not sure I'll ever be truly happy again. Not now that I know what it feels like to be in love. As mad as I am at Helix, I still love the asshole.

"I'd really like for you to stay at the house instead of a hotel, Nicci. It will always be your home," my father is saying, and I snap back to the conversation. I don't even remember getting in the car, but apparently I did because I'm in the passenger's seat and we're pulling onto the highway.

Pop is looking hopefully at me, but the last thing I want is to be in my parents' house, not just because my mother and sister are nightmares, but it's also the first place I slept in a bed with Helix.

He finally told me about the whole situation where he woke up with me holding his dick and sleeptalking about corn dogs. I was mortified at first, but it quickly turned funny, in hindsight. We still laugh about the corn dogging incident sometimes.

No, *laughed*, past tense.

"I'm going to stay at the hotel where the wedding is being held, Pop. It will be more convenient." Then I decide to tell the full truth, finding the strength to stand up for myself. It's ironic that the man who broke my heart is the one who kick-started my ability to do so.

I add, "Ma and Angelica make me miserable, and I don't have to sit around and be treated like shit. Plus, it's not really my home anymore since Angelica has my room now."

Pop's mouth gapes open before he snaps it tightly shut and nods. "I understand."

When we reach the hotel, my dad hops out and gets my suitcase from the trunk. I give him a quick peck on the cheek. "I'll see you at the rehearsal dinner tonight."

When I enter Bridgewater Hall alone that evening, I feel awkward. This is the same place where Angelica's engagement party was held, and I try not to dwell on the fact that the last time I was here, I was much more comfortable because *he who shall not be named but it rhymes with Felix* was with me.

I wish Austin was here. He's the cool cousin everyone likes, and I could have hung out with him tonight. But this dinner is only for the immediate family and the bridal party. I think Pop probably put his foot down about the price for this extravagant wedding Angelica insisted on having.

And you'll probably never get married because you don't have a man.

Paging Nicolette Bell, pity party for one. Your sad little life is ready for you.

I purposely showed up just before dinner was served so I could minimize the amount of time I had to spend mingling, especially with Ma and Angelica. Speak of the devils, Ma is seated directly across from me when I find my seat. Pop is on her left side, and Angelica and Rory to her right.

My mother puts on a fake smile for the other guests. "Nicolette, so nice to see you. That dress is an interesting color choice."

I don't even glance down at my purple fitted dress that hits at a modest length above my knees. I know this color looks amazing with my green eyes. Hel— *he who shall not be named but it rhymes with Felix* told me so often. In fact, he bought me this dress one day when we were shopping at a lovely boutique in Rice Village.

"Thank you, Ma," I say mildly, though I know she didn't mean it as a compliment. "And mustard-yellow fits your personality perfectly."

Her eyes widen and then narrow, like she's trying to figure out whether or not I just insulted her.

Angelica's blue eyes sparkle with that look I've become all too familiar with over the years. "Hello, sister. Where is your *boyfriend*?" The last word is delivered with a nasty sneer, and I feel myself shrinking as I take my seat. I don't want to. I'd rather retreat to the restroom area and touch the wall where *he* and I shared our first kiss.

As I open my mouth to tell my predetermined fib, I smell him, the rich bergamot mixed with hints of vanilla. Jesus, I've gone completely crazy. I see his handsome face in my mind all the time, and now I'm freaking smelling him?

"Sorry, I'm late. Had some things I needed to attend to for my family."

Super-dee-duper. I'm hearing his voice now too. Someone call Tranquil Minds Behavioral Health Center and see if they have an extra bed available.

But then a large body sinks into the chair beside me, and I realize I'm not hallucinating. When I turn my incredulous face to the left, my lips receive the sweetest kiss ever.

"Hello, sweetheart. You look absolutely stunning tonight."

Oh my fucking hell. *He who shall not be named but it rhymes with Felix* is here.

The guy—that's his new moniker because that other is growing tedious to think—sits beside me for the entire dinner. And he won't stop freaking touching me. A casual arm draped over my shoulder. A not-so-casual hand on my thigh.

I hate that I like the warmth it brings to me... the elemental confidence I feel just by having him by my side. Ma and Angelica refrain from any of their snarky barbs, which makes dinner an almost pleasant experience.

The guy keeps up an easy chatter with my father and the other diners as I quietly eat my roast chicken and veggies just to give myself something to do. The food is good, and I realize how hungry I suddenly am. I haven't been eating well the past couple of weeks, and my stomach is pleased I'm no longer neglecting it. My skin, however, feels like someone washed it on hot and ran it through a dryer, shrinking it to the point of discomfort.

"Can we talk?" he whispers in my ear as I pick at my slice of chocolate cake. It feels dry on my tongue but it's probably more to do with my body's response to *the guy* than any fault of the baker.

I risk a glance at him, and that's a fucking mistake. His eyes are a rich cobalt, only made more brilliant by the matching shirt he wears beneath his charcoal-gray suit. His tie is the same dark-gray, and I wonder what it would feel like wrapped around my wrists while he tied me to the bed and worked that beautiful, filthy mouth of his down my body.

Stop. It.

His smirk tells me he knows exactly what I'm thinking. "Or we could act on whatever dirty thoughts are going on in that head of yours," he murmurs so only I can hear. "My tie has a nice texture that would leave the prettiest patterns on the soft skin of your wrists."

That pops my hazy bubble, and I grit my teeth. "Not going to happen."

His smile is easy and devastating. "Okay. We can just talk then. I have a lot of things to say to you."

"I'm sure you do," I shoot back. "The answer is no."

The guy's jaw tightens stubbornly. "I'm coming to the wedding tomorrow. I'd like to be able to get everything out in the open so we can relax and not have so much tension between us."

"You're not coming," I state firmly.

"I am coming," he retorts with just as much vehemence. "Do you really want to sit all night with these people with no buffer?"

He has a point. Tonight hasn't been horrible.

"Fine," I acquiesce through gritted teeth. "You can be my fake date for the wedding."

"And you'll listen to me tonight? I have a room in the hotel, or I could come to yours, if you'd feel more comfortable."

I open my mouth, close it, and open it again as my brain has an all-out battle with my heart. We do need to air our differences, and maybe I would feel better if I got to get some things off my chest too.

We need privacy, but there's no way he's coming to my room. I'll go to his so I can leave whenever I want. That puts me in control. Right?

Fuck if I know, but I hear myself say, "I'll come to yours."

I hope to god I can handle what's about to go down because I feel so vulnerable when he looks at me with those pleading blue eyes.

"Can I get you a drink?"

Of course *the guy* has the penthouse suite, complete with a full bar in the living room. My eyes search the selection and fall on a bottle of my favorite cabernet sauvignon on the top shelf.

"A glass of the cab," I say before reiterating, "Only one glass to take the edge off."

He smirks and expertly uncorks the bottle before pouring us both a healthy glass of the deep red wine. I'd like to down it like a shot of tequila, but I force myself to sip as *the guy* makes himself at home beside me on the burgundy couch. He removed his jacket when we got up here and rolled up the sleeves of his blue dress shirt, showing off his tattoo. He's also wearing gray suspenders, damn him.

"First of all," he says, brushing the backs of his knuckles down my bare arm.

"First of all, no touching," I say pointedly. "You said you wanted to talk."

Looking chagrined, he pulls his hand back and rubs it up and down his own thigh. His thick, muscled thigh that I'm definitely not thinking about right now.

"Okay, first of all, I want to start by apologizing." He wets his lips, and swallows. "I was one-hundred percent wrong, Nicolette. You have more integrity in your pinky finger than most people have in their entire bodies. I know you would never steal or do anything to hurt our company. My issues are my own, and I was projecting them onto you, and that was absolutely a mistake."

I sense he's not done, so I remain quiet as he takes a long sip of his wine. "I haven't trusted anyone outside my family in a long while, but when I fell for you, I gave you my heart and my trust. I let that trust waver, and for that, I'm truly sorry."

Okay, as far as apologies go, that was a good one. He owned his mistakes, apologized for them, and didn't blame anyone else for his fuck up. But I'm still so hurt.

"Thank you," I say quietly. "I accept your apology."

The tight set of his shoulders releases a bit of tension, and he gives me a fleeting smile. "Thank you. I know I don't deserve it, but thank you."

"Is that all?" I ask, feeling the need to flee, and I don't know why. Maybe I can sense something more coming, and it scares me. I want to hold onto my anger for a while longer, and I'm already feeling a tad softer toward *the guy*.

"I'd like to explain, if you'll let me. I don't want you to think I'm making excuses because I'm not. I just want to let you in." He stares down into his glass and swirls the red liquid a few times. "I feel closer to you than I have with anyone except for Phoenix. I shared a womb with him but I feel like I share a soul with you. I've never had that before."

His eyes pin me in place, his tender gaze beseeching.

"Okay," I breathe, taking another drink of my wine for fortification purposes.

The guy gnaws on his bottom lip for a second before beginning. "Five years ago, I was in the best shape of my life. I was headed to the Olympic trials for swimming and was predicted to make the U.S. Team."

My lips part in shock. I know he's said he was a competitive swimmer, but I didn't expect this level. "But you didn't?"

He shakes his head, still looking at his wine. "I had a girlfriend, Kayla, back then. We had been together for about a year and a half."

A year and a half? That sounds serious, and thinking about him with another woman gives me an ache beneath my breastbone. Downing the rest of my wine, I refill my glass about halfway. Fuck it. I'll sleep like a baby when I get back to my room.

"Kayla started getting clingy with me, and it got really old, really fast. To be honest, I was planning to break up with her, but there was a death in her family, so I let it go on for a few more months." His face wrinkles into a grimace. "I was finally ready to break things off around the time of Phoenix's wedding. You remember I told you what happened that day?"

His eyes catch mine, and I nod, taking a small drink of my wine. "I remember. Poor Phoenix."

The guy takes a generous gulp of his own wine and nods. "After all that went down, I thought it might be a good excuse to let her down easy. I told her I had to end things because I needed to be there for my family, and it wasn't fair to string her along when I wouldn't have time to spend with her."

I nod along. "That sounds reasonable."

"I truly thought so. Kayla was one of those fragile types, and I really was trying to let her down easy, like the whole *it's not you, it's me* thing so she wouldn't feel bad about herself." He drags a hand down his face. "I thought it would be the kindest thing to do instead of telling her she was getting on my last nerve."

I can feel the tension thickening like a dense fog in the room as he tops off his glass.

"Kayla didn't take it well. She started clinging harder. I moved in with Phoenix for a bit, just to be there for my brother since he was having such a hard time, and she would randomly show up at his house with food or little gifts for both of us."

"Ahh, a stage-five clinger," I surmise, and he shakes his head.

"I'm not even sure there's a number high enough. I told her over and over to stop it, that things were over between us, but she insisted she could help." *The guy* blows out a deep exhale, and I can smell the sweetness of the wine on his breath. "It got to the point where my family was becoming concerned. Notes on my car every morning. Flowers showing up at the lab. Some notes that were kind of disturbing. She just wasn't taking the hint."

My heart thuds inside my chest. This Kayla chick sounds unhinged.

"What kinds of notes?" I ask.

"Nothing overtly threatening. It was mostly stuff like *I'll never let you go* and *You know your heart belongs to me.*" He shakes his head. "Phoenix was especially worried. He told me I should get a restraining order against her. At that point, he was my entire focus... well him and Reecie. So, to put his mind at ease, I went down to the police station."

I can hear the strain in his voice, so I break my no-touching rule and place my hand on his knee. He immediately covers my hand with his and gives me a grateful look before continuing.

"I told the officer what was going on, about the notes and gifts, how Kayla wouldn't leave me alone."

"Did you get the restraining order?"

His lips turn white with pressure, and he shakes his head. "When I got done, he made me feel stupid. Laughed and asked me what kind of man couldn't handle a little attention from a woman." Staring at the wall, he says quietly, "I felt like less of a man."

I roll my hand over and link my fingers with his. He seems like he needs an extra level of comfort, and no matter how mad I am at him, I do care about him.

"What happened?" I ask, pretty sure this story is about to take a turn.

"I decided not to get the restraining order and went home. I hadn't been home in about a week. I had only gone to the swimming training facility for practices and then back to Phoenix's. That's it, other than going with my brother to shop for baby stuff a couple of times. I was focused on Phoenix and my intense training schedule. That's it. But I needed to get a couple things from my closet."

His eyes gaze unseeingly at the large television mounted on the wall, where "Welcome, Dr. Hale" is bouncing slowly around the screen.

"I was living in an apartment then, and when I entered my living room, something seemed off, but I didn't think much about it. I just chalked it up to that empty feeling homes get when they've sat unoccupied for a while."

He drains his glass, and I do too, sensing things weren't going to end well with this story. He adds more to our wine glasses, emptying the bottle before resuming his stare at the television, which is now listing the hotel's amenities.

"When I got upstairs, I saw immediately that something was really off. All my clothes had been hung on one side, and women's clothes hung on the other. I recognized them as Kayla's."

"Shit," I mumble, and he nods.

"Very shit," he replies. "That's when I realized what was off about my living room. My coffee table was gone, and it had been replaced with Kayla's little spindly-legged one. She had effectively moved herself into my apartment while I was gone."

This tale had officially gone dark, and I clenched tightly to his hand.

"I went downstairs, and she was coming out of my kitchen wearing an apron and one of those dresses that looked straight out of a 1950s sitcom."

"She broke in?" I ask incredulously.

"She had a key, which I took back from her after we broke up. Apparently, she had copies made." He winces. "I know now I should have had the locks changed, but hindsight and all that."

We each take a sip of wine before he starts talking again.

"I asked Kayla what the hell she was doing in my house, and she informed me—very calmly, I might add—that she was taking care of things for me like a good wife should do. I was just flabbergasted and so damn angry. We'd never even gotten close to the marriage level, at least in my eyes. I told her she needed professional help, and she started to cry. That kind of shit used to work on me, but I was beyond caring. I yelled at her to get out."

Helix's head moves side to side as if he still can't believe what happened next. "She told me she couldn't have this discussion right then because she had dinner in the oven. So she wiped her eyes on her frilly apron and went back into the kitchen. I was standing there trying to figure out what the fuck was happening."

I stay quiet, though I want to rage on his behalf. His voice takes on a raspy quality, rough and scratchy.

"I finally followed her into the kitchen and found her holding one of my huge butcher knives. She told me my heart belonged to her, and she planned to take it."

My free hand slaps across my mouth, and I curse into my palm. This bitch had gone completely psycho.

"When she lunged at me, I tried to dodge." Helix's eyes came to me. "I often wonder what would have happened if I'd just punched her. My instincts have always been to never lay an angry hand on a woman, but I still wonder if my life would have turned out differently if I'd done more to protect myself. Then I feel like a horrible person for even thinking it."

Squeezing his hand hard, I say, "There's a difference between abuse and self-defense, Helix. You shouldn't feel bad for thinking about it. Hell, I wouldn't have blamed you a bit if you'd cold-cocked her."

His smile is sad. "That's what Phoenix said. And my therapist. I saw Dr. Shannon for two years afterward. We talked a lot about toxic masculinity and society's standards for how men should act. Like the whole thing with the restraining order. I let myself be shamed into dropping it because *a real man* doesn't need outside help in a relationship."

"Utter bullshit," I grumble.

"Yeah, I know that now. I've grown a lot since then."

My eyes flick to his shoulder, hidden beneath the cobalt-blue of his shirt. "Is that what happened to your shoulder?"

Helix nods and stares at the fringe ringing the rug beneath the coffee table. "Yeah. When I dodged, the knife went into my shoulder, severing my coracoclavicular ligament." His chin trembles, and it hurts me to the depths of my soul. "It ended my swimming career."

Holy. Fucking. Shit.

I can't help myself. I throw my arms around Helix and let him bury his face in my neck. His arms are strong and warm around me, and I realize how much I've missed his hugs.

We cling together, me whispering, "I'm sorry. I'm so sorry," over and over into his thick, dark hair.

"No, I'm sorry," he murmurs. "I should have told you way earlier about all this, but it's not easy for me. My entire life changed that night, and it's not something I like to dwell on. But it definitely caused trust issues."

He pulls back, and I see a tear hanging on his bottom lashes. Helix swipes it away with his thumb before using his index finger to wipe beneath my left eye. I hadn't even realized I'd been crying too. Then he smudges his thumb and forefinger together, melding our tears together. It's such an intimate thing to do, like some kind of weird blood pact but with tears. I don't dislike it.

"I just wanted you to know everything, Nicolette. Yes, I screwed up, but I never stopped loving you, not for a second. I understand if you can't find it inside yourself to forgive me, but I'd like to try and make it up to you." His blue eyes search my face. "Will you let me try?"

Oh my heart. It pounds and it hurts and... it starts to heal. Just the tiniest bit. But I still feel the need to protect it from further damage.

"You hurt me, Helix. You didn't trust me. I've told you how I've always felt I was written in the margins of my own life, and what you did shoved me back to the margins."

"I know." He cups my face, and another tear falls from his eye. "I can never apologize enough. If you say it's over for good, I'll respect that, but if you think there's even a chance you could forgive me, I will fight for you, Nicolette, because you don't belong in the margins. You're front and center of my life, and I want to prove it."

Helix drops to his knees on the rug and sandwiches my hand between his. "I will do anything in my power to get you back, Nicolette Bell." His lips quirk up the tiniest of bits. "Short of stalking. After what happened to me, I understand boundaries, so if you set them, I will follow them. I love you with my entire heart, and if there's a glimmer of hope, I will grab onto it."

I think about that for a long while before speaking. "You've always encouraged me to stand up for myself, and this is me doing exactly that." His face falls until I say, "But there is a glimmer."

He's full-on grinning now. "Say no more. If I overstep, you can tell me, but expect to be wooed, Nicolette. I mean, you need to seriously prepare yourself for the wooing."

Laughing, I say, "I look forward to it."

He pulls me into a hug, and I close my eyes, loving the feel and the scent of him way more than I should.

And then the wine kicks my ass, and I fall asleep with my head on his shoulder.

NICOLETTE

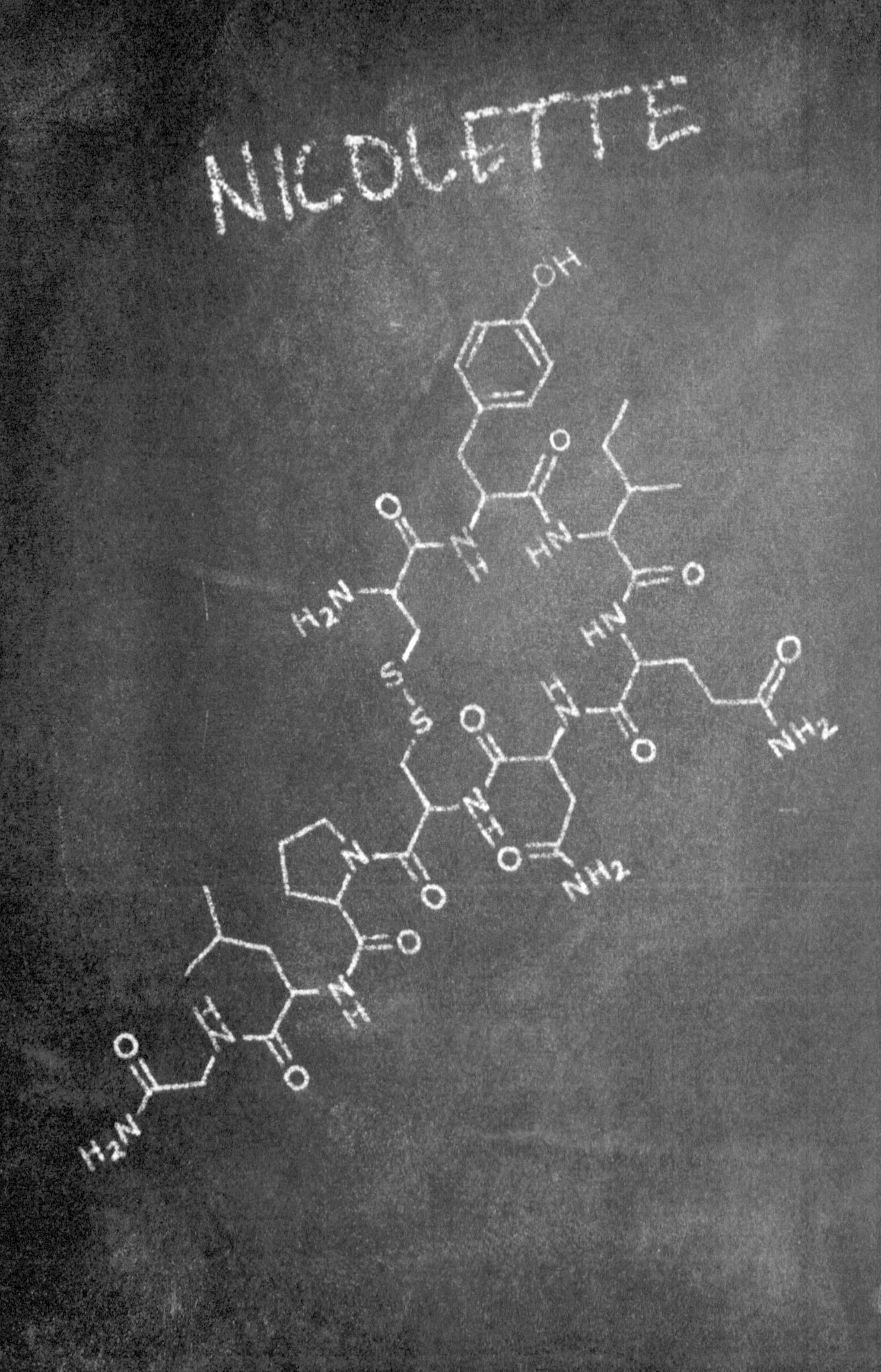

Chapter Thirty-Seven

MY SISTER'S BIG FAT DISASTROUS WEDDING

I awaken in a strange bed and have a moment of panic, my body jackknifing to a sitting position as my head swings from side to side. Then I remember falling asleep in Helix's hotel room. *Damn wine.*

Patting the covers beside me, I find no Helix, and the bed doesn't look disturbed at all on that side. He obviously meant it when he said he was respecting boundaries. Then I look over and see my dress draped across a chair, and my eyes jerk down to find I'm wearing one of Helix's huge T-shirts. Huh. So much for boundaries.

I can't bring myself to be mad about it though because the shirt is baggy and comfortable, and he's seen it all before anyway. Sliding from the bed, I tiptoe on bare feet into the hallway of the suite and find another bedroom with the door slightly ajar. I push it all the way open and see a large form sleeping on a much smaller bed than the one I woke up in. Leaning against the door frame, I watch him.

Helix is on his back, one arm thrown over his head and one leg cocked out to the side. His big frame takes up the entire bed, and the covers are pulled down to his waist, giving me a hint of the gray band of his boxer briefs and a whole lotta damn muscles. This man is devastatingly hot when he sleeps.

He makes a soft grunt and slides his hand down over his chest and abs before resting on a noticeable bulge beneath the covers. Then he squeezes it and moans.

"Thinking about corn dogs?" I ask, and his eyes pop open to find me as a sleepy smile creeps across his lips.

"I think the real question is, have *you* been thinking about corn dogs?"

Okay, he's even hotter when he's awake and flirty.

"Not really," I lie, and he scoots up, leaning against the headboard. My eyes find the scar on his shoulder, but I quickly pull them away and up to his messy hair.

"Come sit with me, queenie."

This is a dangerous proposition, but I do it anyway, resting my butt on the edge of the bed and tugging his shirt down over my thighs. His eyes follow the movement.

"For the record," he says, "I put my shirt on you and then slid your dress down over your legs, so I didn't see you undressed. I'm still amazed by how hard you sleep when the wine hits."

"Thank you for that," I tell him quietly because that was pretty damn respectful of him.

"Boundaries," he says. "You set them, and I'll follow them. Whatever you need." I nod, and he holds his hand out, palm up, an invitation I accept. "Would you like to get some breakfast with me?"

I hesitate before agreeing. "Sure. Just let me go get changed."

"Do you want me to walk you to your room?" The grin he gives me is pure cheekiness. "Or I could help you shower."

"That's really nice of you," I say drolly, "but I believe I can manage."

"Like I said, I'm here for whatever you need." He pulls the covers back and slides from the bed, giving me an excellent view of his round ass when he stands and stretches. "I'll get you some shorts to wear so you don't have to put your dress back on." Then he strides from the room, my eyes following him the entire way.

When he returns, my gaze is still in the same spot, and his penis enters the room first. I hear him chuckle because I am obviously staring at his, uh, corn dog.

"Shut up," I whine, dragging my reluctant eyes away. "I can't *not* look when it's sticking out there like that."

"You won't hear me complaining. I'm here for your viewing pleasure."

I stand and snatch the shorts from him before stomping from the bedroom. "I'll be back in ten. Have some damn clothes on."

"You'll need a key to get back up here. I put one on your purse beside the door," he calls to my retreating back, and I can hear the amusement in his voice.

Stepping into the shorts, I head straight for the exit, snagging my purse and the key card as I do. As soon as I enter the elevator, I realize I'm barefoot because I left my shoes in Helix's room, as well as my dress. The man had me so damned flustered with his sexy ass and rumpled hair and big dick.

I press the button for floor six, but the elevator makes a stop on ten. Angelica's friend, Annette, enters with a bucket of ice, looking me up and down with a raised brow. "Good night?"

"Mmhmm," I say noncommittally before remembering Helix is supposed to be my boyfriend, and I'm obviously doing the barefoot walk of shame from his room. "Helix surprised me, and I already had a room. All my clothes are in there."

"He seems nice," Annette says before fanning herself. "And he totally gives off some serious BDE."

"With good reason," I assure her, staring up at the numbers as the cart descends.

"I had to go get ice for your sister. She's on the warpath this morning."

"Welp, good luck with that," I shoot back, stepping off the elevator as soon as the doors open.

Annette follows and then groans when we both hear Angelica shrieking at a hotel worker. "This is unacceptable. Do you not realize I am *the bride?* You should be bending over backward for me."

Annette jogs to keep up with me as we grow closer to the screaming. Luckily, my bridezilla sister's room is at the very end of the hallway, so I don't have to pass it to get to mine.

"Please don't make me go back in there," Annette hisses, and I give her the most apathetic look I can muster.

"You're the one who's chosen to be her friend all these years," I say, opening my door and stepping inside. The click of the door behind me is so, so satisfying. Those who tolerate bullying are just as guilty as the ones who bully, and I have no sympathy for Annette.

After rinsing off in the shower and dressing, I walk back out of my room to hear the bridezilla still screaming. "This room is shitty. It's just a regular room. Why am I not in the penthouse?"

"Because you didn't pay for the penthouse, Ms. Bell," the hotel worker replies.

"My father will pay. Get it for me." I swear, her audacity is completely over the top.

"I'm sorry, ma'am, but there's already a guest in the penthouse."

She lets out a shriek of frustration, and I laugh as I walk down the hallway, her rant fading away as she insists they kick out the other guest because she's "the bride, goddammit."

Breakfast was nice this morning. Helix and I ate and talked, not about anything significant, and it felt so natural and normal. My heart is still guarded though.

The story he told me last night was heartbreaking, and I can't say it didn't soften my feelings toward him just a bit. I believed him when he said he wasn't making excuses for his behavior, and I honestly think he just wanted me to understand him on a deeper level.

We all have past experiences that color the way we view or respond to things, and that's fair. Having trust issues is completely understandable in his case. Hell, I've had the same problem because I grew up feeling like I had no one I could fully trust. When the people who are supposed to be your baseline means of support constantly let you down, you're left wary of putting your faith in anyone. So I can relate to him on that point.

The problem is that I *did* put my faith in Helix, and he let me down by suspecting me of horrible things. Was what he did unforgivable? I'm honestly not sure, but I'm leaning toward no. I'm not telling him that though because I want to see what this wooing is all about.

Starting now.

We're at Rory and Angelica's reception, and I just escaped an arduous conversation with my long-winded Aunt Bibi about her bladder issues. I see Helix exiting the hallway leading to the restrooms and move to intercept him.

"Come on," I say, taking his hand and leading him toward the light-up dance floor. I'm fully aware Helix Hale doesn't dance. He's told me that on numerous occasions, so this is a bit of a test.

"Where are we going?" he asks nervously.

"I love this song and want to dance," I say, glancing back to see his face pinkening with what I'm sure is panic.

"W-with me?"

I stop, swivel on my heel, and plop a hand on my hip, lifting one eyebrow. "Unless there's someone else here you'd like to see me dance with."

With a frown and a grumbled, "Fine, come on," he leads me to the far corner of the floor, positioning us in a glowing blue square. "Don't blame me if your toes suffer."

Hiding my smile, I look up at him. "Is it really such a hardship to hold me close to you?"

In answer, Helix hauls my body against his and wraps his arms around my waist as the band begins playing "Just the Way You Are" by Bruno Mars. I loop my arms around his neck and rest my cheek against the lapel of his jet-black suit, letting the beautiful melody guide our sway.

He tilts his head down until his nose is buried in the top of my hair, and then he kisses me there. "I wouldn't do this for anyone else," he informs me, keeping one hand on the small of my back, left bare by the deep V of my magenta dress. The other slides up my spine until he's cupping the side of my head, his thumb stroking slowly against my cheek.

I feel completely possessed by him, and I close my eyes as the sweet lyrics play. We don't move our feet at all, but I don't care. Being held like this heals a part of me.

As soon as the song ends, I go up on my tiptoes and reward him with a soft kiss to his lips. "Thank you."

His handsome face breaks into a smile. "Completely worth it for that kiss. What do I have to do to get a little tongue action next time?"

"The Cha Cha," I challenge flatly, and he shudders, making me laugh. "Let's go sit. I think I've tortured you enough for one night."

Helix grabs us a couple drinks, and we find an empty table in a quiet corner. "What was your sister yelling at Rory about earlier?" he asks.

"Apparently," I say, lowering my voice, "Angelica insisted the ice sculptures be delivered and placed by noon, even though the service was a good four hours later. She was devastated that they were already half melted by the time the reception started."

"And how exactly is that Rory's fault?" Helix asks, taking a drink of his drink and wincing at the taste.

"It's not. He was trying to explain to her that ice sculptures were made of, you know, *ice,* which *melts.* And that it was her own fault for insisting they arrive so far ahead of the actual wedding."

Helix blows out a breath through pursed lips. "Bet that went over well." He leans close. "How long do you give this marriage? I say they'll either be divorced or one of them will be in jail within six months."

I glance over at my sister, who's pouting and glaring at her new husband, who seems to be well on his way to complete drunkenness. "To be honest, I'm not sure they're going to make it to the honeymoon."

"Serves her right. Seems like all she's done is complain the entire day."

It makes me a little sad, not because I wish my sister well. I couldn't care less about her happiness. I'm disappointed because my father obviously paid a small fortune for this party to celebrate a marriage that already seems to be on the rocks.

I take a sip of my pink drink and practically gag on the sweetness. "What the fuck is this?" I croak, holding up the glass and staring at it.

"Ah, that, my dear, is the signature cocktail of the wedding. It's called the Clutterbuck Love Fizz. The bartender told me all the ingredients were specifically chosen by the charming new Mrs. Clutterbuck herself. I think he's purposely pointing that out to everyone so no one thinks he came up with it."

"Don't blame the poor guy. It tastes like syrup."

Helix pushes his away. "I'll go get us a beer... unless you'd prefer wine."

I narrow my eyes at him. "Pushing your luck, Hale."

He laughs and heads back to the bar, returning a few minutes later with two IPAs, which we both eagerly glug to get rid of the sugary taste of the Clutterbuck Love Fizz.

"Can I ask you a question about what you told me last night?" I ask, once half of my beer is gone.

He nods. "Of course."

"What happened to Kayla, if it's not too uncomfortable for you to talk about?"

"She was sentenced to three years in a mental health institution."

"Three years? But it's been five. Is she out?" Panic wells up in my chest at the thought of that woman roaming free.

"She's not out. She found out I was paying for her stay at a private facility and decided that meant I loved her. The institution carefully monitors all outgoing mail, but she somehow found a way to start sending me letters."

"Oh my god!" I gasp.

"Yeah, that violation added a few more years to her sentence. Kayla's mom is actually a really nice lady, and she keeps me up to date with what's going on. We talk about once a year after court evaluations are done. She said Kayla refuses to take the prescribed medications, so as long as she's being uncooperative, it's highly unlikely they'll release her. She also refuses to acknowledge what she did was wrong, so that doesn't help her case."

I don't say it aloud, but I hope they never let her out.

Helix changes the subject. "Would you come upstairs with me when this is over?"

"To your room?"

He smiles. "Not for *that*... unless you're offering."

"I'm not." *Am I? No, definitely not.*

"Okay," he says easily. "I have something I'd like to give you. Let's call it phase one of the wooing."

I look around the room. Rory and Angelica are arguing again, my father is hiding out around the corner of the bar, and Ma is running around looking harried. Most of the guests have left already, even though the newlyweds have yet to make their grand exit. I guess all Angelica's antics have left a sour taste in everyone's mouth.

"You know what? Let's just go now," I tell him.

Helix seats me on the couch in his suite while he retreats to his bedroom, returning a moment later with a slender box wrapped in shiny blue paper.

"This is for you."

I stare down at the prettily wrapped package and pick at the tape as Helix sits on the adjacent chair. "What is it?"

"A loaf of bread," he says sarcastically.

Rolling my eyes, I pull off the paper and open the box to find a nameplate like you would see beside an office door. It reads:

Nicolette Bell, M.D., Ph.D.
Laboratory Director and Head of Research and Development
Hale Laboratories

Picking it up, I stare at the words, trying to decipher what exactly is going on here. "What is this, Helix?"

"It's your new job," he says softly.

My head shakes side to side in denial. "No, Director of Research and Development is *your* job."

His blue gaze is intense and piercing. "Not anymore. I've turned in my resignation."

I leap to my feet and gape down at him. "You can't resign, you nimrod." Shaking the metal nameplate at him, I protest, "And you can't give me your job."

"It's already done," he states calmly. "And I'm not giving it to you. You've earned the position. If you reject the offer, we'll have to shut down the lab until we can find someone else to run it."

Blinking about fifty times in the span of two seconds, I scoff. "And what about you?"

"If you'd like me to come work for you, I'd be happy to. If not..." Helix averts his eyes to a spot on the wall to my left.

"If not, what?"

He brings his gaze back to me. "If not, I'm moving to London with Remi."

Alarm bells ring inside my head, and my nerve endings spark into a frenzy. "You're moving?" My voice is about two octaves too high, and I realize how very much I don't want him to go.

Helix wets his lips and stands, taking one long step until he's only an inch away from me. "If things don't work out with us, I can't stay, Nicolette. I can't live close to you if you're not mine."

"B-but Houston is your home."

"You're my home," he retorts, reaching down to tap the plate with the tip of one finger. "You deserve this, and it's what I want more than anything. You're smarter than me, you have more degrees than me, and you're older than me."

"You could have left out that last one," I say wryly, earning me his signature half-cocked smile, but it fades almost as soon as it appears.

"Please accept it. I believe in my heart that you are what's best for the future of Hale Cosmetics."

My feelings are raw on the surface of my skin when I whisper, "I don't want you to move to London."

"Then I would happily apply to be your lab manager. Or whatever position you want me in. Would you like me to send over my resumé?"

I snort out a laugh. "You've officially lost your damn mind."

"There's no rush. Take your time thinking about it and let my father know when you've made your decision." Helix rests a gentle hand on my cheek. "I love you more than anything in the world, Nicolette Bell, but that's not why I'm doing this. I'm doing this because you're the best person for the job."

Inhaling a shaky breath, I say, "I'll think about it."

Taking a step back, he asks, "Would you like to ride home on the jet with me tomorrow?"

Of all the decisions I'm now facing, that one is the hardest to answer, but I finally say, "I think I need some space from you right now. I'll just take my scheduled flight."

Helix nods solemnly. "Whatever you want, queenie."

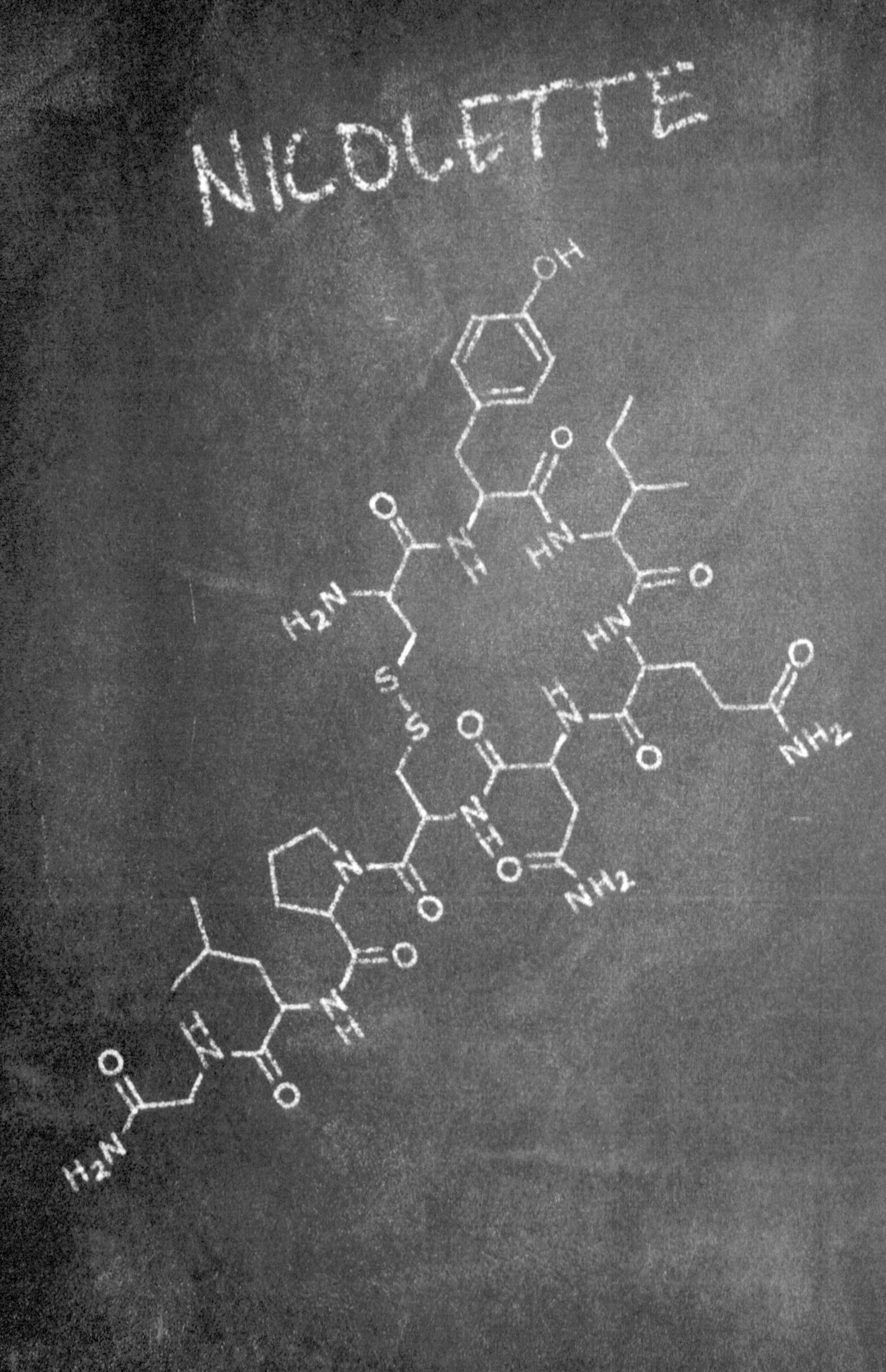

NICOLETTE

Chapter Thirty-Eight

THE WOOING

The day I get home from the wedding, I realize the wooing has already begun. I arrive at my townhome to find Calvin—the man who picked me up from the airport for my interview—waiting in his car with a huge bouquet of flowers.

They are bright and colorful, but what really makes me smile is the attached card.

To my beautiful Nicolette,

These may just look like flowers, but I think of each bloom as a promise from me to you. I selected each type because they all have individual meanings, which I listed below.

Red rose - love

Peony - happy life

Morning glory - affection

Lily of the valley - humility

Heliotrope - devotion

Red Chrysanthemum – I love you (because that one bears repeating)
I hope these brighten your day as much as you brighten my life.
All my love,
Helix

"Well played, Dr. Hale," I say aloud, holding the card to my chest.

The next day, Calvin arrives on my doorstep again, this time with an enormous stuffed elephant. And when I say enormous, I mean almost large enough for me to ride on. It takes Calvin and I both to wrangle it into my living room.

Once he's gone, I stare at the insane gift and giggle. The elephant has green eyes and is wearing glasses exactly like mine. It's obviously been custom-made because there's a tag on the butt that reads *Queenie.*

And so it continues for the next two weeks. Gifts arrive each day, delivered by Calvin. Some are funny, like the case of frozen corn dogs that arrived three days ago. That one had Calvin scratching his head, but there was no way I was explaining it to him.

Today I received a leatherbound journal, the pages filled with Helix's distinctive handwriting. Some of them contain his thoughts, and there are even a couple of poems. I've read through it three times already and decided my favorite was a poem titled *Margins.*

You say you've been written in the margins of your life.
But I see you.
You say your voice doesn't matter.
But I hear you.
I will write your name in the boldest font, not in the margins, but on the front cover of the book.
Then I will fill each page with the pieces of my heart.

Some people are written in pencil and can be erased from memories.

Some people are written in ink, which can fade with time.

But you have been burned into the pages of my life, permanently etched into my soul.

You will not live in my margins.

Yeah, that one made me cry. Helix Hale is a damn good wooer.

The next day, I get up and dress, my eyes falling on my dresser and the nameplate with my name and my new title... if I decide to accept the job. I've thought about it a lot over the past couple weeks and have started to formulate a plan.

I clip on the charm bracelet Calvin delivered five days ago and wiggle my wrist to hear it jingle. There's an elephant charm, as well as an Erlenmeyer flask, a cute pair of glasses, and, of course, a corn dog. I have no idea where the hell Helix even found a corn dog charm, but it made me laugh.

Calvin usually makes his deliveries a little after noon, but when that time comes and goes, I find myself feeling anxious. I definitely don't need any more gifts. I'm well and truly wooed, but I worry that something happened to him.

At two in the afternoon, I hear a knock on my door and sprint to open it, finding a person standing there with a box so large, I can't see his face.

"Good grief, Calvin. What does he have you delivering today?"

"Not Calvin," a voice says from behind the box, and a thrill shoots down my spine. Because I recognize that voice. I've missed that voice.

I haven't heard it in two weeks. Helix and I text every day when I message him to say thank you for whatever gift arrived. But his deep voice resonates inside me and makes me giddy.

"Come on in," I say, stepping back to allow Helix inside. He sets down the box, which is wrapped in the gaudiest snowman Christmas paper I've ever seen and is topped with a sparkly silver bow. "Did I sleep for a few months? Because I'm pretty sure it's early March."

He stands and ruins me with his handsome smile. "Just call me the Spring Santa." Lowering himself to the floor, he gestures for me to do the same. "I wanted to be here when you opened this one."

"What is it?" I ask as I sit cross-legged beside him.

Rolling his eyes, Helix lets out an exaggerated sigh. "Why do you always ask me that when the present is right in front of you? Just open it."

"Fine," I huff, pulling off the bow before diving in to tear off the paper. My heart stalls for a second and then begins beating faster when I start to suspect what's in the box. Removing every scrap of paper, I stare wide-eyed at what's revealed.

"You... you got me a Barbie Dreamhouse?"

"This was the original design. They have newer versions," he says worriedly. "There's one with a slide and a pool. If you don't like—"

His words are cut off by my lips because I dive at him, knocking him onto his back and kissing the fire out of him. And god, how I've missed kissing Helix.

He's startled only momentarily before his hands are on my ass, and he's kissing me back with fervor. I plunge my fingers into his hair to anchor his mouth to mine as I take and taste everything I've been craving.

"I love you," I tell him between kisses. "I love you, and you're not moving to London."

He rolls us, pinning me beneath him as he runs his mouth across my cheek and bites my earlobe. Then his kisses trail down my neck, and one hand pulls my knee over his hip.

"You're awfully fucking bossy since you became lab director."

I shove his shoulders and turn us again, putting me back on top. "Damn straight. And I haven't accepted yet."

"But you will, right?" he asks, his breaths stuttering as I pull down the collar of his dove-gray Henley and lick a line along his collar bone.

Our hands are all over each other, touching and caressing, relearning each other. Biting the side of his neck, I soothe the spot with my tongue before sitting up and bracing my hands on his chest, doing my best to ignore the growing bulge beneath me.

"Only if you'll be my co-director."

Helix's eyebrows raise and then furrow together. "No, I want you to have it."

"And I want us to be partners."

His baby blues search my face. "In all the ways?"

I nod. "In all the ways."

He sits up and cups my face with both hands. "It was the Barbie house that clinched it, wasn't it?"

I burst into laughter and give him a quick kiss. "No, you nut, though I do love it." My eyes fall to his chest, and I shrug before lifting my gaze back to his. "What clinched it was the effort you put in to get me back. No one has ever made me feel so important and loved."

Helix twists one of my curls around his finger. "You are important and loved. Never forget that, Nicolette. And I'm so sorry for—"

I shush him with a finger to his lips. "I don't want you to apologize anymore. That will only serve to drive a wedge between us. Everyone makes mistakes, Helix. What matters is how you fix them." I drag my finger down his lips and tap his chin. "And you went above and beyond. Every gift you sent was so meaningful."

"Even the corn dogs?"

Giggling, I say, "Even the corn dogs." I swing my leg over and off him, seating myself on the floor beside Helix. "Want to help me put together a magnificent Barbie Dreamhouse?"

He wiggles and stretches his fingers. "That's what I'm here for, babe. After all, we're partners now."

"I have no idea who the fuck wrote these instructions, but they need to be shot," Helix grumbles, staring at pink piece of plastic like it had personally insulted him.

"That's the one I've been looking for," I accuse, taking it from him and snapping it into place. "There, that part's done. Only fourteen thousand more pieces to go."

Helix snorts. "The funny part is, you're not even exaggerating." With a tilt of his head, he assesses what we've already spent two hours working on. "Is there a Barbie doll that's a building inspector? If so, I think we're fucked. No way she'll grant us a permit for this."

Picking up another piece, I hold it against the instruction booklet to compare. "I used to think we were smart, but this has proven me dead-ass wrong."

"Aren't there any other toys you wanted as a child? Preferably something that doesn't require a mechanical engineering degree to assemble it?"

"Hmm," I ponder. "I liked puzzle-based toys like Simon. Ooh, and Perfection. Remember that game where you were timed and the whole board would pop up and scare the shit out of you?"

"Oh, yeah. That one was fun."

"I got one for my birthday one year, but Angelica stole all the pieces and buried them in the back yard. It took me three months to find and dig them all up." I snap one of the railings into place. "I never did find that hexagon-shaped piece."

"She was a fucking brat. Still is," Helix says, picking up the instructions and holding them upside down like that might help. "Any news on the newlyweds?"

"Ah, yes. The Clutterbucks returned from their honeymoon, both of them still alive, though barely. They apparently got some kind of virus that tried to destroy their intestines."

"Sucks for them." Though he doesn't really sound very sorry about it.

"Pop said they've been house hunting for months, but Angelica keeps rejecting all of Rory's suggestions. Apparently houses that are within their budget aren't big enough for her." I gesture to the dollhouse. "I think she's dreaming of something more like this."

"A house that will fall over if the wind blows wrong?"

I stick my tongue out at his negative attitude. "Anyway, they're now living in a small room at the back of Angelica's beauty salon because Rory told his landlord he'd be moving out after the wedding. So now his lease is up, and they don't have anywhere else to go. I'm sure he thought they would have secured a house by now. Guess he didn't realize how snotty my sister was going to be about it."

"Has he met her?" Helix scoffs. "I'm sure your parents would let them live at their house."

Cutting my eyes at him, I ask, "Would *you* want to live with my mother?"

"Good point," he says, making a slight gagging noise before getting back to work. "You know, our Aspen trip is coming up in two days. I can postpone it if you're not ready."

I smile over at him. "I'm ready."

Helix stays with me the next two nights. We don't have sex, but we sleep together, and when he holds me against his warm body all night long, I feel like I'm finally at peace.

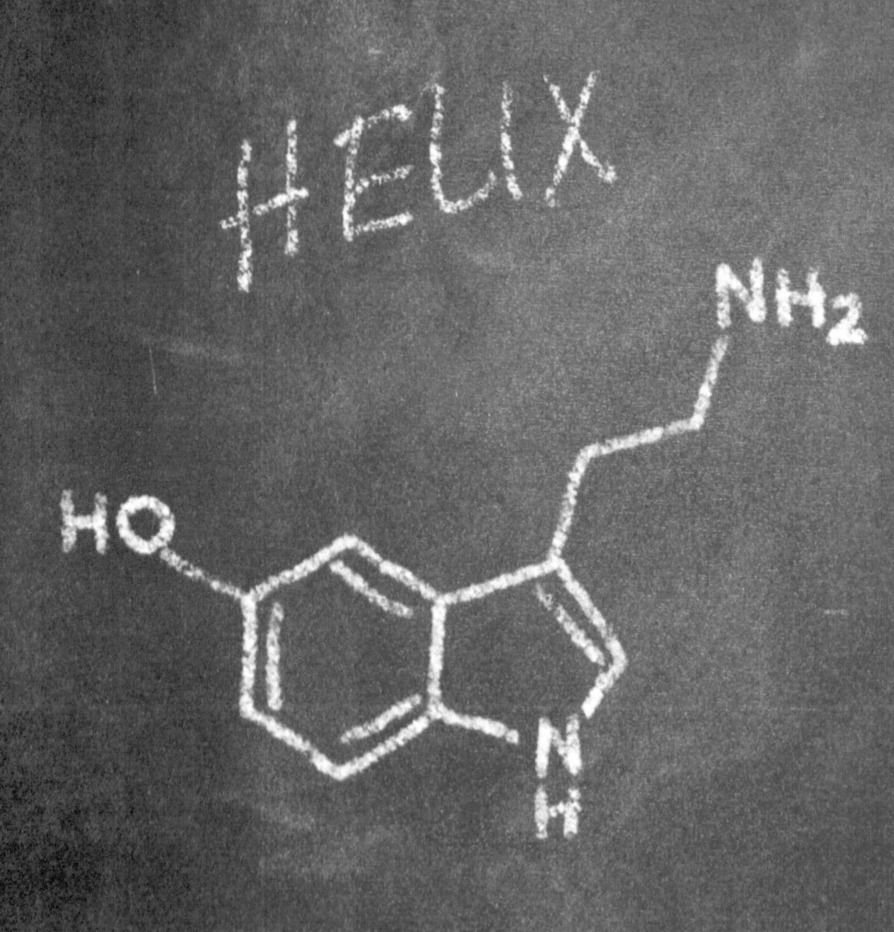
HELIX
NH₂
HO
N
H

Chapter Thirty-Nine

THE CABIN

"This place is beautiful," Nicolette says breathily, her eyes rising up the peaked windows of the great room and all the way to the timber ceiling thirty feet above. The back wall juts out in a V-shape and allows a view of the mountains beyond a thick forest.

"Okay, I'll buy it for us."

Her head snaps down so quickly she stumbles, but she catches herself before she can land on her perfect ass.

"You can't buy this cabin," she insists, looking at me like I just grew a penis out of my forehead.

"Why not? You said you liked it."

She puffs out an exasperated breath. "You can't just buy things because I say I like them."

I walk toward her and rest my hands on her hips. "I can and I will."

Nicolette eyes me skeptically and cocks her head to one side. "Okay, I like Italy."

Pulling out my phone, I say, "Let me make a couple calls. But I'm having that tower straightened. There's no need for it to be leaning like that."

She bursts into laughter and swats my chest. "You're being ridiculous." Then she grabs my hand and begins dragging me to the left side of the cabin. "Let's go explore."

We find a well-stocked kitchen and a dining room with a large table that looks roughhewn but is smooth as silk to the touch. There's also a half bath and two sets of stairs, one leading up and one down. On the other side of the main level, there's a nice sized bedroom with an attached bath.

We head downstairs to find a game room with a pool table and full-sized video games and another bed/bath combo.

The top level consists of a loft living area that overlooks the great room below with a second kitchen off to the right. Heading left, we find two double doors that open into the master suite. The space manages to look cozy despite its size, with a wood-burning fireplace, complete with a furry brown rug. French doors open onto a private balcony that looks like the perfect spot to have our morning coffee.

The bed is four-poster and large enough to fit a lot more than two people, and I get a vision of Nicolette and I sleeping in that bed and being woken up by our five children. Yeah, I said five. I plan to fill her up every chance she'll give me.

Our first evening together in Aspen was sublime. When we cooked dinner together in the beautiful kitchen, it felt like we were an old married couple, but at the same time, it was like a fresh and new rela-tionship. Comfort and excitement... could I ask for anything more?

As I sit on the smooth whiskey-colored couch with Nicolette's head in my lap, my eyes go up and to the left, visualizing the engage-ment ring I brought with me. I'm not sure if it's too soon after our fight and subsequent breakup to ask her to spend the rest of her life with me, but I'm dying to pop the question. I'm dying to officially make her mine.

I definitely want to do it on this trip, despite my reservations about the timing, but when exactly should I do it? I'd pictured something like this... relaxing, having a couple brandies, a fire in the fireplace. The setting is romantic for sure, but do I want to do it on the first night? What if she says no and the rest of the trip is awkward?

Then again, what if she says yes?

I look down at her when she takes a drink from the brandy snifter and sets it aside. She's wearing fitted jeans and a sage-green Henley beneath my unbuttoned flannel shirt. I think I love her in my clothes more than anything else she's ever worn.

As I comb my fingers through her dark hair, Nicolette's eyes rise up to mine, and I see the mischievous glint there a second before she rolls over onto her stomach. Her nose nuzzles against my crotch as she asks, "May I please suck your big dick?"

Fuck me.

"Please do," I answer, my voice little more than a grunt because the blood supply to my brain heads south, leaving my verbal skills somewhere near caveman levels. "Clothes off."

Nicolette stands and begins stripping as I do the same, pulling off my white T-shirt before quickly shucking my jeans. I take her in as she removes piece by piece, revealing her luscious body to my lustful gaze.

When she's completely naked, she drops to her knees and pulls my thighs wide with her hands. I scoot my ass forward to give her better access to my bobbing cock. The cool leather I'm sitting on contrasts with the heat of her mouth when she takes me inside.

"That's my girl," I praise, gathering her hair in one hand to use as a makeshift handle for me to fuck her mouth. This is the first sexual contact we've had in weeks, and I'm already primed to come.

The fire crackles behind her, the orange glow flickering on the creamy skin of her back and ass.

"Do you know how beautiful you look with your mouth stuffed full of my cock? Damn, baby. Fucking this tight little throat makes me want to blow my load so deep in you, you'll taste me for a week."

Nicolette hums around me and the vibration has me lifting my hips from the couch as I hold her down on my cock.

"That's it. Take it deep. You're such a good girl." I lose control, yanking her hair as I use her sexy mouth to get off. My strokes are long and smooth, feeling Nicolette's tight lips sliding from tip to root and back again.

"Goddammit, how the fuck are you taking me so well? You're my perfect girl, aren't you? You're getting my cock so nice and wet so I can spread your pretty legs and slam right in." I pant out a few harsh breaths as I try to hold on for just a few more seconds. "Touch that pretty pussy. Soak your fingers and then give me a taste."

I tilt my head against the back of the couch but keep my gaze downcast on the woman between my spread thighs. She clutches my thigh with one hand, but the other disappears between her legs. I watch her arm move as she pleasures herself at my direction, and it's the hottest damn thing I've ever seen.

"Two fingers inside, baby. I want to taste the deepest part of you." Thirty seconds later, her fingers reappear, her watery green eyes watching me as she holds her hand up. I waste no time, taking her dripping digits into my mouth and sliding my tongue around them. She tastes like the most beautiful heaven I could imagine, and that's what finally pushes me over the edge.

I'm barely able to moan out a warning before I spill myself onto the back of her tongue. Nicolette swallows around me, drinking down every drop of my release as my body shudders violently. My breathing is so fast and labored, I can't even utter a single syllable, only grunts of pure ecstasy.

My body is a giant limp noodle of happiness as I sag onto the leather with a goofy smile on my face. Nicolette rises, and I see the tight pout of her nipples and the slickness coating her thighs. I'm going to fucking eat her up... if I can ever regain muscle control after that monster orgasm.

"Sit on my lap and let me suck your tits while I try to remember how to walk," I command, earning me a giggle. She complies, straddling my thighs and jutting her breasts into my face.

Nicolette has the perfect tits, in my opinion. They are soft with the rosiest nipples that pebble as I stroke them with my tongue. I fill my mouth with one and feel her drip onto my balls. With my tongue and lips, I draw her deeper, using my teeth to scrape against the sensitive tip before moving to the other. She writhes against me, and I feel my cock take notice. He's not quite ready for action yet, but he will be soon.

Releasing her from my mouth, I swivel my body and lay on the couch. "Come ride my face, pretty girl. I need to tongue fuck you."

"Helix," she squeals when I grab her ass with both hands and drag her up my body. "I'll smother you."

With a wicked grin, I ask, "Are you forgetting I'm a swimmer? I've got a lung capacity that will blow your damn mind. Now straddle my fucking face and put that perfect cunt in my mouth."

She spreads her legs over my face, though I notice she's still trying to hover. Pulling her firmly onto me, I proceed to make her forget her own name.

"Jesus," she gasps after the second orgasm, grasping the arm of the couch with both hands. "Consider my mind blown."

The sweet taste of her climaxes on my tongue has reinvigorated my cock and my legs, and I scoop Nicolette into my arms and stand, walking us to the soft rug in front of the gently crackling fire. Then I lay her down and cover her body with my own.

I want to slow things down and take my time with her, make her feel how special she is to me. Reaching between us, I give my dick a couple long pulls before nestling the head between her lower lips. She's so wet, I slide in easily until our pelvises are kissing.

"Put your arms above your head, Nicolette," I demand gently. When she does, I link my fingers with hers and begin to move. Her body fits mine like a glove, and I take her lips in a deep, longing kiss. We move together, our bodies innately knowing what to do.

"I love you," she utters into my mouth, and I feel a surge of emotions so strong, it makes my heart ache.

I pull back and stare into the emerald gems of her eyes. "I love you too. With all that I am."

We make love on that rug, fingers squeezing and bodies slick with perspiration. I feel so fucking lucky that this woman loves me, that she lets me love her back. My hips roll and thrust as she meets me move for move until we're right on the edge of something unfathomable.

"Fall with me, queenie," I beg, as her legs bind around my middle.

And she does.

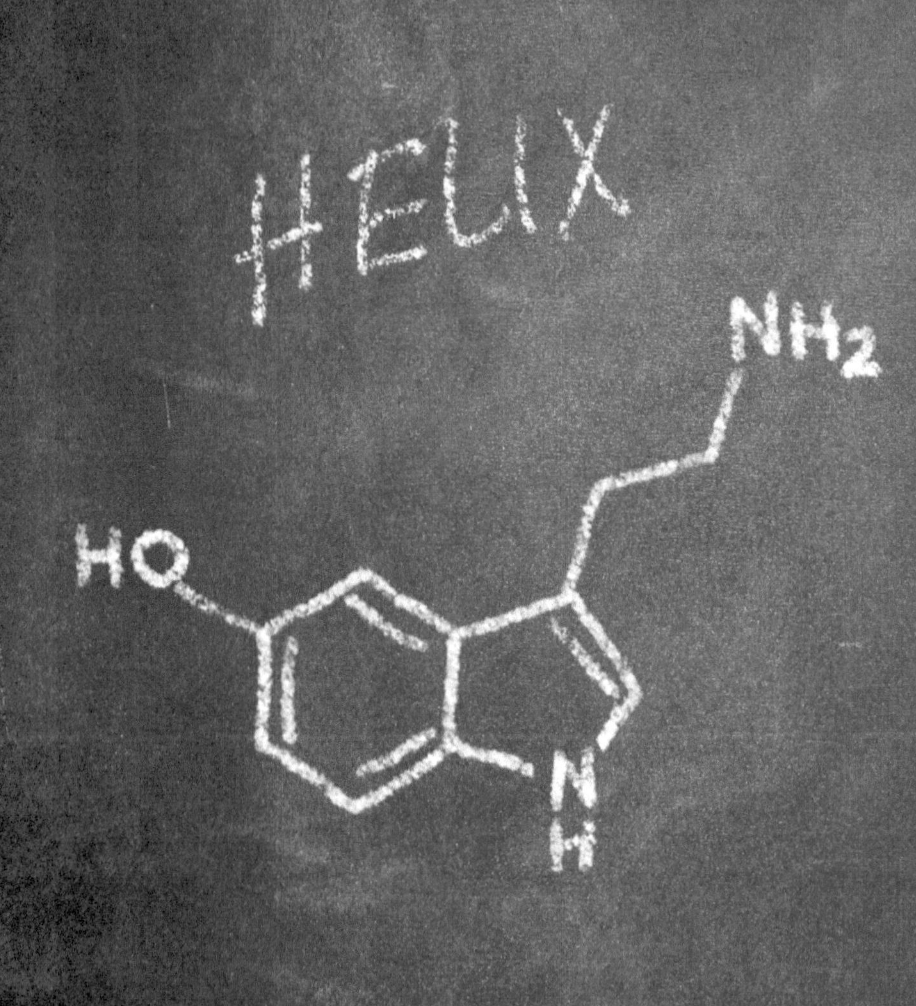

HELIX
NH2
HO
N
H

Chapter Forty

FINDING MY PEACE

Well, we finally found something Nicolette Bell isn't good at… snow skiing. She warned me that she had only skied twice in her life, and one of those days had been spent in ski school with a bunch of kiddos. The other day had been spent falling down.

I thought maybe she was exaggerating. She wasn't.

We hit the slopes on our third day in Aspen, though maybe "hit the slopes" isn't quite the correct term here. She fell over trying to put her skis on. I helped her up, and she asked if I was going to kiss all her bruises later. I told her of course and asked if she could try to fall on her pussy every time. She laughed and threw her pole at me, which made her lose her balance and end up on the ground once more.

She did pretty well getting to the ski lift line, and I was encouraged, but as we waited our turn, she fell again. While standing still.

It only took one look at the misery on her face as I pulled her to her feet, and that was it. I kneeled down and immediately removed her skis. Then we rented a couple snowmobiles, spending the rest of the day riding and laughing together.

In the evenings, we cuddle on the private balcony or by one of the fireplaces in what I now think of as "our cabin." Sometimes we go to a small bar we found and drink spiked hot cocoa with mounds of

393

whipped cream and chocolate shavings. We're in a really good place now.

I still feel the incessant need to apologize, but she shuts me down every time, reminding me that once a person is forgiven, you put past mistakes behind you. And she's right. Every time I apologized, it only brought up feelings of guilt inside me, which in turn made her feel guilty because I felt guilty. It was a vicious cycle and didn't allow for full healing.

The only problem is we're now on day six of our vacation, and I still haven't proposed. I keep thinking the right time will occur, and I'll just know. Maybe I'm stressing too much over trying to make it perfect. I should probably just man up and ask the damn question.

We rented a two-person snowmobile this evening for a nighttime ride up a small mountain. Nicolette is behind me with her arms wrapped tightly around my middle, sharing my warmth.

I reach the top of the mountain and stop the vehicle, climbing off before helping Nicolette. She's dressed in tight black waterproof pants and a puffy red jacket. Her curls stick out beneath her red knitted hat, and her smile is radiant and exhilarated.

There's a small frozen lake here, but we don't walk on it because we don't know how thick the ice actually is. Instead, we walk around the perimeter with her tucked beneath my arm. There's a nice coating of snow on the ground, and we're surrounded by evergreens and a stand of aspens that only add to the feeling of seclusion.

"This mountain and lake are also included with the cabin," I tell her. I'm still intent on buying this place for us.

"The cabin comes with its own freaking mountain?" she asks, incredulity coloring her voice.

"Yes, there's quite a bit of acreage. The place was built with privacy in mind. The couple that owns it is getting older and have chosen to live full-time in Florida where it's warm."

Nicolette stops walking and turns to me. "You really want to buy this place?"

She looks so beautiful in the nighttime, her skin an almost ethereal blue with the moonlight beaming down.

"I do want to. Not to live permanently but as our own private getaway." I pull her closer and kiss her forehead. "And one day we can bring our kids here. You can teach them to ski."

She laughs and pinches my ass, though I barely feel it because I'm wearing thick pants too. "How many hypothetical kids are we talking about?"

"Five," I answer without pause.

Nicolette raises a skeptical eyebrow. "And who do you think is going to birth these five children?"

"Well, since my beautiful wife will be the only one with that particular talent, I'm going to leave that up to her."

"And what will you be doing while your wife bears your very own basketball team?"

I smile proudly. "I will have the esteemed titles of chief foot rubber and captain of the ice cream retrieval squad." Nuzzling against her ear, I whisper, "I will also be commander of all orgasms."

"Commander, huh? That sounds important."

"The Orgasm Commander is the most paramount position I will hold. Would you like a demonstration of my skills?"

"So what... you're gonna run some drills for me?"

"I'm gonna run my drill *into* you," I promise, making her laugh. "Sorry, queenie, but you walked right into that one."

And suddenly, I know. Now is the perfect time. We're alone in a beautifully romantic setting. We're happy and bantering, tossing out innuendos to make each other laugh. This moment is... us.

Unzipping the pocket of my jacket, I reach inside as I sink to one knee. Nicolette looks confused until she sees the distinctive Tiffany-blue box.

"Oh my god, Helix."

I'm not sure if that's an *oh my god, Helix, this is the best thing ever* or if it's more of an *oh my god, Helix, get up because you're embarrassing yourself*. But the bright joy in her eyes tells me it's the former, and I press on.

Only... I forgot everything I was going to say. I've been going over it in my mind for what seems like forever, but in the moment, my brain can't remember a bit of it. So I wing it.

"Nicolette Bell, I love you so much more than I ever thought myself capable." *That's it, buddy. A strong start. Telling her you love her. Keep it going.*

"We started as coworkers, and I was immediately attracted to your beautiful brain. But it wasn't long until I fell even harder for your incredible heart. I love that we were friends first and built a foundation we could grow on."

The aspens are behind Nicolette and slightly to the right, and the leaves blowing in the breeze remind me of something I learned back in college.

"You probably already know this, but a single aspen tree is only one part of a larger organism. The life force of it is below the ground, and the entire stand is considered a single organism. I feel like that describes how I feel about you. I'm no longer a single tree living on my own. We share a life force, Nicolette. On the surface we look like two, but there's something deeper, below the surface, that binds us together and makes us one."

My heart almost bursts when she smiles. "I love that you're proposing with biology facts."

I can't hold back my chuckle. "You can take the nerd out of the lab..." Popping open the ring box, I see the reflection of the diamond in her wide eyes. "Nicolette Bell, will you allow me the honor of calling you my wife?"

She gasps and covers her mouth with her hand, and I panic that she's going to say no.

"I know this may seem soon. We've only known each other for less than a year, but it's been the best nine months of my life. You're the best friend I've ever had, and I promise to always put you first."

I'm babbling. I know I'm babbling, and yet I can't seem to stop.

"If you think it's too soon, I can save the ring and wait a while. I understand you might need more time, and that's perfectly fine. I'll wait forever for you. Or if you don't like the ring, I can get another one. Maybe I should have taken you with me to pick it out. That probably would have—"

I'm silenced by her bare hand over my mouth. She apparently removed her glove sometime during my blabbering speech.

"Would you just put the ring on my finger already, Hale? I'm trying to say yes."

"You are?" I ask, and she bites her bottom lip and nods.

"Yes, yes, yes."

Sliding that ring onto her finger gives me a peace like I've never known, and as I pick her up and kiss her on top of our mountain, I know I've found my forever.

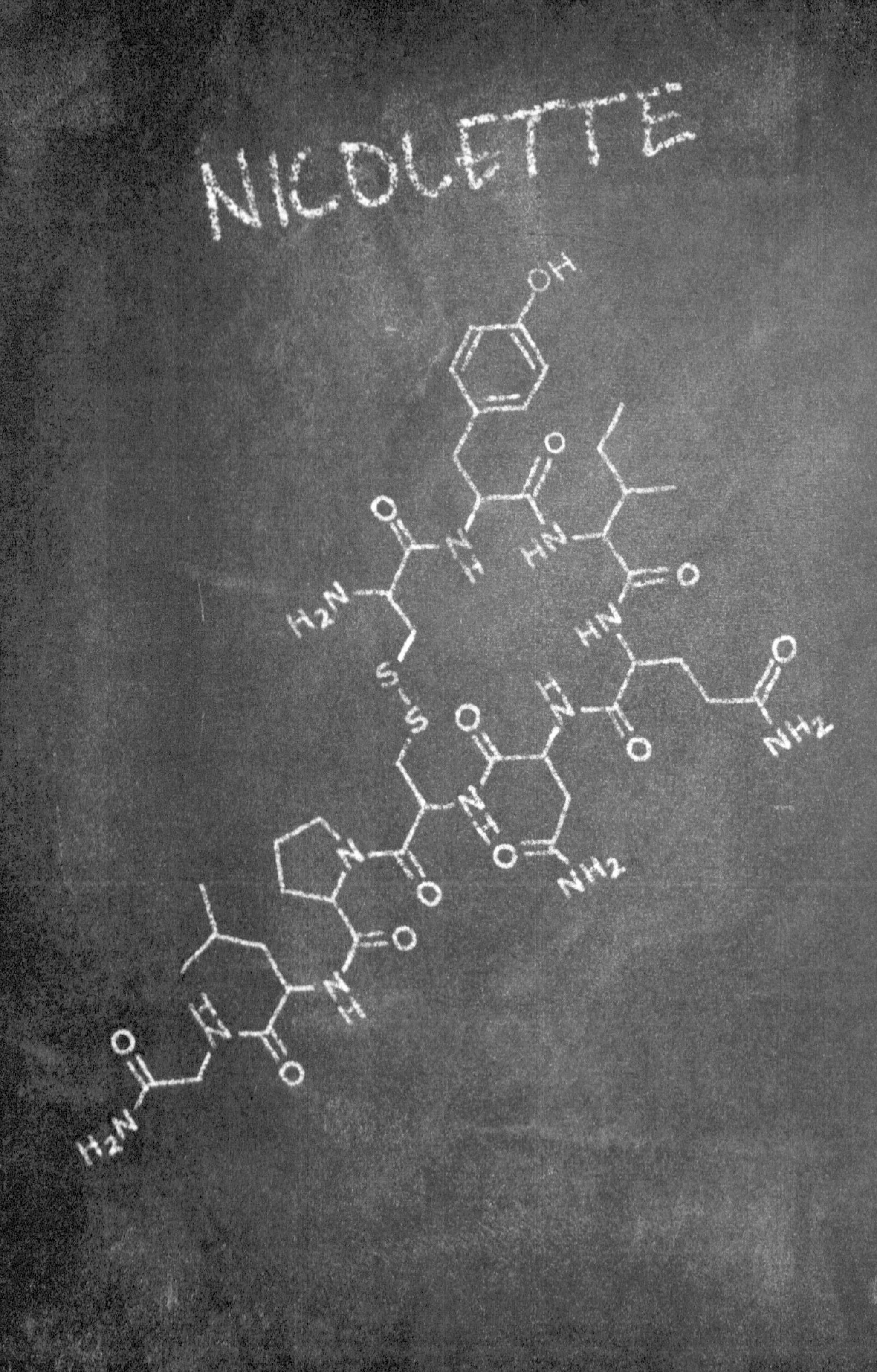

NICOLETTE

Chapter Forty-One

HELIX SHOULD DEFINITELY BUY THIS CABIN

My eyes slowly open, and I smile, remembering the events of last night. I am an engaged woman, and I repress the need to kick my feet in delight.

After the romantic proposal, Helix and I came back to the cabin and drank brandy out on the balcony that juts off our room. There's a lounge chair out there, and I'd sat with my back pressed against his chest as we watched the stars.

And then one thing led to another—or more accurately, his hands inside my fluffy bathrobe led to me turning around and riding him like he was my own personal pony. The cold combined with my desire had my nipples hard as pebbles, but he warmed them with his hot mouth as his hands heated my skin. God that had felt good, the icy night air sizzling with the steam of our lovemaking. Then we'd come inside and taken a candlelit bath together.

"You're turned on," a raspy voice comes from behind me, snapping me out of my memories of last night.

"What? No, I'm not," I say, feigning innocence.

Helix chuckles against the back of my neck in the dark room. The sun hasn't come up yet, but my internal clock can sense that dawn is just around the corner.

"You think I can't feel the wet spot you're leaving on my thigh right now, baby girl?"

I shift my hips slightly and notice his leg is indeed between mine as he holds me from behind. The coarse hairs on his leg rub against my bare pussy, and I feel his lips curl against my shoulder.

"Sorry," I whisper.

"Were you under the impression I was complaining, queenie?" His hand slides up my belly to cup my breast. "Ride it out."

"What?" I ask again because surely he's not wanting me to—

"Grind that cunt on my leg until you come. And then I'm going to fuck your wet pussy until you drench the sheets."

Okay, apparently that *is* what he wants me to do.

Tilting my pelvis downward, I press my clit against the strong muscle of his thigh and rotate my hips in a small circle.

"Mmm," I moan as Helix plucks at one nipple and then the other.

"That's it, Nicolette. Take what you need from me." He peppers kisses along my shoulder, occasionally tasting my skin with his velvet tongue. "You're going to be my wife, so I expect you to use any part of my anatomy to get yourself off. I'm here for your pleasure, and I'll always take care of your filthy little needs."

"Oh god." I ride against his leg with absolutely no shame. "I never knew this could feel so good."

"I like being your sex toy, baby." He scrapes his teeth up and down my neck before sucking on a spot that goes straight to my clit. "I like when you use me to get yourself off."

I grind down harder, turning my face to search for his lips. Helix cups my cheek and takes sweet command of my mouth, his tongue fucking into me as my pussy drips juices all over his leg. A hard rod throbs against my backside, and it turns me on even more knowing he wants me.

When he presses his thigh more tightly against me, I lose it, churning my hips faster and faster as I break apart with a loud cry. Helix swallows it, dropping his hand to rest on my lower belly, which only intensifies my orgasm.

Before I've even recovered, he slips his hard cock inside me and stills, allowing my inner walls to contract and quiver around him. "Such a good girl," he coos, nuzzling his face into my neck. "There's nothing better than the feel of you coming around me."

Helix hitches my knee up and drapes my leg over his, allowing him to go an inch deeper. When his hand slides lower, I tense.

"Too sensitive," I warn, and he chuckles.

"I know your body, Nicolette. I know your clit is extra buzzy after an orgasm." Instead of touching that tingling bundle of nerves like I thought, he makes a V with his fingers and rests them on my pussy lips. "I just wanted to feel myself plunging into the most perfect cunt in the world. Put your hand on mine. See how good we feel together."

I lower my hand and drape my first two fingers over his, feeling the slide of his dick between my fingers as he moves slowly in and out of me. It's intimate and sexy as all hell.

"Harder, Helix," I groan. "Be rough with me."

With a soft growl, he rolls us until I'm flat on my stomach with him draped over my back. "Spread those pretty legs for me, queenie. I'm about to tear this pussy up."

Oh hell yeah.

I widen my legs, flattening my inner thighs against the mattress as Helix slams into me with a deep thrust. "That's my good little wife. Taking your husband's cock so well."

I don't point out that we're not married yet because he seems to be getting off on calling me his wife. And if I'm being honest, I like it just as much. Burying my face in the downy pillow, I lift my hips an inch off the bed and cry out into the softness.

The wide crown of his cock hits me exactly where I need it, and I clench the sheets so hard, they pull from the corners of the bed. "Shit, that's good," I groan, my voice muffled as his hips begin slapping against my ass with the force of his fucking.

Helix presses his knees into the mattress and surges forward again and again while I hang onto the crumpled sheets in my fists. The sounds of his feral grunts mix with the squeaking of the bedframe and the banging of the headboard to create the perfect symphony of a good, hard fuck.

I come again, and Helix rises up onto his knees before grasping my hair and pulling me up with him until my back is flush with his chest.

His churning hips never stop their brutal momentum. Dragging one hand up my body, he wraps it around the front of my throat to feel my vocal cords vibrate with my low sound of approval. I can feel him smile against my neck.

"My wife loves her necklaces, doesn't she?" he asks, pushing up into me over and over. His words are hot against my ear, and I reach back with one hand to hold the back of his head.

"Yes," I pant as Helix's teeth latch onto the curve where my neck meets my shoulder. My body bucks when he applies suction, and I feel his cock swell and jerk inside me. "Come inside me, Helix. Fill me up."

The first warm jet coats my insides as Helix tightens his grip on my neck. A jolt of adrenaline shoves me into yet another orgasm, and I get the sensation of levitating above the bed.

"God, I love you," he groans as he continues spilling into me.

My smile is loose and satisfied when I turn my face to kiss his jaw. "I love you too."

Then we collapse onto the bed as the sun begins to rise on our last day in Aspen. And I decide Helix should definitely buy this cabin.

The next two months pass quickly, and before I know it, it's May. Helix has thrown every spare minute into planning our upcoming nuptials. I'm not sure I've ever seen a groom so invested in a wedding before, but he's intent on giving me the fairytale wedding I mentioned when we were fake dating at Angelica and Rory's engagement party.

I assured him a simple ceremony was fine with me, but he just kissed me and told me his queen would have the day she always dreamed of as a little girl. Yeah, I melted.

And then I gave him a blow job that left him shuddering for a full minute after I was done.

His family is ecstatic that we're getting married on New Year's Eve this year, but no one more than Helix's mother. Ophelia has been invaluable to me as I've tried to navigate the intricacies of a high-profile wedding. The woman should seriously consider a career as an event planner because she has a wonderful eye for detail.

We've hired a professional wedding planner, a man named Blaze with an over-the-top accent of indistinguishable origin and a flair for the dramatic. He reminds me of Martin Short's character, Franck, from those *Father of the Bride* movies. I seriously have no idea what he's saying half the time, but Ophelia seems to understand him, so maybe it's just me.

My family... well, we got mixed results when we told them we were getting married. Pop was happy, Ma looked like someone pissed in her green bean casserole, and Angelica pouted because she said I was copying her and only getting married because she did. Like she single-handedly invented the entire institution of marriage.

A couple days after we told them, Ma called and said she's not sure New Year's Eve will work for her because one of the neighbors is having a party she doesn't want to miss. I called her bluff and politely told her that was too bad and I hoped she had fun eating spinach dip and mini quiches from Costco. She got huffy that I didn't appear to be upset at the thought of her absence and said she *supposed* she could manage to show up.

I honestly don't give a fuck. Truth be told, I'd rather her not come. My elephant is strong inside me, and I'm not putting up with any more of her bullshit. Helix asked for my permission to "handle" my mother if she got out of line at the wedding, and I told him to go for it. I'd be too busy getting ready to marry the man of my dreams to deal with her foolishness.

Ophelia and I are on the way to meet with Blaze. Helix usually attends, but today we're discussing bridal clothing, so he's not invited. Apparently, Blaze will be helping to style my wardrobe from top to bottom, including clothing for the engagement party all the way through the honeymoon.

Other than his thick accent, I've found Blaze super easy to work with. I've been blessed with a scientific mind and not an artsy one, so I'm grateful for his help. He never oversteps; he simply presents ideas to Helix and me and lets us decide. He also has tons of photos so I can picture what he's talking about.

I was nervous the first time we met because he was prattling on about aesthetics, and I had not a fucking clue. I mean, I know the meaning of the word, but I had no idea of specifically what a "wedding aesthetic" was. But he showed us lots of examples of classic, vintage elegance, art deco, minimalist, and so on.

Helix and I both loved the vintage elegance style and decided on the colors of off-white and silver, though Helix also requested accents of scarlet. He told me later that it was because it's the color of my aura. He got Cinco de Mayo anal for that sweet idea.

"Nicolette, I have a question for you, and feel free to say no," Ophelia says as her driver winds the black Mercedes through the streets of Houston.

"Sure, go ahead," I tell her.

She takes my hand and squeezes. "I would like to buy your wedding dress." I'm a little stunned. Maybe she thinks I can't afford something that would be suitable for such an elegant wedding.

"That's so kind of you, but it's not necessary. I have some money allocated for that in my budget."

"Oh, I know, sweetheart, and I'm not asking because I think you can't afford it." She smiles shyly. "I wanted to buy it as my gift to my new daughter."

And that gets me all in the feels. I'm not accustomed to having a true mother figure in my life, but Ophelia and I are slowly working toward that type of relationship.

"Thank you," I say softly. "That means a lot to me."

She claps her hands beneath her chin like a giddy schoolgirl. "Excellent! I know you said you wanted a Bouvier dress. Would you prefer I get a designer to fly down here to Houston, or do you want to go to New York for a consultation?"

I think it over for about two seconds. "In New York since most of my bridal party live there already. My other bridesmaid, Shay, can fly up with us. Oh, and I'd like to bring Perri, even though she's a groomswoman for Helix and not a bridesmaid."

"Of course. That sounds perfect. Will your family be joining us, dear?" she asks delicately.

"No, I'd prefer my mother and sister not be there," I reply simply.

Ophelia nods in understanding. " Are you okay with me tagging along? I promise I won't be a bother. I'd just like to be there to support you."

So much affection for this woman rises up in my throat and threatens to choke me. She has been very helpful but never oversteps or tries to take over. She lets Helix and me choose and doesn't offer suggestions unless she's asked.

"I wouldn't have it any other way," I tell my future mother-in-law.

I was a little apprehensive about the whole wardrobe selection thing. After all, I'm a grown woman who has been picking out her own clothes for years. But it turns out, having a consultant, a.k.a. Blaze, takes a lot of the pressure off me.

So far, we've selected a chic white jumpsuit for the engagement party next month, a pretty pink dress for the bridal shower, and a classy white dress for the rehearsal dinner. Now that I've chosen all that, I don't have to worry about a single thing. Blaze will pair each outfit with the perfect shoes, jewelry, and bags, which will keep me from having to take off work and scramble around Houston to shop for accessories.

Then everything will be delivered to Helix's house... or actually *our* house since I'll be moving in with him once the lease on my townhome is up in June.

Ophelia and I are going through several racks of sample clothes to pick out some things for the honeymoon. She holds up a simple but beautiful blue sundress.

"What about this, Nicolette? There's a lovely little café I've been to in Santorini, and I can just picture you wearing this for a casual brunch there. But maybe in green to match your eyes?"

"I love it," I tell her, and she hands it to Blaze.

"I think that should be enough dresses. Let's find some casual things since you want to be comfortable while you're exploring. The evenings in Santorini can get cool in December, so I suggest long sleeves or a few light jackets."

"Ahh, zhou're going to Greece." Blaze comments. "Zhou deedn't want to be sooprised as to zee location of zee honeymoon?"

I shudder. "No way. I've never understood that whole thing where the bride has no idea where she'll be spending some of the most exciting weeks of her life. I like to be prepared."

"I oonderstand," Blaze says in his thick accent. The man has a soft, lilting voice, but he's built like Arnold Schwarzenegger, which doesn't match at all. I'm convinced there's some kind of ventriloquism going on.

Ophelia helps me select some nice but functional casual clothing, which Blaze notes on his tablet. Then he claps excitedly.

"Now eet is time to sink about your... bedtime attire. Vee have several directions vee can go. Zhou have zhour classy, or zhour sweet, innocent look, or zhou can go totally slooty."

It takes me a second to realize he's saying *slutty*, and I feel my cheeks heat.

"I think I'll go get a cup of coffee," Ophelia says diplomatically, patting my shoulder before exiting the room.

Blaze looks at me expectantly, and I whisper, "Let's go with slooty."

"That was so much fun," Ophelia says once we've left Blaze's headquarters. "Thank you for allowing me to be a part of it."

"Oh, please! I wouldn't have wanted to go without you." I pause and chew my bottom lip for a second before speaking again. "You told me before I can call you Mom. Is that still okay with you?"

Tears fill her brown eyes, and she nods as she reaches for a monogrammed handkerchief in her designer bag. "Nothing would make me happier. Now, let's go grab some lunch together, daughter."

The word doesn't feel at all foreign on my tongue when I reply, "Okay, Mom."

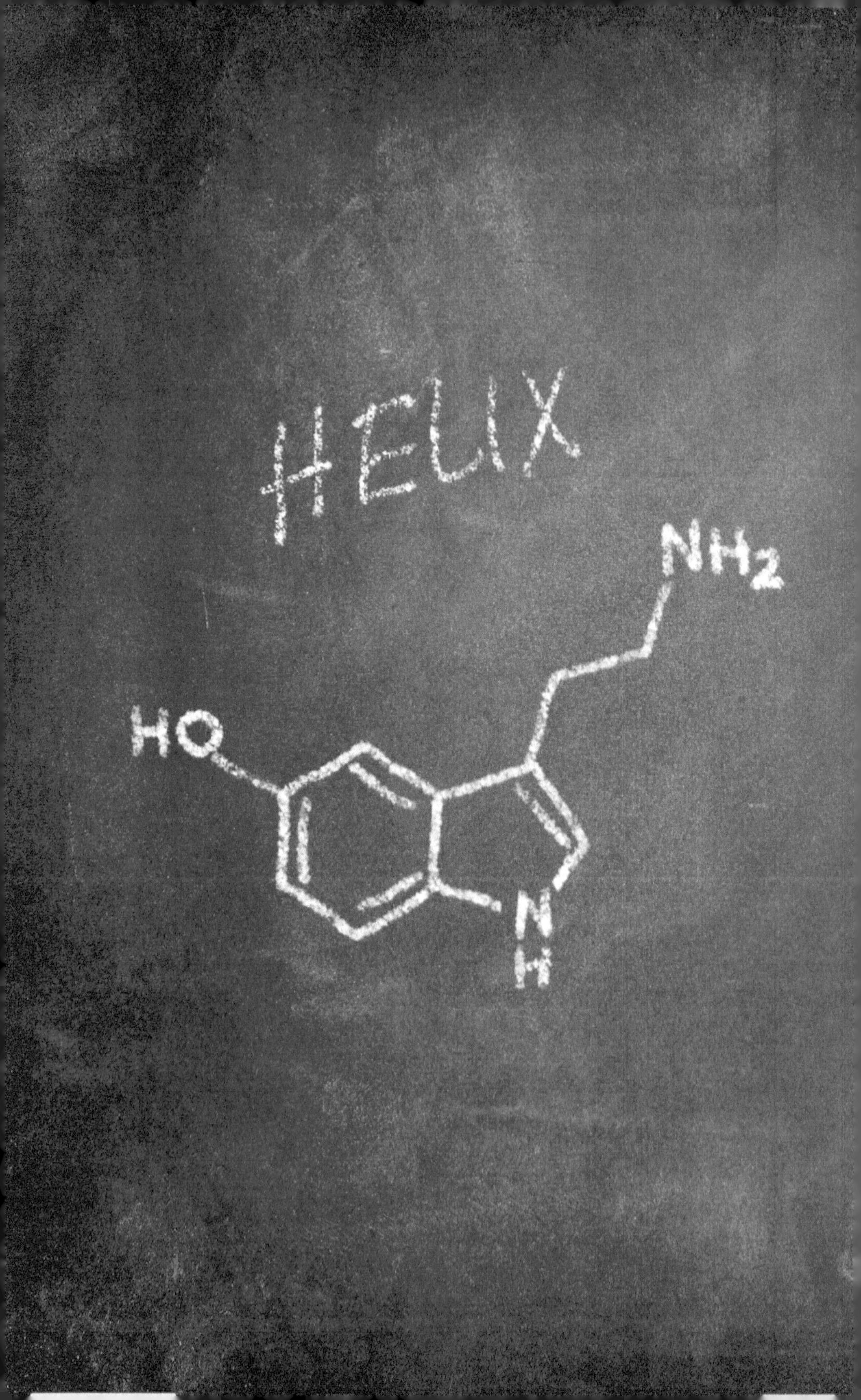

HELIX
NH2
HO
N
H

Chapter Forty-Two

NEW YEAR'S EVE

"It's your wedding day, Uncle Helix!"

"Really? Is that why I'm wearing this tuxedo?" I ask Reece, patting myself and looking confused. I pick her up and press a kiss to her cheek.

"You're silly," she accuses, wrapping one small arm around the back of my neck. "Do you like my flower girl dress?" She pats the layers of fluffy tulle.

"It is the most beautiful dress for the prettiest girl I've ever seen, and are you wearing lip gloss?"

"Yes, Auntie Nicolette put it on me. Daddy said it was okay cuz it's a special 'casion." She pooches her little lips out so I can see.

"It is a special occasion," I tell her. "Where's your basket of flowers?"

She points at Phoenix who is holding a delicate white basket adorned with bows and filled with scarlet rose petals. "I'm feeling quite fancy. Maybe I should have been the flower boy," he teases.

Reece rolls her eyes, something she's been doing more and more lately. She's a whopping five years old now, but half the time she acts like a teenager.

Remington walks up and holds out his arms for Reece. "Let's walk outside. Dutton and River are out there looking at the ducks in the pond."

She goes willingly, and Phoenix calls after them, "Don't get dirty. Or fall in the pond. The wedding starts in less than two hours."

"Where's Mom?" I ask my twin, and he points a thumb toward the hallway.

"Down in the Galleria ballroom making sure everything is perfect for the ceremony."

I nod. "I'll go check on her. Maybe grab her a glass of wine to calm her nerves." Eyeing my brother, I wonder if he's struggling with all the wedding-day festivities since his own wedding went so wrong six years ago. "You doing okay, Phe?"

"Never better. I'm excited to have a new sister to pick on." His face turns serious. "I'm really happy for you, Helix. You deserve to be happy."

Pulling him into a tight hug, I tell him, "Thank you for being my best man."

When I release him, he straightens his black bow tie and flashes me a cheesy grin. "Well, since I'm the best brother who ever lived, it only makes sense."

I head off down the hallway, pausing beside the bridal room where I know Nicolette is getting ready. I hear laughter from inside and smile, so happy she's having a good time on what I know can be a stressful day. I credit her friends for that. Lehra, Artie, Gianna Bouvier, and Nicolette's pharmacist friend, Shay, make up her bridal party. They have all been nothing but supportive to my bride.

Kissing my fingertips, I lay them against the wooden door and whisper. "Love you, baby. See you at the altar."

Then I wind through the hallways of the luxurious Ashworth hotel to the sunlit atrium, where our reception will take place after the ceremony. It looks stunning, with intricate off-white and scarlet flowers on every flat surface.

Blaze runs up, a look of panic on his face. "What is zee groom doing here? Is somezing wrong? Is it zee centerpieces? I promise zhou, zee candles will be lit at zee end of zee ceremony so everyzing will be..." He makes a chef's kiss motion with his fingers.

I pat his shoulder. "Everyzing, I mean, *everything* looks perfect,

Blaze. You and your team have done an amazing job. I was just going to see if I could grab a glass of wine for my mother."

His panicked demeanor settles, and he pats his chest in relief. "Whew. I vas vorried." He smiles widely. "And Ms. Ophelia, ahhh, how I've tried to recruit her for my team. Amaaaaazing lady!"

"I couldn't agree more. Can you tell me where to get a glass of red?"

Blaze twiddles his fingers toward the back. "In zee keetchen back there. Vould you like me to get eet for zhou?"

"No, it's fine. I know you have plenty to do. Thanks again, Blaze."

After grabbing my mother a glass of her favorite shiraz, I trek down the hallway to find the Galleria ballroom. Seriously, this place is like a damn maze.

The fashion tycoon, Auburn Bouvier, is walking up and down a wide corridor with his nine-year-old twins, Jaxon and Jane, and his younger daughter, Eliana, holding onto his finger. I think the little toddling one is a bit over a year old.

"Hey, man," he says when he sees me. "A little anxious aren't you? The wedding doesn't start for a while."

I laugh and hold up the glass I'm holding. "An offering for the wedding goddess," I tell him before explaining, "My mother."

He nods his dark head. Auburn looks dapper as hell in a navy-blue tuxedo that's obviously been custom-made to fit him like a glove. I guess that's not unexpected when you're the CEO of a major fashion company.

"I saw Ophelia a couple minutes ago. She was down that adjoining hallway. I'm just walking some energy off of these kids before they have to sit still."

We look at his two older children, who have linked their hands with their little sister and are playing ring around the rosy. "Good plan. There's a duck pond back that way," I tell him, jerking my head.

"Really? Okay, thanks for letting me know. Dad is in the bathroom, so I'll wait for him so he can help me watch Eliana. She's fast on the breakaway."

As if on cue, the little one takes off running down the carpeted hallway with her brother and sister chasing her. Paul Bouvier, the patriarch of their family, steps out of the restroom just in time to intercept his grandbaby before she can escape.

Auburn chuckles. "That's why we keep the old guy around. He's an excellent baby-catcher. And don't worry, I'm taking Eliana to the nursery room before the ceremony. That was a nice touch, by the way."

"Hey, the Hales do it classy," I joke, popping my cuffs.

He eyes my attire appraisingly. "You look good. Monty did an excellent job with that tux." Monty is his younger brother and one of the top designers at Bouvier.

"I'm sure he did a great job with Nicolette's dress as well," I say. It's possible I'm fishing for details.

Auburn sees right through my weak attempt and shakes his head in disappointment. "Nice try, bud, but I'm not saying shit except you're going to be a very happy man in less than two hours."

My heart jackhammers in my chest at the thought of my bride in her fancy gown. "I can't wait."

We start off at a stroll down toward Paul and the kids, and my old friend says, "Hey, I was recently approached by an organization that provides free medical care for kids whose families can't afford it. They mostly focus on children who need orthopedic surgery of some sort."

I notice his eyes are firmly on Jane. He and Gianna adopted their twins from a children's home a few years ago. Little Jane was in a wheelchair due to having a couple pieces of shit as their birth parents. I recall that she had extensive surgery just to be able to walk. Now she's able to run and play with the other kids.

"How can I help, Auburn?"

He turns his blue gaze on me. "It's still in the works, but they're looking for businesses to partner with for a huge event. They wanted a cosmetics company, and I recommended Hale." His eyes go back to his older daughter who is laughing as she skips around her grandfather. With a soft voice, he says, "We were lucky we were able to afford everything Janie needed. Some families aren't so fortunate."

I rest my hand on his shoulder. "I'll mention it to Dad. I'm sure he'll want to be involved."

After greeting Paul and the kids, I stride toward the ballroom. As soon as I near the corner, I hear Rory and Angelica, who seem to be in some kind of argument.

"You're being ridiculous, Angelica."

"Oh, shut the fuck up, Rory. I'm tired of listening to your shit."

I plaster myself against the wall and eavesdrop without shame as Rory replies.

"I'm serious. You know this is wrong, and you're doing it anyway."

"Read my lips. I. Don't. Care. And who's going to stop me?"

"You should be stopping yourself. You're acting like a spoiled little brat."

I'd like to yell, "Amen, dude," even though I have no idea what they're arguing about. It's pretty much a given that Nicolette's sister is acting like an asshole in any given situation. But I keep my mouth shut and listen.

"Whatever, Rory. My sister thinks she's so goddamn special marrying into some rich family. It should be me who has fancy houses and private planes. And she's going to Greece for her honeymoon. Greece! You took me to fucking Mexico."

Aw hell, I wish I had some popcorn for this show. I can hear the hurt and anger in Rory's voice when he lowers his voice.

"That's it. I'm done with you and your entitled ass. I've tried and I've tried, but nothing is ever enough for you. Expect to hear from my lawyer first thing Monday morning."

"Fine, I didn't want to be married to you anyway. I only went after you because I didn't want Nicolette to have you," she shoots back. "You can't even buy me a decent house, Rory. Maybe I'll hook up with one of the other Hale brothers. I bet they would buy me anything I wanted, especially if one of them knocks me up."

Yikes! Making a mental note to warn Remi and Phoenix to steer far, far away from this crazy bitch, I step around the corner. Rory is storming off in the other direction while Angelica stands there looking after him, her face reddened with anger.

But what catches my attention is what she's wearing. It's a long white formal gown with lace and beading all over the bodice, very obviously a wedding dress. Rage boils up my chest and onto my neck, heating the skin there.

Oh no she fucking didn't.

"Angelica," I say, and she whirls around, her eyes widening with surprise before her lips morph into a flirty smile.

"Hi, Helix. You look handsome."

I don't crack so much as a grin in return. "You should really go get changed. The wedding will be starting soon."

She giggles and smacks my chest. "I've already changed, silly. This is what I'm wearing. Do you like it?" she coos, batting her eyelashes at me.

I know she's used to getting her way when she uses that baby voice, but I only feel disgust toward her. Coldness coats my voice even though my anger is red hot.

"Was audacity on sale the day you bought that dress?"

Angelica looks taken aback. "Wh-what are you talking about?"

My eyes narrow into slits as I repeat the exact words she said to her sister at the engagement party in New Jersey. "You know it's against wedding etiquette to wear white, right? Only the bride is supposed to wear white."

She has the nerve to roll her eyes. "Pshht, that's such an outdated concept. I think guests should wear what looks best on them, and I look amazing in this dress."

Without a second thought, I tip my hand forward and pour the entire glass of red wine down the front of her dress. Then I sling it by the stem until every single crimson drop stains the shiny fabric.

Angelica lets out a shriek I'm surprised doesn't shatter the glass in my hand. "What the hell is wrong with you?"

I hear footsteps running toward us, and turn to find Albert Bell approaching, a glass of what looks like whiskey sloshing in one hand. "What is all this yelling?"

Angelica points an accusing finger at me. "Daddy, he poured wine all over my dress," she whines.

"My hand slipped," I lie, flexing my fingers for effect. "I'm going to have to get that looked at."

Nicolette's father seethes, and I'm afraid it's directed at me until he surprises the shit out of me and whirls on his oldest daughter. "What the hell are you wearing, Angelica?"

She lets out a noise of frustration and gestures wildly at her stained dress. "This *was* the dress I was wearing to the wedding until *he* ruined it." The look she throws at me is full of pure venom.

Albert lowers his voice to a scary level. "You know better than to wear white to a wedding, Angelica Ann. Hell, I'm a man, and I know the bride is the only woman that should wear white. What were you thinking?"

Before she can answer, Bridget Bell joins the festivities, her eyes wide. It should have come as no surprise to me that she'd also be wearing an inappropriate color for someone else's wedding, but here she is in an ivory formal gown.

"Oh my god, baby," she squawks, batting ineffectively at Angelica's dress. "What happened?"

"Helix dumped wine on me," the brat tattles, and her mother spins on me, eyes glowing like a demon in a B-rate movie.

"How dare you?" she spits, taking a menacing step toward me, but her husband steps in between us and blocks her path.

"What is this, Bridget?" he demands, gesturing at her dress. "Where is the pink dress you showed me?"

Her chin lifts haughtily as she turns her attention from me to Albert. "I changed my mind because I thought this one suited me better. Angelica helped me to pick it out."

"Figures," he mutters. "You two did this on purpose, didn't you? To ruin Nicolette's wedding."

"I—what? How dare you," she splutters, propping her hands on her hips. "You are out of line, Albert Bell."

"No, Bridget, *you're* the one who's out of line," he shouts. "You and this little monster you created," he says, waving a hand toward Angelica. The little monster in question gasps in outrage, but Albert isn't done. "I've stood by for too many years while you two treated Nicolette like garbage, but that ends *today*. Both of you go change right now, and if you put a single toe out of line for the rest of this wedding, you'll have me to answer to."

Bridget doubles down, squinting at her husband. "I didn't bring another dress. This is the one I'm wearing."

They're nose to nose, having an epic staredown, a war of the wills, and I wouldn't have been surprised to hear Michael Jackson's "Beat It" start up in the background.

What happens next surprises the hell out of me. Albert Bell slowly lifts his arm and deliberately dumps the contents of his glass over his wife's head. It drenches her hair and drips brown liquid all over the light-colored material of her dress. I resist the urge to applaud. Barely.

Then Bridget draws back her hand and slaps her husband's face just as three security guards round the corner. *Ho-ly hell. This is like some Jerry Springer shit.*

"Whoa, whoa. Back up, ma'am," one of them calls as another gets between the couple with his hands outstretched. The third guard I recognize as Tessa Blanchard, head of security for the wedding. We've had a few problems with the paparazzi following us since news broke of my upcoming marriage to Nicolette, so we have an entire team on hand to keep everyone safe and our wedding as private as possible.

"Dr. Hale, what's going on?" she asks, approaching me on brisk feet.

"These two women were attempting to sabotage our wedding," I tell her. "I want them removed." Tessa immediately spins on her heel, barking orders into the device on her collar, and seconds later, four more guards sprint toward us.

"I didn't do anything!" Bridget protests. The guards surround her and Angelica as the team awaits their orders.

Tessa ignores the screeching and looks to Albert. "Sir, would you like to press charges on that woman for assault?"

He hesitates for a moment before saying, "Yes, I think I would."

"What? You piece of shit," his wife yells. Angelica is squalling like a baby as Bridget attempts to stomp over to her husband, but she's stopped once again by a guard, this one built like a mountain.

"Unless," Albert adds, "Bridget and Angelica go directly to the airport and leave. Then I won't press charges."

"You don't mean that," Bridget says. I notice she's a lot quieter now that she's been threatened with jail time. It's probably still an act.

"I do mean it," Albert replies. "You two have bullied Nicolette since she was a little girl, and I blame myself as much as you because I could have stopped it at any time. But I was too weak. I wanted to keep the peace in the house. You and Angelica were the loudest, squeakiest wheels, and I allowed you to get the grease, and sweet Nicolette was the one who suffered because of it. She tolerated your passive-aggressive bullshit because I wasn't strong enough to put a stop to it. But it stops right fucking now." His chest is heaving with emotion, and I notice tears streaming down his face. "I won't allow you to ruin the best day of her life because she deserves this happiness. Go home, Bridget, and let Nicolette have her day in the sun. I'll deal with you when I get home."

Then he spins around and walks swiftly away, leaving his wife and older daughter stunned in his wake. I'm pretty sure they've never been talked to like that, but it was about damn time.

I say a quick word to Tessa, telling her to take the two women to the airport and leave them there and to make sure the staff are all aware to keep them from the hotel. And I follow Albert, seeing him disappear into a men's room ahead.

I wait by the door until he emerges ten minutes later with reddened eyes. He shoots me a guilty look.

"Would it be inappropriate for me to clap right now?" I ask, earning me a small smile from the man.

"Yes, because it was too little, too late. I should have done that years ago." Albert clears his throat. "I understand if you don't want me here. I'll leave if you think that's what's best for Nicolette."

"I'd like you to stay, and I think Nicolette would as well." I clap him on the shoulder. "Now let's both go get a drink. I have a little story about a baby elephant I want to tell you."

My wife brings tears to my eyes when she walks down the aisle. Auburn was correct; I'm ecstatic. Nicolette's creamy ivory dress is a ballgown style with a fitted bodice and sweetheart neckline. Layer upon layer of sumptuous silk make up the skirt, which gives her the appearance of floating toward me.

It's a dress fit for a queen, which is fitting because that's what she is to me... my queenie.

Her hair is down, her curls wide and loose, like it was styled with hot rollers. And of course, her makeup is perfect. I can barely get through the vows without dipping her low and kissing her, but when the moment finally comes, I do just that. I kiss my wife.

Once we've walked up the aisle after being introduced as Dr. and Dr. Hale for the first time, I kiss her again.

"You are absolutely stunning, Nicolette. I'm the luckiest man in the world."

She smiles up at me, the flowers of her huge bridal bouquet tickling the back of my neck. "I'm the lucky one, husband. I love you so much."

I rub my nose against hers. "I love you too." My hands slide down over the thick layers of fabric over her hips. "And I can't wait to see what you're hiding beneath these skirts."

"I think you'll be pleased, husband." My wife's smile turns sexy, and she goes up on tiptoe to whisper in my ear as the bridal party recessional begins. "It's very slooty."

I have no idea what that means, but I'm pretty sure I'm going to love it.

PHOENIX HALE

ABOUT TEN MONTHS PRIOR

I'm sitting at my desk in the executive offices of Hale Cosmetics, thinking about the woman I want but can't have. She's so much younger than me, though to be honest, she doesn't seem like it when we spend time together.

As they often do, my thoughts turn dirty, and I reach beneath my desk to cup my hardening cock through my pants. I shouldn't think about Jordie McNamara like this. And I sure as hell shouldn't stroke myself off to thoughts of her every fucking morning in the shower like a teenager with a crush. I'm a grown man with a child.

Okay, tomorrow is the day. I won't think about her at all while I'm naked. But today, maybe just once more won't hurt.

I stand, intent on heading to the bathroom to think about my forbidden fruit and jerk out a quick one, when my office door flies open. Quickly sitting to hide the evidence in my pants, I relax a little when I see my twin. Then my heart rate picks up when I see the panicked look on his face.

"Helix, what's wrong?"

"She didn't do it," he says, his breaths heaving out of his chest. "Nicolette didn't steal the formula."

We've talked this subject to death the past couple days. "I know. I thought we already established you don't believe she did all that shit."

"Yeah, but now I have proof." He waves his laptop around. "I have a video of the thief."

"The security company dug it out already? I thought they said it would take a while."

"It's... well, it doesn't matter how I got it. I've watched it about fifty times, and the woman looks familiar to me somehow. Not her face, but there's something niggling in the back of my mind." He places the device on my desk and opens it. "Will you watch it with me and give me your thoughts?"

"Of course," I say soothingly as he takes a seat on the edge of my desk. I can feel his anxiety as if it were my own. "Have you heard from Nicolette?"

"She's not answering me," he says tersely, "but I have a plan. I'm going to show up at her sister's wedding. The rehearsal dinner is Friday night."

I try not to visibly wince at this plan. "Are you sure that's the best idea, bro? Didn't you tell me her sister treats her like shit?"

He nods, his focus intent on the screen as he locates and clicks on an MP4 file. "That's why I have to show up."

"You don't think you being there would only add to her stress?"

He glances at me and shakes his head solemnly. "She needs me." Directing his attention back to the screen, he orders, "Watch."

The screen is filled with a view of the hallway outside Helix's office in the laboratory building. We're both silent as a woman in all black approaches the camera with her head tilted down. Helix is right; there's something familiar about the way she moves. She's short, and despite her bulky clothing, I can see she's quite thin.

The hairs on the back of my neck stand at attention, though I can't quite place why.

The woman enters the office, and I stay silent as Helix fast forwards through seven minutes of nothing. When the figure emerges, she's holding a thick manila envelope, which she stuffs beneath her sweatshirt. A sliver of skin is revealed, and my blood cells all seem to pause mid-flow.

When a bit of platinum hair slips from her hood, she quickly hides it and jogs off toward the exit as I sit there trying to get my circulatory system to come back to life.

"Back it up," I say around a dry tongue. "To where she puts the envelope under her shirt."

Helix looks at me curiously and slides the little bar back a bit. "Here?"

I nod dumbly and point. "Can you zoom in right there?"

"Whoa, I didn't even notice the tattoo," he murmurs when the patch of skin fills the screen. "Let me see if I can clear it up a bit."

It seems like it takes him forever, but in actuality, it's probably only a few seconds before the ink comes into focus and I see my own name in a cursive script. I recognize it instantly because I had a similar one once, though I had it removed years ago.

"Phoenix?" my brother calls, and it sounds like his voice is coming from the bottom of a well. Or maybe I'm the one in the well and he's trying to save me.

I manage to drag myself to the surface and look at the face that matches my own. Helix looks concerned, and I can only imagine the expression on my face right now.

"Phoenix," he says again, "are you all right? What's happening here?"

"I know who it is," I tell him, my eyes going back and forth from the image to my twin.

His hand is warm on my shoulder, and I close my eyes to absorb the comfort. Because inside, my organs are hosting a rave.

"Can you tell me who it is?"

I can, but I don't want to, though I open my mouth to say it anyway as my gaze once again focuses on the tattoo.

"That's the woman I was going to marry," I tell Helix, bringing my eyes back to his widening ones. "That's Beatrice fucking Bettencourt."

Well, isn't that an interesting turn of events? If you want a sneak peek of what happened on Phoenix's wedding day all those years ago, check out the prologue to **Hale No** by typing this into your browser: https://dl. bookfunnel.com/yyvfwavio1

To be one of the first to get **Hale No (Phoenix and Jordie's story)** in your hot little hands, you can preorder it now on Amazon.

For an introduction to Jordie McNamara, star of the WNFL and Phoenix's young forbidden fruit, you can read her sister's book, **The "Kinda" Secret Pineapple Island Swingers' Resort.** Be ready to laugh your ass off when a romance author accidentally books her writing retreat at a swingers' resort – and meets a hockey hottie who definitely knows how to handle his (hockey) stick. (Also available on Amazon)

And yes, I know I was vague as shit about the Hale cousin, Dutton, but I did it on purpose [insert evil author laugh here]. If you like Cowboy romances, watch for Dutton's book coming in the future. I'll let him tell you the whooooole sordid story.

Other characters from **Hale Yes** with their own books:

Auburn and Gianna Bouvier in **Love Without Numbers**

Lehra and Cruz Estrada in **Love Without Demands** (also plenty of Artie in this one!)

Also by Jade

The Bouvier Family Saga

Love Without Numbers

Love Without Influence

Love Without Demands

Love Without Control

Highway to Hale

Hale Yes

Hale No

Hale Damage

All Hale the Queen

Fierce Protectors Series

Dauntless Protector

Devoted Protector

Deadly Protector

Young Protector (prequel novella to Deadly)

Disgruntled Protector

Determined Protector

Damaged Protector

Standalones

The "Kinda" Secret Pineapple Island Swingers' Resort

Delay of Game

Rating the Book Boyfriend

I Dream of Johnny

One of the best ways you can help indie authors is to leave a review on Amazon, so if you'd be so kind, hop on over there now, rate this book, and leave me a review. It doesn't have to be fancy, just a few words to let other readers know what you thought. —Much love, Jade

About the Author

Jade Dollston is a Texas author who loves reading, writing, Doritos, and rum. She is married to her high school sweetheart, and they have one amazing daughter.

Her love of reading all things smutty has turned into a love of writing all things smutty. She enjoys a diverse selection of romance, and this is reflected in her writing style. Be prepared to laugh, cry, cringe, and fan your face, possibly all in a single chapter.

Jade is so excited to share her work with the world and hopes that you enjoy reading the words from her heart.